Rainbow in the Dark

Rainbow in the Dark

Wade McCoy, MD and
Patrick Chalfant

Copyright © 2011 by Wade McCoy, MD and Patrick Chalfant.

Library of Congress Control Number: 2011902307
ISBN: Hardcover   978-1-4568-6974-8
              Softcover   978-1-4568-6973-1
              Ebook   978-1-4568-6975-5

All rights reserved. No part of this book may be reproduced or transmitted in any form or by any means, electronic or mechanical, including photocopying, recording, or by any information storage and retrieval system, without permission in writing from the copyright owner.

1. Though this work is based on some true events, this book is a work of fiction with much artistic license taken within the framework of actual places and times. The characters are fictional though there may be actual people who bear resemblance to the characters, and whether living or dead, is purely coincidental.
2. Cover photography by Emily Brashier
   Urban Exposure Photography
3. *www.arainbowinthedark.com*

This book was printed in the United States of America.

To order additional copies of this book, contact:
Xlibris Corporation
1-888-795-4274
www.Xlibris.com
Orders@Xlibris.com
93499

To the women who have loved me through my life—my mother, my wife Sarah, and our girls.

Wade McCoy

For Cooper

May you always reach above and beyond the comforts of your world and allow your imagination to boldly shake the tree of ingenuity.

Patrick Chalfant

Because you love me I have much achieved,
  Had you despised me then I must have failed,
    But since I knew you trusted and believed,
      I could not disappoint you and so prevailed.

          —Paul Laurence Dunbar, "Encouraged"

Dr. Henry Kirkland Jr.

Chapter 1

Weatherford, Oklahoma

1989

Running with all his might, Kirk strove to reach the end of the buildings. He heard his friend's voice only a few feet in front of him screaming, "Run, Pee Wee, run! Run before you get yo' ass blown off!" Kirk glanced back and saw the shadow of his pursuer. He turned the corner and ran like the wind. The harder he tried to run, however, the more resistance he encountered. He suddenly felt as though his legs were stuck in Jell-O.

"Stop right there, or I'll fill your ass full of lead!" shouted the tall man who pursued him.

Knowing a decision had to be made, Kirk's thoughts raced. He knew he couldn't outrun the man. For some reason, his usual speed was gone. I must use my wits, thought Kirk. Since he'd walked through this dark alley every day for the past several years, it was as familiar as his own home. Kirk suddenly saw his escape. He ducked into a small crack between two buildings and watched as the man ran by, still holding the gun in front of him.

Kirk let out a breath of relief but was sweating heavily and so scared he could hear his own heart pounding. Assuming the man had probably reached the other end of the alley, Kirk stepped out of the crack and headed back in the same direction from which he had come. Again, he tried to run, but try as he might, his legs just wouldn't work. Out of nowhere, he felt the tall man grab his shoulder, spin him around, and cram the gun in his face. There was no escape. He was as good as gone. As he closed his eyes, he heard a deafening "boom, boom."

# # #

Dr. Kirkland jumped out of his chair. Hearing loud knocks, he looked to his office door. Assuming a student was outside, he quickly tried to orientate himself by rubbing his eyes, then splashing ice water on his face. He shook his head at his strange dream. His 180 pound body and six foot, two inch frame slowly arose from the chair and walked to his office door. Dr. Kirkland opened the door, but found no one outside. Throughout his tenured career at Southwestern Oklahoma State University, he'd encountered this phenomena many times. Early in his career, he didn't mind such things, but nearing sixty years old, he was growing weary of the students' youthful antics.

Since his first general biology class of the semester was about to begin, he decided it was time to meet his new students, and grabbed his briefcase. His office sat atop the first flight of stairs, right on the way to the second floor of the Old Science Building at SWOSU.

As Dr. Kirkland walked down the worn marble stairs, his clothes fluttered from the breeze blowing down the hall. His attire was the same as he wore thirty years ago, when he started teaching at Booker T. Washington High School, the segregated school for blacks in El Reno, Oklahoma. He wore dress slacks, a button-up shirt, and a white coat with "Dr. Henry Kirkland—Department of Biological Sciences" sewn on the left breast pocket.

Today was the first day of the 1989 spring semester. As Dr. Kirkland entered the room, he found the class about half full of college students, all sitting in neat rows. He wasted little time walking to the front of the room, laying his briefcase on the desk, then turning around to face the full-length chalkboard. After writing his name on the chalkboard, he then wrote "Intro to Basket Weaving" on the board. Many of the students pulled their schedules out of their backpacks and examined them. Dr. Kirkland ignored their confusion. Instead, he opened his briefcase and removed a sack lunch, which contained a sandwich. Dr. Kirkland took a bite of the sandwich, then laid it back on his desk. Next, he grabbed an apple and shined it on his coat.

As more students entered the room, Dr. Kirkland continued to empty things from his briefcase. He then removed a new box of chalk and a toy revolver, which he laid on the desk without saying a word. The sight brought instant silence from the group.

"My name is Dr. Henry Kirkland. I will be your professor for the next several months."

Dr. Kirkland turned to the chalkboard and erased "Intro to Basket Weaving". With a big smile on his face, he wrote, "Intro to Biology".

As Dr. Kirkland spoke to the students, a slight movement at the door caught his eye. He turned and saw Wade McCoy, a senior at Southwestern and a former student, standing in the hall. As soon as McCoy made eye contact, he began pacing back and forth, occasionally looking into the room through the open door.

"You will receive four examinations and a final in this class," Dr. Kirkland announced to the class. "The only acceptable reason for you to miss an exam is in the case of a death, and that must be your own death, not your great-aunt or best friend or even mine. If I die, I will have made plans for the exam to be given."

With a straight face, Dr. Kirkland proceeded to write the rules and the plan for the class on the chalkboard. After he finished, he looked at his watch and saw that it was ten 'til nine o'clock, so he excused the class. After the last student left the room, Dr. Kirkland walked out into the hallway.

"Wade, how are you doin', my boy?"

Holding an eight by ten envelope in his hand, Wade held up the package, with tears in his eyes. Dr. Kirkland acted as though he had no idea what was in Wade's hand.

"What's that, an eviction notice?" asked Dr. Kirkland as he walked back to his office, with Wade following like a puppy.

"Dr. Kirkland, I was accepted to medical school. This is my acceptance letter!" said Wade.

Dr. Kirkland stopped walking and smiled. "I knew you would! Come in my office. Let's take a look at that letter."

Dr. Kirkland unlocked the door and reached up, touching the office number 303 with a smile. They entered the office. Like he had so many times over the years, he offered Wade a chair. They both sat down, but the office was so small their legs touched.

"Well, I'll be . . . it's snowing, I didn't think it would today," Dr. Kirkland said as he looked out the window. He then took the envelope from Wade and slowly opened it. In silence, he read the letter. He then looked at Wade.

"You did it! I'm proud of you, Young Wade."

"Dr. Kirkland, I couldn't have done it without you," Wade said, crying lightly. "Remember the first time we sat in this room several years ago? You asked me what I was planning on doing with my life. It was then that you told me to go to medical school."

"I remember," said Dr. Kirkland.

"You didn't know it at the time, but I thought I could never go to medical school. I grew up on the farm. I graduated high school with ten people in my class. There wasn't a snowball chance in hell I could have gone to med. school. But you helped me again and again, and here we are! I'm going to medical school!"

"I always knew you could do it, Wade."

"Do you remember when you bailed me out of that algebra class and called the professor to get me into a prep class? You had to talk the professor into taking me two weeks into the semester."

"I didn't do the work, you did," replied Dr. Kirkland.

"Why did you call me to your office and fight for me over the last several years?" said a sincere Wade.

"Because someone had to," replied Dr. Kirkland. He stood and extended a hand. "Congratulations, Young Wade. You are on your way!"

Dr. Kirkland reached into this back pocket and pulled out a notebook. He turned the pages in the book until stopping at one with a long list of names. Wade noticed that some of the names had check marks, while others didn't, but no names had been crossed out. Dr. Kirkland allowed Wade to see him put a check by the name 'Wade McCoy'.

"What's that about?" asked Wade with curiosity.

Dr. Kirkland failed to respond. Instead, he gathered his briefcase.

"Dr. Kirkland, why did you check off my name?"

"Over the years, I've come across many students. I've pulled many aside and encouraged them to go into various studies. Some were more suited for dentistry or physical therapy, or even forestry. For the past thirty years I've climbed those stairs thinking about which student had what it takes to make it."

"Really?" said Wade. "You told me that by my second test."

"That's right, Wade. That was three years ago and now here you are, a future doctor."

"But why did you do it? Hardly any other professor does. Most of them delight in telling students how hard graduate school is, how they don't have what it takes."

"Maybe I'll tell you sometime," said Kirkland.

"Ah, tell me now," begged Wade. "As you know, you're getting old and you might not be here the next time I stop by."

"I'm not that old and don't get smart with me, boy. I could put a stop to that little letter you just got," Kirkland said with a stony face.

"I'm sorry," said Wade. "Please accept my apology. I got carried away with . . ."

Dr. Kirkland smiled. "I'm just giving you a hard time," he said. "You're still gullible, Wade!"

"You get me every time. When am I going to learn?"

Dr. Kirkland looked out the small second-story window. He saw it was snowing hard outside, which sparked a distant memory. He reached into his pocket and retrieved three worn-slick silver dollars. He flipped them through his fingers while Wade watched.

"To understand, you'd have to understand these silver dollars," said Dr. Kirkland.

"I'm guessing by all the snow falling outside that school will soon get called, so why don't you tell me about them."

"But it's such a long story," replied Dr. Kirkland.

Wade smiled. "I've got all the time in the world."

"I'd have to start way back when I was a kid. I was left alone in my small hometown of Atoka because I convinced my folks I didn't want to move. That was a different world. You see Wade, we don't just live one life in this world. We live several lives at different stages. You've just gone through a couple. I've lived many lives. Back then I wasn't Dr. Kirkland, I was just Kirk, a poor kid trying not to starve to death."

Dr. Kirkland leaned back in his chair, a sign he was willing to talk. Wade knew he was in for a treat.

"To understand how it all fell together, you have to go back to Kirk in the winter of 1945."

"Sounds great. I'm listening."

"Kirk had just begun his employment at the . . ."

"Who's Kirk?" interrupted Wade.

"Like I said, that was a different time. I was a different person. I wasn't Dr. Kirkland, I was just Kirk. And Wade?"

"Yes, Dr. Kirkland."

"Don't interrupt me again, if you want to hear this story."

Chapter 2

Atoka, Oklahoma, 1945

Kirk's shoulders throbbed in pain as he scrubbed the counter of the drugstore fountain in perpetual motions that seemed to have no end. It was as if he were in the middle of some wretched new physical workout, using muscles repetitiously he'd never before used. To move his mind away from the pain, Kirk thought of his high-school basketball team and all the ridiculous conditioning drills his coach forced upon them each day. After a few moments, Kirk smiled. Just thinking about practicing basketball made his arms hurt more than scrubbing the counter.

"You're making progress," said Carney. "Now, give your rag a good rinsing over at the sink and I think you'll be on your way."

"Yes sir," replied Kirk.

As Kirk walked to the fountain's sink, he gave the counter a quick look over to gauge his work. So far, his work looked great, but he was faced with a colossal deposit of gunk on the soda-fountain countertop. It was a mess like he'd never before seen: cherry syrup, malt, vanilla ice cream, soda pop, and lime seeds all mixed together and dried over the countertop that ran the length of the soda fountain.

"Ever seen such a mess?" asked Carney with a smile.

"Sure haven't, Mr. Carney," said Kirk, in a delayed response. He never looked at Carney, nor changed his facial expression. The cluttered countertop was frustrating, but he was too reserved to show it.

Carney placed his hand on Kirk's shoulder. "I don't like being called Mr. Carney. My friends call me Skeet."

Kirk absorbed the words. Without thinking, he blurted out: "My friends call me . . ." but couldn't muster the courage.

"Your friends call you what?" Carney asked politely.

"They call me . . . well, sir, they call me lots of things, so Henry will probably do just fine."

Kirk wanted to tell Carney his friends refer to him as Kirk, not Henry. As a matter of fact, only his folks and a few close friends still called him Henry. He'd been known as Kirk since he started at Dunbar School, the black segregated school on the east side of Atoka, many years ago. Most of his friends wouldn't even know his name is Henry Kirkland, Jr.

"So Henry it is," said Carney with a smile.

"Yes sir, Mr. Carney. I mean, Skeet."

"I'd better get back to my job. If you have any problems or need any help, don't hesitate to let me know. Being your first day here, I expect you'll have questions."

The cowbells on the front door rang out, signaling that someone was either entering or exiting the drugstore. Kirk looked up and noticed a white man, dressed in an expensive suit, complete with a dress hat, walking toward him. Kirk assumed that it was a customer, so he went back to scrubbing the counter.

Carney gave Kirk the thumbs up as he walked back to the pharmacy, where two fat bearded men, appearing to be father and son, impatiently waited for their prescription to be filled.

"I got better things to do than to stand here and watch you coach that boy on how to do your dirty work," snapped the older man.

"I'm sorry for the wait," said Carney, with a forced smile. "This is Henry's first day and I was just helping him get started."

"First day, huh?"

"Sure is," replied Carney. He took the prescription from the older man, then walked behind the counter and started gathering pills. "Henry will be coming in before and after school to help out."

A scowl shot across upon the old man's bearded face. "What's the matter, weren't there no white boys needin' a job?"

The younger bearded man ran his hands over his face and fidgeted with his coat. Kirk sensed his nervousness.

Carney paused, and then forced another smile. "Actually, Henry's going to be doing the job I used to do when I was a kid workin' at Atoka Drug, cleaning and what not. His parents moved to Langston this morning, leaving Henry to fend for himself and I kinda figured he might need a way to make ends meet, so I . . ."

"His parents left him here, alone?" asked the younger man, visibly shocked.

Carney grabbed a wholesale bottle of pills from the shelf and began dispensing. "Yeah, but the decision to stay was his own. His folks are good people, they just had a better opportunity in Langston. His stepfather, Henry Colbert, is one heck of a bricklayer. He got a great job teaching masonry at Langston College. Henry just turned fourteen and figured he was old enough to look after himself. Somehow, he convinced his parents he should stay in Atoka so he could play ball with his friends."

Kirk scrubbed as quietly as he could in order to hear the conversation. The talk made him uncomfortable, but he was still trying to gauge his employer. Carney's reaction to the bearded men would be telling.

"I don't reckon it makes a damn to me," replied the old man, "but I don't see why in the world it makes a damn to you. You some kinda guardian angel?"

The younger man rolled his eyes and let out a loud sigh. Kirk sensed the son becoming more uncomfortable.

Carney shook his head. "Of course not."

"Then why you takin' in a colored boy of all people?"

Carney thought for a moment. "The same reason I'd take in your son if he were in the same boat."

"I can smell what you're standing in, but if you ask me he won't be worth a damn. Figure he'll end up like the rest of 'em across the tracks. Too lazy to work, just livin' hand to mouth their whole lives."

"There's plenty of white folks 'round here who aren't worth a damn, Dad," the son said in a weak voice. Kirk could tell the words took every bit of the young man's courage.

The older man gave a look to his son so nasty it seemed to freeze time. While the tension grew more and more uncomfortable with each passing second, Kirk quickly realized he'd become lost in the conversation. As a matter of fact, he was no longer scrubbing the counter, he was leaning against it, staring at the men. He soon made eye contact with the son, which sent Kirk's stomach into summersaults. He began scrubbing again.

"Will there be anything else?" Carney asked. He placed the bottle of pills in a sack and rang up the register.

"I reckon not," said the old bearded man.

The man quietly paid for his prescription, grabbed the bag, and led his son toward the door. Kirk tried to look busy as they passed by. He breathed a sigh of relief as the old man walked by first. He quickly decided to make a gesture of recognition to the younger man, just something small that would let the son know he appreciated his courage. Even though the younger man didn't really say much to thwart the old man's nasty bias, Kirk at least wanted to acknowledge it by a wave or a smile.

As the younger man passed by slowly, Kirk's stomach turned. Now's the time, he thought. His brain was sending the signal to look up and smile, but his body wasn't cooperating. He tried to raise his head and open his mouth, but instead found himself pretending to be more engaged in his work. No matter how hard he tried, he couldn't muster the movements. It was as if something more powerful were in control.

The cowbells on the front door soon sounded. Knowing the opportunity was missed, Kirk frowned. He glanced to the back and saw Carney still in the pharmacy, organizing bottles and listening to the well-dressed white man behind the counter. While the suited man spoke to Carney, he gave Kirk the evil eye and stared endlessly at him. The sight made Kirk feel uneasy, so he shifted his focus back to the counter.

After scrubbing on the counter for several minutes, Kirk finally felt a sense of ease, primarily because his apprehensions about Carney were subsiding. He was nice enough, he thought. As a matter of fact, Carney seemed as though there wasn't a mean bone in his body. After all, he took up for Kirk to the bearded man. He certainly wasn't forced to do so. Maybe he's not so bad, thought Kirk.

"Better get back to that counter, boy," called out a voice from the far end of the fountain. "It ain't gonna scrub itself."

Although Kirk didn't know where it came from, he nonetheless ignored the comment. He let out a sigh and started scrubbing on the counter again.

"I've seen orangutans who scrub better than that," the voice sounded again.

Kirk bit his lip and let the comment fly right on by. He felt sweat on his brow and knew molten-hot anger was on its way, but he maintained his composure.

"What's a matter, boy? Can't you hear?"

Kirk's fist clenched. A flash of rage shot across his forehead. He breathed slowly and quietly begged it to pass. After a few moments, he scrubbed the counter, but every impulse in his body was directing him to strut over to the heckler and give him a sound thrashin'.

While a confrontation with a customer would surely seal his fate and make his first day at the drugstore his last, it didn't matter. A man could only take so much. Kirk's pulse quickened as he pretended not to hear the comment and continued scrubbing.

"Excuse me," said the voice again.

Kirk's focus remained on the countertop.

"What in the world is a dirty nigger boy like you doin' in a nice place like this?"

Kirk's heart erupted into a frenzied pace. He felt his eyes vibrating like jackhammers in his head. He threw the rag down, clenched his fists, and then jumped over the counter. He was upon the man before the fevered anger in his head allowed his eyes to recognize the identity of who he was about to flog.

"Hold on, hold on!" said the man, as he broke into heavy laughter.

Kirk stopped dead in his tracks.

"Uncle Willie, you're a sum bitch," Kirk said while breathing a sigh of relief.

Consumed by fits of laughter, Uncle Willie struggled to make a straight face. "They ain't no doubt that little Henry's balls have dropped," he said while chuckling.

Kirk smiled. "You were about to find out up close and personal just how much they've dropped."

"Damn!" yelled Uncle Willie. "For a twelve-year-old, you sure can walk the walk. I thought I was about to get mauled by a damned grizzly bear!"

Kirk laughed. "I'm fourteen now, and you're lucky you're my uncle. If not, I would've pasted pieces of your black ass all over this store."

Willie clapped his hands and bellowed out a raucous laughter. The noise that emanated from the middle-aged black man sounded like a sick elephant. Nonetheless, it was music to Kirk's ears. It had been a rough first day. Willie's presence definitely eased Kirk's mind.

After several moments, the laughter faded. Kirk walked back to the soda fountain and scrubbed the next section of counter space.

"I guess your folks already left town?" Uncle Willie asked with a sober face.

Kirk's expressionless face never wavered. He just nodded. Uncle Willie immediately sensed Kirk was close to tears.

"You alright with it?"

Kirk continued working. After a short while, he looked up. "I reckon."

Uncle Willie walked over and placed his arm around Kirk's neck. "Now, you know if things don't work out or if you get lonely, or whatever, you've got a bed over at our house," he said.

His eyes watering, Kirk nodded.

Willie's face turned stoic. "Matter of fact, I'm gonna get the red ass if you don't come. You got that?"

Kirk nodded.

Willie could immediately sense duress. He'd known Kirk his whole life and struggling for words just wasn't his nature. As a matter of fact, he'd often wished Kirk wouldn't talk so much. Uncle Willie found a stool at the counter and sat down.

"What's the matter, Henry? Why ain't you sayin' nothin'? Do you miss your family that much?"

"No," Kirk immediately replied.

"You sure?"

"Maybe a little."

"Is they something else?"

Kirk stopped scrubbing and stepped closer to Uncle Willie. "It's this place."

Uncle Willie immediately stood up. "Is somebody messin' with you?" he flared.

"Not really. I just feel outta place, you know. This really ain't a place for colored folks."

Willie stroked his chin. "Yeah, I understand, I really do. I kinda feel outta place myself. Is Mr. Carney treatin' you right?"

"Yeah, he is, but that's just it. I don't know why he's being so nice to me."

Uncle Willie gave Kirk a puzzled look. "I don't understand what you mean."

"Why is he takin' a chance on a black boy when he could get a rich white kid or even himself to do the job?" asked Kirk.

"Look, I've known Carney for a lot of years, and I don't think you have anything to worry about."

"Yes, but it just has me thinkin', that's all," said Kirk. "Why is he drawin' all this attention to me and to himself? I have to believe most white folks aren't gonna take kindly to havin' a black kid down here."

"Maybe he believes in you. Maybe he feels like you got a chance to get the hell out of Little Dixie and do somethin' fo' yo'self," said an animated Uncle Willie. "Maybe he's one of these white folks who feels bad about all the terrible shit that's happened in the past."

Kirk stared at the floor. "Maybe so."

"What did yo' daddy say? Did you talk to him about this b'foe they left?"

"Yeah. Both he and Mama thought it was all right, but what do you expect them to say? They're leavin' they son alone in a Southern town that's filled with mainly whites. I expect they'd go along with damned near anything."

An air of serenity fell over Uncle Willie. "I'll tell you this. Normally I'd be with you and agree you can't never trust any nester, but I think Carney is different. I think he's alright."

"Yeah, maybe you're right," Kirk said, still staring at the floor.

"But don't you never forget, this is 1945 and things are still bad for blacks, especially in the south. Separate may be fine, but it damned sure ain't equal. It wasn't that long ago when the Klan was marching right through downtown."

"Really?" said a surprised Kirk. "They were here?"

"Hell yeah, they was here," said Uncle Willie. "Trust me, Henry, I remember when the Klan was crackin' the skulls of black kids in this town. No one likes to remember, but it did happen, right out there on Court Street."

"Damn," said Kirk. "I'm glad it was before my time."

"While I believe Carney to be a good man, sometimes good men do bad things when they face pressure from they peers. You know what I mean?"

"I do," replied Kirk.

"But don't let that get in yo' way. I think you'll be alright, plus I'm never gonna be too far away."

Kirk stared at the floor in silence, lost in his thoughts.

"Everything's gonna be fine. Understand?"

Kirk slowly nodded. "I guess you're right."

Uncle Willie smiled, then raised his hat and stroked his hair. "You damned right I'm right," he said. "Willie's always right. Now get yo' black ass back to work." He laughed.

Kirk smiled as he watched Uncle Willie exit the building.

"Excuse me, Henry," said a voice from behind.

Kirk quickly turned around and spotted Carney standing with the suited white man.

"Yes sir," replied Kirk.

"I want you to meet someone," said Carney. "This is Duke Russo."

Kirk looked up and found Russo, still giving him the evil eye, had extended his hand. Kirk shook it reluctantly.

"Russo is the owner of the building," said Carney. "He and I are partners in this pharmacy."

"Nice to meet you," said Kirk.

"Have you ever done anything like this before?" asked Russo.

"No, sir."

"Never?" asked Russo, condescendingly.

"No. I'm used to doing hard work with my father, like choppin' wood, haulin' brick, and workin' cattle out at the Brooks Ranch."

"Well," said Russo sternly, "you'll be expected to work here. I'll not have any loafers on my payroll."

"Of course not," said Kirk.

Carney was quick to intervene. "You'll not have anything to worry about with Young Henry," he said. "I know for a fact he's a great worker, a good student, and an all-around good kid."

"He'd better be," said Russo. "Cause I'll be watchin'."

Carney smiled. "You have absolutely nothing to worry about with Henry. I promise."

"We'll see," said Russo. He buttoned his coat and headed for the door. "I'll not tolerate stealing or any other tomfoolery."

As Russo walked to the door, Carney called out, "Duke."

As soon as Russo turned around, Carney was right in his face. "Duke, I'm having a hard time understanding why you're being so indignant to Young Henry," said Carney. "Has he done something to offend you?"

"It's nothing personal," said Russo. "I just want this young man to know our rules."

"I think he understands our rules and I know he will be a fine asset to our company. Are we clear on this issue?"

Russo nodded. "I'll see you in the morning, Skeet."

"We can talk more about this then," replied Carney.

As soon as the cowbells rang, Carney grabbed Henry by the shoulder.

"Don't worry about him. He's a businessman and sees the world through that perspective. He means no harm to you, he's just trying to protect his money and his investments."

"Sure thing," said Kirk. "Easy come, easy go."

With his hands in his slacks pockets, Carney smiled and then extended his arms out, forcing his elbows down to his belt, as if he were trying to pull up his slacks without using his hands. He then raised his right hand to his mouth, swiping his extended finger across his upper lip. "I think you and I are going to get along great," he said with a big smile.

Kirk noticed the unusual act and wondered if it were a nervous tic. "Me, too."

"Oh, and one more thing: My wife needs me at home, so we're going to close up early tonight."

Carney reached inside his coat and retrieved an envelope, which had Kirk's name written across the top.

"I want you to have this," said Carney with a soft smile.

A little hesitant at first, Kirk slowly reached out and retrieved the envelope. "What is . . ."

"It's just something to help you get started. It's not an advance, so you don't have to pay it back. It's a gift."

Kirk felt a blast of humility explode in his stomach. "You didn't have to . . ."

"I know, I know, but I wanted to," said Carney.

"Well, thanks."

"Don't mention it. Now finish up quick so we can get out of here."

With rag in hand, Kirk was quick to finish the counter. He rinsed his rag, put on his coat, then met Carney at the front door.

A brisk wind greeted them as they both walked into the cold night air.

"I didn't realize it was so cold," said Carney, as he locked the front door. "This is much colder than this morning. A blue northerner must have blown in."

"I'll say. Gonna be cold tonight."

"Wait here. I'll pull the car around and give you a ride home."

"Thanks, but I have a few things I need to do."

"Suit yourself. I'll see you in the morning."

Carney sprinted over to his car, then slowly wheeled down Court Street. As soon as he was out of sight, Kirk retrieved the envelope from his pocket and looked inside. He found five dollars, which was a hell of a lot of money to a broke and lonely kid.

"Wow," he muttered to himself.

Kirk looked through the darkness and noticed most of the town was just about shut down. It was after five and there were no visible signs of life. As he walked down the sidewalk, he felt the wind blowing through his thin worn-out coat. The coldness, which seemed to permeate his bones, worsened his tired and hungry state of consciousness.

He buttoned up his coat and kicked his pace into a lope. He knew of only one place able to make things better: Johnny's Cafe. He couldn't get there fast enough.

As Henry jogged past the front entrance to the cafe, he smelled the aroma of freshly-cooked food through the open front door, reserved for whites only. He sprinted around the corner, into the alley, and finally arrived at the back door.

Warm air greeted Kirk as he made his way toward the kitchen. Knowing him as a regular, the cooks smiled and said hi as he walked to the back, where he sat at the only table where the establishment allowed blacks to eat.

Rosna, the waitress, was on her way up front to take some orders when she stopped at Kirk's table. "Are you having your regular?" she asked.

Kirk smiled. "Yes ma'am. And please make it a double."

After a brief wait, two bowls of chili arrived complete with crackers, cheese, and a bottle of ice-cold Coke. Kirk tore through the chili like a lost dog.

"Are you a little hungry tonight, sugar?" joked Rosna.

"Indeed I am," said Kirk. "Been lookin' forward to this all day."

"Would you like another?"

Kirk had eaten so much he wasn't sure he could walk, much less find the energy to sit up straight and eat more. "I don't think so. I best be gettin' on home."

"Suit yourself."

After a few moments, he finally found the energy to stand. He reached into the envelope, removed a dollar, and placed it on the table. He then grabbed his Coke and walked to the back door.

"You take care now, Kirk," said one of the cooks. "It's gonna get cold tonight, so keep warm."

"I'll do my best. Thank you."

Kirk left through the back door, then past the dock, and into the dark alley behind Johnny's. The miserable cold-night air instantly reminded him of the creepy short walk through the alley that awaited him. Home was only a couple of miles away, but the walk through the alley was the part that he dreaded the most. Nightlights stood on the docks of each of the businesses, so the entire walk down the alley wouldn't be in total darkness. However, after passing through the light of one of the nightlights, the way would instantly turn to complete darkness until the next nightlight appeared. Kirk didn't mind the portions of the alley that were lit, but he sincerely disliked the few steps afterward which were in total darkness. He often feared someone could be waiting.

Kirk said a prayer, then quickly ran down the alley. As he encountered quick flashes of lightness and darkness, he breathed in short bursts, just like in basketball. In an instant, it was over. He turned the corner and was back on Court Street. He let out a sigh and slowed his gait to a walk. The cold walk was miserable, but at least he wasn't hungry.

As he made his way to the railroad tracks, he felt snow softly trickle down onto his head. He looked up and noticed thick, heavy clouds filled the night skyline, indicating a big storm was looming. With his family gone, he sensed intuitively that perhaps other storms were coming, too.

Maybe the snow storm was God's way of telling him to be strong because his world was about to get turbulent.

Kirk did his best to shake off the chill and braced himself for the longest leg of his journey home, the jog down the railroad tracks. He looked at his wristwatch and waited until the second hand reached twelve. As soon as it did, he lowered his head and began his brisk jog into the wind. His two-mile journey would be long and cold, but he would be home soon. A thought which made him smile.

Chapter 3

Knowing his house was near, Kirk stopped jogging and stepped off the train tracks. He looked at his watch. His run took just under sixteen minutes. It was no record but he was proud, given the adverse conditions.

Kirk watched as his breath rose into the night air, indicating the temperature was still dropping. He wasn't too bothered by the cold, however, because he had finally reached the two giant oak trees beside the tracks. These landmarks were always a happy sight because their presence indicated that his house was close. He passed through the opening between the oak trees and walked until he reached his backyard. After quickly darting around the house, he stopped in the front driveway and looked across the road. Snow was already accumulating on the roof of Dunbar, his school. Although it was just beginning, Kirk hoped the storm would produce enough snowfall to cancel school.

With his first day of work still fresh in his mind, he gazed around the area surrounding his house. He saw a stark contrast between the area behind the drugstore and the neighborhood he called home. He quickly understood why this area was known as the other side of the tracks. Since only a few of his neighbors had electricity, the streets and houses were pitch dark, ironic since the area was known as "Black Town." Kirk wasn't ashamed, but for the first time in his life, he certainly recognized the difference.

As he approached the house he'd helped his father build, the feeling was bittersweet. Since his family was gone, he was now the man of the house, but wasn't so sure he was ready. Everything seemed new, including the same old routines he'd been following for years. Even the sight of his house was different. He wondered if the place would ever feel like home again.

Kirk walked onto the front porch and looked through the front door's small window. He saw nothing but darkness, a bleak reminder that the house was empty. Due to the numbness in his hands caused by the cold temperature, he fumbled with the keys but was finally able to open the door and walk inside. Upon his arrival, he immediately sensed the house seemed colder than the air outside.

He relied on his memory to find his way through the dark and locate the coal-oil lamp, and then slowly made his way over to the old oak desk and felt around for the drawer which contained the matches. As he reached down to open the drawer, he heard a ghastly sound. Scared, Kirk froze in his tracks.

"Henry."

Kirk couldn't move. The voice was a whisper, yet it shattered the silence like breaking glass. It was the eeriest thing Kirk had ever heard. In an evasive move, he silently dropped to the floor. He reckoned if an intruder were in the house and meant to do him harm, he'd have a harder time finding him on the floor.

Since he'd fallen to the floor with little sound, his confidence grew. He decided it would be best to get to the front door. The only problem was the house was so dark, he had no idea where the front door stood.

"Hennnnnnnnnnnnnnn-reeeeeeeeee," the voice sounded again.

Kirk felt sweat pouring off his body. Even though his limbs were still frozen from fright, they shook violently.

"I'm comin' to get you, Henry," said the voice, now growing louder, as if it were coming closer.

Kirk exhaled, helping him gain control of his arms. After a few moments, all the feeling in his limbs came back. He felt around in the darkness and finally found something firm. He wasn't sure what it was, but it weighed a couple of pounds and could be used as a weapon.

"I'm gonna get ya, boy."

The voice was very near now. Kirk assumed it was only a few feet away. He knew any sound he made would give away his position, so he closed his mouth and breathed through his nose. With the weapon drawn back, he waited.

Suddenly, he heard a cracking sound. After a quick assessment, he recognized it as the sound of a match striking a hard surface. He knew in a matter of moments, he would be forced to make a fight or flight decision.

As he contemplated his next move, the words of his father rang out in his head: "Junior, it's time to be a man!" Within a split second, a gust of courage swept over Kirk. It was time to fight.

He calculated the intruder's position by the sound of the match. No sparks showed, but he knew enough of the intruder's location to at least make contact with the object he held in his hand. He rose to his feet, exhaled silently, and threw the object with all his might at the intruder.

To his surprise, the intruder began to laugh. Not a quiet, controlled laugh, but a boisterous man-laugh, a laugh only a friend could muster from an inside joke. A best friend, like Ralph. But that was impossible. Ralph was in Langston, attending college.

"Who the hell are you and what do you want?" Kirk screamed into the darkness.

The laughter continued, growing louder and louder. It almost sounded forced, as if someone was tormenting him before bringing harm.

"I've got a gun," threatened Kirk, "and I'm not afraid to use it!"

The laughter stopped.

"I don't see no point in pullin' yo' gun," said the voice.

Kirk exhaled and breathed easy.

"Ralph, what the hell are you doin' in my house?"

Ralph successfully struck a match. He walked over and lit the coal-oil lamp.

"Kirk, you haven't called me Ralph since you were in kindergarten. The name is Ripp."

"I know that," said Kirk, still upset. "But when you break and enter, don't expect me to be your pal!"

Ripp picked up the object Kirk had just thrown at him. It was a girl's doll.

"Is this how you're gettin' by now that yo' family is gone? Playing with little girl's dolls?"

Kirk grabbed the doll. "This belongs to my little sister. It must have fallen out of a box when they moved this morning."

Ripp smiled. "Uh huh," he said with sarcasm. "Sure it's your little sister's. Oh yeah, I believe that. Oh, and by the way, there are deadlier weapons than a little girl's doll."

"Har har," replied Kirk. "You don't know how close you came to getting maimed. If only I had my gun in my hands . . ."

"Shit. If I knew you had a gun, you think I would have even thought about comin' in here and scarin' you?"

"Hey . . . I just realized something," said Kirk. "Why aren't you at Langston? Did they cancel Friday classes?"

Ripp hung his head low. He cleared his throat.

"What's wrong?" said Kirk.

"I'm done with that."

"What do you mean?"

"It just didn't work out. College ain't for me."

"But what about baseball? You're givin' that up?"

"I don't know," replied Ripp. "I'm thinkin' 'bout trying out for a semi-pro team."

"What's wrong with college? Too hard?"

"Hell, yeah. I tried, Kirk, I promise. It's just too much for a dumb old black kid like myself. Ain't no way I can go to school and play baseball for the college. Ain't no way. The class work is just too much."

Ripp had just dropped a bombshell and Kirk wasn't sure how to react. Should he be compassionate and sympathize with his best friend, or should he act in Ripp's best interests and scold him for quitting? Tough decision, he thought.

"I'm sorry to hear that," said Kirk. "You know Carney ain't gonna like it."

"He's already been over to the house and spoke to Mom and Dad."

"What? How did he know?" asked Kirk.

"That's just it," Ripp said and pointed his finger at Kirk. "Hell, if I know. That white man must have some kinda special powers, 'cause I didn't tell no one I was quittin' school. I came home earlier today, planning to tell my folks when I got here, but Carney beat me to it."

"No lie?" Kirk asked as a chill went up his spine. "Maybe he does have special powers."

"Wouldn't surprise me," said Ripp.

"Maybe Carney knows one of your professors."

"I'm tellin' you, Kirk, I haven't told a soul."

"That's weird."

Ripp replied with a soft voice, "Maybe he's clairvoyant!"

"Clarawhatant?" Kirk quickly asked.

"Clairvoyant."

Kirk shook his head. "You go off to school and come home usin' big words. What are you sayin'?"

"Aw hell, it's nothin'. Just a word I learned last month. It means someone who can predict the future or has special senses about things that are happenin' or will happen in the future," Ripp said.

Kirk shook his head. "I don't know about all that. I just know it spooks me wondering how he knew. I'll see if I can find out tomorrow. So, what did Carney say?"

"He wasn't mad, more like disappointed, I guess. He told me and my folks he'd do whatever he needed to do to make me stay. Of course, Dad was pretty hot about me leavin', so it wasn't a good situation for me. I left and came here."

Kirk let silence hang in the air for a moment while he pondered Ripp's plight. "What are you planning to do?" Kirk finally asked.

Ripp stroked his chin in thought. "I don't know. Probably help Dad down at the Chevrolet place. Make some money, try to get my shit together. You know, take my time to get a plan."

"I've got to be honest with you. It's sad that you left college, but I am glad you're back."

"Me, too."

Kirk finally felt the warmth from the coal-oil lamp. He rubbed his hands together to get the full effect.

"Damn, it's cold in here, Kirk," said Ripp. "You're not really gonna stay in here tonight, are you?"

"I have to. It's my home."

"But it's so cold. How can you stand it?"

"You'd be surprised at how much heat that lamp gives off when it gets going. It just takes a while. Normally, my mom would have it on all day, so when I get home from school, it would be pretty nice in here. The pot belly stove adds a lot of heat, too," Kirk said, then paused. "Of course, she's not gonna be here anymore so . . ."

"Are you gonna be alright with not havin' family nearby?" Ripp asked.

"Yeah, I think so. I don't expect it to be easy, but I'll get by."

"How did you talk them into lettin' you stay?"

"I had to beg 'em," said Kirk, with a stoic face. "It wasn't easy. Dad was offered a real good job up at the college in Langston, teachin' folks how to lay bricks. He didn't want it at first, but they offered him some pretty decent money. Anyway, he and Mom told me we were moving and I told them I wanted to stay."

"That doesn't sound so bad."

"I had to beg for several days straight. I think they finally got tired of arguing with me."

"And this is your first day to be all alone?"

"Sure is," Kirk said with a forced smile. "I think I'll be okay."

"I know you will. But if you ever miss people, you're more than welcome at our house," Ripp said as he walked to the front door of the shack. "Oh, and by the way, how 'bout we go to the river tomorrow night? We can build a bonfire, just like in the old days."

"You're on. Of course, the old days were just last winter," laughed Kirk.

Ripp shook his head. "It seems longer than that."

"Time flies, doesn't it?"

"Well, I best be gone. I'll give you a holler tomorrow." Ripp walked outside into the cold night air.

Kirk walked to the small window by the front door. As he spotted Ripp entering his car, his mind wandered. Although he did his best to hide his emotions, he felt very disappointed Ripp failed at college. For most of his life, Kirk wondered if he himself would go to college. With this in mind, his friend's early departure caused doubt. If Ripp couldn't make it, how could I, thought Kirk. Ripp was a smart guy. Sure, he sometimes allowed baseball or the girls to sway his priorities away from his studies, but he was smart enough to never allow that to hurt his grades in high school. Evidently college was much more challenging than Kirk previously thought. He felt the disappointment weighing down on him.

As he walked into the living room to get ready for bed, Ripp's failure remained on his mind. College was a few years away, so maybe there was time to prepare. Maybe Ripp just didn't want it badly enough. It was a lot for a fourteen year-old boy to think about in a cold house all by himself.

Kirk picked up the coal-oil lamp and placed it on the table next to his bed in the living room. He kicked off his shoes and frantically covered himself with four thick blankets. After he finally found a comfortable spot, he looked up. Since the old shack didn't have a finished ceiling, Kirk could see through the small holes in the roof. He saw whirlwinds of snow blowing through the air, some of it even falling right on top of him. This was a usual occurrence with the shack's worn roof. Be it snow, rain, or sleet, Kirk and his family were used to seeing Mother Nature up close and personal through the roof in their home. As always, there was only one person to make things right. The dearest of the dear, his mother, Laura Colbert.

"Mom!" called Kirk. "Mom!" he shouted again.

Kirk's face cracked a smile as he remembered that his protector/cook/doctor and every other service provider a boy needs was miles away.

"This is probably gonna take some getting used to," he muttered to himself.

Feelings of sadness and isolation engulfed him, but Kirk reminded himself he'd asked for this arrangement. He would be fine, he thought. It would take some getting used to, but things would work out.

A big believer in the power of imagination, Kirk's thoughts soon shifted to basketball. Soon, he was knocking down buckets for the University of Oklahoma's basketball team. The crowd roared as he led his team in the final seconds of the NCAA Championship Game. With seconds counting down, Kirk dribbled down the court, jumped up, and shot a thirty-five footer, swooshing the net as the buzzer sounded, bringing victory for the OU Sooners. The crowd went crazy! His teammates hoisted him on their shoulders as they cut down the net. All was well in the mind of Kirk.

He opened his eyes and saw more snow falling down lightly through the roof, a cold reminder the daydream was just that, a daydream, especially since he was only fourteen years old and black, two traits that had never been allowed on the Sooner's basketball team in 1945.

In the past, when feelings of despair crept into his psyche, Kirk relied on his imagination to find a happier place. As he grew older and encountered more and more of life's turmoil, he used this trick often. Kirk rolled the blankets around him tight. He then prayed his imagination would stay strong and vibrant. He had a bad feeling he would need it.

Chapter 4

Kirk opened his eyes. He quickly realized he was at home, lying on the cot in the living room. His brain reeled, and he looked around to familiarize himself with his surroundings. He quickly spotted the roof and remembered how the snow fell on top of him during the night.

"Damn," he said, recalling a strange dream about a large snowman hitting on his girlfriend, Vanessa.

Kirk quickly uncovered and got up while looking at his shoes and noted they were still worn and tattered. They hadn't been magically repaired during his sleep.

He walked to the kitchen counter and grabbed a knife from a drawer, then picked up an unused moving box from the small kitchen table. With great skill, Kirk used his knife on the cardboard boxes to cut out some new soles for his shoes. After that task was completed, he grabbed some wire from his notebook and used it to sew up the larger holes in his shoes. Kirk was well schooled at this trick as he'd done it multiple times in the past.

After he'd repaired his shoes, he walked over to the sink, washed his face from the water bucket, preparing himself to start his day. He turned off the coal oil lamp, made a quick dash for the front door, and stepped out into the dark and cold early-morning air.

As he walked toward the tracks, Kirk looked at his watch and saw it read five a.m. Since he'd often worried about having the ability to get up on his own, the sight made him smile. Normally, his mother would awaken him. He'd wondered if he would have the fortitude to do it by himself. As he stepped onto the tracks, he realized he'd passed the first test with flying colors. The smile on his face seemed to beam into the early morning air as he jogged the two-mile journey to his first stop.

By the time Kirk reached the front of the newspaper shop, his blood circulated throughout his body. Even though the temperature was just below freezing, he felt no discomfort. As a matter of fact, he actually felt fantastic and grateful to be alive. He looked to the nearby drugstore. It was dark inside, signaling that Carney had not yet arrived. He felt proud he was out and about before the old man.

Kirk jogged down the alley, turned the corner, then stopped at the back of the newspaper shop, near the dock. As always, Mark Maston, the owner of the newspaper shop, left the large stack of papers behind the dumpster for Kirk's early-morning delivery. Kirk picked up the stack to load them onto a small wagon he used for transporting the papers for delivery. There was only one small problem: The wagon was nowhere to be found. He searched the dock and its surrounding area for several minutes. He even opened the big dumpster and looked inside, but the wagon simply wasn't there.

Kirk knew he didn't have the strength to carry and deliver so many papers without the wagon. He thought about walking to Mark's house, but given the early morning hour, he quickly ascertained that Mark would still be asleep and probably wouldn't have much interest in helping the paperboy.

While sitting on the dock steps trying to figure out what to do, he gave a big sigh.

"I don't give a damn what he says," shouted a voice from around the corner. "He may have dreamed up this plan, but I'm the one running this show and we'll do it my way!"

Frightened, Kirk quickly jumped behind the trash dumpster.

"I'm not askin' you to change the plan," said another voice. "I'm simply telling you we have to be compliant with his wishes. Without him, we can't pull this off."

Knowing his position behind the dumpster was hidden in the darkness, Kirk stared intently in the direction of the voices. He could hear them growing louder and louder. Fear shot up his spine.

"You're not listening to me!" shouted a short man, turning the corner.

Kirk immediately recognized his boss, Mark. "I don't give a damn about what he wants!"

"Easy, easy," said the accomplice. "This can all be worked out among the three of us, I promise."

At first, Kirk couldn't place the other man, but as soon as the man stepped into the dock's night lights, Kirk remembered the face. It was Russo, Carney's partner at the drugstore.

What the hell are these two men doing out here this early in the morning, thought Kirk.

Mark removed his keys and unlocked the back door. "Persistence and a strong hand are the only things this fellow understands. Trust me, you don't know him like I do."

"He's a man of reason," replied Russo. "And I promise I can get through to him."

"You'd better," said Mark, "because if the public finds out about this, we're all through. Our lives will be over. Our businesses, our families, everything we hold dear in Atoka will be finished."

"You're not tellin' me anything I already didn't know," said Russo.

"Good. Let's get this loaded and get it on over to Stringtown."

Both men entered the newspaper shop. The door closed behind them.

Kirk was uncertain as to what to do. He wasn't sure what Mark and Russo were up to, but he was sure it was no good. Kirk had been throwing papers for Mark for three years. Even though Mark was small, Kirk knew he was extremely mean and vindictive. Kirk never saw him use violence on anyone, but he heard the threats many times. Of course, Kirk didn't know Duke Russo, but what he'd learned from him the day before was more than enough to know to stay away.

His interest was piqued, but he was still unsure. He feared both men and knew that if they caught him spying, there would be hell to pay. But then again, he thought, chances like this don't come along very often.

He braced himself with a drain pipe that ran down the side of the building, then climbed up the trash dumpster. A significant amount of snow and ice covered the top of the dumpster, so he was extra cautious not to shift weight too quickly as he slowly straightened his torso. After mustering his courage, he peered through the high window and looked down into the back of the newspaper shop.

Kirk saw the two men loading something into the trunk of Russo's black Studebaker. The item looked to be several feet long, wrapped in blankets, and heavy enough that it took both men to load it. Again, fear shot through Kirk's spine. He had no way of knowing for certain, but it appeared the men were loading a body into the trunk of Russo's car.

Kirk's mind was whirling and racing. What if they saw him? Would they kill him, too? He felt sweaty inside his coat.

Finally, rationality set in. This whole thing is absurd, he thought. These men were two of Atoka's most prominent businessmen. Why would they be discarding a body? Kirk shivered, as an epiphany hit him. Maybe that's how they became two of Atoka's most prominent businessmen.

A flood of emotions hit Kirk. Gone was his daring confidence. If caught spying, he was a goner. He quickly decided that it was time to leave.

He tried to step down, but his foot slipped on the snow and he crashed onto the dumpster. A loud thud resonated throughout the alley and into the newspaper shop. Kirk ran to the pile of newspapers and lifted with all his might. As he rounded the corner of the building and ran into the dark alley, he heard men's voices at the newspaper shop's back door. Like a flash, he sprinted down the dark alley, crossed Court Street to the south, then ducked into another dark alley on the other side of the street. He then headed east to deliver his papers.

"What the hell was that?" quipped Mark as he stepped out to the dock. His temper flared, and he frantically searched the surroundings for anything suspicious. "Who would be out and about this early in the morning?"

"You got me, but I aim to find out," said Russo as he retrieved a pistol from his coat. Gun in hand, he walked around the dock.

Mark lowered Russo's pistol. "I know who it was."

"Who?" demanded Russo.

"It was that boy who delivers newspapers." Mark walked over to the dumpster. "See, the newspapers are gone. I put them out here just before you got here. I'll bet he slipped on the ice while he was carrying them away."

"You think he saw anything?" asked Russo.

"Naw," replied Mark. "Besides, he's harmless."

Russo walked over and inspected the dumpster. A look of surprise filled his face when he noticed footprints all over the top of the dumpster. Russo looked up and spotted the small window, which hung high on the wall.

"Harmless, huh?" he said to himself.

"What was that?" asked Mark, oblivious to Russo's discovery.

Russo gave Mark a long stare. "Nothing."

"Let's get the hell outta here."

"Agreed," said Russo.

The two men entered the back door of the newspaper shop. While Russo started the car, Mark slid open the massive back door. Russo slowly pulled the car through. After closing and latching the door, Mark jumped into the passenger side.

"I know the roads are slick, but we need to hurry. I told Battle Axe to meet us at five-forty-five at the corner."

Russo remained silent.

"Something buggin' you?" asked Mark.

"Witnesses always bug me and they should bug you, too."

"Relax, you have nothing to fear. The kid didn't see anything. And even if he did, he wouldn't have the faintest idea what we're doing."

Russo responded with a long, deep stare. Mark had seen the look before and knew it meant that he should just shut up.

Russo shook his head, then looked forward. He steered the car onto Highway 69, which led north out of town. He exhaled a deep breath as the reality of the situation set in. He now had a new problem to deal with.

# # #

Walking briskly, Kirk entered the east side of town near his home. Located on the other side of the railroad tracks, this area was the primary location for black housing in Atoka. He knew this area well and could move through it quickly. Judging by the weight difference of the stack of papers, Kirk figured he'd thrown about half of the papers. He was grateful the run was going so smoothly without the wagon. As a matter of fact, the process was actually going better than usual. With the wagon, he could only travel on streets and sidewalks. Now he had the freedom to travel through back yards and over fences, which saved time. Although the process of carrying the heavy stack of papers was much more strenuous, he loved the mobility. Since he was getting older and stronger, Kirk decided he'd try this routine again the next day.

He walked down Elgin Street and threw papers until he came to the cross street of Mackay Avenue. Kirk sighed as he stepped onto the yard of Mrs. Parker. His quickened pace was about to face a major hurdle.

Kirk dearly loved Mrs. Parker, but was politely leery of her, due to her affliction. She was seventy-three years old and probably the greatest cook in the free world, even better than his mother. Sometimes after church, Kirk and his family would go to Mrs. Parker's house and eat lunch until they simply could eat no more. The food and hospitality were awe inspiring, but there was a drawback—Mrs. Parker's love of oration.

In all his life, Kirk never encountered a human being who liked to talk so much. Just when he and his family thought the conversation was over, she'd get her second wind and talk some more. Of course, her words were harmless, but she had a way of grating through people's nerves like the slow drip drip dripping of water torture. Others described it as fingernails on a chalkboard. Sometimes during summer walks, Kirk's dad would lead the family around Mrs. Parker's house, even if it meant walking an additional mile when everyone was dog tired.

As Kirk entered Mrs. Parker's yard, he was careful not to make a sound. There was still enough darkness outside to hide a young agile man who moved in stealth-like strides, so he felt he could get away if she suddenly opened the door. Instead of throwing the newspaper, he silently crept up the sidewalk and laid the newspaper on the porch. He looked around the premises and noticed no movement.

Since the curtains were closed, he couldn't tell if the lights inside Mrs. Parker's home were on or not. Her house was the envy of her neighbors as it was the only home in the all-black neighborhood that had electricity. Mrs. Parker's husband was the unofficial mayor of Dunbar. Since he had a little money and some influence, he was able to sweet talk the electric company into wiring their house.

He turned and quietly crept to the sidewalk, then walked toward the next house. For once, it appeared he was about to get away.

"Henry Kirkland, don't you even think for a minute that you's gonna deliver my paper without sayin' hi," bellowed a voice from behind.

Kirk rolled his eyes because he instantly knew it was Mrs. Parker. She was one of only a few who called him Henry. He knew he was caught, but it really wasn't so bad. He felt a familiar feeling, like when his mother would call him in to dinner, which made him smile. He turned around.

"Oh, no, no, that's not what I was tryin' to do," said Kirk. "I didn't see the lights were on in your house, so I assumed you were asleep. I didn't want to disturb you, so I . . ."

"Get yo' ass in this house right now and eat some breakfast. I promised yo' momma I'd look after you when they left, and I ain't about to go back on my word," Mrs. Parker said with fire in her voice.

Kirk knew if he dared to tell her he didn't have time to stop, her feelings would be hurt. She was a lonely woman. Her husband recently passed on and all her kids were grown and living in nearby towns. Kirk and the church were about all she had.

"Of course," said Kirk, fixing a smile. "I've been lookin' forward to your cookin' all morning."

"Damned right," said Mrs. Parker.

He followed Mrs. Parker into the kitchen. He sat down and was immediately served. After chomping down two servings of ham and eggs, grits and cheese, and biscuits and gravy, he stopped for a moment to catch his breath. Mrs. Parker sat beside him at the table, sporadically falling asleep.

"Say Mrs. Parker, what do you know about the man who owns the drugstore?"

Mrs. Parker quickly opened her eyes.

"You should call me Joyce. Mrs. Parker is my mom's name."

"All right, Joyce. What do you know about the fellow who owns the drugstore?"

"Are you talking about Mr. Carney?"

"No, Mr. Carney is a co-owner and the pharmacist. I'm talking about Russo, the man who owns the building."

"That Mr. Carney is a very nice fellow," said Mrs. Parker. "But I don't know much about Russo. He's never said much to me. Why?"

"Oh, I was just wonderin', that's all. You know I took a job down there."

"At the drugstore?"

"Yes'am. Before and after school, then all day on Saturdays."

"How you like it?" asked Mrs. Parker.

"So far, it's alright," replied Kirk while drinking some milk. "Don't reckon I've been there long enough to really know. How long has Russo been here in Atoka?"

Not hearing a reply, Kirk looked up to see Mrs. Parker sitting back in her chair with her eyes closed.

Kirk really wanted to know more about Russo, but he had much to do. He put the empty plate in the sink and walked to the front door. Mrs. Parker's snoring indicated she was now engaged in deep sleep. Kirk slipped on his coat, then opened the door and walked out into the cold early morning air. He felt much better now that he'd eaten, but his morning was only starting.

Chapter 5

As expected, Battle Axe Masters was waiting for the men at the corner of Liberty Road and Highway Sixty Nine, just north of Atoka. It was five forty-five-a.m. when Russo turned his Studebaker onto Liberty Road. Battle Axe started the engine as soon as he saw the car and drove onto a small path that led into the woods. Russo's car followed. When both cars were well into the woods, far from the eyes of any passersby, they stopped and exited their vehicles.

"Mornin', Battle Axe," said Mark. "How's life treatin' you?"

Battle Axe smiled. "Any better and I'd be institutionalized."

"I hear that," Mark replied.

"Enough of the small talk," said Russo in a stern voice. "Let's get this done."

"Sure thing," said Battle Axe.

Russo's anger over the possibility that Kirk had spotted him and his car at the newspaper shop began to fester during the short drive to the woods. For months, their actions had remained covert and now it seemed as though the kid could blow their cover.

Russo and Mark quickly unloaded the cargo, and placed it in Battle Axe's open trunk. Both men stepped away from the car, while Battle Axe closed the trunk.

"Did you get this car from the Chevy shop?" asked Russo.

"I did," replied Battle Axe.

"Who does the car belong to?"

"Old Man Thomas," replied Battle Axe. "We doin' some work on it this afternoon."

The remark caught Russo's attention. "Who's we?" he asked with wide eyes.

"Me and my boy, Ripp."

"What other mechanics are working there?"

"Just me and Ripp," replied Battle Axe.

"So, no one else knows about it?" asked Russo.

"Nope," Battle Axe said with a smile.

Russo nodded. He bent down and looked at the license plate. After spending a few seconds inspecting the tag, he stood.

"Why haven't you removed the license tag?" Russo demanded, "I've told you to always remove the tag when you pull off the highway!"

"I'm sorry. I was in a hurry this morning and must have forgotten."

With his jaw muscles twitching, Russo walked to Battle Axe. He raised his hand and shoved his finger into Battle Axe's face.

"How many times have I told you about removing all traces?" he shouted.

Battle Axe rolled his eyes. "I'm sorry. Again, I was in a hurry this morning."

"How many times have I told you to remove all traces?" Russo shouted in an even louder voice.

"Several times."

"And how long have we been doin' this?"

"I don't know," said Battle Axe. "A few months."

"Do you have a poor memory?" Russo asked.

"No."

"Then tell me why you failed to remove all traces? Tell me why you left a license plate."

"I forgot. It's as simple as that."

"Do you know what will happen to us if anyone finds out what we're doing?"

Battle Axe's patience was growing thin. He didn't mind getting yelled at for his obvious mistake, but as usual, Russo was taking it too far.

"I suspect we'll be in a lot of trouble, and while we's on the subject of what we're doing, I don't appreciate not having a damned clue!" Battle Axe bellowed.

"First of all, the less you know about this, the better," said Russo, with growing anger in his voice. "And you're damned right, we'd be in a shitload of trouble if we're ever found out!"

Mark was quick to intervene. "I think you've made your point. Let's just calm down and get this deal done."

Battle Axe could feel his heart pounding. Russo had crossed the line. The repeated screams were more than he could take.

"Do I make myself very clear?" barked Russo.

"You know what, Mr. Russo?" shouted Battle Axe as he shoved his finger into Russo's face. "I think I've had enough of yo' bullshit. Matter of fact, I think I'm done with this."

"What?" exclaimed a shocked Russo.

"You promised me what we was doin' here was on the up and up, but you refuse to tell me. And since you be actin' more paranoid than ever before, I'm not sure I want to be seen with you!"

Battle Axe walked to the car and got behind the wheel. As he tried to close the door, Russo grabbed his arm.

"You best get yo' hand off me, white boy. You mess with the bull, you'll get the horns!" thundered Battle Axe's voice.

Even though Battle Axe was only five feet seven inches tall and weighed 140 pounds soaking wet, everyone knew when he gave a command, he meant it.

"I ain't afraid of nobody, you understand?" Battle Axe continued as he jumped out of the car. "And I'll tell you something else, I done had my fill of this horseshit."

"How about everyone just calm down for a few moments," said Mark.

"I don't know who's supplying the brains and money behind this operation, but I know you nesters ain't smart enough to do it alone," fumed Battle Axe. "So you go and tell Mr. Moneybags that Battle Axe has had enough. Tell him Battle Axe is takin' a walk."

Russo wiped his hands over his eyes and let out a deep breath.

"Look. I'm sorry about yelling at you. I lost my temper. I'm just a little nervous about all this," Russo said, then paused. "I'm sorry. Can we forget what just happened?"

Battle Axe walked in small circles shaking his head, trying to cool down. Russo knew he was agitated, so he walked to Battle Axe and put his hand on his shoulder.

"I was out of line," said Russo. "Way out of line. Can we just forget about this?"

Battle Axe looked Russo straight in the eyes. "They's a couple of things we need to get straight right now."

"Like what?" asked Russo, with a smirk on his face.

"For starters, I been doin' yo' dirty work for the last few months and you always tell me the check is in the mail. I been checkin' my mail every day now and I ain't once got no damned check. The whole reason you axed me to do this was because I have access to a different car every time. Well, every month, I produce a different car, yet I get no damned check. Seems to me I'm offering you a unique service, yet I'm not feeling any appreciation."

Russo reached into his pocket and pulled out a roll of twenty dollar bills. He peeled off three twenties and handed it to Russo.

"How's this for appreciation?" he asked.

Battle Axe smiled. "I'm feeling a little more appreciation," he said. He inspected the money, folded it, then placed it in his pocket.

"What else is bothering you?" asked Russo in a calm voice.

"I'm getting tired of making this run by myself. Why should I be the only visible one in all this?"

"What would you like us to do?" asked Mark.

"I want you to come with me."

Russo wiped his brow, then shook his head. "I don't know about that. What if someone sees us?"

"Shit," said Battle Axe. "They ain't no body gonna see you. I've always been real careful 'bout that. The only thing I've ever seen on the trip are rats and coons."

Russo looked at Mark, who shrugged.

"I don't mind," replied Mark. "I don't think it would take too long to run it up there."

Russo stroked his chin for several moments.

"If we're seen, it will greatly complicate matters," he said.

"Come on," said Battle Axe. "No one will see us and we'll be back before they even turn on the grill at Johnny's, I promise."

Russo threw his hands in the air. "All right," he replied curtly.

"Alright indeed," said Battle Axe with a smile.

Battle Axe took a screwdriver from inside the car, then walked to the back and removed the license plate. He threw the plate on the back seat, then walked to the cab and started the car. Russo and Mark reluctantly entered the vehicle. As Russo sat down in the passenger seat, he looked to the sky and saw the sun had just crested the horizon.

"The older I get, the less I understand you nesters," said Battle Axe. "You shore get riled up easy."

Russo wore a confused look on his face. "What does he mean by nesters?" he asked.

"It means white folk," replied Mark.

Russo shook his head while he shut the door to the car. "I'm gettin' too old for this shit," he said.

Battle Axe laughed. "We's just gettin' started."

Chapter 6

After Kirk finished his paper route, he jogged downtown to the pharmacy. He reached the front door then stopped to take a look at his surroundings. The sun had just crested over the horizon, giving the newly fallen snow on Court Street a soft glow. It was quite a sight. With no footprints nor tire tracks disturbing the pristine scene, Court Street was a work of fine art. Kirk stood for just a moment and watched his breath move through the chilled air.

The contrast of the sight before him intrigued Kirk. On Saturdays, Court Street would be filled with folks from every corner of the county to trade, shop, and socialize. The three blocks of various retail stores and barber shops would be hoppin' with people, but this morning, it was quiet and empty. For just a moment, Kirk felt like he owned the place. Still loaded with Mrs. Parker's biscuits, Kirk felt content and inspired by the work of Mother Nature. He smiled as he entered the drugstore.

The distinct smells of the store greeted Kirk upon his entrance. He wasn't sure if it was from the drugs in the back or all the merchandise up front, but the store definitely had a unique smell. The faint and favorable odor reminded Kirk of Christmas at home. It gave him a warm feeling of contentment.

Since the store was far deeper than it was wide, he had to make several steps before he actually made his way to the pharmacy. Along the way, he passed the counter, which stood parallel to the center aisle and housed various merchandise items. On the opposite side of the counter was the real-life fantasy of every kid in Atoka, the soda fountain. Down its counter sat several stools, which were bolted to the floor and used more as mini-merry-go-rounds than places to sit. The counter and stools were strategically placed to be easily accessible from either the ice-cream freezer, the candy-bar rack, or the soda cooler. Many an afternoon was wasted by kids admiring or partaking in the wonders of Carney's candy land while their parents waited on prescriptions in the back of the store.

"You're late," bellowed a nearby voice in the darkness.

"Mr. Carney, is that you?" asked a startled Kirk.

"You told me you'd be here at seven. It's now four minutes after, which means you're late."

Kirk recognized Carney's voice and assumed he was teasing.

"You can deduct it from my pay," Kirk jokingly responded.

"I'm not laughing," said Carney.

"Oh," said a startled Kirk. "I didn't realize being four minutes late was . . . I'm really sorry."

"Sorry doesn't cut it here, Henry. Our deal was for you to be here at seven. Not a minute later. Now, if you think that's too early, perhaps we should rethink this arrangement. Is that what this tardiness implies?" Carney asked with a stern voice.

Kirk wanted to blurt out the real reason he was late. He wanted to tell Carney he'd been the sole witness to the early morning dirty deeds of Russo and Maston. Instead, he refrained and quietly replied, "No, sir."

"Can I then assume this won't happen again? Can I assume you'll be on time as promised?"

"Yes, sir."

"Good, then let's get to work," said Carney as he turned and walked to the pharmacy area. As he stepped through the door and disappeared into the darkness, Carney shook his head.

Kirk's fear of disappointing others was just as adamant as his fear of things that go bump in the night. His parents had instilled a system of values, which he earnestly tried to incorporate into his everyday life, but sometimes things just didn't work out. It occurred on a seldom basis, but when it did, it always stung Kirk's ego.

"Do you remember my instructions on how to mix the cough syrup?" asked Carney.

Kirk nodded. "Yes, sir," he replied.

"Good. I'd like for you to mix up a batch. Let me know if you have any problems or questions."

"Will do."

After Carney turned on the lights, Kirk walked to the pharmacy and located the empty gallon jar of cough syrup. He tried to recall the previous day's instructions on mixing up fresh cough syrup.

Since it was a big seller in the winter, Carney wanted cough syrup mixed fresh often in order for the most active ingredient, tincture of opium, to stay more stable and potent. Carney even let Kirk in on a little company secret. When Carney and Russo moved into the pharmacy building a few years ago, they found the mother lode of all stashes in the attic: gallons and gallons of pure opium. After devising a recipe, they began producing their own cough syrup and it became a big seller. Every winter since, Russo would employ his sales skills to move the cough syrup. He spent time walking around the store in search of folks afflicted with the cough. The syrup was a weak narcotic, but was excellent at breaking up the old winter cough. Most folks loved it.

Kirk searched the shelves until he located the opium jug and the cherry syrup jug, and carried the contents out to the soda fountain. He earnestly tried to remember Carney's words from the day before on how to mix the elixir. Try as he might, however, he couldn't remember if it was one part opium, three-parts water, and a half part cherry syrup, or three parts opium, one part water, and a half part of cherry syrup. Kirk let out a long sigh and scratched his head. He really should ask Carney, he thought, but with the morning's mood already soured that probably wasn't such a good idea.

Staring at the elixir before him, Kirk's mind began to race. It wasn't too late, he thought. If Carney was going to act like a jackass just for being four minutes late, what would he do in times of real catastrophe? Maybe Kirk should run to the front door and never come back. Maybe Carney's compassion over the previous days was just an act and deep down, he was just another white son of a bitch who threw around his temper like drunken fathers threw horse-shoes at a Sunday picnic. Maybe you really can't trust the nesters, like Uncle Willie sometimes said.

It was a lot for a young man to absorb.

"Havin' problems, Young Henry?" asked Carney.

Kirk paused. "No sir," he replied. "I think I can manage."

Kirk quickly uncapped the opium jug and poured in three pints, then added a little cherry syrup for taste and three pints of water. He figured he had a 50 percent chance of getting the concoction right.

Feeling like a mad scientist, he shrugged and gave the jug a shake, then carried all the items back into the pharmacy. Carney had stepped into the back to retrieve something, so Kirk's presence was never noticed.

After spending over an hour at the soda fountain doing odd jobs, Kirk looked at his watch. The timepiece read seven-forty-five, which signaled it was time to get back home so he could get ready for school. His ego still stinging from Carney's tardy talk, he looked to the frosted glass door that led to Court Street and wondered if this was all a big mistake.

Before leaving the pharmacy, he walked to the sink and washed his hands. The thought of going home instantly eased his mind because he knew the greatest therapist in the whole world was there, his mom. No matter how big or small the problem, his mother always had a knack for easing his troubled mind and quelling his fears. She always knew what to say, and above all, she loved him, unconditionally.

Kirk smiled as he dried his hands. He looked down to his watch, an heirloom given to his mother by her grandad, a man born into slavery but freed after the Civil War. His mother gave him the watch on the day they departed for Langston. The sight of the beautiful timepiece struck him cold as he instantly remembered his mother was gone. His father was gone. His brothers and sisters were gone. The world in which Kirk had existed for fourteen years was gone.

He felt his eyes welling as he zipped up his coat. The lump in his stomach suddenly felt the size of the Oklahoma Panhandle. He wanted to fall to his knees and cry. Atoka suddenly seemed different. It was no longer his hometown. It was a cold, dark place where terrible things happened. Things like bodies being wrapped up and transported to God knows where to be dumped by the owner of the town's newspaper, who happened to be his boss. Maybe Langston wouldn't be so bad, he thought. Sure, there would be changes, but at least he'd have the security of his mom, dad, and his brothers and sisters. And no dead bodies.

There was still time, he thought. His mom and dad hadn't even settled in Langston yet, so his arrival wouldn't disrupt their routine the least bit. It would be a new start with new friends, a new job, a new school, a new everything. He truly loved his friends and routine in Atoka but more important than his routine was his inner peace, which was suffering something fierce at the moment.

As Kirk walked to front door, his mind was made up. As soon as Woods' Brothers General Store opened at eight, he would go there and call his mom collect. He would explain everything had gone to hell in a hand basket. She would drive to Atoka and pick him up, and he would be back with his family by nightfall. Tears came to Kirk's eyes as he reached for the door handle. Before he could walk outside however, something grabbed him from behind.

"What's bothering you, Kirk?" asked Carney with soft eyes.

Kirk turned around and wiped his nose. "Nothing, sir."

Carney laughed. "You should give up on lying, 'cause you aren't very good at it."

A slow smile found its way to Kirk's face. "Yes, sir."

Carney placed his arm around Kirk and looked him in the eye. "I wasn't trying to break you this morning. I'm just trying to help you. Let me tell you a quick story."

Both Carney and Kirk walked to the soda fountain and sat down.

"When I was your age, I didn't have a pa. He was a real rascal who left me and my family when I was about ten years old. I understood I was the oldest boy in the family and it was my job to take care of everyone. I freely accepted this inherited burden. I didn't ask for it but I also didn't try to evade it, either."

Kirk slowly began to regain his composure. While he listened, he grabbed a Baby Ruth candy bar, leaving a nickel on the counter.

"I can't tell you how or why exactly, but being in that position made me grow up real fast. Like you, I was forced to have several jobs and I quickly learned it really didn't matter if I had a good excuse, what mattered is that I arrived to work on time, worked hard all day, and went home when the work was finished. If not, I was fired and my whole family went hungry. Do you understand where I'm coming from?"

Kirk nodded. "I think so."

"Back then, everyone in my world, and I do mean everyone, depended on me. There was no one else who would take the responsibility. Just me."

Kirk sat motionless, lost in Carney's speech. The reality of his predicament became very clear and he felt as though he was making a connection to Carney's words.

"It's vitally important for you to understand it's going to be rough. Life ain't always fair, Young Henry. The system will not change to fit your needs; you must change to fit the system's needs."

"The system? You mean the white man's world?" said a confused Kirk. For years, he had heard Uncle Willie complain about the white man's world. He never really understood the term.

"I guess 'round here the system is the white man's world, but there's a whole big world outside of Atoka. The system is the same everywhere. It's about getting a job, paying your bills, going to college, buying a house, getting married and having kids."

"I don't know," said Kirk while shaking his head. "I'm not so sure I'll ever be able to buy a house. Not so sure about college, either."

"That's because you need confidence and you'll gain that. Stick with me and I'll show you the way."

Kirk was more confused than ever, but decided he'd stretched his own emotions far enough for one day. He sat in silence and tinkered with the candy bar wrapper.

"Are you thinking you might want to go to Langston to be with your family?" asked Carney.

"The thought did cross my mind."

"Look Henry, if you want to go back to your family, I'll personally drive you to Langston myself. And what's more, I'll completely understand. That's your family and only God comes before that. But I urge you to give Atoka another try."

Kirk remained silent.

"Do you want to go?"

After a long pause, Kirk shook his head. "No sir. I think I want to stay here."

"Good. Head on to school and I'll see you this evening."

"Will do," replied Kirk.

"Do you want me to give you a ride? It's awful cold out there."

"Naw," said Kirk. "Dad says it builds character."

"Young Henry, there's something else," Carney said quietly.

"Yes?" said Kirk.

Carney reached into his pocket and retrieved a shiny 1921 silver Peace Dollar. He handed it to Kirk.

"What's this?"

"It's a souvenir. It's not to spend, it's to keep."

In all of Kirk's fourteen years, he'd never received such a gift. "I don't understand. What does this mean?"

Carney smiled. "It means I believe in you. Life is a very unpredictable venture, but one thing that's always constant is faith. With faith, anything is possible."

"I think I understand."

"Good. I realize right now, there is a lot of uncertainty swirling around in that young mind of yours. You're probably wondering what the future holds and if you'll be able to survive on your own. In the future, whenever you're faced with uncertainty, I want you to pull this silver dollar out of your pocket and hold it. Hopefully it will remind you of this moment."

Kirk smiled. "Thanks," he said softly. "This means a lot."

"I knew it would."

Chapter 7

Kirk sat back on the couch in the living room of his house and closed his eyes. He'd propped open the front door slightly in order to hear the eight o'clock bell from the schoolyard. Since his school was no more than one hundred yards away, Kirk made a morning routine of sitting down and relaxing for a moment before the bell.

Just as he was drifting off to sleep, he heard a car pull into the driveway. At first, he thought it was his parents. Perhaps they had came back to pick up some miscellaneous items. But as Kirk arose to his feet, he heard the car's engine rev up, signaling it must be Ripp.

"What brings you out so early in the morning?" asked Kirk from the front porch.

"The early bird catches the worm," said Ripp with a smile. He exited the car and jogged to the porch.

"How was the drive? Did you slide around on the snow and ice?" asked Kirk as they entered the house.

"Yeah," said Ripp. "I'm sure they'll call off school. Have you heard anything?"

"No," said Kirk. "I figure I'll run up there when the bell rings and find out. What about you? What're you doing today?"

"Since I quit school, Mom and Dad have really been up my ass about finding work, so yesterday, I started down at the Chevy house with Dad. I'm going down there in a little bit. Geez, you're lucky you don't have to put up with parents."

"It's funny you say that," said Kirk with a solemn facial expression. "I always envisioned it would great, but after experiencing it, I have to say that being on my own ain't so great."

"Get the hell outta here!"

"No, no, I'm serious. It's kinda lonely."

A smile shot across Ripp's face. "Then I got just the thing. You, me, some pretty girls, and a bonfire. Whatta ya say?"

Kirk's eyes grew wide. "When? Tonight?"

"Hell, yeah."

"But it's freezing out there."

"I know it's cold, but the fire and the girls will keep us warm."

"I need to think about that," said Kirk. "I'll definitely have to think about that."

"Think to your heart's content," said Ripp. "But yo' ass is going."

Kirk smiled just as the school bell rang. "Alright. What time you pickin' me up?"

"About seven."

"Seven it is. Come hell or high water, right?"

Ripp smiled. "That's right."

They walked to the porch. Wearing a long face, Ripp cleared his throat several times. Kirk knew this habit as a nervous tic that often foreshadowed strong emotions.

"Something buggin' you?" asked Kirk.

"Sorta. Has Carney said anything about me?"

"No, why?"

"Just curious."

"Why would Carney be asking about you? Are you in trouble?"

"No, no. I used to work at the drugstore in the summers, you know, and I was just wondering if . . ."

"Is everything alright?" asked Kirk.

"Fine, fine. I was just wondering, that's all."

"I'll keep my ears open. Are you sure you aren't keeping something from me?"

As Ripp cleared his throat again, the second bell rang from the schoolyard.

"I best get up there and make sure they cancelled school," said Kirk. "Why don't you stay here and we can talk about whatever it is that's buggin' you when I get back."

Ripp's demeanor quickly changed to nonchalant. He acted as if he hadn't a care in the world. Kirk knew the opportunity to speak was over.

"Naw, I best be gettin' on," replied Ripp.

"We'll talk about it tonight, then, right?"

"It ain't nuthin'," said Ripp. "And hopefully we won't be wasting time talking tonight, if you know what I mean."

Kirk laughed. "We'll see."

# # #

By the time Kirk finished his jog to the drugstore, Court Street was a far cry from the unspoiled beauty that it had been earlier in the morning. Now the snow was flawed with tire tracks, footprints, and dirty mounds pushed aside from the morning snow plow. It was still a beautiful sight, thought Kirk. Even though it was tainted, it was still a beautiful sight.

Upon entering the drugstore, Kirk walked straight back to the pharmacy. He noticed Mr. Carney helping an older gentleman.

"It was the damndest thing," said the old man, who was wobbling as he stood. "Right after I picked up my cough syrup this morning, I went home and was about to pour myself a little sip, when all of the sudden, my big St. Bernard came running through the living room and jumped right in my lap."

"You don't say," said Carney.

"If I'm lyin', I'm dyin'," said the old man.

Carney spotted Kirk walking to the pharmacy counter.

Kirk tried to keep a straight face, but the old man's story made him laugh.

"Thanks for all your help," said the old man. He picked up his sack from the counter and walked away.

"That's going to have to last you awhile. Make sure your dog stays out of it," said Carney.

"My dog?" asked the old man, puzzled. "Oh, my dog. Yes, yes, of course."

After the old man left the building, Kirk walked closer to Carney.

"Is that man alright?" asked Kirk.

"Mr. Lucas? Oh, he's fine. He just likes your syrup." Carney then made a gesture of bringing an imaginary bottle to his lips. "Mr. Lucas has an affinity for the hooch and a little cough syrup every now and then."

"Really?" Kirk's heart raced even more. "Doesn't he need a prescription for the cough syrup?"

"No, it's up to the pharmacist. If I feel like they need it and they are legitimate, it's my call. Don't worry though, he won't be getting any more for quite a while," said Carney. "So, why aren't you at school? Did they call it off?"

"Yes sir. I didn't have anything else to do and thought you might need a hand."

"As a matter of fact, I do," said Carney, while filling another bottle of cough syrup from the jug. "I was planning to go up to the attic today and file away all the Christmas decorations. We were very busy over the new year and I never had a chance to place the boxes back where they're supposed to go. They're scattered all around up there and they need to be stacked in an orderly fashion. Does that interest you?"

"Sure," said Kirk. "I'll get right on it. By the way, Ripp came by this morning."

Kirk was very interested in Carney's reaction to hearing Ripp's name. He still had no idea what was bothering his best friend so much. He hoped Carney would shed some light.

"How is Ripp?" asked Carney nonchalantly.

Here it comes, thought Kirk. He's about to give me the dope. "He's fine. I think he's helping his dad, down at the Chevy house."

"I see," Carney said while placing the filled cough-syrup bottle in a sack. "Kirk, would you mind refilling my coffee?"

Coffee cup in hand, Kirk quietly walked to the soda fountain, refilled the cup, and returned to the pharmacy. As he opened the pharmacy door, he ran into Russo. As the coffee splashed onto Russo, Kirk took immediate evasive action by directing the rest onto the floor.

Embarrassment and fear overcame Kirk. "I'm sorry. I didn't see you there."

The image of Russo's face at the newspaper warehouse earlier in the morning was etched into his mind. He was still afraid Russo knew he was spying on their conversation.

Instead of speaking, Russo was silent. His eyes seemed to pierce through Kirk's soul.

"I'll uh . . . I'll clean that up," said Kirk.

"I think that's a good idea," said Russo in a stern voice. "I don't like messes, if you know what I mean."

"Of course not. I'll get right on it."

He felt fear shooting out of every nerve ending in his body. His hands shook as he walked back to the soda fountain. He refilled the coffee cup and quickly took it to the pharmacy.

"You alright?" asked Carney.

"Uh, huh."

"You look as though you've seen a ghost."

Kirk could only shake his head.

"The traffic has slowed down here, so why don't you head on up to the attic. You'll understand what I mean when you get there. Just take all the Christmas boxes and stack them along the east wall."

"Okay," said Kirk. He let out a deep sigh. Slowly, he started regaining his composure.

"And don't worry about the coffee mess on the floor. I'll take care of it."

Kirk hurried to the back of the store and practically ran up the stairs to put as much distance as possible between himself and Russo. As soon as he reached the attic, he shut the door behind him, which immediately swung back open. Since the temperature in the attic was much colder than in the drugstore, he locked the door to prevent the cold air from escaping.

Kirk let out a huge sigh as he turned on the lights. He looked around and saw many decorations and boxes scattered around the attic. It was hard to believe a mess like this could be owned by Carney. He began picking up decorations, then neatly stacked them on shelves running along one of the walls. After gathering decorations for quite some time, he made his way to the boxes, which he neatly stacked on the opposite side of the shelves.

His back ached as he stacked an especially large box on the shelf. In hopes of warming up and resting, he decided to go downstairs and take a quick break. At the attic door, however, an unusual sight caught his eye. He spotted a smaller door on the west wall of the attic. Kirk inspected the door and found it was stuck. After nudging the door slightly, he was surprised to find the door swing open.

Curious of the purpose of this little room inside the attic, Kirk ducked his head and entered. The area was caked with dust, appearing to be unvisited for decades. He walked to the far corner and spotted an old chest lying at the bottom of a bookshelf. Kirk wanted to see what lay inside, so he enthusiastically opened the chest.

The chest was topped with letters from people he didn't know and names he didn't recognize. As he dug through the contents, he spotted some old postcards, many dating back to the early 1920s. The postcards lifted his spirits and even made him smile as he assumed that the contents of the chest were probably long forgotten by Carney.

The smile must have dropped a thousand miles, though, when Kirk saw what lie next in the chest. Fear and confusion swept over him like a tidal wave as he stared. Just as he reached down to pick up the object for a closer look, a loud pounding on the attic door blasted through the area like a sonic boom. Kirk froze.

Chapter 8

Weatherford, Oklahoma, 1989

"So what was in the chest?" Wade asked with great anticipation.

Dr. Kirkland frowned. "What did I tell you about interrupting me?"

"Sorry," replied Wade. "So what did the coin Mr. Carney gave you in the drugstore mean?"

"It came to mean faith," replied Dr. Kirkland. "He gave me that coin at a crucial time in my life. I was strongly leaning toward calling my mom and moving to Langston with them. Had it not been for the coin and that talk from Mr. Carney, I don't know if I would have stayed in Atoka."

"But it was only a coin."

"Wade, you're just a pup. You'll learn you can't live without faith. Someday, you'll learn what I mean and remember the ramblings of an old man."

"But you had Ripp, too," said Wade. "He probably helped your decision to stay at least a little."

"His presence in Atoka made a difference," said Dr. Kirkland. "But it didn't really matter so much. When you're as young as I was, all that really matters is your family. Looking back on it now, I'm surprised I stayed. The coin represented Carney's faith in me, which was something I'd never experienced before. It was a very very powerful icon."

"So what was in the chest?" asked Wade.

"You don't have much patience, do you?"

"No," Wade said with a laugh, "I'm not old enough to have patience."

Dr. Kirkland thought for a moment. "I was already in a fractured emotional state," he said, "and what I saw completely turned me upside down and made it much worse."

"Were you upset because you saw them load the body?"

"Among other things."

"Was that your first time to see a dead body?" asked Wade with hesitancy.

"It was, but sadly, not my last dead body to see in Atoka. You've got to remember, things in Atoka, in America, in 1945 were very different than they are today."

"Are you referring to civil rights?"

"Yes."

"The Civil Rights Act passed in 1964 and since Atoka is located in a part of Oklahoma known as 'Little Dixie', I'm guessing you saw your fair share of discrimination."

Dr. Kirkland looked deep into Wade's eyes. "Not overtly," he said.

"Really?" said a confused Wade. "I don't understand."

"There were rules," said Dr. Kirkland. "We black folk knew the rules and usually didn't break them, so there generally weren't many problems."

"Rules?" asked Wade.

"Yes, there were rules, but none of them made any sense. For example, blacks could go into the drugstore and buy ice cream, but we weren't allowed to lick it until we went outside. I followed the rules, just like everyone else from East Atoka. Another rule was I could work in the drugstore, but I wouldn't dare have served food or drinks."

"Are you serious?" said a shocked Wade.

"Oh, yeah. The rules were the rules. They weren't posted anywhere, you just knew them. Now, don't get me wrong, the black and white water fountains and waiting rooms were clearly stated. But mainly, the rules were just known by tradition."

"Like eating in the back of the restaurant?"

"Exactly, but you have to remember, blacks weren't allowed in all the restaurants. For example, I ate in the back room of Johnny's all the time, but wasn't allowed in the other restaurant, the Corner Café."

"I see," said Wade. "What would have happened if you went in there?"

Dr. Kirkland shook his head letting out a loud laugh. "Oh, there would have been hell to pay, I'm sure."

Wade scratched his head in confusion. "So, you weren't allowed to go into The Corner Café, but Mr. Carney hired you to work in the drugstore. That must have made you feel strange."

"Now you're starting to get it, Mr. McCoy. Hiring me was unusual, but what you're about to hear will truly amaze you!" Dr. Kirkland said in a low tone as he raised his eyebrows.

Chapter 9

Atoka, Oklahoma,

1945

The wind howled around the large pillars that formed the base for the main entrance of the Stringtown Internment Camp, just seven miles north of Atoka. The prison was originally built as an overflow facility for the large state prison at McAlester, known to locals as "Big Mac." When Big Mac would overfill, the residents of Stringtown would be burdened with some of the nastiest criminals in the state. Since the prison was only seven miles north of Atoka, most people in the area kept an eye on it. If a prisoner managed to escape, the entire area was notified and every family within a one hundred mile radius would go to bed with their shotguns.

World War II brought changes to the Stringtown Prison. As American forces progressed through Europe, space was needed for prisoners of war. Because of its sparse population and lower prisoner numbers, Oklahoma was chosen. Since only a few high-security prisons existed in the state, Stringtown seemed to be the most appropriate location to house German prisoners. The locals referred to Stringtown as "the German POW prison" or "Krautville". The federal government staffed the prison with a mixture of military police and local citizens, all hired to perform the various functions.

In an office deep within the prison walls, Josephine, Carney's wife, stared at a receipt she found in the mail. Her concentration was broken by the sound of footsteps coming down the hallway. She looked up and realized she'd been gazing at the receipt for at least the last ten minutes.

For the past couple of years, Josephine had served as the secretary to the auditor of the prison, Geddy Wainscott. Part of her job duties called for her to sort through his mail. On this occasion, however, she was confused to find a mysterious receipt. She noticed the sound of footsteps seemed to be growing louder as she stared at the receipt in front of her. She rubbed her eyes, then turned around and focused her attention to the hallway. Within moments, she saw the source of the footsteps, Karl Bartz.

"Good morning, Karl," said Josephine.

"*Guten Morgen*," Karl replied.

"You're a little late this morning. Is everything alright?"

"Maybe not so much," replied the former Nazi soldier. Karl walked close to Josephine and whispered. "I think that maybe they suspect me."

Josephine noticed Karl's face was pale and rigid. He looked as though he hadn't slept in days.

"What happened?" Josephine asked, concerned.

"They are vatching me." He wiped the beaded sweat from his forehead, then suddenly became animated. "*Wir kämen alle um!*" he shouted.

"What? What are you talking about?"

Karl grabbed Josephine's arm. "They will kill us all," he said. "Me, you, zee guards, zee administration, all of us."

"Who? Who will kill us?" Josephine asked, very concerned.

"Zee Nazis. They are not finished with their madness."

"But they're under guard," said Josephine. "There's no way they can harm us. The MP's will protect us."

Karl's eyes starting twitching. "I shouldn't have spoken to zee intelligence officer."

"What intelligence officer? What are you talking about?" asked Josephine.

"Last week. I live with so much of zee . . . zee guilt. I know where many of zee high ranking Nazis fled. I told the Americans everything."

"Fled? You mean when the Allies stormed into Germany?"

"*Ja.*"

"Where did they go?" asked Josephine.

"Candido Godoi, Brazil. There are many Deutschlanders there from the beginning. They blend in perfectly."

Realizing a passersby in the hallways might see him spending too much time collecting the trash, Karl reached down, grabbed the trashcan, then dumped it into his portable trash bin.

"And you think the other Nazi prisoners know you talked?"

"They threw dishes at me last night," replied Karl. "They know and now we are all going to be killed."

"They can't kill anyone now. The war is almost over and they're prisoners on American soil."

Karl shifted his eyes nervously. "Silly American, you do not know their power. They will fight to the death. No one can stop these animals."

"Did you tell the guards you fear for your life?"

Karl turned and looked to the hall. "*Ja*, but it makes no difference. No one can protect me now."

"I'll talk to the guards."

"I beg you, please," said Karl. He returned the trashcan to the floor, then crouched low. "Please. I have not seen *meiner kinders* in ages," he whispered.

"Your kids?"

"Yes. *Und meiner* wife. I miss them so. You must keep me alive so I can return."

"I'll do my best," said Josephine. "By the way, how are the ponies?"

Karl thought for a moment. "They need much to eat."

Josephine nodded as Karl exited the room. She picked up the receipt from the desk and studied the contents again. While she shook her head in disbelief, the phone rang.

"Stringtown Internment Camp, this is Josephine."

"Hey Jo, how's my first lady?" said Carney.

"Hi, Skeet. How are things at the drugstore?"

"Fine. I'm hearing the roads are pretty bad. Did you make it in alright?" asked Carney.

"I did. Have you heard from our kids?" asked Josephine.

"They're fine. I talked to JoAnne on the phone and she said Carolyn invited a friend over and they're havin' a big time playing in the snow."

"Glad to hear they're alright."

"School's out, there's snow on the ground, and they have the house to themselves, so I think they're doing pretty fine."

"Good. Look, I just spoke to Sooner Schooner. The ponies are restless."

"You just spoke to who?" asked a confused Carney.

"You know, the Sooner Schooner."

"I don't know what . . . oh, that Sooner Schooner."

"The ponies are restless."

"Understood. I'll see what I can do."

Geddy Wainscott entered the office and removed his coat. He brushed away the snow, then hung it on the coat rack.

"Look, I need to go. I'll call you later," Josephine said into the phone. She placed the phone on the receiver, then gathered the mail.

"Hello Geddy."

"Mornin'. It's a bit frosty out there. I was afraid I was never going to make it in."

"Me, too," Josephine said with a big smile. "Not to change the subject, but I was going through the mail this morning and found something of interest. I came across some receipts for rationing stamps I don't understand."

Geddy raised his eyebrows. "Rationing stamps?"

"Yeah, there's a receipt for $11,368 a Jereboam Industries paid to this camp. I didn't think . . ."

"This doesn't concern you," Geddy replied in a stern tone. "I'll take care of this myself."

He grabbed the receipt out of her hand and shoved it into his pocket. He walked to the doorway and turned down the hall.

Josephine shook her head. "Jereboam, Jereboam," said muttered to herself. "Where have I heard that name?"

"Don't forget," said a voice from the hallway.

Josephine turned her head and saw Karl watching her.

"Please don't forget to speak to zee guards," he said. The fear in his eyes was so intense, it could pierce walls.

"I will," replied Josephine. "I will."

# # #

Karl quickly made his rounds and gathered trash from all the front offices of the prison. As soon as he'd dumped the last trashcan into the portable bin, he pushed the bin down the hallway, toward the janitor's closet. Along the way, he passed a hallway which led to the cell block. Out of the corner of his eye, he spotted several Germans gathered on the other side of the bars, waiting for him to pass.

As soon as the former SS guards noticed Karl, they clicked their metal cups on the bars and began screaming.

"*Landesverraeter!*" a tall, unshaven man yelled.

Karl did his best to ignore them. He picked up his pace.

"*Landesverraeter!*" he heard again.

Now past the entrance, Karl stopped the portable trash bin, and walked back to face the prisoners.

"I am no traitor!" he screamed.

Seeing Karl's face up close invigorated the former SS guards' anger. They screamed and jumped around like monkeys.

"I am no traitor!" Karl screamed again.

The tall, unshaven man reached into his pocket and removed a rock he'd previously retrieved from the prison grounds. He hurled the rock with all his might. Karl never saw it coming until it struck him square on his forehead.

He covered his face with his hands and ran to the safety of the hall. Their jeers and laughter followed him and seemed to heighten the sting of his wound. He removed his hands from his face and found them covered in blood. Not aware of the damage of his wound, he grabbed a towel from his portable trash bin and placed it against his forehead.

"Animals," Karl said, while he slowly pushed the trash bin down the hall. When he arrived at the end of the hallway, he removed the trash bag, then opened the back door. He stepped outside and walked through the snow, his trail splattered with drops of blood.

Chapter 10

Kirk found the dancing flames of the roaring fire to be mesmerizing, at least for a moment. The crackling of the wood provided a natural percussion for the flames as they leaped high into the cold night air. An occasional hissing sound would emanate from the wet, dead branches, which accentuated the eeriness that dominated his already bleak mood.

"Kirk, my man, what are you doing? The ladies are beginning to worry," whispered a concerned Ripp.

Kirk turned around and noticed the two girls behind them, several yards away from the fire. Standing near the trees in the dark, they looked cold and bored.

"Got a lot on my mind," said Kirk. His eyes remained fixated on the fire.

"Come on, man. Get up and get it together. We don't get a chance like this too often."

Kirk looked at Ripp. "A chance like what?"

"A chance to hang out with two beautiful girls here at The Bog. And not just girls, but girls who want to be with no one but us," Ripp said, then paused. "I know you've been seeing Vanessa for a while and this ain't nuthin' new for you, but my brother, I've been after Clarice since I was in the tenth grade. I've been dreaming about this for a long time."

Kirk shifted his eyes back to the fire and mulled over Ripp's words. He's right, thought Kirk. North Boggy Creek, or The Bog, as they called it, was a sacred place for Ripp and Kirk. They'd been frequenting it for over three years, ever since Ripp was old enough to drive. They first discovered the area one summer while on a scouting mission to find a place to catch crawdads. The first trip out with a seine proved so bountiful they had visited The Bog almost every weekend since. During the warm months, their weekends were spent catching and boiling crawdads, while the winter months usually found them gathered around a bonfire with dreams of someday sharing The Bog with their dates.

"Alright," he finally said. "I'll try to smile more."

Both girls stepped forward and approached Ripp and Kirk. "Hey guys, we're gettin' scared," said Vanessa. "Maybe we should head on back to town."

"Now ladies," Ripp said, wearing a used-car-salesman's smile, "you ain't got nuthin' to worry about. "You're with two of the strongest young men in Atoka County. There ain't nothin' nor nobody that will harm you, 'cause they gots to come through us first."

The two girls seemed surprisingly comforted by Ripp's words. Vanessa walked over and sat down on the old log beside Kirk. Clarice soon found a seat next to Ripp, who stretched an arm around her.

"Where are we, exactly?" asked Clarice.

Ripp pointed to the creek, which was frozen over from the cold. "That there is North Boggy Creek. Me and Kirk call this place The Bog."

Clarice rolled her eyes. "That doesn't really help me. Where are we from Atoka?"

"We're just north east of Atoka," said Kirk. "Not far from Stringtown."

"Oh," said Clarice. "I think I know where we are now. We're not far from Atoka Lake."

"That's right," said Ripp. "And even closer to the Stringtown Internment Camp."

"What's that?" asked Vanessa.

"That's where they keepin' them Nazis."

Frightened, Clarice instantly pressed her body next to Ripp. He smiled.

"You lyin', Ripp Masters. They ain't no Nazis in America."

"I give you my word," said Ripp. "When our boys took Normandy last summer, they captured all those that they didn't kill. We had to send 'em somewhere, so they sent some of 'em here."

"Why would they send them to Oklahoma?" asked Vanessa.

"Don't know," replied Ripp. "But as sure as I'm sitting here now, I promise you, they's Nazis housed just right up the road."

Vanessa looked to Kirk. "Is he telling the truth?"

"'Fraid so. Skeet's wife, Jo, works there at the prison. She talks to 'em everyday."

"Oh my God," said Clarice.

"Wait a minute," said Vanessa. "Are we talking about the same Nazis who murdered all those poor Jews?"

"The same," replied Ripp. "And what's more, they's been a couple that have escaped and they ain't never been found. They could be livin' in these woods."

Clarice and Vanessa both wrapped their arms around their dates.

"Maybe we best get on outta here," said Clarice with a frail voice.

"Trust me, girls, you're in good hands. Just hold on tight and we'll protect you. Besides, the real danger ain't Nazis anyway," said a confident Ripp.

"What do you mean?" asked Vanessa.

"The real threat is ghosts."

"Ghosts!" screamed Clarice. "What're you talkin' 'bout?"

"Ever hear of Bonnie and Clyde?" asked Ripp.

"Sure," said Vanessa. "Who hasn't?"

"Yeah, but did you know they came right through here?"

"So," replied Clarice. "I'm sure lots of criminals have driven by Atoka on the way to Dallas. Big deal."

"Well, Ms. Clarice, they just so happened to have attended a Stringtown dance back in 1932. Bonnie wasn't there, but Clyde Barrow was, and he was accompanied by a man named Ray Hamilton. During the dance, Hamilton and Clyde stayed out in their stolen car drinkin' moonshine they were bootleggin'. They were confronted by two Stringtown lawmen, Sheriff Maxwell and Deputy Eugene Moore."

"Then what happened?" asked Vanessa.

"Clyde and Hamilton murdered Deputy Moore in cold blood, and seriously wounded Sheriff Maxwell with all the gunfire."

Shaking, both girls tightened their hold on their dates.

"And this happened in Stringtown?" asked Clarice.

"Just right up the road, and Clyde was known to have said he did shoot the Sheriff, but it was in self-defense," said Kirk.

"Yep, that's what the rumor is," chimed in a jovial Ripp.

"And they killed the deputy?" asked Vanessa.

"But those bad boys both got what was comin' to 'em. The law caught Hamilton. He was fried in ol' Sparky in 1935 over at the prison, Big Mac. People say they've seen ol' Ray roaming these hills ever since," said Ripp with big eyes.

"That's it," said Clarice. "We gettin' the hell outta here, right now!"

"Hold on, hold on," said Ripp. "I need to go see a man about a dog."

Still frightened, Clarice and Vanessa held on to Kirk as Ripp walked into the dark woods.

"Excuse my language," said Clarice, "but is Ripp bull-shittin' us about all this stuff?"

"I'm afraid not," replied Kirk. "I wish he was."

"Then why ain't you scared of them ghosts and Nazis?"

"I don't know," Kirk replied nonchalantly. "I guess I've got a lot on my mind."

"Want to talk about it?" asked Vanessa.

Kirk stared at the fire for a moment, then turned and faced Vanessa. "I don't think it would do any good," he said.

With sincerity, Vanessa looked into Kirk's eyes. "What's botherin' you, Kirk? Are you missin' your family?"

After silent contemplation, he finally determined he should at least try to talk to Vanessa.

"When I was at the drugstore today I found something that really bothered me. I was up in the attic and found . . ."

Suddenly, three small trees behind them began to shake violently, sending the snow from their branches down onto the scared girls. A loud, shrieking sound shredded the cold night air.

"I am the ghost of The Bog. I have come to suck your blood!" sounded the voice.

The girls both jumped to their feet and flailed their arms wildly, as if some wicked ectoplasm was attacking from the heavens. The two raced across the campground, in the direction of the parked car.

"You don't know much about the paranormal, do you?" asked Kirk.

"What?" asked Ripp.

"Ghosts don't suck blood. You're thinking about a vampire."

"Oh," said Ripp. "Doesn't matter, though. I think I got the job done."

Kirk arose from the log. "We probably ought to go find the girls. They were running so fast, they might be in Arkansas by now."

The two men walked briskly to the car, surprised to find the girls waiting.

"Did you guys hear that ghost?" Ripp said, with a smile.

"Get in here and turn on this car," said Clarice. "'Fore I kick yo' butt, Ripp Masters."

"Yes ma'am," replied Ripp, still smiling. He sat behind the wheel, across from Clarice. Shivering from the cold, Kirk and Vanessa cuddled together in the backseat.

Ripp started the car and drove through the maze of county roads that led to Highway Sixty-Nine. When they reached the highway, they drove south toward Atoka. Ripp looked over to Clarice and noticed she still wore a scowl, indicating she was still a little miffed about his joke.

"I read in a magazine that ninety-three percent of women are attracted to men that make them laugh," said Ripp. "As a matter of fact, the survey said that ninety-seven percent of married women want to be married to a man that can make them laugh."

Ripp's knowledge of gender statistics seemed to have no effect on Clarice. As the car sped through the night, silence filled the cab of the vehicle.

"Whose car is this?" asked Kirk. "Is it from the Chevrolet place where your dad works?"

"Don't forget, I work there, too. The car belongs to old man Thomas. Me and Dad did some work on the transmission this afternoon. I told Dad I would test drive it. He almost didn't let me have it, because of the slick roads, but we really did need to see if the tranny was gonna work."

"You gotta be the luckiest guy in the world," said Kirk. "Not a day goes by when you don't have a different car to drive."

"Well, I ain't complaining. The bad part is, I hope I don't end up working there for the rest of my life. My dad has been there for fifteen years; another one of the mechanics has been there for twenty."

"You'd better get used to it," said Clarice.

The comment hit Ripp in the face like scalding water.

"What choo talkin' 'bout, girl?" he said curtly.

"That's what you get when you don't have an education. You don't find a job that you want, you take any job you can get. I read that most women are repulsed by uneducated fools."

"Ouch," replied Kirk with a smile.

"Why did you quit school, anyway?" asked Clarice. She shook her head and stuck out her chest as would an over-protective mother.

"Well, I . . . I ugh . . ."

"Did the goin' get too rough?"

"As a matter of fact, it did. College ain't like high school, Clarice. You'll find out next year, after you graduate."

"I'm lookin' forward to it," said Clarice. "And I hope you find the courage to try it again."

Ripp cleared his throat as he struggled for words.

"I think, uh, you're gonna be pleasantly surprised this coming fall," he said, then cleared his throat again. "I'm uh, making plans to uh . . ."

"It looks like we're getting close to my house," said Kirk. "I think I'm ready to get home."

"Yeah, that's a good idea," said Ripp. "We can all stop off at your house and . . ."

"Not tonight," said Kirk. "I'm sorry, but I'm just not up for any social activities."

"Are you sure?" said Vanessa. "It's kinda early and I don't really have much to do tonight."

"I'm sorry, but not tonight. Maybe tomorrow."

"All right," said Vanessa.

Ripp stopped the car in front of Kirk's house.

"Thanks guys. I had a good time," he said as he rubbed Vanessa's hand, then reached over and opened the door. "Hope to see you tomorrow."

The group watched Kirk as he stepped out of the car and walked toward his house.

"What's bothering Kirk?" asked Vanessa.

"Not sure," said Ripp. "Maybe he's missing his family."

"You should take us home, then go back and talk to him," said Clarice. "You're his best friend. He needs you."

"Aw, he'll be alright," said Ripp. "That's one thing about ol' Kirk, he's tough. He'll be fine."

Clarice gave Ripp a hard stare, but said nothing. The vehicle roared on through town.

Kirk unlocked the front door and walked inside his house. Before leaving with his friends earlier that evening, he'd built a fire in the pot-belly stove, so at least the house was relatively warm. Guided by the glow of the stove, he lit the coal-oil lamp, then walked to the back door and gathered logs for the fire.

After stoking the fire and eating a Baby Ruth he'd stashed in the cupboard, Kirk decided the day had provided more than its fair share of stress. He went straight to the living room and lay down on the cot, covering himself with the thick blankets. Kirk reached over and twisted the knob of the coal-oil lamp, extinguishing its fire.

He could feel the tension in his stomach as he stared at the heavenly stars through the holes in the roof of his house. He remembered the cumbersome task of convincing his parents he was old enough to stay behind, that he could take care of himself, and better yet, he would thrive in school, get a job, and lead a productive life, all on his own. Even though he'd endured many hardships over the last couple of days, he took great solace in the fact he was making his own path. As a black American, he knew he would encounter more than his fair share of obstacles in life, but his life was his own to live and no one would ever take that away. The thought gave him comfort as he grew drowsy.

Just before he found sleep, a terrible little thought began to fester in his mind. He remembered Ripp's story about the ghosts and the Nazis. He'd heard both of these stories before and they always made him scared, but his mom or dad was always around to quell his fears.

As the irrational thoughts fired rapidly in his mind, he quickly realized he would be the perfect victim for either an escaped Nazi or a pissed-off ghost. Being a black kid living alone with hardly anyone checking in to see if he was alright made him feel extremely vulnerable.

Suddenly, a loud thud hit the door. Kirk's heart rate shot into the stratosphere. He was so scared he couldn't move. A few moments later, he heard the thud again, only this time the dull noise sounded just outside the wall where he lie. Sweating ice, Kirk realized he had no defenses. The Nazi ghost could come right to his bed and he had no way to stop it.

He exhaled a deep breath when he remembered the gun. On the day his parents left town, Uncle Willie brought over a shotgun, just in case he needed to defend himself. Kirk knew that was his only chance.

He quietly arose, bent down, and grabbed the shotgun from underneath the bed. He cracked open the double-barrel .410 shotgun. Both barrels were loaded with bullets.

As he quietly slammed the shotgun shut, he heard yet another thud, only this time, the sound was much louder and just outside his position. There was no mistaking it. Someone had come for him.

Who could it be, thought Kirk. Ripp? Did he have enough time to drop off Vanessa, then take Clarice to Stringtown and come back? Kirk wiped sweat from his forehead. What should I do?

Rather than waiting on the intruder to come and get him, Kirk decided to go on the offensive. He crept over to the door and quietly unlocked the knob. He steadily opened the door, but only a crack.

Another thud sounded outside the walls of his house. Kirk ascertained the intruder was just outside his house, hitting the exterior with his hand. The sound was too dull to be a rock. With this in mind, Kirk pulled back the hammers on the .410, took in a deep breath, then opened the door and charged outside into the cold, dark, night air.

"Back to hell with you, you Nazi son of a bitch!" he screamed as he crammed the barrels of the gun into the throat of the intruder.

"Holy shit!" screamed the intruder. "Holy shit!"

Kirk pressed the cold steel farther into the intruder's throat, pushing the intruder's head onto the walls of the house. The intruder now had nowhere to go.

"What choo want with me?" screamed Kirk.

The intruder couldn't speak. He could only clear his throat repeatedly.

"Aw, hell. Ripp, is that you?"

"Y-y-y-y-y-y-y-yessssssss."

"What the hell you tryin' to do, get yo'self shot?" Kirk said as he removed the gun from Ripp's throat.

Ripp spent several moments clearing his throat.

"Just relax, man. You're out of harm's way."

"I'm sorry," Ripp said. "I wanted to talk to you. I just didn't want to knock loud and scare you, being that we was talking about Nazis and what not back in the woods."

"It's alright. What do you want to talk about?"

"Can I come in?"

"Of course."

Kirk and Ripp entered the house. After turning up the coal-oil lamp, Kirk sat in a chair, across the living room from Ripp.

"The girls and I are getting worried about you, Kirk. What's going on?"

"I had a bad day."

"Tell me about it. That's why I'm here."

Kirk thought for a moment. "You sure Clarice didn't tell you to get yo'self back here and find out what was buggin' me?"

Ripp sighed. "You're too damned smart for your age, Henry Kirkland. How'd you know?"

"'Cause, like Vanessa, she's a nice girl."

"Well, now that I'm here, you might as well tell me what's got your brain all tied up," said Ripp.

"First of all, what I tell you stays between you and I. No agreeing, then runnin' and tellin' Clarice or your mama."

"You have my word."

"Alright. Being that we didn't have school today, I went in to the drugstore. Skeet was surprised to see me, so he racked his brain to find something for me to do."

"Alright. What happened?"

"He sent me up to the attic to tidy up. They was lots of Christmas stuff and whatnot lyin' around. He wanted me to clean it all up, which I did."

"So what's wrong with that?" asked Ripp.

Kirk could tell he wasn't really listening; he was merely going through the motions.

"I came across an old chest. I thought it looked pretty neat, so I opened it up," said Kirk. Ripp was staring at the fire through an open vent of the pot-bellied stove. Kirk decided to test his attention span by remaining quiet. After a few moments, Ripp looked at Kirk.

"So what was inside the chest?" he asked.

"I found some pictures, really bad pictures."

"What, like pictures of naked movie stars?"

"No, you pervert. I think the pictures were of Skeet, when he was younger, before he opened the pharmacy. But I'm not sure."

"Well, I'm sorry to tell you this, Kirk, but they ain't no laws against having pictures of yo'self in the attic."

"Even if the pictures depict someone as being in the Klan?"

Ripp's eyes suddenly grew bigger than silver dollars. "Mr. Carney was in the KKK!"

"I don't know for sure. That's why you got to keep your mouth shut about all this. It might not have been him, but it kinda looked like him," said a shattered Kirk.

Ripp mulled over Kirk's words. "Wait a minute," he said. "If Carney is a KKKer, then why did he hire you? Hell, I even worked for him for a little while."

"That's what I can't figure out."

"Can you tell me where it was taken?" asked Ripp. "Maybe it's from another town or something."

"No," said Kirk. "The picture was taken in Atoka, right on Court Street in front of the Dime Store. They was several of the Klansmen, carrying torches. The man who looked like Carney stood in front, holding a cross. And not only that, there was an old white hood in there. It was awful."

"Damn," said Ripp. "Hard to believe."

"Yeah. It makes me wonder what's going on. I mean, if it was Skeet and he does hate black folks, why did he hire me?"

Ripp shook his head. "I just can't believe Carney would be in something like that."

"Then why are those photos in his attic? Why else would he have such pictures?"

"Maybe he doesn't know," said Ripp.

"Yeah, maybe so," Kirk said, finally finding some comfort. "Maybe it's just a man who looks like Carney."

"I got to be honest with you, Kirk, Carney's been nothin' but good to us colored folk. I'd have a real hard time believing he's involved in something nefarious."

"Nefarious?"

"It's one of them three-dollar words. It means evil."

"Oh," said Kirk.

"Was there any writing on the photo? Did it say anything?" asked Ripp.

"Yeah," replied Kirk. "It said Jereboam. Don't know what that means."

Ripp stared at the stove for a moment. "I don't think you have anything to worry about," he said.

"Maybe you're right."

"So, you feel better?"

"A little."

"What's got you now?" asked Ripp.

"They's something else."

"What?"

"I did my newspaper route this morning."

"And?"

"You know that fellow Russo, the one who owns part of the drugstore?" asked Kirk.

"Yeah."

"It was early in the morning, before the sunrise. I saw him and Mark Maston doing something nefarious."

Ripp smiled. "You picked that up quick. Who's Mark Maston?" he said.

"My boss. The fellow who owns the newspaper shop."

"What were they doing?" asked Ripp.

"It sounds crazy, but it looked like they were loading a body into the trunk of a car."

"No way!" said Ripp.

"I think they was."

"Are you sure?"

"It sure looked like a body. It was covered in something, but it really looked . . ."

"Did they see you?" interrupted Ripp.

Kirk looked down the floor. "I don't know. I was up high on the trash dumpster, lookin' through the window. I slipped and made some noise. They heard it and came runnin' out, but I was already gone."

"Think they know it was you?"

"I do," said Kirk while shaking his head. "I saw Russo in the drugstore later that morning and he acted real strange."

"Damn," said Ripp. "What choo gonna do?"

"I don't know."

"You going to the drugstore tomorrow?"

"Yeah," replied Kirk. "Being it's Saturday, I'm going in early and staying all day."

"You think you'll be safe?" asked Ripp.

"I reckon. I don't figure he'll do anything to me while I'm in a public place."

"I don't know what to tell you. I can't rightly see Russo hidin' a body, but then again, I don't really know him, either. You want me to go to the store with you?"

"No. I think I'll be okay."

"Alright," said Ripp while standing. He walked to the door. "I asked the girls if they want to go out tomorrow night. They said yes, so let's plan on doing something after work."

"Sounds good."

Ripp turned the handle to the front door. "Oh, and Kirk."

"Yes."

"Just 'cause you hear something outside yo' door in the middle of the night don't mean that you can shoot they ass."

"Sorry about that," said Kirk. "I was a little scared. Some fool told me a scary story about a Nazi ghost out in the woods."

"I think I heard the same story." Ripp smiled, then walked through the door and headed out into the night.

After closing and locking the front door, Kirk fell onto the mattress. It had been a very long day.

Chapter 11

Kirk focused on touching each of the railroad tracks with his feet as he made his way to the drugstore. It was another stupid self-amusement game he'd improvised to fill a boring activity. Not only did it take his mind away from the tedious tasks, but it also seemed to diminish the pain in his legs that always came with long walks.

The sun was just beginning to crest the horizon and while the air temperature was still very cold, this morning was much warmer than previous days. This observation prompted hopes that maybe a break in the weather was coming with an end to the dreary snow.

A quick glance down to his watch showed the time was ten minutes until seven. The paper route had gone much faster than normal, thanks to Kirk's decision to abandon the wagon once again and deliver the newspapers by foot. He was also able to use stealth and completely avoid Mrs. Parker.

The thought of being early forced a smile upon Kirk's face as he now had a decent chance to arrive at the drugstore before Carney. Carney, he thought. Kirk's pace slowed. He suddenly remembered Carney, Russo, and the picture. The thought stopped him dead in his tracks.

What if all this is true, he thought. What if things weren't as they seemed and both his bosses were only posing as legitimate businessmen to hide their true identity? What if this all were just a game and he was the poor bastard caught in the middle, to be used as a pawn in one of their schemes? Or what if things were even worse?

Kirk looked ahead and saw the tracks running straight ahead, almost as far as the eye could see, but then turned and ran out of his view. The bend in the tracks enticed his imagination. He then turned his head around and looked behind him. In the distance, he spotted the two giant oak trees, the icons he always relied on to signal that his house was near.

Kirk expelled a deep breath, turned, and continued walking toward the bend in the tracks. I wonder what's around that bend, he thought.

# # #

Kirk's dream of beating his boss to work was dashed when he reached the front door of the pharmacy. As usual, Skeet was already inside, beginning the morning activities. Kirk quickly made his way through the front door and walked to the pharmacy.

"Mornin' Mr. Carney."

Lost in his daily tasks of organizing the day's prescriptions to fill, Carney failed to hear Kirk's words.

"Good morning, Mr. Carney," said Kirk, in a much louder voice.

Carney looked up from his paperwork.

"Oh, hi, Young Henry," he said with a big smile. "How are you doing this morning?"

The smile instantly brought relief to Kirk's apprehension about his boss. "Fine, and you?"

"I'm doing great. Are you ready to get started this morning?"

"Yes sir. Where would you like for me to begin?"

"Well, I've already started brewing the coffee. There will be a bunch of folks in here pretty soon. There will probably be a big lot in here to pick up their prescriptions, too, so we're liable to be pretty busy for a good while."

"No problem," said Kirk. "Anything else?"

"Well, the damndest thing has happened over the last couple of days," said Skeet. "It seems as though we've almost sold out of that cough syrup you made."

Kirk's heart raced.

"I think I'd like for you to mix up some more, if you don't mind," said Carney.

"Sure thing. I'll get right on it."

Kirk walked away from Carney as fast as he could. He grabbed the near-empty bottle of syrup, dragged it to a corner, and began mixing the concoction. Being that Kirk had mixed the elixir far too potent last time around, he decided to change his formula. This time, he used one part opium, three parts water and a half part cherry to taste. The thought of someone overdosing on his mistake frightened him to the bone. If this mixture was wrong, at least it would be too weak and wouldn't bring harm.

By the time Kirk finished making his opium-based syrup and cleaning up the mess, the drugstore was showing signs of life. He looked up and saw Carney serving coffee at the soda fountain. He made his way to help. Several folks were gathered at the pharmacy window, making small talk and waiting on Carney. Others sat at the bar of the soda fountain, waiting to order coffee. Most of the patrons were elderly people who'd never seen Kirk before. They were surprised when he walked behind the counter to help Carney. The person who normally handled the coffee rush was Barbara Ellen, but she'd been out sick for the last week.

"I normally wouldn't ask you to do this but with Barbara Ellen being out, I'm in a jam. Can you take over?" asked Carney. "I need to get back to the pharmacy window."

Kirk was surprised. "Are you sure that would be a good idea?"

"Of course. I think it'll be fine."

"Well, with me being black and all, I didn't think we were supposed to . . ."

"Nonsense. You're a human being, same as me. Although maybe not as good looking," Carney said with a laugh. "If anyone gives you any problems, you come straight to me."

"Yes sir," replied Kirk, now more confused than ever. If Carney were a Klansman, Kirk thought, he was doing a great job of hiding his hatred of black people.

"And remember, speak to everybody you see and always remain courteous and keep a smile on your face. They'll come around, I promise," Carney said with authority.

"Understood."

An elderly white lady hobbled on crutches to the counter. Kirk was quick to help.

"What'll it be, ma'am?" he asked.

"What happened to Mr. Carney?"

"He was needed back at the pharmacy, but I can help you."

"Where's Barbara Ellen?"

"She's out sick, but I'm more than happy to help."

"Oh," replied the lady, somewhat taken aback. "I suppose."

Kirk could easily see the lady was definitely shaken by the thought of being served by a black boy. Even though he wanted to walk away, he knew Carney expected him to do his job.

"What can I get for you, ma'am?"

"Well," said the lady, still visibly shaken, "I sure would like to have a coffee while I'm waiting on my prescriptions, but . . ."

"I'd be more than happy to get that for you ma'am."

"What's the goin' price?"

"Five cents," replied Kirk. He sensed she was finally becoming more comfortable.

"Then fill 'er up, young man," she said with a somewhat forced smile.

After Kirk poured the coffee, the old woman gave him a long hard gaze.

"I don't remember seeing you in here," she said. "Just . . . who are you?" she asked.

Kirk laughed. "I work for Mr. Carney. I just started a couple of days ago."

"Oh, so you work here?"

"Yes ma'am," Kirk replied with a smile.

"Oh." After a few moments of silence, the lady continued. "Well, I guess I should pay for this, shouldn't I?"

Kirk laughed. "The coffee is five cents, ma'am."

The lady propped herself up with her crutches, then struggled to find a nickel in her purse. After a few moments of searching, she looked up with sincere eyes.

"I'm afraid I'm having a hard time here finding money in my purse. These crutches really make life difficult for me."

Kirk bent down, across the counter. "This one's on me," he whispered into her ear.

"Oh, my. I wasn't expecting that."

"It's no problem," Kirk said as he handed her the cup of coffee. The old lady looked down and inspected the coffee. She hesitantly smelled the coffee, as if it were laced with cyanide. After a few moments, she looked up and smiled. Kirk noticed the old lady struggling.

"Do you need any help carrying that back to the pharmacy counter?" asked Kirk.

The old woman nodded. She handed Kirk the coffee and then placed her purse's handles around her shoulder. After much struggling, she propped herself up with her crutches and hobbled briskly back to the pharmacy. Once she sat down, Kirk handed her the coffee, then returned to the soda fountain.

The woman stared at her cup of coffee. After a few moments, she inched her nose forward and smelled the coffee. In an effort to be inconspicuous, she made eye contact with other patrons. A second later, she sat the coffee on the pharmacy counter.

Kirk was wiping the soda fountain when he noticed a nice-looking middle-aged man, wearing a business suit.

"I see you're doing a great job," said the man.

"I'm sure tryin'," replied Kirk.

"My name's Butch. I work down at the bank. I'm one of Skeet's friends."

"Nice to meet you."

Butch extended his hand. Kirk looked him in the eye and noticed a long scar across the right side of his forehead. Undeterred, Kirk shook his hand.

"Looks like you have your hands full," said Butch with a smile. "I'd say you're doing a great job."

"Thanks. My first day to serve coffee."

"Looks like you're fitting right in. Heck, before long, you'll be running this place."

Kirk smiled. "Thanks."

"Well, I'd better get back to the bank."

"Don't you want to order some coffee?"

"I'm actually running way behind. I'll take a rain check."

"Oh, okay."

"Gotta run," Butch replied. He patted Kirk on the shoulder. "It was very nice to meet you. Keep up the good work." The man practically ran to the door.

Kirk shook his head. As he greeted the next person in line for coffee, an old man wearing thick glasses, he noticed the once long line had now dispersed either to the pharmacy or out of the store completely. Once again, Kirk shook his head.

Carney made his way through the prescriptions with lightning speed. He wiped his brow as the last man in line, a farmer named Drake Cooper, walked to the pharmacy window.

"What can I help you with?"

"I just bought me a pig and I reckon I need some medicines. I heard you was the veterinarian around these parts."

Carney laughed. "No, I'm a pharmacist, not a veterinarian, but I do carry livestock vaccines and medicine. How old is the pig?"

"Just been weaned. I had me some extra gasoline rationing coupons, so I traded them with old man Boswell for one of his little piglets."

"If he's just been weaned, you're gonna need to vaccinate him. I have erysipelas, bordatella, and pasturella. Have you ever vaccinated a pig before?" asked Carney.

"No sir. I'm a cowboy, not a pig farmer."

"Alright then, I have some syringes you can borrow, but I'll need for you to bring them back. What you'll need to do is throw your leg over the pig and twist his head a little. Be sure to get a good clamp on his head.

Then you might have to put his ear in your mouth and pull real hard to keep him still. Give the shots in the fat of the neck."

The young man smiled and nodded. "I reckon that explains it," he said.

Carney rang up the medicine and collected the money. The young man tipped his hat and casually walked out of the drugstore.

Kirk had been listening to the story and was in awe of Carney's instructions. He seamlessly went from pharmacist to veterinarian.

"You really are a jack of all trades," said Kirk. "I didn't know you used to vaccinate pigs."

"Who me? Hell no. I've never vaccinated a pig in my life, you think I'm crazy?"

"Then how did you know?"

Carney smiled. "Let me tell you something. When those cowboys come in the store, always look at their boots. The ones with the most shit on their boots are probably the ones with the most head of cattle and therefore, the ones with the money. I've listened to the farmers' stories over the years and know how to talk the talk. So, when a rich cowboy comes in, I go out of my way to make a friend."

"I see," said Kirk, while scratching his chin.

"It looks like the morning rush has come and gone. I have a special job for you. Follow me."

Carney led Kirk into his small office behind the pharmacy. Kirk felt privileged to be invited into such a special place. Carney walked over to his small safe, which sat by his desk. He spun the wheel back and forth a few times, then opened the door. He retrieved a small deposit bag.

"I need you to do something for me," said Carney.

"Sure," said Kirk, not having the faintest idea what it could be.

"I'd like for you to take this over to the bank and give it to Sharon or Darlene. One of them will be sitting at the windows up front. Tell her your name and tell her you're from the drugstore. And don't worry, these ladies are both real nice."

"Are you sure you want me to do that? I mean, there's probably a lot of money in there and you don't even really know me and . . ."

Carney grabbed Kirk's hand. "If I didn't trust you, I wouldn't have hired you, Henry."

"Well, okay, I suppose."

"Good," Carney said. "Now hurry on back. There's a lot to do here today."

Kirk grabbed the deposit bag and walked toward the door. "I'll be back as soon as I can."

As Kirk left the drugstore, his mind swirled at tornadic speeds. "Sharon, Darlene, Sharon, Darlene," he said. When he stepped through the front door and the cowbells rang, a thought hit him right between the eyes. What if I can't remember all this? He reckoned his only hope was to write down the instructions. But since he carried no pen, the only way to do so would be to walk back to the pharmacy, find a pen, then locate something to write it on. Carney would see him and surely suspect he was incompetent. His only shot was to rely on his memory.

A mixture of warm morning sun and cold air hit Kirk as he stepped out onto the sidewalk on Court Street, then headed east. As he walked down the street, gazing at all the businesses' windows, he wondered what he could buy with all the money in the bag. It would probably be more than enough to set up him and his family for months in Langston. The thought made him tighten his grip on the bag. He crossed Court Street at the corner and took a deep breath as he looked up at the towering bricks of the bank.

After Kirk opened the door to the bank, he stopped. Since he'd never been in the bank before, his heart began to race. What would the folks inside think of a black boy bringing in God knows how much money? Did Carney call ahead and tell them he was coming? Kirk took a deep breath and took his first step inside the bank.

He only saw one woman working, so he walked toward her and noticed a wooden plaque with her name on it.

"Hi, my name is Henry Kirkland. Mr. Carney sent me here to deposit some money from the drugstore. Is your name Darlene?"

Darlene was speechless. "Uh . . . yeah," she said.

With a troubled look upon her face, Darlene sat in silence. With each passing second Kirk grew more and more uncomfortable.

"Do you have the deposit bag?" asked Darlene.

"Oh, of course." Kirk removed the bag from his coat. "I'm sorry, I wasn't . . ."

From out of nowhere, Butch appeared directly in front of Kirk.

"Just what do you think you're doing, young man?" Butch snapped.

"Oh, hi, Butch," Kirk responded.

"Don't 'Hi, Butch' me. What in the hell are you doing with all that money, boy?"

If aliens suddenly landed on Court Street and began blasting Atoka with cosmic lasers, Kirk would be no less surprised and shocked. What happened to the pleasant man he'd just met in the drugstore? Confusion fogged Kirk's mind as he struggled for something to say.

"Uhm . . . Mr. Carney asked me to come here and give you the deposit money."

Butch violently ripped the bag from Kirk's hand.

"Darlene, I want you to count this money and make sure this boy didn't take a little for himself." Butch tossed Darlene the deposit bag.

"Oh, no sir. I would never do that. I was only doing what Mr. Carney said, honest," said Kirk. He felt his heart racing so fast it seemed to pound out of his chest.

"I'll have you know if you've taken one dime, I'll see to it that you spend the rest of your adolescence in a detention center, young man," said Butch.

"It's all here," said Darlene. "On the deposit slip, Skeet wrote down fifty-seven dollars and thirteen cents. I just counted it. It's all here."

Kirk let out a deep sigh.

"It's a damned good thing, boy," said Butch. He clenched his jaw as he stared at Kirk.

"I reckon I'll be on my way," Kirk said. "Much obliged."

Darlene signed the deposit slip, placed it back in the bag and handed it to Kirk. He shoved the bag into his coat and hurried out the door.

For the first time in his life, Kirk felt he'd looked into the eyes of evil, a monster in disguise. Butch's pre-disposed opinion of him left behind a feeling of emptiness Kirk had never experienced in his whole life. As he walked through the cold air, he couldn't determine which was colder, the winter air or the way he felt inside.

# # #

It was almost seven o'clock before Kirk actually had the time to sit down at the soda fountain and think about how busy the day had been. Ever since he'd returned from the bank, the action at the drugstore was non-stop. He hadn't even had a moment to tell Carney about his experience with Butch.

While Kirk sipped on a soda, he pondered the events of the day. He looked up and saw Carney had just turned off the back lights in the building, which included the pharmacy. That was a good indication the store was about to close.

"I'm glad every Saturday is not like this," Carney said as he walked up to the soda fountain.

"Me, too," replied Kirk. "Can I pour you a soda?"

"Fill 'er up, partner."

Kirk wasted no time retrieving a cold Coke from the refrigerator and pouring it into a mug for Carney. He slid it down the counter, just like a pro.

"My, you sure are catching on fast. I didn't know you were such a fast learner."

"Thanks," said Kirk. "You've made it easy. I've been practicing when no one is around. I know I'm not the new soda jerk, but I can pretend, I suppose."

After Carney took a big drink from his soda, he smiled at Kirk. "That's the stuff."

"For sure."

Carney took a long sip on his ice-cold Coke and sat back deep on the stool at the counter. He looked down at Kirk's shoes.

"Your shoes are just, well, awful. They are worn completely through," said Carney.

Embarrassed, Kirk's first instinct was to protect his parents. "It's my fault," said Kirk. "Momma gave me some money for shoes before they left, but I used it for something stupid. She's probably gonna kill me when she sees . . ."

"Are those the same shoes you play basketball in?" Carney interrupted.

"Yeah, but I'm sure Mom will take care of it."

"No worries," said Carney. "Do you need some help?"

"Oh, no. I have some money saved back, so I'm pretty sure I can buy some soon."

"You sure?" said Carney, just after taking a drink.

"Thanks, but I'm fine. Besides, Momma will be sending some money soon, I'm sure."

"Alright," said Carney. "But you know if you ever need anything, let me know."

"Will do."

"Speaking of basketball, when's your next game?"

"Monday night."

"When and where?"

Kirk paused for a moment. "At the Dunbar gym at seven o'clock."

"That's good," Carney said. "You won't have far to travel. How was your visit to the bank?"

"Oh," said Kirk. "I almost forgot." He walked over to his coat and retrieved the deposit bag. He grabbed the receipt and handed it to Carney.

"It's all there," said Kirk. "Take a look at the receipt. Darlene counted it up and everything, just like you said."

"I never had any doubts," replied Carney. "Did you have any problems?"

Kirk pondered for a moment. Telling Carney about Butch's viciousness would at best sound unbelievable. After all, Butch was a respected and prominent man in Atoka. Kirk instantly recognized a Pandora's Box. And he was fairly certain that it didn't need to be opened.

"No," replied Kirk after much thought. "It was awful stuffy inside that place, though. I got quite a few strange looks."

"Oh?" Carney said with a raised eyebrow.

"I'm not so sure those bankers were expecting a black boy to come in with a bag of money like that."

"Did anyone give you any grief?"

"Well," said Kirk, "I think I might have caught Butch in a bad mood."

"He's like that," said Carney. "Old Butch isn't nearly as slick as he reckons himself."

Carney walked over and put his arm around Kirk's shoulders. "A great man once said, 'you can fool all the people some of the time and some of the people all of the time, but you'll never fool all of the people all of the time,'" he said with a smile. "Butch has yet to learn that lesson. Do you know what I mean?"

"I think I do," said Kirk.

"Good," replied Carney. "What do you say we get on outta here?"

"I'm right behind you."

Both men exited the building and stood on the sidewalk in front of the store. Carney fumbled with his keys until he found the one to the front door. He locked the door and smiled.

"Do you need a ride home?" he asked.

"No," replied Kirk, "It's a ritual of mine to go to Johnny's on Saturday night. I'm addicted to their chili."

"It's mighty cold. You sure?"

"I'll be alright."

"Great. I'll see you Monday."

The thought of a bowl of Johnny's chili was already making Kirk's mouth water. As he jogged past several blocks, he could feel his stomach turning with each step. Finally, he reached the entrance to Johnny's. As always, he turned the corner and made his way to the alley, then on to the back door, but something caught his eye. There were no lights on when he passed the front entrance. That's strange, thought Kirk as he stepped to the back door. His stomach dropped when he tried to pull open the back door, but found it locked. He quickly walked around the building to the front door and found that it too was locked. A note on the front door read "Due to the weather, we're closing at six o'clock."

"Damn," replied Kirk. "Now, what am I gonna do?"

Kirk searched for options. The only other restaurant in town was The Corner Café, but it had a reputation for not being black-friendly. Normally, Kirk would figure out another option, but The Café was near and he was damned hungry.

Kirk blazed a trail through the two blocks south until he reached The Corner Café. As he arrived, he noticed that the lights were on, which gave him hope, but the parking lot was empty. He walked past the front entrance, turned the corner, and walked down the length of the building, to the alley. As he turned the corner, he saw a young white man wearing a chef's apron walking away from a large trashcan in the alley. The white man never noticed Kirk as he entered The Corner Café's back door entrance. Kirk quickly approached the back door. He tried to pull it open, but found it was locked. Kirk knocked on the door.

"Yes," replied the young white man.

"I'd like to get something to eat."

"Uhm, I'm sorry, but we don't serve . . ."

"I don't understand," said Kirk.

"We don't serve blacks."

"I've heard that about this place," Kirk said calmly. "But there are no cars parked out front, which means you have little or no customers. Now, I know you're not inclined to serve my kind, but it's damned cold, I'm damned hungry, and there are no damned witnesses, so what do you say we forget about your rule, just for tonight?"

"I'm sorry," said the man with sincerity, "I truly am, but I can't let you in."

Kirk pulled out a wad of dollar bills. "I have the money right here. I'll pay you double."

The young man shook his head. "I'm sorry, but I just can't."

"Please," pleaded Kirk. "Look man, I haven't eaten all day and I'm starved," he said, as his eyes welled. "I know you've got to do what you've got to do, but I'm desperate. Please give me a hand here."

Kirk heard loud voices from inside the café. Judging by the young man's facial expressions, it appeared his boss was yelling at him from inside the building. The young man quickly closed and locked the door.

"Well, don't that beat all," said Kirk in disgust. He felt his knees weakening as he stood in the alley, trying to figure out what to do. He sighed deeply, then turned to walk home. As he passed The Corner

Café's large trash container, something caught his eye. He stopped and looked inside.

Throughout his young life, Kirk had heard of miracles. At Sunday School, he heard stories of times throughout history when the faithful were in need and God intervened by parting the Red Sea or vanquishing enemies, or even when Jesus turned water into wine. As Kirk looked down into the large trashcan, he wondered if he were witnessing such a thing, but on a much smaller scale.

There, on top of the trash, sat two pristine biscuits on a white plate. Kirk was really amazed by the sight because the plate almost seemed to emit a faint white glow. And what was even more amazing was the fact the biscuits were still hot. So hot, they were emitting stream into the cold night air.

Kirk had always considered himself to be a proud person who was above eating out of a trashcan, but he had a feeling more was at play here than what it seemed. As a matter of fact, he even felt a strange warm feeling that emanated in his chest and seemed to radiate throughout his body. It was as if God was lending a hand, perhaps not just to satisfy his hunger, but also to let Kirk know that He was there. With this in mind, Kirk grabbed the biscuits. He looked up toward the heavens, nodded, and walked down the alley toward the railroad tracks.

Chapter 12

Kirk wiped the sweat from his eyes, then tried his best to rub his hands dry on his shorts. He walked to the free throw line, placed his feet perfectly behind the black line, and flashed his hands to the referee, indicating he was ready. After receiving the ball, he dribbled twice, let out a deep breath, and shot toward the goal. A thunder erupted from the all-black crowd in the Dunbar School Gymnasium as they applauded and cheered when the ball swished through the bucket. Kirk's free throw tied the game with only two seconds left on the clock. If he made the next free throw, Dunbar school would pull off the biggest upset in generations.

The coach for Crescent, the visiting team, called a time out in order to put pressure on Kirk. This action was a staple in high school basketball, meant to give the opposing school's athlete too much time to think about the free throw, and in the process falter under the pressure and miss the shot. Kirk smiled as he trotted over to the sidelines to meet with his coach and teammates. Tension grated the crowd as indeed, on this Monday evening game, there was much pressure.

For starters, Kirk's Dunbar team was good with a record of thirty-three wins and five loses, but still expected to be blown out by the undefeated Crescent team. Crescent had been on a roll all year, mainly because they had the ringer of all ringers, Hubert Ausbie, who scored seventy-five points in his previous game last week. No one really thought Dunbar had much of a chance, but the crowd showed up anyway. The ten-row bleachers on both sides of the basketball court were packed, plus standing-room only on the ends. All eyes were on Kirk as he stood in the huddle and listened to his coach, also his science teacher, Willard Dallas.

"Alright, Pee Wee," Coach Dallas shouted, "it's all up to you."

The crowd was so loud, he found it difficult to hear the coach's words.

"As soon as Pee Wee shoots the free throw, I want everyone back. Regardless of whether he makes it or misses, I want Hoss, Robert, Linus, and Carl back to defend our goal. Pee Wee, after you shoot the ball, I want you and only you to stay on Ausbie like white on rice, just like you been doin' all night."

Due to Kirk's skinny stature, he had been branded with the name Pee Wee when he started playing basketball. Even though Kirk was over six feet tall, he was so thin people sometimes mistakenly thought him small. As was the case this evening, Kirk always disproved this misconception. He'd already scored twenty-nine points and, most importantly, he'd held the ringer Ausbie, to only twenty-five.

Ivory Moore threw Kirk a towel. "It might be time for some new shoes, Pee Wee," said the assistant coach. "You're sliding all over the place tonight. Use that towel to clean the soles."

Kirk nodded and wiped his feet. He threw the towel back over to Coach Dallas.

"You've practiced and made this shot at least ten thousand times," said Coach Dallas. "Forget about the crowd, forget about Ausbie, forget about everything. Just put yourself on automatic."

He nodded and trotted back to the court. When the crowd noticed him they clapped and cheered. As Kirk made his way to the free-throw line, he looked into the home side of the stands and saw a sea of black faces below a haze of cigarette smoke. Most of them he knew, either as parents and relatives of his teammates or just acquaintances.

"Go get 'em Young Henry," a voice bellowed from the crowd. Hearing the voice stopped Kirk cold. He knew of only one person who referred to him as Young Henry, but that couldn't be, he thought. He'd stand out like a sore thumb, especially in this gym, where everyone is packed together like sardines.

"Give it to 'em, Young Henry," the voice said again.

Now Kirk was sure of it. As his teammates and the Crescent players walked to the lane, Kirk looked to the visitor's side of the stands. It only took a moment of scanning through the cloud of cigarette smoke to find the only white face in the building. It was Carney.

Kirk smiled and Carney smiled back. Sitting to Carney's immediate right was Uncle Willie, who nodded. The sight of Carney and Uncle Willie gave Kirk the confidence of a thousand men. As he lined up on the free-throw line, he knew what the outcome would be before he even touched the ball. The referee blew the whistle, then bounced the ball to Kirk. He took two dribbles, came up in perfect form, and nailed the shot.

The Crescent players scrambled to throw the ball inbounds. Ausbie already had it by the time Kirk ran to him. With one second remaining, and standing on the other team's free-throw line, Ausbie jumped up and launched the ball. As the ball soared through the air, time on the game clock expired. The ball was thrown with such might it traveled over the backboard and slammed into the brick wall. The game was over. The crowd ran onto the floor. Teammates lifted Kirk's lanky body up on their shoulders. Everyone cheered for the Wildcats. Dunbar had done it again and Kirk was the hero.

# # #

Coming out of the dressing room afterward was always one of the highlights of basketball games, because every team member received special treatment. As players emerged from the dressing room into the cold night air, a crowd made up of friends and family usually gathered to wait on the players. Now that Kirk's family was gone, he wasn't expecting to be greeted by anyone, but he was wrong. As he walked outside, a whole crowd of people began clapping and cheering. For once in his life, he honestly felt like a hero.

"Very good, Young Henry," said Carney. "Looks like you might have another career on your hands."

"Same here," said Uncle Willie. "You showed 'em how we play ball here in Dunbar."

"Thanks, guys," said Kirk. "I really appreciate you coming down. That was quite a game, huh?"

"Damned right," replied Willie. "That ringer ain't got nothin' on you. Ausbie walked in here with his head cocked up like a rooster, but the whole team got on their bus with heads hanging like a bunch of geese!"

"Well, Ausbie is one heck of a player, but you shut him down. You watch," said Carney, "the whole globe will be seein' more of Ausbie, I'll bet. He's a special kind of player, and you'll always know you were the one who held him to twenty-five points."

"Thanks," said Kirk.

Carney looked to his watch. "Josephine is expecting me. I'd better get." He shook Kirk's hand. "I'll be seeing you in the morning?"

"Yes sir."

As Carney walked to the parking lot, Vanessa snuck up behind Kirk.

"Look at you!" she exclaimed. "I didn't realize that you were such a rainbow."

"Everyone gets lucky every once in a while," Kirk humbly replied.

"It wasn't luck," Vanessa said in a very matter-of-fact tone. "You're just that good."

"Get outta here," said Kirk. "You're embarrassing me."

"Do you have time to walk a girl home?" Vanessa asked.

"Sure," said Kirk.

Uncle Willie was quick to interject. "Do you have a minute to talk?" he asked, with a somber face.

"Sure," said Kirk.

Uncle Willie led the way to the parking lot. While Kirk followed, he could sense he was about to be exposed to something heavy. He'd seen Uncle Willie act like this before and it usually wasn't good. His present demeanor reminded Kirk of the way he acted just a few months ago, when he visited the Kirklands' house after being bailed out of jail.

The incident occurred in Boggy Bend, at a bar called UL Washington's Place in the country near Stringtown. Uncle Willie was there one Sunday afternoon, enjoying the day with some of his friends. He wasn't one for drinking, but liked making the rounds at the bars.

While he sat peacefully in the tavern, a troublemaker came into the bar looking for Willie. The man entered the bar sporting a hammer in one hand and a gun in the other. The stranger then placed the gun in his pants. Holding the hammer, the man walked straight up to Willie. "If this doesn't get you," said the man while reaching into his pants and retrieving the pistol, "then this will!" Everyone in the bar was terrified. Everyone, except Uncle Willie. Uncle Willie walked up to the gentleman and smiled, as if he were acting in a movie.

He then took a Colt .45 from his coat pocket, crammed the pistol in the man's mouth and started pulling the trigger. After the man fell to the floor, Uncle Willie wanted to make sure he was dead, so he shot him two more times.

Uncle Willie was immediately taken to jail, but Battle Axe quickly bailed him out. One of the first stops he made out of jail was to the Kirklands' house. Kirk answered the door that night and noticed Uncle Willie was acting odd. Of course, Kirk's parents were shocked, but Uncle Willie assured them he'd get off because he was provoked. No one in Kirk's family shared his positive outlook. Two years prior to the incident at Boggy Bend, Uncle Willie shot another man in the leg at Boyette's Bar in Atoka, just because he thought the man said something negative about his mom. Due to the extent of the injury, doctors had to amputate the man's leg. Uncle Willie never served time for the incident because of some connections Kirk's mother, Laura Colbert, had at the Sheriff's office. However, Kirk's family knew he wouldn't be so lucky for the murder.

The thought sent shivers up Kirk's spine as he wondered what Uncle Willie was about to drop on him.

When they reached his car, Uncle Willie walked to the trunk.

"What's going on?" asked Kirk as the two men stood over the trunk.

Uncle Willie remained silent while he reached into the trunk and removed a paper bag.

"They's something we need to talk about," said Uncle Willie.

"What's wrong?" Kirk asked.

"Did you hear about the James boy?"

Kirk shook his head. "You mean Rudy?"

"Yeah. Did you know him?"

"Well, kind of. He's a little bit older than me. What happened?"

"They found him tonight," Uncle Willie said slowly.

"What do you mean?"

"Those bastards killed him."

"What! We knew he was missin', but I figured he'd just split for a while!" yelled Kirk.

"Well, them thugs done killed his ass. They found his body a little while ago, just up the road."

Kirk was shell shocked. He didn't really know Rudy, other than an occasional pickup basketball game, but he always seemed to be a pretty nice fellow. And to be murdered, especially in Atoka, was just unbelievable."

"Do you know why?" asked Kirk.

Uncle Willie stroked his chin. "I heard he was gettin' too close to some white girl or something. I don't know who these thugs are. I just know they slipped him a mickey and when he fell asleep, they broke his neck."

"Oh my gosh," said Kirk. "I probably won't sleep tonight."

"That's why I wanted to talk to you," said Uncle Willie.

Uncle Willie reached into the brown bag and retrieved a pistol. Rather than handing it over, he placed it in Kirk's front pocket.

"But I already have a gun," said Kirk.

"You have a shotgun," replied Uncle Willie. "By the time you get that damned thing out, they'll have enough time to clean your clock."

Kirk reached into his pocket and pulled out the pistol. It appeared to be a .45 caliber revolver.

"A pistol is different," explained Uncle Willie. "Keep it loaded. That way, if anyone ever jumps you, just pull it out and you have six friends."

Uncle Willie spent a few moments showing how to hold, reload, and clean the gun. Kirk finally felt more comfortable handling the weapon, but he was still apprehensive.

"I don't know, Uncle Willie," Kirk said while holding the pistol. "Momma says these things are just an invitation to trouble."

"Maybe so," said Uncle Willie. "But if trouble ever tries to find you, this is your answer. Trust me."

"Who are these guys who jumped Rudy?"

"Just thugs. They probably don't even live here. They probably live up in the hills. Don't matter though. They wait 'till late at night, then strike when you're not ready."

All the fear Kirk experienced when his family left came rushing back in a giant tidal wave. If some thugs did away with Rudy, why wouldn't they do away with me, he thought. It was almost too much to think about. Suddenly, he had a cold realization.

"Do you think I'm safe in my house?" Kirk asked.

Uncle Willie stepped close and placed an arm over his shoulders. "I don't think anyone's safe in they home," he said. "Carry this gun with you at all times. Sleep with it under yo' pillow. Make it become yo' best friend."

Kirk stared at the gun and thought for a moment. "Maybe so."

"Your circumstances are quite a bit different from everyone else's. With yo' momma and dad gone, you gots to be extra cautious. The world is full of bad people. Always remember that."

"I will," said Kirk.

Uncle Willie handed Kirk the brown bag. "They's lots of bullets inside," he said. "If you need more, let me know."

"Alright," said Kirk.

"Well, I gots to get. You take care now and remember, if anything goes wrong or you need anything at all, you know where I live."

"Understood."

Uncle Willie closed the trunk, stepped inside his car, then drove off into the night. Kirk met Vanessa halfway back to the gym.

"You ready to head back?" he asked.

"I'm always ready to go with you, my rainbow," she said with a laugh.

Kirk gave Vanessa a hard stare. "More like a rainbow who's been left on his own. A rainbow in the dark."

A puzzled look was plastered on Vanessa's face. "What does that mean?" she asked.

Kirk simply looked to the ground and began walking.

Chapter 13

Josephine walked with minced steps down the hallway deep within the Stringtown Internment Camp. As she walked toward Geddy Wainscott's office, her hopes were dwindling with each step. Over the past few days, she'd learned just how difficult it was for a civilian to meet with the military brass. She'd tried in vain to setup an appointment with prison officials. After all her phone calls went unreturned, she decided to try her luck with a high-ranking civilian, a person who had the officials' ears and was accessible. Josephine decided to talk to her boss.

"Hi, Mr. Wainscott. Do you have a minute?" Josephine asked from the doorway.

"Sure," replied Geddy. "You're my secretary. Why wouldn't I have a moment for you?"

Josephine entered the office, which wasn't like the others inside the prison. While all the others were a collection of cheap, lowest-bidder and bland amenities, Geddy's mirrored an expensive trial-lawyer's domain. The entire suite was encased in mahogany. When Geddy was hired to work as a contractor for the government, his office was just as tasteless as the others, but over a couple years time, he managed to find justifications for replacing the carpet, the shelves, the desks, and every other item inside the government walls of his allotted space. And he did it all on Uncle Sam's dime. Geddy made a mockery of thrifty spending in a time when the entire nation was trying to save for the war effort. But he was worth it. Or so he thought.

Standing in front of his desk, Josephine's plan was to sound as sad and pitiful as possible. She faced a mammoth task and would have to be inventive to succeed.

"I have a problem and I need your help," she said.

Geddy wasn't paying her much attention. With his back to her, he sat polishing his new twelve gauge shotgun.

"Shoot," he said. "Excuse the pun."

"There's a prisoner here that needs some protection."

Geddy dabbed a little oil on his rag and rubbed it into the gun's metal barrel. "I'm sure they all need some protection, if you listen to them."

"I think this is serious," said Josephine. "And I'm sorry to ask you, but I can't seem to get anyone's attention in the army."

"Well, they are trying to win a war," Geddy replied nonchalantly. "I figure they've got bigger and better things to worry about."

Josephine felt the dejection as clearly as Geddy was handing it out. All the frustrations she'd encountered for the past week seemed to press down on her, all at once.

"But, can't you do something?"

Geddy didn't respond. He looked at his reflection in the gun and smiled.

"Don't you see they're very liable to hurt poor Karl?" she pleaded.

Geddy instantly set his shotgun on the floor and spun his chair around to face Josephine.

"What did you say?"

Surprised that Geddy suddenly decided to pay attention to the conversation, Josephine wiped the tears from her eyes. "That they're very liable to hurt poor Karl."

"Karl who?" he asked.

"Karl Bartz, one of the prisoners."

"What do you know about Karl Bartz?" he asked. He placed his hands together on the desk. Josephine noted the change in his demeanor. The fake grin, coupled with his coat, tie, and short haircut, made him resemble a politician who just got caught in a whore house.

"I know he's very scared he's going to be attacked by the other prisoners."

"I don't think it's such a good idea talking to Karl Bartz. From what I understand, he's delusional."

"Delusional or not, isn't there a way to help him?" pleaded Josephine.

"I'm sure the officials are doing everything they can to protect him, but remember, this is a prison," said Geddy.

"What about isolating him?"

"There's no way of doing that, either," said Geddy. "They simply don't have enough room in this facility. This prison was established to serve as a sub-prison, meant only to relieve the over-crowding at the state prison in McAlester. Stringtown was never intended to be an interment camp for World War II prisoners."

Josephine was biting her nails and showing real signs of anxiety. She felt as though her pleadings fell on deaf ears.

"What about solitary confinement? That would keep him safe from the Nazis, wouldn't it?" she said with sincerity. "Look, Karl is not an evil Nazi. He's a farmer that just happened to be born in Germany. He's no different than anyone you and I see in town."

Geddy rolled his eyes. "Look, we don't have the room. Solitary is already filled up with the Germans and Italians who are too dangerous to deal with. I know you like Karl and I know he does a fine job emptying your trashcan, but he's a murderer who's on his own."

"But he's been a model prisoner. He's done everything that's been asked of him, and more."

"And that's why he gets to work and pretty much have the run of the place. The officials know he's no threat."

"Then why not give him some protection?" pleaded Josephine.

Geddy's stare pierced Josephine. "You may see him as a nice German, but most of us don't give a shit about these dirty Krauts," he declared.

Josephine sensed Geddy's annoyance with her questions, but didn't care. "How can you say that?" she asked with misty eyes. "He's a human being, same as you. Can't you muster up at least a little compassion for him?"

"No," Geddy said with a smile. "I can't. He's a Nazi, same as all the others. In my opinion, those heartless bastards should all die."

Geddy's words struck Josephine cold. "But Karl has a wife and kids back in Germany. You can't be telling me you have no empathy at all for them?"

"I don't," said Geddy. "Karl is likely to die. It doesn't matter if he's hung by the military or if his throat is cut by his fellow Nazi brothers with a crude knife that was mysteriously smuggled into this prison by . . ." Geddy stopped himself.

Josephine's eyes widened. "What would you know about a crude knife?" she asked.

"Oh, I don't know anything about a crude knife. I'm just saying that they might use something like that to kill him."

"But how do you know they're going to kill him? I never told you that. All I said was that they might hurt him."

Instantly, Geddy became uncomfortable. He began rubbing his face with his hands. Beads of sweat broke out across his forehead. "I just assumed they would kill him because he's a traitor. I'm sure someone has told the Nazis by now."

"But who would tell them?" asked Josephine. "What good would it do for the Army to tell his fellow soldiers he talked?"

"I doubt it was the Army that told them," said Geddy. "I'm sure it was someone from the outside."

Josephine was now more suspicious than ever. Judging by his change in demeanor, she knew Geddy was hiding something.

"Look, I don't know who told them or why, but I do know he's fearful about his life. I'm just asking you to talk to the military officials and ask them for some protection."

"I really don't think they're going to care," said Geddy. "And besides, because of his good behavior, Karl is already a trustee who's not in with the main population. He's relatively safe."

"I realize that," said Josephine, "but if he's ever placed back in with them, they'll tear him to shreds."

Geddy turned his chair around and picked up his shotgun. "I'll see what I can do. But I really think he'll be just fine."

As Josephine turned to leave, she felt faint. She'd always known Geddy was a cold man, but the apathy he showed toward a practically helpless fellow human being left her reeling in disbelief. Geddy had just revealed his true character and it made Josephine nauseous. As she reached for the door, Geddy spun around in his leather chair.

"And Josephine, I think you might just have bigger problems to worry about than poor Karl."

Puzzled, Josephine turned around.

"What sort of problems?" she asked.

"Well, no one in town would tell you or Skeet this, but . . ." Geddy said, then paused. Josephine felt her stomach turn as she watched him transform from a ruthless uncaring bastard into someone who actually cared about her.

"But what?" asked Josephine.

"I'll just come out and say it."

"Please do."

"There are plenty of people in town none too happy about that nigger boy workin' in the store. They really don't like havin' him around the soda counter."

The jolt of toxic rage completely consumed Josephine. She clenched her fist and tried her best to stay calm, but she quivered with raw anger.

"Mr. Wainscott, I appreciate you letting me know of this concern," she said with a stone face. "I'm sure Skeet would not have imagined having Henry down at the drugstore would be a problem."

Geddy arose from his chair and walked to Josephine. He smiled and placed his arm around her.

"Jo, you and Skeet are friends of mine. Our kids are in school together. We go to church together. I have only your best interest in mind," he said softly.

"I'm sure you do," she replied.

Josephine's fists were so tightly clenched she could no longer feel her hands. The anger she felt inside had engulfed her so much, she was growing dizzy. Her instincts told her to run away, so Josephine stepped out of Geddy's hold and walked toward the hallway. However, Geddy grabbed her right shoulder. She turned around and faced him again.

"And while we're clearing the air here," Geddy continued, "there are some folks in town who are also concerned about Skeet opening the drugstore on Sundays. We all know the Blue Laws are no longer in place, but it's just an understanding in our community that business should not be done on Sunday. Some people feel the Sabbath is no longer holy to Skeet."

Josephine exhaled a deep breath. "You know, Mr. Wainscott, I've never in my life heard the same tongue move so effortlessly from apathy to bigotry and then rest in the cradle of our Lord. I'll not look at you the same, ever again."

A confused look swelled upon Geddy's face. He looked to the floor as he searched for words.

"Don't mention it. I'm just trying to help. Maybe someday you could return the favor," Geddy said, then looked up. Josephine was nowhere to be found.

# # #

After finishing his trash rounds, Karl walked down the hallway and into the main recreation room for the prisoners. Verifying all the prisoners had been placed in their cells, he walked back down the hallway and stopped at a janitor's closet. After determining no one was watching, he retrieved a set of keys from his pocket, then unlocked the door. He entered the windowless room and turned on the lights.

Karl walked to the state-of-the-art printing press and flipped on the switch. The low hum indicated it was warming up. After checking the levels of ink, he walked over to the shelf and removed a gasoline war coupon. He loaded the machine with a template he'd been working on for several weeks. After the machine had warmed up, he loaded it with blank paper and hit the print button. Once the machine printed the page, he removed it and compared the duplicate to the gasoline coupon. It was a perfect match.

Karl rubbed his eyes. It would be a long day.

Chapter 14

Kirk took a deep breath and dried his face with the bathroom's community towel. He looked down to the sink and noticed something was clogging the drain, so he turned the stopper with his hand, but the water refused to drain. It just sat there, unmotivated to do anything. He smiled as he rolled his eyes and reached for the doorknob.

He could hear Carney's boisterous laugh as soon as he stepped out of the drugstore's bathroom. As usual, he was wearing the mask of a politician, asking the patrons how they were, how their kids were doing at school, and laughing in general at their feeble attempts at humor. Kirk was relieved to hear his laugh, as he was counting on Carney to be in a good mood.

Early that morning, he had entered the drugstore while Carney was busy in the pharmacy. His entire early-morning shift was spent unloading pharmaceutical items off the supply truck, so he never had an opportunity to speak to the boss. The thought made his stomach jump. Ever since the previous night's basketball game, Carney had been on Kirk's mind almost non-stop. After several hours of lying in bed awake, he decided he must speak to Carney alone. The reasons were two-fold.

For starters, Kirk was still in awe Carney braved the environment and actually attended last night's basketball game. That took some guts. Not just because it was a bit dicey for a white man to attend an all-black event, but because many considered it to be beneath a white man to attend a black event, especially to see a black kid play. For such a respected man in the white community, his presence at the basketball game showed Carney was a man of great humility. He didn't see himself above blacks or above anything or anyone. Carney did an admirable thing and Kirk really wanted to express his appreciation.

Because Kirk had never actually expressed his gratitude to anyone outside of his family, the thought made him nervous. He wasn't so sure he would convey his emotions clearly without sounding like a total sap. Adding to this anxiety was the fact he actually needed a favor from Carney. He needed to borrow money, which added a whole new layer of turmoil to his angst. It was all tearing him apart.

Kirk walked past the pharmacy and noticed many patrons were gathered around Carney at the soda fountain. They were listening intently as he regaled them with stories, captivating their interest much like Bob Hope at a recent USO event in France. Kirk walked softly through the crowd of people until he reached the fountain, where he scrubbed the ice-cream freezer with a wet rag. Carney was so engaged in his story, he didn't even notice. He wore a stoic face as he told his story.

"So these high-school students from Antlers were in town attending this basketball tournament. They were between games and had some time to kill, so the principal decided to bring them to this soda fountain. They were here for a while and I didn't think too much about it, but after they all left the store, I got to lookin' around and noticed every pair of sunglasses from the racks were gone. I mean, every damned pair," he said with emphasis. "I immediately ran to the phone, called the superintendent at Antlers and I said, 'Hank, if I don't get all those sunglasses back immediately, your school buses will be grounded in Atoka until these kids graduate.'"

Jeff Spiva, a high-school student with aspirations of someday becoming a doctor, was captivated by the story, as were all the others.

"What'd the superintendent say?" asked Jeff.

"He says, 'I know who took 'em,'" said Carney with a confident smile.

"What happened then?" asked Jeff.

"Well, it wasn't long until the principle brought back the sunglasses and apologized. I told him I didn't need an apology from him, I wanted it from the kids who committed the crime. So I made the principal march out there to the buses and round up the kids who did the actual stealing. I made each and every one of them come to my little office in the pharmacy, where I gave 'em a good talkin' to about what they did and the future they can expect if they continued a life of crime."

"Those poor kids didn't know who they were messin' with," said Mark Richmond, someone Kirk knew was a life-long friend of Carney's.

"I didn't want to cause any trouble," Carney said, "but it just angered me that a group of kids could behave so badly. I didn't really care so much about the sunglasses. I just wanted to teach them a lesson."

"I'll bet you did," said Jeff.

"I like to think so," Carney replied. A lull in the conversation came over the group. Searching for the next topic, Carney looked up and spotted Kirk. "Well, there's the basketball star."

The crowd looked confused.

"Last night, Young Henry held Hubert Ausbie to twenty-five points," Carney said proudly, "which was quite remarkable, as Ausbie scored seventy-five the night before."

The crowd sat expressionless and did not utter a sound.

"Young Henry is quite the athlete," said Carney. "Quite the athlete, indeed."

After another few moments of uncomfortable silence, the crowd began to disperse. Carney thanked everyone for their business, then walked back to the pharmacy. While Kirk continued to scrub the ice-cream freezer, he noticed a familiar face that alerted his senses: Butch was sitting near the end of the counter, speaking to a gentleman he'd never seen before. The two were sitting by themselves and were speaking very quietly to each other, almost whispering. Before Kirk could look away, Butch waved his hand. Kirk hesitantly walked over to the two men.

"I don't really care to hear that you held that other boy to twenty-five points," said Butch with a nasty scowl on his face. "As a matter of fact, I'd rather not hear anything about you."

Kirk's immediate response was to duck and run, but then he remembered Uncle Willie's words that directed him to never take any guff off of anyone.

"I'll keep that in mind," said Kirk with confidence. "Thanks for lettin' me know. I'll be sure and let Mr. Carney know that talking about me should be avoided when you're in his presence. As a matter of fact, I'll go tell him right now."

Kirk smiled and turned to walk back to the pharmacy to tell Carney. Before he could take a step, however, Butch grabbed his arm, wheeling him around for a face-to-face confrontation.

"If you know what's good for you, you'll not say a word about this to Carney," Butch said. He began shaking his finger at Kirk. "I know how to deal with troublemakers like you and believe you me, I'll do it."

Kirk noticed that the man sitting next to Butch wasn't saying anything, but judging by his scornful look, he probably shared Butch's agitated disposition. His stare seemed to pierce through Kirk while he drank his cherry limeade.

"Look man," said a calm Kirk, "I don't know what I've done to offend you, but whatever it was, I'm sorry. I got no problem with you and I don't know why you have problems with me."

"'Cause I don't trust you," said Butch. "I've seen your kind before. You got no business bein' in a nice place like this. You're takin' unfair advantage of Mr. Carney's generosity and kindness and it makes me sick to my stomach."

Kirk knew he was in a bad place. He quickly reckoned his only hope of escaping the confrontation was to eat some crow and get back to the ice-cream freezer.

"I'm real sorry to hear that," said Kirk. "Can I can make it up to you by buying you a soda?"

Butch ignored Kirk's kind words and looked ready to erupt. He leaned forward in his chair and, just as he was about to open his mouth to lambast Kirk, Carney approached with lightening speed. Butch instantly knew he was caught, so he smiled and sat back down in his chair. As if he were expecting to be flogged by Carney, Butch closed his eyes and braced himself.

But Carney continued walking toward the front of the store. Kirk looked up and immediately noticed why. Josephine had entered. She was carrying a bag and smiling from ear to ear.

"Why, hello, Jo," said Carney. He suddenly had a jump in his step and seemed ecstatic to see her.

"Afternoon," replied Josephine. "This place looks pretty dead."

"You just missed the rush," said Carney. "It was hoppin' until a few moments ago."

Josephine looked toward the soda fountain and spotted Kirk. She and Carney walked over to him.

"Well, hello," she said. "You must be Henry."

"Yes ma'am," replied Kirk. "It's very nice to meet you."

"Same here," she replied.

Josephine immediately recognized Butch and the man sitting next to him. "Well, I didn't know you were coming here," she said. "Why didn't you let me know? I could have picked up your prescription and brought it to work tomorrow."

"I needed to speak to Butch anyway," said the man, showing no emotion.

Carney walked over to Kirk. "Young Henry, this is Geddy Wainscott. He's Josephine's boss up at the Stringtown Prison Camp," he said. "He's an auditor."

Kirk nodded. "Nice to meet you," he said.

Geddy gave no response. Kirk looked over and saw Butch wiping his brow, still shaking at the thought of being caught by Carney.

"You feelin' alright?" Carney asked.

"Me? Oh, yeah," he replied with a smile. "We were just talkin' to Kirk about his big game last night. Ain't that right, Kirk?"

"Yes sir," Kirk replied in monotone.

"Not only is this young man a natural at running the soda fountain, sounds like he's a natural ball player, too," said Butch. "I'd love to come down and watch a game."

"Sure, sure," said Carney. "Next time I go, I'll let you know."

"Great."

Butch and Geddy arose to their feet. "We must be going," said Butch. "It was very nice seeing you, Josephine."

Both men quickly put on their coats and walked out of the building. Only Josephine, Carney, and Kirk remained.

"Whew," said Josephine. "I'm glad those jerks are gone," she said. "Imagine my surprise at finding both of those degenerates in one place."

"Oh, let's not fret over it. What'd you say we get outta here a little early tonight?" asked Carney.

"Sounds good to me," replied Kirk.

"If my lady doesn't mind helping, we'll close down the pharmacy. I'll bet that'll give you just enough time to clean the soda fountain."

"I'm on it," replied Kirk.

Josephine placed the sack of goods on the watch counter, then joined her husband in the back. Kirk grabbed his rag and continued his cleaning in double-time. He quickly wiped down the counter, cleaned the ice-cream freezer, wiped off the soda tray, and mopped the tile floor. Making record time, he finished just as Carney and Josephine walked to the soda fountain.

"Let's get outta here," said Carney.

"Sounds great," replied Kirk.

After the group walked to the front door, Kirk recognized the opportunity. *Now's the time*, he thought. *Carney will be softer now that she's with him. Now's definitely the time.*

"Uhm, Mr. Carney," said Kirk, "Could I . . ."

"Call me Skeet."

"Sorry," Kirk said with a smile. "Skeet, could I ask you a favor?"

"Sure," replied Carney. "I'm not so sure I can help you, but shoot."

"Remember the other day when we were talking about my shoes and you mentioned maybe it was time to get some new ones?"

"Sure," said Carney. "I remember."

"Well, I kinda think maybe you were right. I'm having a heck of a time gettin' any traction when I'm playin' ball and besides that, they're only held together by pieces of wire and tape. I'm thinking maybe it's time to get some new shoes."

"I'm glad you came to that conclusion," said Carney. "I couldn't agree with you more."

Kirk let out a sigh of relief. "Good," he said. "'Cause I went to Woods' to look at some to buy and I had some problems."

"Like what?" asked Josephine.

"First of all, due to the war, they won't sell me any unless I have a book of coupons. Mom and Dad didn't leave me with any coupons and I don't have a way to get any."

"Well, Young Henry, our boys are out in the killing fields braving this cold winter and fighting for our freedom. Those coupons are meant for us to conserve and to ultimately do our part to contribute to the war."

"Oh," said Kirk. He looked down to his shoes and shrugged. "I never thought of it like that," he said.

"You learn something new everyday, huh?" asked Carney.

"I guess so," Kirk said, still ogling his shoes. "The thing is, my feet get real wet and real cold every time I step in the snow or the slush. They generally stay that way all day, too. I'm starting to get these sores that make it painful to walk."

Carney placed his arm around Kirk. "Just think how bad those soldiers have it."

"Yeah, I guess so," said Kirk. "How long do you think the shortage will last?"

"Until the war is over," said Carney. "Could be awhile."

Kirk felt totally dejected. "I see," he said. "I hate to ask you this, but would it be possible for me to get an advance on my pay so I could go on down to Woods' and give them the money for some new shoes, just in case some extra shoes come in?"

"I have an even better idea," said Carney.

For a moment, Kirk felt a ray of hope. "Oh yeah?"

"After watching you play ball last night, I went home and told Josephine about you sliding around the floor in those old shoes. I also told her how over time, you use wire and tape to keep those shoes goin'."

"It really made me sad," said Josephine.

"That's when I came up with a great idea," Carney said.

"What's that?" Kirk asked with eager anticipation.

"I asked her to go down to Woods' today and to buy you some new tape and wire," Carney said with a big smile.

"It's right there in the bag I brought in," Josephine said while pointing to the watch counter.

Kirk turned around and saw the bag on the counter. "Oh, thanks," he said very slowly. "This will give me something to do tonight, I suppose."

"After you finish your studies, of course," said Carney.

His hope shattered, Kirk tried to maintain his composure. "That's right," he said. "Right after I finish my studies."

"Great," said Carney. "They'll be good as new tomorrow."

"You bet," Kirk smiled.

Carney reached into his pocket and removed the keys to the front door. Kirk casually walked to the watch counter and picked up the bag.

"How 'bout me and Jo give you a ride home?" asked Carney.

"Thanks, but I've got a bowl of chili waiting on me over at Johnny's."

"Suit yourself," said Carney as the group walked through the front door. Carney locked up and walked Kirk to the curb.

"I'll see you in the morning?" he asked.

"Sure thing," said Kirk.

"It was very nice meeting you," said Josephine.

"You, too."

"Oh, and I hope the color of that tape matches up with your shoes," she said.

"I'm sure it will. Thanks again for thinking about me."

Carney walked over to Kirk and slapped him on the back. "No problem, Young Henry. Anytime you need tape and wire, you know who to call," Carney said with a smile.

Kirk stood and watched them step into their car and drive off into the night. He looked up the street and noticed the lights at Johnny's. "At least I won't go hungry tonight," he said. Kirk's disappointment had clouded his judgment so much he'd forgotten just how slippery the ice had become on the streets. As he stepped toward Johnny's, his foot turned, which shifted his balance, and down to the ground he went.

He lay there for a few moments. Feeling the water seeping through his pants and into his underwear, he finally decided it was time to get up. He got to his feet, then reached down to pickup the contents of the sack strewn along the street. As he felt around on the dark street, he tried in vain to locate the tape and wire, but instead only found a brand new pair of PF Flyers basketball shoes laying on the cold icy street.

Kirk looked up and saw the Carney's taillights driving into the night. He smiled.

Chapter 15

"So, what do you think?" asked Kirk, with great anticipation. While Ripp studied the photograph, Kirk paced back and forth across the living-room floor of his house.

"I don't know," said Ripp. "This picture is old and faded. It's difficult to determine."

"Difficult to determine?" quipped Kirk. "You wanna know what's difficult? How 'bout smuggling this picture out of the drugstore this afternoon. That's difficult. You're just lookin' at a picture. They ain't nothin' difficult 'bout that."

Ripp smiled. Through the years, he'd learned when his best friend was agitated, the best way to calm him down was to simply let him talk.

"Tell me how 'difficult' it was," said Ripp.

"I had it all planned out. I'd been waiting all week to try it today, because it's Thursday. Carney is always telling me Thursdays are the slowest day of the week, so I knew I'd have a better chance if there wasn't much to do," Kirk said.

After hearing no reply, he gave Ripp a hard stare.

In order to get a closer look, Ripp had moved the picture just a couple inches away from his face.

"Are you listening to me?" asked Kirk with raised eyebrows.

Lost in his investigation, Ripp failed to hear Kirk's words.

"Ripp Masters, are you listening to me?" yelled Kirk.

"Yeah, yeah, I'm listening," said Ripp, while never taking his eyes away from the picture. "We should've done this during the day, when there's some sunlight. Your house is so dark that I'm struggling to see the details of this picture."

"Sorry about that, but I didn't want to wait."

Ripp laughed. "You done got obsessed with this, huh?"

"Probably," said Kirk. "Are you through asking me dumb questions?"

"Go ahead with your story."

"So anyway, since there wasn't anything to do at the drugstore, I told Carney I wanted to go back up to the attic and tidy up," said Kirk.

"Then what happened?"

"I walked up the stairs, found the picture, placed it under my coat, then walked back down."

"So?" asked Ripp. "What's so damned difficult about that?"

"As soon as I walked back in the drugstore, Carney asked me to help him move the ice-cream cooler. There's a repair man coming in the morning to look at it."

"And?"

"I bent down and grabbed the cooler and the picture came flying out from underneath my coat. It fell on the floor, right in front of Carney."

Ripp placed his hand over his mouth. "Oh no," he said. "What'd you do?"

"I reached down real fast, picked it up, and put it back in my coat."

"Did Carney see it?"

"Yeah, he definitely saw something," said Kirk. "I don't know if he saw it was a picture of The Klan, but he knew it was a picture of something. He said, 'what's that?'"

"Not good," said Ripp.

"I know, I know. I told him it was a picture from school. I said I didn't have anywhere to put it, so I put it under my coat."

Ripp gave Kirk a hard stare. "Do you think he bought into that?"

"Not sure. Not sure."

"Well, I've got to tell you this, your life is anything but boring now," Ripp said with a smile.

"For sure," Kirk replied. "So what do you think about the picture? Is it Carney?"

"It does kind of look like Skeet," said Ripp. "But I'm not sure."

"Doesn't help much."

"I'm sorry, but I can't say for certain, just by looking at a picture. It does kind of look like him," said Ripp, "but I wouldn't bet my life on it."

Kirk let out a sigh of frustration. "I was hoping we could definitely prove it wasn't him in the picture."

"Me, too," said Ripp. "I still believe he would never have anything to do with The Klan, but we need to know for sure."

"But how?" asked Kirk.

"I don't know."

Kirk and Ripp turned their attention to the photo again.

"Wait a minute," said Kirk.

"What is it?"

"Take another look at the man in the middle, the one who we think could be Carney."

Ripp looked at the man holding a cross.

"What are you thinking?" asked Ripp.

"How tall is Carney? He can't be over five-foot-seven."

"He's five-foot-four inches. I know because one day we both measured ourselves on the scale down at the Dime Store that measures your height and weight."

"Does the man in the picture look like he's five-foot-five?" asked Kirk.

A smile jumped onto Ripp's face. "No, he doesn't, and I bet we can prove it."

"How?"

"Higher learning," said Ripp with a smile.

"Do you mean stuff you weren't smart enough for in college?"

"It's called Algebra," said Ripp. "Do you have a pencil and paper?"

"Sure," Kirk replied.

"Do you have a tape measure?"

"I do," said Kirk.

"Then that's all we need. We'll go down to the Dime Store tomorrow and do some measurin' and put this dog to bed."

"Tomorrow?" said a disgruntled Kirk.

"Yeah. You don't want to be goin' to the Dime Store now, do you?"

"Absolutely. Why not?"

Ripp shook his head. "'Cause it's ten-thirty at night and we're two blacks who probably don't need to be seen downtown. It might look a little suspicious to a police officer, if you know what I mean."

"Aw, hell, they won't do nuthin' to us as long as we stay outta trouble," Kirk said, confidently.

"They is if you's black," quipped Ripp. "You just ain't gonna let this go, are you?"

Kirk's face was somber. Ripp could tell that he felt passionately about this issue and desperately needed to know. Ripp looked at Kirk, then shook his head.

"Then let's go," he said.

# # #

It was almost midnight by the time Kirk and Ripp pulled in front of the Dime Store on Court Street at the exact place the photo was taken years ago. The town was practically deserted. The only visible movement occurred when an occasional trucker passed.

They stepped out of Ripp's car and made their way to the parking meters.

"Did you bring the tape measure?" asked Ripp.

Kirk removed the tape from his coat and handed it to Ripp, who quickly measured the meter.

"It's fifty-inches tall," said Ripp.

"So, what does that mean?" asked Kirk.

"Let me see that picture."

After returning to the car and inspecting the picture with some light, Ripp measured the meter.

Kirk took the tape measure and picture from Ripp's hands, and measured the Klansmen in the picture.

Ripp grabbed a pencil and paper and started scratching out something that looked like he was cracking some Nazi code. He looked up at Kirk with a big smile and said, "There's not a man in here shorter than five-feet-seven inches."

"How can you know that?" inquired Kirk.

"It's just a problem of proportionality, my friend, which proves Carney is not in this picture," Ripp proclaimed proudly.

Kirk shot back, "You know, you're not as stupid as you look!"

"And look at that fellow holdin' the cross. He must be six feet three at least."

"He is, indeed," replied Kirk, still excited.

Engaged with the picture, they never noticed what was going on around them. A tap on the driver's side door grabbed their attention, and they found a police officer standing outside the car with a nightstick in his hand.

Ripp was quick to roll down the window.

"Yes, sir," said Ripp.

"Just what in the world are two boys doin' out so late?" asked the officer.

"Uh . . . we were just measuring the parking meter," said Ripp.

The police office laughed. "Yeah, right. And I'm Nat King Cole."

Kirk quickly tried to diffuse the confrontation. "Honest, Mr. Cole, we were measuring the . . ."

"Get out of the car!" snapped the officer.

After patting them down and finding no weapons, the officer searched Ripp's car.

"Lucky you're not driving one from the shop," Kirk whispered. Ripp nodded.

After the officer finished his search and found nothing, he walked back around to Ripp and Kirk.

"What are your names?" asked the officer.

"I'm Ralph Masters and this is Henry Kirkland. My daddy's name is Battle Axe. He works down at the Chevy place," said Ripp. He pulled his driver's license from his wallet and handed it to the police officer. After writing down the boys' names, the officer gave Ripp his ID.

"Henry is going to school at Dunbar and came across an old photo. He was just trying to see how tall the folks were in the picture. That's why we measured the parking meter."

"My name is Officer Earnest. If I find there's been any tomfoolery at any of these businesses tonight, you can both expect to go directly to jail. I wrote down your information, so I know where you live."

"Yes, sir," replied Ripp with a smile.

The officer gave them both a cold stare, then continued.

"There's recently been some unfortunate things happenin' to colored boys about your age," said Earnest. "I reckon you might ought to watch out."

"Yes, sir," said both Kirk and Ripp.

The police officer nodded his head, then walked back to his car. After taking his time, he slowly placed his car in drive and eased down Court Street.

"Whew," said Kirk. "Glad that's over."

"Me, too," said Ripp. He started the car and began the drive to Kirk's house. "I was beginning to wonder if he was gonna take us in. I don't think he bought our story."

"I'm not so sure," said Kirk. "I think he was worried about us."

"What?" replied Ripp.

"You know, what with Rudy James getting it and all. I'll bet the cop was worried about us being out late by ourselves. It sounded to me like he was concerned."

"Concerned about us stealin' his shit," laughed Ripp. "I really don't think he gives much of a damn about us."

"You never know," said Kirk. "After all, he did take an oath to protect and serve."

"By the way," said Ripp with a weak voice, "I heard more about poor Rudy."

"Like what?" asked Kirk.

"It wasn't random what happened to him. Evidently, he'd gotten to be friends with a white girl here in Atoka. Word is some thugs beat him up and it got out of control."

"You mean someone beat him to death for bein' friends with a white girl?"

"I heard he was at the bar drinkin' and someone slipped a mickey into his beer. They took him outside and when he passed out, they dropped a cement block on his head, only it missed and hit his neck and killed him.

"They ended up disposing his body at the prison in Stringtown."

"Oh my God!" exclaimed Kirk. "That's terrible."

As the car passed over the tracks, Kirk felt a lump in his throat that wouldn't go away. What if that was me, he thought. As they drove slowly down his street, he looked out and saw nothing but dark houses. The thought scared him a little, but then he remembered the pistol Willie gave him. He would definitely take that out of his dresser drawer and sleep with it when he got home.

"You just watch yo'self," said Ripp as the car pulled into Kirk's driveway. "I don't want to have to go out on a manhunt 'cause someone popped my best friend."

The car stopped. Kirk took a long look at his house's lone dark window. The sight sent shivers up his spine.

"Don't worry 'bout me," said Kirk. "I can take care of myself."

Ripp looked into Kirk's eyes. "You sure?" he asked.

"Positive," said Kirk as he stepped out of the car. As Kirk walked to his house, Ripp rolled down his window and shouted:

"Are we takin' the ladies to Stringtown this weekend?"

"Fo' sure," said Kirk. "As I always say, 'we are runnin' buddies. You got the car so you do the drivin', I'll do the runnin!"

The thought of taking girls out on a double date with Ripp usually made Kirk smile, but Ripp noticed his face was expressionless.

"You sure you're alright?" asked Ripp.

"Don't worry, I'll be fine."

Chapter 16

Broom in hand, Kirk walked to the front of the drugstore and looked out the window. He smiled when he noticed not a single cloud appeared in the sky. It meant today would probably be a nice warm day, a wonderful break from the terrible cold spell that had loomed for so long. He glanced over to Court Street and saw water trickling onto the sides of the street, a sign the snow was beginning to melt.

"It's a great big world out there," said a voice from behind Kirk. Startled, he looked around. Carney had managed to sneak up behind him.

"You scared me, boss," said Kirk. He then pointed to the street. "Think the snow will melt off today?"

"I think there's a great chance," said Carney. "And I'll be none too sad if it does."

"Me, too," said Kirk. "I think I've had my fill of the Arctic for awhile."

"I see you've already done all the sweeping," replied Carney. "That's my Young Henry, always getting things done ahead of time."

"Thanks."

Carney looked to Kirk's new shoes he and Jo purchased and smiled.

"Wow," said Carney. "You sure know how to fix up a pair of old shoes with some new wire and tape."

Kirk recognized Carney's joke. The thought made him feel guilty he hadn't already thanked Carney for the gift.

"Oh yeah," said a smiling Kirk. "Thank you and Jo very, very much for the shoes. That was quite a pleasant surprise."

"What shoes?" said Carney with a big smile.

"That act of kindness really made an impact on my life," Kirk said as his eyes grew misty. "I can't tell you how much I appreciate it."

Carney gave Kirk a long stare. He smiled, and then lightly punched Kirk on the arm. "Glad they helped," he said.

"You and Jo really didn't have to . . ."

"I'm caught up in the pharmacy, so I'm going next door to have a coffee with some friends," interrupted Carney. "If you need anything, just come by and let me know."

Kirk wore a puzzled look.

"Something bothering you?" asked Carney.

"Why don't you have coffee here?"

Carney laughed. "That's a great question," he said. "To tell you the truth, it's more of a good-will gesture than anything else. Joni Nugent, the girl who owns the coffee shop, is a nice girl and I really like her. I was good friends with her parents. More than anything, we go there just to help support her. I know she doesn't make a whole lot on a cup of coffee, but we tip her real good."

"I see," said Kirk.

"Besides, we've been going next door for years and years. I guess we really are creatures of habit."

"Guess so."

"Do you have plenty to keep you busy?" asked Carney.

"I do. The soda fountain's clean and ready for the Saturday morning rush, but I have a few other things to do."

"Good. Barbara Ellen should be here any moment to run the fountain."

"Okay. I have some cleaning to do in the back."

"Right," said Carney. "If you get finished before I get back, go to the pharmacy and restock the medicine shelves. I received a shipment last night. You'll find the boxes by the door."

"Will do."

Kirk had no more walked to the soda fountain and began wiping down the already clean counter, when he heard clanging from the front door cowbells. He turned and saw it was Barbara Ellen.

"Good morning, Kirk," she replied as she walked to the fountain.

"Mornin'."

"And how are you today?"

"Good," replied Kirk. "Just tryin' to get goin'."

"Me, too."

As Barbara Ellen started scooping ice and polishing the soda glasses, Kirk twirled his broom and walked to the pharmacy. He swept all the loose dust on the back room's old wooden floor, and noticed not much else needed his attention, so he grabbed the two boxes of freight by the door and carried them into the pharmacy.

Kirk had unloaded the first box with no problems and had almost made his way through the second when he encountered a bottle of medicine he'd never seen before. He assumed it might be something for pigs, but he wasn't sure.

Barbara Ellen was in the middle of making coffee when Kirk approached her.

"Do you know what this is?" Kirk asked and handed her the bottle of medicine.

"I don't know," replied Barbara Ellen, after studying the label for a moment. "Don't think I've ever seen it before."

"Me, either," said Kirk. "And there's no other bottle of medicine like it on the shelves."

"Are you caught up with all your chores?"

"I am," responded Kirk.

"Why don't you go next door and ask Skeet. He'll know where it goes."

"Yes ma'am."

Barbara Ellen smiled. "Thanks, but you don't have to call me ma'am."

"Yes ma'am. I mean, yes . . . Barbara Ellen."

Barbara Ellen smiled as Kirk walked past her and on to the front door.

# # #

"So, I was goin' through the newspaper and read about this new chemical a company was using for weed killer," said Carney. "I did the research and found it wasn't harmful to anything other than weeds. I was really sold on the stuff, but it was way too expensive to buy. Then I thought, hey, I can order that chemical through the drugstore and make it myself."

Russo, Mark, and Butch sat around the table, drinking their coffee and listening intently. Folks in Atoka respected Carney for many things, including his success as a business man, his leadership in the community, and his uncompromising values, but none of those accolades compared to his legendary status as a storyteller. Whether it be at the drugstore, the coffee shop, or after Sunday School, when Carney talked, people listened. As usual, he captivated his small audience on this morning at the coffee shop.

"So, did you order it?" asked Mark.

"I did," replied Carney.

Needing his coffee refilled, Mark looked around the coffee shop for Joni. Even though the coffee shop was rather small and occupied by only a few inhabitants, he couldn't seem to spot her. Finally, he heard the old hard-wood floorboards creaking in the back of the establishment, near the kitchen. Due to his need for a refill, he hoped she had gone back to gather another hot pot.

"As soon as the shipment came in, Skeet put on his lab coat, goggles, and top hat," laughed Russo. "You should have seen him in the back of the drugstore. He looked like part-mad scientist, part-Mad Hatter."

Everyone at the table laughed.

"I felt like one, too," said Carney. "I was winging it completely. If I didn't have something the recipe called for, I substituted it with something on the shelves. Let me tell you, I was a rogue scientist. But that wasn't the worst part."

"The story gets worse?" asked Mark.

"Oh yeah. Right in all the middle of this, Mrs. Johnson barges in the drugstore, demanding I sell her some cough medicine. She was in a hurry and was in no mood to wait."

"So, what did you do?" asked Butch.

"He took off his gloves, washed his hands, then went to the back and mixed her some cough medicine," said Russo.

"Which gave Russo the perfect opportunity to satisfy his fancy to mix dangerous chemicals," said Carney, pointing at Russo. "You think I was a mad scientist? Let me tell you, Bela Lugosi's got nothin' on this guy."

Embarrassed, Russo covered his face with his hand. "I was just trying to help out," he muttered.

"Dare I should try to understand what would compel Russo to want to become a master chemist, but . . ." said Mark with a smile. "But I'm going to try to get this straight. Russo decides to take over your job of mixing deadly chemicals, while you're in the back, mixing cough medicine for Mrs. Johnston?"

"Right," said Carney.

Butch smiled. "How many died in the explosion?"

"There was no explosion," replied Carney. "But there might as well have been. As soon as I finished mixing the cough medicine and pouring Mrs. Johnston's bottle, I hurried back to the counter. Let me just say I sensed a problem as soon as I opened the back door to the pharmacy and spotted green smoke."

"Oh, my gosh! What did you see?" asked Butch.

"Lots of green smoke and I could smell the noxious fumes. I knew right away hydrochloric acid was somehow put into the mixture. I could smell it."

Russo's face turned red. "It seemed like a great idea at the time."

"Dear God!" said Mark. "What did you do, Skeet?"

"I ran over to the counter and guess what I saw?"

"Little green men?" laughed Butch.

"A huge hole had burnt itself clean through the counter."

"Dear Lord," said Mark.

"I ran like a wild man to the back door and opened it up, then I told Mrs. Johnston to get out of the building. After we fanned a lot of air through the building, everything was fine. But it got a little scary there for a minute."

"What a funny story," said Butch. "I never knew."

"Oh, that's not the funny part of the story," said Russo, still embarrassed.

"Do tell," said Mark.

"Well, after we got everything cleaned up and patched the hole in the counter, I decided to go back and try to finish what I started," said Carney. "I must say, I was impressed with how fast I mixed up the concoction. I was so impressed, I took my new weed killer home that evening."

"How'd it work?" asked Butch.

"First let me say the job in front of me was of almost insurmountable odds. It occurred around the first week of last July, so the weed problem in my yard was nothing short of colossal. I mean, it was right out of the Old Testament."

Everyone around the table laughed.

"As soon as I got home, I sprayed everything in my front and back yard. I mean, I doused those miserable weeds. Then I walked back in the house and went right on with my life."

"Did it kill the weeds?" asked Mark.

"Oh yeah," replied Carney. "In a couple of days, they were wiped out. And that's where the real problems started."

"How so?"

"About two days later, old Man Perkins knocked on my door. I could tell right away he was upset, so I asked him to come inside. After Jo poured him a glass of tea, he proceeded to tell me, 'Skeet you killed my tomaters.'"

Laughter consumed the table.

"Well, what did you tell him?" asked Butch.

"I told him I never even came close to spraying my concoction anywhere near his garden and besides, the weed killer I used was harmless on everything except weeds."

Butch smiled. "I'm not so sure hydrochloric acid is real good for tomatoes."

"I wondered that, too, but my mixture had no acid. After Russo's accident, I started all over, just to make sure no acid got into the mix."

"Did Perkins believe you?"

"No. I smoothed it over and we ended the meeting as friends, but I don't think he believed me. So, later that night, I got an idea that would really wreak havoc with his noodle."

"What'd you do?" asked Mark, laughing.

"When I got home the next evening, I saw him sitting on his front porch. He was pretending to read the newspaper, but I could tell he was on the warpath to protect his garden."

"Now this is Old Man Perkins we're dealing with," said Russo. "For those who don't know, he's not the shiniest spoon in the silverware drawer."

"As soon as I drove into my driveway, he started watchin' me. When I opened the door to my car and stepped out, I got a closer look and what I saw just about caused me to bust a gut from laughing so hard," said Carney. He placed his hands over his face to contain his laughter.

"What was so funny?" asked Mark.

"The old man had actually cut several holes in the newspaper so he could covertly spy on me." Carney was laughing so hard, he could barely speak. "And these holes . . ." Carney stopped to catch his breath. "These holes were as big as tomatoes."

Again, the table erupted in laughter. Mark laughed so hard, he fell out of his chair.

"I'll never get that image out of my mind," said Carney. "I was looking straight at him, but he never knew I was watching him. He thought he was invisible. It was the damndest thing I'd ever seen in my life."

After several minutes of laughter, the table finally quieted down.

"I changed my clothes and went back to the shop, where I rinsed out that sprayer real good. It was so clean, you could've drank out of it. I then walked back outside and found he was still sitting in his rockin' chair, just watchin."

"This is where it gets real interesting," said Russo.

Both Butch and Mark were clinging to Carney's words.

"So I grabbed my sprayer and walked out in the yard. I sprayed down everything with water, front yard and back. I could see Perkins out of the corner of my eye. By this time, he was using binoculars to watch me. It also looked like he was takin' notes. I could see him twitching a little bit more and more with each passing second."

Russo's face was red from his failed attempts to conceal his laughter, but both Mark and Butch were confused.

"I don't get it," said Butch. "So you sprayed your yard with water, what's the big deal?"

"I knew I was runnin' low on water, so I walked back to the front yard and twisted off the cap to the sprayer. Just as I poured the rest of the water on the ground, I looked over to Perkins and gave him a big country wave."

"What did he do?" asked Mark.

"He couldn't believe I could see him," Carney laughed. "He turned around to see if there was someone behind him I was waving to. Due to the newspaper, he thought his identity was concealed and I couldn't see him."

"This is the craziest damned thing I've ever heard," said Butch.

"Oh, it gets better," said Russo. "Skeet, tell 'em what happened the next day."

"The next evening, we were visited again by Perkins, only this time he was angrier than all get out."

"But why?" asked Mark.

Carney smiled. "'Cause he said all the spraying I'd done the day before done killed all his watermelons."

Everyone at the table burst out in laughter.

"And it was only water?" said Mark, slapping the table with his hand.

"Just good ol' H20," said Carney.

After a few minutes of bellying laughing, Russo grabbed his cup and walked toward the back of the shop.

"I'm gonna shrivel up if I don't get some coffee," Russo said, still laughing randomly as he walked out around the corner.

"Where is Joni?" asked Mark.

"Russo will find her," replied Butch.

"Hope so," replied Mark. "Well, this stuff is running right through me. Think I'm gonna go relieve myself."

"I'm right behind you," said Carney.

As the two men stood, Kirk opened the front door to the coffee shop. He was quick to spot Carney, so he made his way over to the table.

"Sorry to bother you, but I have a question about the inventory."

"No problem," said Carney. "Have a seat. I'm going to the bathroom, but will be right back."

Kirk immediately noticed Butch's piercing eyes. His angry face was so cold and evil, he resembled a marble statue of the devil.

"Go ahead, sit down," Carney said as he walked toward the bathroom. "If you're thirsty, have Joni get you something."

Kirk reluctantly pulled back a chair and sat down. Butch's facial expression never changed.

"Mornin'," Kirk said without establishing eye contact.

"I don't think your kind is welcome here," Butch growled.

"Of course they are," Joni said, suddenly appearing out of nowhere. She carried a hot pot of coffee and a million-dollar smile.

"My doors are open to everyone," she said as she refilled empty coffee cups on the table. Shocked and embarrassed, Butch searched for a lifeline.

"I didn't realize you were standing there," Butch said with a big, fake smile. "You must have misheard what I said. I was just telling Henry he was more than welcome to sit down here. Ain't that right, Henry?"

Kirk's heart was pounding out of his chest. He knew the smart thing to do was to go along with Butch's lie and allow him to save face. It might actually quell some of the tension he felt each time he was in Butch's presence. But then again, Kirk wasn't always known for doing the right thing. Just as he opened his mouth to utter his response, he was interrupted.

"Your charming line of bullshit won't fly here," said Joni. Her innocent and happy face instantly hardened. "I know who you are, banker. They might let your bigotry go unnoticed down at that evil bank, but if your mouth ever spews such vile language here, in my place of business, I'll personally escort you to the door and will mail you your teeth, after I sweep them up from the floor."

Butch and Kirk sat in a numbed state, their eyes as big as silver dollars. Joni towered over Butch, expecting a response, but he was too shocked to speak. No one, especially a woman, had ever spoken to him in such a tone.

"Do I make myself clear?" Joni's voice thundered.

Kirk noticed the scar on the right side of Butch's face seemed to take on a life of its own. It appeared to be deeper and darker, emitting a sinister appearance.

"Yes, ma'am," Butch replied.

"Good." Joni walked gracefully to another table and turned back into the beautiful, hospitable host. Kirk smiled.

"So how are things going, Young Henry?" said Carney as he approached the table.

"They're going fine," said Kirk. "I just have a question about a new bottle of medicine I found."

"Joni, could you bring Young Henry a bottle of pop?" Carney shouted. He looked to Kirk. "Why don't you take a load off and have a Coke with us?"

Kirk looked to Butch, who still looked to be in a state of shock. Russo and Mark soon sat down at the table.

"Sure," Kirk said hesitantly.

"Hello, Kirk. How's my favorite newspaper delivery boy doing?" asked Mark.

"Good morning, Mark. I'm doin' fine, thanks," replied Kirk.

"You know, Skeet, ol' Henry is the best newspaper thrower I've ever had. Did you know he's not missed a day of work since I hired him? Doesn't matter if it's raining, sleeting, snowing, or just hotter than a day in Hades, I can always count on Henry to get my newspapers out each morning."

Russo sat there and continued to drink his coffee, as if he never heard Mark's words. Butch's face started twitching and beads of sweat popped out on his forehead.

"Young Henry was quite a find," said Carney. "Wish I had ten more like him."

Joni flashed Kirk a big smile as she placed his Coke on the table. The sight made Kirk blush. He almost felt as if she was flirting with him a little, but he knew that to be very dangerous waters.

"Don't let these fellows rub off on you," Joni said. "Next thing you know, you'll be in here, drinking coffee with them while everyone else is havin' to work."

Everyone at the table laughed.

"It may not look like we're working," said Mark, "but we're actually making some big decisions *about* work."

"About how to get out of work," Carney said, while the table laughed.

Kirk was quick to reach into his pocket and retrieve a quarter. He handed it to Joni.

"Oh, no," said Carney. "The Coke's on me."

"It's actually on the house," Joni replied. "So put your money away."

Kirk looked up and saw Butch's face was so red, he looked as though he was going to pass out.

"Excuse me," Butch said. "But I need to go to the bathroom."

"Thank you, Joni," Kirk replied. "I appreciate it very much."

"No worries," said Joni. "I'd like to see you in here more."

"Yes, ma'am," replied Kirk.

"And stop calling me ma'am," Joni said with a smile.

Kirk smiled and nodded.

For once, Kirk's world was nothing but sunshine. He didn't know if it was from Joni's flirting or because, for once, he felt accepted by his bosses, Mark and Carney. And to make matters even better, Butch had been put in his place by Joni. Kirk smiled and took a big drink of Coke. Things were starting to look up in his world.

"Oh, by the way," said Carney, "I ran into Gail Bert at the store yesterday."

"How is Gail Bert?" asked Mark. "Is he still raisin' them chickens?"

"I think so," replied Carney. "But that's not what we talked about."

"What did Gail Bert have to allow?" asked Russo.

"Well, actually, he was telling me about that murdered boy they recently found in Stringtown," said Carney. "Turns out, it was on Gail Bert's land."

"You don't say," said Russo.

The feeling of euphoria Kirk had been enjoying blasted away into the stratosphere. He suddenly felt cold and empty as he relived that cold snowy morning when he watched as Russo and Mark loaded what appeared to be a body in their car. And now he was sitting down at the same table with the two men who perpetrated that ghastly crime. Kirk looked over to Mark and Russo.

"Gail Bert said he just happened upon the body," said Carney. "He was out on his land feeding his cows by that tree row you can see from the prison. He saw something had been dragged over to the trees. He was pretty shaken when he realized what it was."

"Is that right?" said Russo, nonchalantly. He reached into his jacket and retrieved a small fingernail file, then started filing his fingernails. He seemed to be hardly paying any attention to Carney's words.

"Gail Bert said he just can't get that image out of his head. The poor black boy was frozen to the tree. Gail Bert actually helped the county coroner thaw out his body enough to remove it from the tree."

Needing acute precision, Russo was now wearing his reading glasses to make certain each fingernail was filed exactly the same on both sides. Flabbergasted by his indifference, Kirk looked to Mark, who was fiddling with the sugar bowl. Judging by the sound effects he uttered, he appeared to be pretending his spoon was huge scoop that was loading a dump truck semi (his coffee cup) with several tons of sugar. After he successfully unloaded two tons of sugar into the truck, he used the scoop to stir the contents. When finished, he smiled at his accomplishment.

Kirk was beside himself. They acted as though they had no interest in this news. After mulling their reactions around in his head for awhile, Kirk came to a startling conclusion: Maybe they've done this before. Maybe they're acting this way because, in their minds, they've removed themselves completely from the event. The thought chilled him to the bone.

Carney looked to his watch. "Well, I reckon we'd better get back to work," he said.

Almost finished with his Coke, Kirk took one final big gulp. As he gently laid the glass back on the table, Butch returned to his seat.

"Anyone have big plans for the weekend?" asked Carney.

"You'll have to speak to my wife," said Russo, still filing away at his fingernails.

"How 'bout you, Young Henry?" asked Carney.

"Me and Ripp are goin' dancin' tonight," said Kirk.

"Where abouts?" asked Carney.

As Kirk looked up, he could see the question caught Butch's attention.

"Over at Stringtown," Kirk replied.

"Got a big date?" asked Mark, with a sly smile.

"Oh, I reckon I'll meet up with Vanessa. I usually do."

"Sounds like fun," said Carney. "Maybe things will slow down at the drugstore and you can leave a little early."

"That'd be great," Kirk replied.

"Well, I suppose we'd better get back to work," said Russo. "Skeet, I'm off to do things with the wife. I doubt I'll be back to the drugstore today."

Carney placed his hand on Kirk's shoulder.

"I think we'll get by. With Young Henry beside me, there ain't no mountain we can't climb."

Kirk smiled, then stood and pushed his chair under the table. He saw Butch staring at him with piercing eyes. His angry face was so cold and evil-looking, the sight reminded Kirk of a marble statue of the devil.

Chapter 17

One final wring of the mop and Kirk stepped back and smiled. It was just past eleven o'clock in the morning and for the last hour and a half, he had been faced with the cumbersome task of performing the Saturday clean up, which was particularly daunting on this particular day. Due to the melt-off from the massive snow drifts on Court Street and beyond, a great deal of mud, water, and grime had been tracked into the drugstore. The tile floor around the soda fountain was especially bad. Normally an off shade of white, the entire area looked more like a collage of black and brown swirls.

Kirk turned and looked at the floor, happy to see he had transformed it back into sparkling tile. It always gave him a sense of fulfillment to complete a task and then step back and see he'd made a difference.

Kirk went over to the RCA radio, sitting atop the ice-cream cooler. A smile mounted on his face as he turned on the box. This time of year was his most favorite. In years past, he'd sit with his family on every Saturday afternoon in the winter and listen to the Oklahoma Sooners play basketball. All time seemed to stop, as it was the family's favorite activity. Kirk turned the knob until he found the game. When he heard the familiar voice of the OU announcer, he smiled. In the background, he could hear the Kansas crowd cheer, "Rock chalk, Jayhawk". Kirk knew that the Sooners were in for a fight against the spirited KU team. He turned up the volume, then walked to the fountain.

"Could I talk you into fixin' me a soda?"

"Why, sure," said Barbara Ellen. "Coming right up."

As Kirk took his first drink from the soda, he felt a warmness encompass his body. So far, it had been a great day. He was still riding high from the major breakthrough he'd serendipitously made at the coffee shop. For the first time in his life, he felt like white people saw him as their equal. And not just any white people, but well-accomplished white people. White people who actually mattered in the community. It was quite a high for Kirk. Never in his life had he felt so invigorated. Things were beginning to look up.

The victory was short lived, though. The normal Saturday cleanup usually took place around closing time, but not today. Due to the melting snow, the whole town was nothing but slop. In all likelihood, he'd probably have to mop and sweep again when the day ended, but he held out hope that traffic would be light for the remainder of the day. Just as he let out a sigh, he heard the infamous cowbells from the front door. Kirk turned and found his greatest fear materialized. A group of white high-school kids entered the store, and as usual, they weren't wiping their feet on the rug. He watched as they walked right to the soda fountain and sat down. His clean-floor masterpiece was instantly wrecked. Kirk wiped his brow and shook his head.

"How fares ye, young swashbuckler?" Carney asked, while walking to the soda fountain.

"Argh!" replied Kirk.

"How are the Sooners doing?"

"They're up by ten."

"Who we playin'?" asked Carney.

"The University of Kansas. It's a Big 8 game. Should be a good'un."

"Let's hope for a win," Carney said, then paused. "Oh, I'm almost ready for you to make 'the delivery'," said Carney. "I have a few more things to write down and it'll be ready to go."

"Just let me know," replied Kirk. "If it's alright with you, I'll do it during halftime."

"No problem."

Since Kirk had done so well with last week's deposit at the bank, Carney decided to make it a part of his normal Saturday routine. Carney didn't particularly want customers in the store to know he was sending a young kid with a sack full of money on a trip by himself, so he referred to the deposit trips to the bank as "the delivery." Kirk really liked the code talk. With World War II roaring in full gear and much in newspapers and magazines about the war effort, "the delivery" made Kirk feel like a spy or a special agent. He felt as though he was on a secret mission only he could perform.

Kirk looked to Carney and smiled. He'd never imagined in such a short amount of time, he would earn so much of Carney's trust. The thought made him almost giddy.

Carney looked at the mop and bucket, then to the now-soiled tile floor. He smiled. "All that hard work, destroyed in just a few minutes. Makes you wonder why we do it, huh?"

"I suppose so," said Kirk.

"It's Sod's Law," replied Carney.

Kirk flashed Carney a puzzled look.

"Sod's Law is an invisible force that exists out there in our universe. Sod's Law declares if anything can go wrong, it will," Carney said with a smile.

"Never heard of it," replied Kirk.

"It's an old saying, handed down from the British. The saying insists that a catastrophe will occur to any poor sod who needs it the least."

"Makes sense to me."

Carney smiled. "Me, too. I can personally attest that Sod's Law is very real."

"I don't doubt it," replied Kirk.

Once again, the front door's cowbells sounded. Kirk and Carney looked to the front of the store. In walked a bearded old man Kirk had never seen before. Due to the cast on his leg, he was walking with crutches. He also wore an eye patch.

"Who's that?" asked Kirk, as he walked to the radio and turned down the volume.

"Old Man Lister," said Carney.

"Friend of yours?"

"Not really. "I've been fillin' his prescriptions for years. He and his family live over by Stringtown, up in the hills. Bad luck seems to follow the man around like a shadow."

"Why do you say that?" asked Kirk.

"I know it sounds crazy, but . . ." Carney said, then whispered: "It's like the universe hates him. Bad stuff happens to him all the time."

Old Man Lister approached Kirk and Carney. "Hello, Skeet."

"Good afternoon, Mr. Lister. What can I do for you today?"

"Well, it seems as though I've gotten myself into a bit of a predicament."

"Oh?" replied Carney.

"Yeah," Old Man Lister replied. "The weather's been so nice, I decided to have my coffee out on the front porch this morning."

"That's understandable," replied Carney.

"So I pulled up my old rockin' chair and was just sittin' there on the front porch, enjoyin' the mornin' breeze with a hot cup of coffee and the wondrous beauty of nature and then I remembered I needed to take my heart medication."

"I'm glad to hear you remembered that," said Carney.

"Right," said Old Man Lister. "So I got the pill out of the bottle and was about to take it, but then I heard somethin' flutterin' on the porch's roof. I didn't rightly know what it was, so I walked over to the front of the porch and looked up to find that it was a bird just sittin' there, flappin' its wings. He weren't going nowhere. He was just a flappin' his wings."

"What do you suppose was wrong?" Carney asked.

"I didn't know. So I says, 'What the hell's wrong with you, bird, you stupid sum bitch!'" screamed Old Man Lister.

"Did that scare him away?" asked Carney.

"No," Old Man Lister said somberly. "It surely didn't."

Old Man Lister stood there, lost in thought. Staring at the floor, he wiped his eye several times, as if he were about to start crying. Kirk was afraid he was on the verge of breaking down. After several seconds of silence, Carney reignited the conversation.

"So, what happened?" Carney asked with a smile.

"Well," said Old Man Lister, "That got-damned bird flew over to the edge of the roof, right toward me, and then he just up and shit, right in my eye."

Old Man Lister just shook his head in disgust, but then paused. Kirk could see that his one good eye was welling up, about to cry, so he looked to Carney, who was doing everything in his power not to laugh.

"So I went to hootin' and a hollerin' at that bird, which must have scared him, 'cause he jumped back, then flew away. All that movement must have broke loose the icicles, 'cause next thing I know, one came fallin' straight down and hit me in the other eye. I fell onto the steps of the porch and broke my leg. Of course, I dropped my medication into the mud. The wife then had to take me to ol' Doc Buster."

Carney's face was as red as a beet. Kirk could see that he was pulling out all the stops to keep a straight face.

"I'm very sorry to hear that, Mr. Lister. Come on back and we'll get you . . ." Carney said, then stopped. He struggled so hard to hold his laughter in, he had to place his hands over his face. "We'll get you taken care of."

As Carney walked to the pharmacy, he flashed Kirk the "I told you so" look.

Kirk watched the old man limp on his crutches and slowly make his way to the pharmacy. He then walked over to the radio and turned up the volume. While listening to the game, he checked out the floor surrounding the soda fountain, in disbelief that the tile floor was caked in mud and grime so soon after its cleaning. The white high-school kids will be gone soon, he thought. He could mop the tile after they left. He decided to focus his energy on listening to the game and sweeping the hardwood floor, which covered almost all of the drugstore, with the exception of the soda-fountain area.

As he swept, the high-school students sat at the counter looking at an advanced physiology book. Judging by the frustration he read in their body language, they appeared to be having problems with their homework. He recognized the boys to be Jeff Spiva, Scott Leeper, and Harold Cole. He'd seen the boys around town before in the drugstore and knew them to be fairly nice guys. Kirk's first thought was to go over and say hi, just to test their reaction. If all went well, maybe he would try to help them with their problem. After all, Kirk had spent an enormous amount of time studying with his science teacher/basketball coach Willard Dallas, and if there was one thing he excelled at, it was advanced science.

As he walked over, a little voice sounded off in his head. It reminded Kirk he'd made a major breakthrough just hours earlier with some powerful white adults. Why did he want to taint that victory by intruding into this conversation, especially when a high likelihood existed that they would refuse his help? After all, he was just a black kid living in the white man's world, a world which wasn't quite ready to break down racial barriers.

As he approached the white kids, Kirk took a deep breath, then exhaled slowly. When he reached them, Kirk's gut warned him to keep going. He had felt this strange whirling in his stomach before and had grown to trust its guidance. Kirk's gait slowed, but he continued to sweep and did not stop. He did, however, manage to eavesdrop on their conversation.

"Damn, this is hard," said Scott.

"Read it again," asked Harold.

"A forty-four year old alcoholic man is admitted to the hospital for detox," read Jeff. "His chemistry levels are checked and everything appears in normal range except he is very acidic. His bicarbonate level is only ten, which is very low. He seems to be doing okay with IV fluids and meds to help him detox, but after about thirty-six hours, he collapses and dies."

"I think I understand that part," said Harold. "Now read the question."

"Here it is," said Jeff. "What killed the man?"

Scott was pulling so hard on his hair, he actually extracted a few strands. "This is driving me crazy!" he boldly said. "How can Mr. Rush expect us to get this?"

"Remember," said Harold, "this is advanced physiology. It's ain't supposed to be easy."

Jeff scratched his head. "Mr. Rush said we have been taught everything we need to answer this question."

"You remember how Mr. Rush always tells us to break down the problem with all the known information, then to diagram the problem and to break it down into small pieces?" asked Harold.

Jeff nodded his head.

"Maybe we should try that," replied Harold.

Jeff grabbed a pencil and began drawing out the problem on a tablet notebook.

Kirk looked down and realized he was paying so much attention to the students' problem, he forgot to sweep. He cleaned up a small area a few feet behind the white boys. After they drew out a diagram of the problem and scratched their heads, Kirk could stand it no longer.

While sweeping by the boys, he paused for a moment.

"Wonder what that ol' drunk's chemistry would have been if they had checked it a few hours after a little IV fluid," Kirk said, then continued to sweep right on past the students.

The boys looked at one another with shocked gazes. Kirk didn't know if it was because a black kid had the stones to talk to them with the presumption that he had the answer, or if his words might have actually helped.

All the students turned around for a moment and looked at Kirk, but just as fast, they resumed their studies. As Kirk continued to sweep, he felt he should have listened to his stomach.

"Boy, what did you mean by what you just said? That thing about chemistry?" asked Harold.

Kirk suddenly felt his shield of invisibility vanish.

"Callin' him 'boy' is an insult, you asshole," replied Jeff. "How would you like it if he said, 'Hey nester, why don't you listen to the teacher and maybe you'll know?'"

"I didn't mean it like that," said Harold. "I just didn't know his name and didn't know what to call him."

Kirk walked over to the counter with confidence. Now he had their attention. He was ready to deliver.

"You said, 'what would the chemistry have been'? We all think it would have been normal. Everything was normal except the bicarb," said Scott.

Knowing he now had them hooked, Kirk smiled.

"Any of you heard anything about acid-base balance?" asked Kirk. "There are several mechanisms involved in the human body to keep the pH level in a narrow normal range, one of which is the proton-potassium cellular exchange."

Hiding in a corner, Carney smiled as he listened to Kirk help the boys. Rather than saying a word, Carney silently walked back to the pharmacy.

Kirk looked up to the radio and heard the half-time buzzer sound. He quickly surmised if he hurried, he could take "the delivery" to the bank, grab a bowl of chili at Johnnie's, and be back to the store with ample time to clean up.

"Mr. Rush is right. You have enough information," said Kirk.

Like Humphrey Bogart in Casablanca, Kirk turned into a cool cat as he left the soda fountain and casually walked to the back of the store to check on "the delivery".

"Holy shit," cried Jeff, "I know what the black kid meant! Look at this first chemistry. It appeared everything is normal except the bicarb. In light of the acidosis, the protons were being pushed into the cells and the potassium was being pushed out of the cells, the part we measure."

"So, what are you getting at?" asked Harold.

"I'm sayin' that this ol' boy's potassium should have been high at first if his total body potassium level was normal. Then as his acidosis was corrected, his potassium would have dropped."

Harold and Scott were quick to catch on.

"And as he was given IV fluids, his acidosis was corrected, the potassium was pushed into the cells, and the blood level of potassium dropped through the floor," said Harold. "When his potassium hit about one point five, his heart stopped. No one ever bothered to check another chemistry on this poor old bastard."

"Ha!" exclaimed Scott. "Mr. Rush thought he was being clever. I'll bet he never imagined we could figure it out."

"Well, in all honestly, we didn't," said Jeff.

All three students looked to the back of the store and watched Kirk gather up the deposits and other bank information.

"That black kid is pretty smart," said Scott. "I'm amazed he knew how to figure that out. Wonder where he goes to school?"

"Over at Dunbar," said Jeff.

"I guess we now know who to ask the next time Mr. Rush gets carried away with his advanced physiology questions."

From the back of the store, Kirk watched the three students slam their sodas, gather their books, and exit the building. He smiled as he watched them walk out into Court Street.

#

Kirk let out a small silent belch as he opened the back door to Johnny's and stepped into the alley. He looked to his watch and saw it was a little after one o'clock. Knowing that the second half of the OU basketball game was already underway, he jogged back to the drugstore. Just as he turned the corner, however, he saw Uncle Willie walking toward him.

"Hey Uncle Willie, what are you doing?"

Uncle Willie walked to Kirk and grabbed his hand. He led him back to the alley.

"Lookin' for you," replied Uncle Willie. "I went over to the drugstore and talked to Mr. Carney. He said you was probably grabbing something to eat over at Johnny's."

"I just annihilated a bowl of their chili," said Kirk. "Man, did it ever hit the spot. What have you been up to today?"

"Been down at the bar," said Uncle Willie.

"It's a little early to be drinkin', wouldn't you say?"

"Hell, I don't drink no more."

"Why's that?"

Uncle Willie smiled. "When I have a drink, I feel like a new man, then the new man feels like he needs a drink, and so on. Pretty soon, things get outta hand."

Kirk laughed.

"I still go to the bars cause it's a fun place to hang out, but that don't mean I have to drink."

"I see," said Kirk. "So, what's on your mind?"

Uncle Willie didn't respond. Instead, he walked over and stared down at Kirk's pants' pocket for a few seconds. Evidently, he didn't find what he was looking for, as he then frisked Kirk from head to toe.

"Would you mind tellin' me what you're doing?" asked Kirk, a little miffed.

"Where's yo' gun?"

"At my house. Why?"

Kirk could tell Uncle Willie was becoming agitated. Uncle Willie took a step forward. He was now face-to-face with Kirk.

"I thought I told you to carry that gun with you at all times," snapped Uncle Willie.

Kirk rolled his eyes. "I'm not so sure I feel good about doin' that."

"To hell with feelin' good, boy," shouted Uncle Willie. "This is yo' life we talkin' 'bout here! Don't you get it?"

Kirk pushed Uncle Willie back. "What's the matter with you?"

"What's the matter with me? What's the matter with you? Don't you remember what I told you at the basketball game? Don't you remember what happened to Rudy? You're a man now, Henry. You gots to pay attention."

Kirk was more confused than mad. Nonetheless, he'd never seen Uncle Willie this angry. He tried to diffuse the confrontation.

"I know you mean well, but I'm just not so sure it's a good idea for me to carry a gun."

Uncle Willie stepped toward Kirk again.

"Damnit boy, don't you know what they'll do to you?" Uncle Willie said with fire in his voice. He grabbed Kirk by the shoulders, lifted him off the ground, and pinned him onto the wall of the building.

His eyes widened. He was now scared beyond belief. Even though Uncle Willie denied it, Kirk was afraid he might be drunk and was unaware of what he was doing. Due to fear, Kirk's arms started to shake.

Seeing the fear in his eyes, Uncle Willie quickly let go of Kirk's shoulders. As soon as his feet touched the ground, Kirk moved a few steps back.

"I'm sorry, Henry. I'm sorry," said Uncle Willie. "I'm just concerned for you."

"I don't think I understand. Is there something you know that I don't know?"

Uncle Willie shook his head. Kirk sensed he was hiding something.

"Please tell me, Uncle Willie. If my life is in danger, please tell me."

"Look Henry, I'm a man of the streets, so I'm privy to a lot of things that you're not."

"So what have you been hearing on the streets?" asked a concerned Kirk.

"I haven't rightly heard nuthin' that pertains directly to you, but what I'm trying to tell you is that they's some thugs roaming 'round Atoka that are makin' it they business to be up to no good."

Kirk paused for a moment. When thinking about enemies and those who wish to do him harm, the first name that popped into his mind was Butch.

"Speaking of thugs, what do you know about Butch, the fellow who works in the bank? Ever had problems with him?"

Uncle Willie paused. Kirk definitely sensed he'd hit a nerve.

"Do you know something I should know? And please don't tell me because you're afraid I'll worry. If he's after me, I need to know," said Kirk.

Uncle Willy took a deep breath. "About what happened a moment ago, when I pinned you against the wall. I want to apologize about that," he said. "When that happened, I was in a frame of mind I call 'seein' red'. It don't happen very often, but when it does, it makes me do stupid things, kind of like what you just saw."

"You saw red?" asked Kirk

"More or less," replied Uncle Willie. "It's times like those when my inner demons make they presence known. Sometimes, when I get real mad, they come out from the abyss and take control over me."

"Is that what happened when you killed the fellow in the bar a few months back? Did he make you mad, then your anger took over your body and you began to see red?"

"That's right," said Uncle Willie. "It's also what happened last summer when my brother brought home a goat and put it in the front yard. I had just mowed the yard and was out back. By the time I got up to the front yard to see the goat, I found he'd been eatin' the grass and pulled most of it out by the root. I'd been workin' to make that damned yard pretty for Momma all summer long, then my brother's new goat comes in and ruint the entire yard in less than a few minutes."

"I'll bet you were mad," said Kirk.

"You damned right. I went right in the house to tell my brother to get that damned monster off the yard. You know what my brother did?"

"No, sir," said Kirk.

"He laughed at me," Uncle Willie said with cold eyes. "The man laughed at me. Pretty soon, I was seein' red. So I went back to the front yard with my gun and I shot the damned goat right between the eyes. After that happened, Momma told me they was evil in her house. She asked me to leave."

"Damn," said Kirk. "I thought you said you were getting better."

"That was a year ago. That's what began to open my eyes. Then, of course, I had the incident with the man in the bar a few months ago. He messed with me, caused me to start seein' red, and I smoked his ass. I promise you, Henry, it's not something I feel good about. I'm ashamed of it, on every level."

Kirk had a sick feeling in his stomach. He looked to his watch, hoping Uncle Willie would get the hint he needed to leave.

"I know you've got to get back to work, Henry, and I'm not trying to dump all my problems on you. My life is different now. After killin' that man and then the goat incident, my eyes were opened to the light. I'm strivin' to get close to that light every day. I've been through a lot, but I'm trying to be a better man."

Kirk looked at the ground. "I know you are," he said.

"The point of what I'm sayin,'" replied Uncle Willie, "is I go to seein' red from time to time and it makes me do crazy shit. It doesn't happen very often, but it happens occasionally. Some folks, like you and Mr. Carney, never go to seein' red, and if they do, they have control over it. Then they's folks like me, who sees it more often than not. But Butch . . . Butch is different. Butch is always seein' red."

Kirk took a hard swallow. "You don't say?"

"You watch out for that man, Henry. He's been eat up by the dumbass and he ain't right in the head. Is he givin' you problems?"

"I'm not sure. He definitely doesn't like me. Ever since I began workin' at the drugstore, he's been messing with me. For example, he was gettin' real mouthy at the coffee shop this morning, and I just saw him at the bank and he just stared at me, real evil like. He acts like the kind of guy who don't care none for colored folk."

"And that's why you need to carry that gun, Henry. In case he catches you somewhere when your back is against the wall."

"But Momma said . . ."

"I know what yo' mamma said, and she's right, a gun can get you killed, but it can also save your life."

"Alright," said Kirk. "I'll do some more thinking."

"Please do," Uncle Willie said, then looked at the large stones that made up the wall behind their position. "Damn," he said.

"What's wrong?" asked Kirk.

"That wall," said Uncle Willie, lost in thought. "It brings back some bad memories somethin' fierce."

Kirk turned around. The wall behind them was tall, made up of hand-cut tan stones cemented together by masons. Bars covered the windows, and made the wall resemble that of an inescapable prison.

"Does it remind you of the joint?" asked Kirk.

"It sure does," replied Uncle Willie. "I had to stare at a wall like that for years and years. It looked like it got taller each day."

Kirk looked down to his watch. It read one-twenty.

"Mr. Carney's probably lookin' for me," said Kirk.

"You best get on," Uncle Willie said. "Sorry for taking so much of yo' time."

"Don't worry about it." Kirk shook hands with Uncle Willie, and then walked toward the street.

"You remember what I said," said Uncle Willie.

"I will," said Kirk. "I promise."

Chapter 18

"So has he done anything that makes you think he'll come after you?" Ripp asked while flooring the gas pedal. The car quickened its pace as it blazed a trail down a country road to Stringtown.

Kirk thought for a moment. "Well, nothin' I could point to as proof," he said. "Other than just acting like a jackass when Skeet leaves the room."

Ripp raised his eyebrow. "You already callin' him Skeet?"

"Well . . . sometimes, but that's really beside the point."

"So he's done nothing to you overtly? Is that what you're sayin'?"

"He hasn't hit me upside the head with a baseball bat, if that's what you're asking," said Kirk.

Ripp sighed as he drove the old beat-up Buick down a dirt road between Atoka and Stringtown. As the car approached each desolate intersection, rather than stopping, he would momentarily turn off the headlights to see if lights were visible in the dark intersection. As soon as he saw no other lights coming, Ripp pressed down the pedal and zipped right on through the intersection. Kirk was never really a fan of this approach, but arguing with Ripp about his driving was off limits. He'd learned his lesson the hard way long ago.

"I think it's all in yo' head," Ripp said as he pulled the light switch. "I mean, I hear what you're sayin', but I don't think the man could hurt a fly."

Kirk rolled his eyes. "I call bullshit on that one, Ripp. Butch is a madman. I guarantee you he's dangerous."

"But we can't rightly do anything unless we have some proof. We got to know he's done something or is planning to do something."

"Proof, huh?"

"Yeah, we need some proof," Ripp replied.

"What about goin' to the police?" asked Kirk.

Ripp laughed. "Yeah, that's a great idea. "Tell the Sheriff one of the town fathers is makin' ugly faces at a black kid. I'm sure he'll haul his ass right to jail, and give you a reward for the tip."

"Yeah . . . Maybe that's not such a good idea."

Kirk looked out the car window. Since all signs of daylight were gone and the night clear and void of clouds, the quarter moon shined down and reflected light on the few patches of snow that sat alongside the road. He looked at his watch and saw it read six o'clock. They were making good time and would arrive early to meet the girls at the dance.

"We're gonna be early for a change. Imagine that," said Kirk.

"I guess they's a first for everything," Ripp replied with a smile. "And this car ain't slowin' us down, either."

"Who's car is it?"

"Some old fellow named Lister," said Ripp.

Kirk winced. "Not a good sign for the evening."

"Why you say that?" asked Ripp.

"It's a long story. What part of the car did you and your dad fix?"

"It was a simple job. We had to re-align the front end. Evidently, he had some sort of accident and his wife had to take him to Doc Buster. Seems she was in such a rush, she crashed right into Buster's clinic. I heard Doc came running out and asked if Marge was trying to make a drive-in out of his clinic. He was pretty surly."

Kirk laughed. "Definitely sounds like Doc Buster."

"Yeah," Ripp replied. "I'm just glad no one got hurt."

As they approached another intersection, Ripp slowed the old Buick, then wheeled it onto the highway. They were now only a few minutes away from Stringtown.

"Can I ask you a question?" said Kirk in a solemn tone.

"Of course," said Ripp. "What's on your mind?"

"How do I look?"

Ripp gave Kirk a hard stare.

"You gettin' fruity on me, Kirkland?" Ripp said with a laugh.

"That's not what I mean. I'm asking how do I look?"

"I'd go out with you, but I ain't promising anything farther than first base," Ripp said with a laugh.

Kirk rolled his eyes. "Would you be serious for a moment?"

"What the hell do you mean?" Ripp said in a flared voice. "When did I become the guy who knows about fashion?"

"This is the first time I've dressed up in fancy clothes without help from my mom. It's the kind of thing you take for granted."

"Oh," replied Ripp. He looked Kirk over. "I'd say you look nice. Where did you get the duds?"

"They're my Sunday-going-to-meeting clothes. Same ones I've worn to Stringtown for the last three thousand times we've gone."

"Oh," replied Ripp. "I guess I didn't notice."

Several moments of silence passed as the old Buick rolled through the night.

"You missin' yo' family?" asked Ripp.

Kirk opened his mouth, but failed to utter any words. After a few moments, he nodded. "Yes," he said. "I do miss them."

"Is it eatin' away at yo' head?"

"Well, kind of. It's not in the normal way you would think, like packin' my lunch or fixin' supper, I miss that, but it's more like the smaller things. It's times like this, when I'm going out to see Vanessa or how happy I was to get the job down at the drugstore. I miss Mom smiling and kissin' me on the cheek and Dad laughing his stupid laugh. I miss my sisters tellin' me boys are stupid," Kirk said, then paused. "I don't really have anyone to share my life with anymore."

Ripp patted Kirk on the shoulder. "You know you've always got me."

"Yeah, I know, but it's different. I just feel . . . a little insignificant, I guess. And scared sometimes, too, knowing what happened to Rudy and all. It ain't always so easy to go to sleep at night, knowin' Mom and Dad aren't there in case something . . ."

"So it's the banker who's eating away at yo' head?"

Kirk thought for moment. "Yeah, maybe a little."

The old Buick turned off the highway and rolled down the street which led to the Essie Hugh's Dance Hall. Kirk could see several cars parked outside.

"They's something else I need to tell you," said Kirk.

"Shoot."

"Uncle Willie gave me a gun and told me to carry it, but I'm not so sure," said Kirk.

"Carrying a gat is an awful burden," said Ripp. "If word got out, you'd just be askin' for trouble."

Kirk sighed. "I know. That's one of my many worries."

"Well, I don't really think things are bad enough you need to carry hardware, but if yo' scared, I could stay with you at your house," Ripp said with sincerity.

Kirk laughed. "And be called a fruit? What do you think?"

"Better to be thought a fruit than to be dead."

"I'll keep that in mind," Kirk said with a smile.

Ripp parked the old Buick directly in front of the dance hall. As they got out of the car, they looked ahead and saw Vanessa and Clarice waiting for them at the front door.

"Look at the gams on those ladies," said Ripp with a smile.

"Gams? They're wearing dresses. You can't even see they legs."

"Maybe we will later," Ripp said with an evil grin.

Kirk shook his head as the two walked confidently to the building, a trait they'd been practicing at Essie Hugh's Dance Hall on Friday or Saturday nights for the last few years. The dance hall was the exclusive meeting place for black kids, ranging in age from junior high to high school. There was hardly ever a band, but the old Wurlitzer jukebox provided a variety of sound for dancing to just about anything, especially rhythm and blues. As long as the jukebox was fed with nickels and dimes, there was ample entertainment for the kids.

"This must be a sign of the apocalypse. Ripp and Kirk are actually on time," said Clarice.

"Don't get used to it," Ripp said with a smile as he kissed her on the cheek. Kirk walked to Vanessa and placed his arm around her shoulders.

"You guys have got to get inside and hear this," exclaimed Vanessa.

"What happened? Did we get a new juke box?" asked Kirk.

"No," said Clarice. "They's a white boy inside, playin' his guitar, just a tearin' it up. Come and see."

Kirk and Ripp were astounded as they entered the dance hall. The crowd of around thirty teenagers were dancing and watching in awe. A young white boy with blond hair was playing his electric Log guitar and a white girl with curly red hair was singing. The audience was mesmerized. Never had they heard before such a heavy sound coupled with blazing harmonic riffs. And the white girl's singing was sensational. The crowd was eating it up.

"Who are these folks?" shouted Kirk.

"Not sure, but I think the boy is from Boggy Depot," said Vanessa. "And I believe the girl is from here in Stringtown."

"Wow. That boy can play," said Ripp. "And that gal's quite a singer."

After the song ended, the couple thanked the audience, picked up their guitar, amplifier, and microphone, and walked to the door. As they walked, the crowd shouted for more, but the couple continued to walk out the door and, like magic, disappeared into the darkness.

"Why're they leaving?" asked Kirk.

"Probably got a bigger gig somewhere else," replied Ripp. "To bad we didn't know they was gonna be playing. We could have arrived earlier."

"I second that," said Kirk.

Someone from the crowd walked over and put some change in the juke box.

"Looks like a decent crowd," said Kirk.

"The night is ripe for the takin'." Ripp smiled and popped the joints in his fingers.

As kids walked to the dance floor, the old Wurlitzer began playing a Tex Ritter song. Couples joined together and began dancing to "I'm Wasting My Tears on You". About thirty seconds into the song, however, the dancing stopped.

"Is this a dance or flat tire?" a voice bellowed from the crowd.

The crowd laughed. One of the young men unplugged the jukebox from the wall, and when it restarted, he put in some coins. The crowd reassembled on the dance floor. Soon the Wurlitzer sounded with the "Harlem Debutante" and the crowd swung right into the Jitterbug. As the dance-floor players did the swing, Kirk and Ripp looked to each other and smiled.

"That's what I'm talking about!" Ripp shouted as he and Kirk danced with Clarice and Vanessa.

After a solid hour without a break, the foursome decided to have a soda and sit down. Clarice was hot, due to Ripp's advancing hands on the dance floor. Vanessa and Kirk silently laughed at their bickering. Ripp and Clarice sat next to each other on one side of the table, while the other side was shared by Kirk and Vanessa. As soon as everyone was seated, Ripp tried to shift Clarice's mood.

"So what're we up for tonight, ladies?" asked Ripp with a smile.

"Don't be gettin' any ideas, Ripp Masters," Clarice said with authority.

"I'm not gettin' any ideas, baby," Ripp innocently replied. "I was just thinking we could maybe go up to Boggy Bend and maybe have a drink, you know, relax a little."

"You wanna get us drunk, that's what you wanna do. Uh hum, I know you Ripp Masters. And I knows what you'll wanna be doin' after we get all 'relaxed', too. Fool!"

Vanessa slid her hand under the table and patted Kirk on the leg. She then leaned over and whispered:

"I think these two were meant for each other."

"They'll definitely be getting married soon," Kirk whispered back.

"All's I'm saying is we could drive up to Boggy Bend and just enjoy the atmosphere," said Ripp. "It's not too far away and it'd be fun to drive through the country."

"Actually, I'm staying with Clarice tonight and her dad wants us in early," said Vanessa. "We're getting up at the crack of dawn to go see her grandparents out in Roger Mills County."

"That's no problem," said Ripp. "We can walk you home, then the three of us can go on over to Boggy Bend and . . ."

"You want me to drop Vanessa off at my house and then run off with you?" asked Clarice.

Ripp rubbed his hands together and smiled. "That sounds great," he said. "Kirk has some friends in Boggy Bend he can go see while you and I have some relaxation time. See, everything worked out perfectly."

"Are you out of your damned mind!" shouted Clarice. "You can cease your sinful thoughts right there," she said while shaking her finger. "To think I would ask Vanessa to come over, then leave her to go out with you. You got some nerve, Ripp Masters!"

Once again, Ripp was reminded of how little he understood women. His only option was to change the topic of the conversation. "Where exactly are you going?" he asked.

"It's out in western Oklahoma," Clarice said, still agitated, but surprisingly much calmer.

"Is it a farm?" asked Kirk.

"No, my grandparents work at the Warren Ranch, which is an old ranch between the towns of Cheyenne and Reydon."

"So tell me Clarice," asked a suspicious Ripp, "what exactly are you gonna do?"

"Help out with the ranch, I suppose."

An old ranch hand himself, Ripp smiled confidently. "That sounds interesting. Are you gonna work the cattle?"

"I'll do whatever they want, 'cause you know I ain't afraid of a little work," Clarice said with authority.

"So you have no problem with cuttin' off them calves' horns?"

"Uh, no, that's not a problem for me," Clarice said with hesitancy.

"And brandin' them with a hot iron?"

"That uh . . . that sounds fine," said Clarice.

Ripp knew his questions were getting to Clarice. She had a weak stomach and it was beginning to show.

"Have you ever dehorned cattle before?"

"Uh, no," replied Clarice.

"I've dehorned cattle on several occasions and let me tell you, that is a bloody mess. Trust me, by the time the day is over, you'll be covered in cow shit, sweat, and blood."

Clarice looked nauseated. She wiped sweat from her brow, then fanned her face with her hands. Ripp took great pride that he was able to evoke such a response. His inner voice of reason told him it was time to stop. However, Ripp was never a fan of listening to his inner voice of reason.

"And how 'bout castrating them calves? Are you gonna help your granddad cut off they testicles?" said Ripp, beaming an arrogant smile.

Clarice had reached her boiling point. She reached into her purse and pulled out a six inch pocket knife. "Maybe I'll get me some practice tonight?"

The smile on Ripp's face dropped a thousand miles. He repeatedly cleared his throat.

"Uh, you know what? I, uh, think we should all probably turn in early tonight," Ripp said, then cleared his throat again. He looked at the blade of the pocket knife. "Yeah, I should probably get you ladies on home."

"You damned right," said Clarice. Gloating in victory, she slowly rocked her head back and forth.

Kirk knew even though the confrontation was over, the tension needed to be diffused. "Well, we'd better get going," he said.

The four put on their coats and finished their sodas. They each said their goodbyes to their friends and walked out the front door.

Kirk could tell Ripp was still shaken from the conversation because he continued to clear his throat. Out of sympathy, Kirk decided to take control.

"Shall we drive you home, or would you rather walk?"

"Let's walk," said Vanessa. "It's just a few blocks and it will give us more time together."

"Sure thing," responded Kirk. "Ripp, are you and Clarice good with walking?"

Clarice nodded her head while Ripp continued clearing his throat.

The foursome exited Essie Hugh's Dance Hall and walked north, beyond the line of parked cars. Along the way, Kirk noticed something strange. A yellow Chrysler Highlander was parked on the street by itself, away from the other cars. He stopped walking for a moment and gazed at the car. It wasn't uncommon to see teenagers sitting in a parked car smoking cigarettes and talking after the dance, but this car caught his attention because it was parked by itself, at a strange angle which indicated the people inside were watching those who exited the building. As his group walked closer to the car, Kirk decided to be safe.

"Let's take the scenic route," Kirk said. "We can walk past the spot where Clyde shot the deputy."

Without responding, the group heeded Kirk's advice and walked toward the west, away from the parked Highlander.

"Is something the matter?" asked Vanessa.

"I'm not sure," Kirk responded. "Just stay close."

He relaxed as they made it all the way over to the next street and walked northbound. The Highlander was out of their sight. He let out a breath of relief and reached for Vanessa's hand.

As they passed the old landmark, Kirk pointed to the side of the street. "That's where Clyde Barrows shot the deputy."

Still smarting from their argument, neither Clarice nor Ripp said a word.

"That's so sad," Vanessa replied. "It's hard to imagine that Bonnie and Clyde killed the poor deputy right here, just blocks from where Clarice lives."

"Actually, Bonnie wasn't here," said Kirk. "A guy named Ray Hamilton was with Clyde at the Stringtown dance when he shot the lawmen."

"It's very sad," said Vanessa.

"That it is," Kirk said, then pulled Vanessa close while they walked.

Kirk saw Clarice's house a few blocks ahead. Suddenly, from the east, the Highlander roared around the corner, headed south toward Kirk's group. Kirk froze when he recognized the vehicle.

"Everyone to the side of the street!" he shouted.

As the group rushed over, the Highlander raced like a bullet toward them. Fearing they would get struck, the group hightailed it even farther off the pavement. Just as the Highlander neared their position, however, it skidded on its brakes, sliding sideways in front of them.

Before Kirk could even let go of Vanessa's hand, three men jumped out of the vehicle. One man stood just outside the Highlander, while the other two walked toward Kirk and his friends.

"We come with a message for the boy who now works for the slave master," said one of the men.

It was too dark for Kirk to recognize any of the black men, but he estimated they were older, probably in their midtwenties. He quickly tried to size them up. The one speaking wore a sleeveless vest and looked confident. The other, shorter man, was fidgeting, showing he was nervous. Kirk released Vanessa's hand, then made a quick glance to Ripp. He, along with the girls, looked terrified.

"Everyone get behind me," Kirk said and placed his hand in his pocket. Ripp and the girls quickly obeyed.

"We don't want any trouble," Kirk said with a friendly voice. "You probably have us mistaken for someone else."

"I'm afraid not, Young Henry," said the man wearing the vest.

"It seems as though you know my name, but I don't know yours," Kirk said, again in a friendly tone.

"And that's the way it's gonna stay," said the shorter man who pulled out a butcher knife and flashed it at Kirk.

The man with the vest stepped toward Kirk and company. They were now only a few yards away from each other.

"We came here to teach you a lesson," said the vested man.

"Oh?" said Kirk. "And what lesson might that be?"

"That your days of working for the slave master are over."

Kirk heard Vanessa and Clarice scream behind him. He then overheard Ripp ask Clarice for her knife. As Kirk assessed the situation, he focused on containing his anger. He knew that was the one variable in the situation that was under his control.

"If you're asking me to quit my job, I'm afraid I can't help you."

The shorter man with the knife smiled and again flashed the knife. "We were afraid you might say that."

The two men started walking toward Kirk and his group. They stopped after only a few steps, however, when Kirk pulled Uncle Willie's gun from his pocket. He aimed it right at the short one's head.

"I tell you now," said Kirk sternly, "that I'd rather not shoot two fools on this fine evening. But hear me loud and clear. If you take another step closer, it will be your last."

"Holy shit, Kirk, I didn't know you were carryin' a gat tonight! What the hell?" exclaimed Ripp.

Both men stopped walking. The man with the vest smiled.

"It's real brave of you to carry a gun," he said "But you ain't got the balls to use it."

With his heart beating faster and faster, Kirk's attempt to temper his anger waned. He raised the gun slightly.

"Back off, or I will show you how we do it at Dunbar!" Kirk's voice thundered. He was surprised his voice boomed so loudly. Ripp's mouth was wide open as he stood and watched.

Standing their ground, Kirk knew he must take decisive action. He raised the pistol a little higher in the air and pulled the trigger. The hammer on the gun made a clicking sound, but the gun failed to fire.

The thugs laughed. Kirk looked down at the gun. What's happening, he thought. Did Uncle Willie give him old bullets that didn't work? Why didn't the gun fire?

As the men stepped closer, Vanessa burst out in tears. She pushed Ripp out of the way and reached for Kirk's chest, which accidently brushed his right arm.

The bullet from the gun exploded and cracked through the cold night air. Both men ducked for cover as the bullet whizzed over their heads.

"This sumbitch is crazy," said the short man, as both turned and ran back to the Highlander. The third man joined them as they jumped into the vehicle.

"That's right!" Kirk screamed. "And you tell the nester who sent you I will smoke all your asses if you ever come back! Tell him next time, I won't shoot to scare. Next time I'll aim right between yo' big white eyes."

As the vested man struggled to start the Highlander, Ripp cracked a big smile. The ordeal was so surreal, it was almost comical.

"Tell the nester he started this battle but I'll finish it Dunbar style!" screamed Kirk.

He shoved the gun back into his front pocket and watched as the yellow Highlander's taillights raced away from the group. Vanessa held on to Kirk with all her might.

"Dear Lord, I thought that was the end," cried Vanessa.

"Jesus, I was so scared," cried Clarice.

Kirk let out a breath of relief and shook his head. Even though he fully comprehended his previous actions, he almost felt as if a stranger had entered his body during the conflict. He wondered what had taken control and given him the courage to stand his ground. Perhaps it was just instinct, he thought. As the incident resurfaced in his mind, fear engulfed his body, making his hands and legs shake violently.

"I was scared, too," Kirk said. "I'm just glad it's over."

Ripp walked over and gave him a big hug. Rather than hugging back, Kirk's body was so weak, he practically fell into Ripp's arms for several seconds. He wiped his brow and tried to calm himself.

"You know what we just saw?" Kirk asked while looking up at Ripp.

"No," replied Ripp. "What was it?"

"Proof. Now we have our proof!" exclaimed Kirk.

"I'll say," Ripp replied. "We can talk about it tonight at your place."

Kirk playing basketball at Dunbar High

Henry Kirkland Jr.'s senior portrait

House similar to Kirk's

Kirk, Battle Axe, and Ripp

F.K. "Skeet" Carney

The Drug Store by Caleb Mild

Downtown Atoka, Oklahoma

Kirk returns to the tracks

Dr. Henry and Viola Kirkland

Chapter 19

As the car slowly approached downtown, Kirk looked through the windshield at the early-morning sun beaming radiant light throughout the cloudless sky over McAlester. The old brick buildings ahead looked isolated and deserted, a manifestation of the way he felt inside.

After spending several minutes trying to understand why the town was so desolate, Kirk remembered it was Sunday. Sunday mornings in McAlester were just like Sunday mornings in Atoka and every other rural community in America: The only activity was church. Everything else took a backseat, even the bars.

The town's lackadaisical mood lifted Kirk's spirits. He'd been trying diligently to calm himself since they left Atoka, but his mind was still on edge. After all, less than twelve hours ago he actually fired his weapon at some unknown thugs at Stringtown. Kirk shook his head in disbelief as the memory resurfaced.

Noticing an approaching speed-limit sign, Ripp took his foot off the gas and pressed down on the old Buick's brake pedal, bringing its speed into compliance. Kirk looked out the window and saw a police car parked on the side of the road.

"Dad used to tell me about the speed limits in McAlester," said Kirk. "He called it a 'speed trap', 'cause you really don't have time to slow down. He said giving out speeding tickets is a major source of revenue for the city."

"Thanks for the warning," said Ripp as the Buick drove by the cruiser.

"Getting pulled over by a cop is all we need right now," said Kirk.

As the old Buick passed the sitting police car, Kirk looked out the window to see if the officer noticed them. Kirk was surprised to see the officer had sat up and pointed his finger at the two as they drove by.

"Is he pointing at us?" asked Kirk.

"Yeah," said Ripp, while looking in the rear-view mirror. "Looks like he wants to say hi, too."

Kirk twisted around and looked behind them. The police car was in hot pursuit, with lights flashing and siren blaring. He felt his stomach drop.

"Damn," replied Ripp. "We don't need this." He slowed the car and pulled off the highway.

"What're you gonna tell him? He's probably not gonna believe a couple of black kids are test driving a car for the Chevrolet place in Atoka."

"I don't know," replied Ripp. "Help me think of something."

As the Buick rolled to a stop, the police officer made no haste in approaching the vehicle.

"Dad's gonna kill me!" Ripp muttered.

"Just be nice," Kirk whispered. "Use some of them three-dollar words you learned in college."

"You think that will work?" asked Ripp.

"It's our only chance," Kirk replied.

As the police officer reached up to tap on the window, Ripp quickly rolled it down.

"Good day, kind sir," Ripp said with a big smile. When Kirk realized that Ripp was using a British accent to strengthen his sophisticated vocabulary, he covered his face with his hands and laughed silently so the officer wouldn't see him.

"I need to see your license and registration," replied the stone-faced officer.

"Certainly, ol' boy," said Ripp. He reached into his wallet and retrieved his driver's license. "About that registration. I'm in a bit of a quandary."

Again, Kirk covered his face.

"You're in a bit of a what?" asked the police officer, looking a little annoyed.

"Quandary. It means predicament. You see, I happen to be a college student who's on holiday for the weekend. I'm presently assisting my father, who just so happens to be a mechanic at the Chevrolet place in Atoka."

"So?" said the officer. Kirk sensed he wasn't all that impressed with Ripp's college talk.

"This auto belongs to a one Mr. Lister of Atoka. The old chap brought this very auto into the Chevrolet place a few days ago. I have been assisting my father in said auto's repair. My colleague and I are currently embarked on a test drive and I must say, it's quite dashing."

"So you repaired it, and you and your buddy decided to test drive this 'auto' all the way over here, to McAlester?"

Ripp smiled. "That is correct, sir. Indeed."

"That's almost fifty miles away. It's gonna take you a hundred miles round trip to see if your father fixed this car correctly?" the officer said, growing angrier with each word. "Are you aware there's a war going on, boy? A world war, I might add. Speaking of which, where did you get the coupons to buy fuel? Are you using some of those counterfeit coupons that have been goin' around?"

Ripp was beginning to lose confidence in his performance. "Well," he said in his normal voice. "Actually, we drove here to McAlester to pickup a spare part for the grill. And the coupons came from the Chevrolet place, uh, sir."

The police officer looked at Ripp's driver's license.

"This all sounds fishy to me," said the officer. "Boy, get your black ass out of the car."

Kirk knew the jig was up and they were going to jail. And to make matters worse, Battle Axe would kill Ripp when he found out he'd taken a customer's car to McAlester for a joyride. Kirk's heart raced as he awaited their doom.

The officer wheeled Ripp around and cuffed him.

"Would it help if my boss, F.K. Carney vouched for us?" said Kirk with a frail voice.

"Who?" said the police officer.

"F.K. Carney."

"You talkin' 'bout Skeet?" asked the officer.

Kirk felt a ray of hope. "You must know him," he said.

"You boys work for Skeet?" asked the cop. "Down at the drugstore?"

"We certainly do," said Ripp, once again using his British accent. "I worked for him for years before I went away to college. Henry just began his employment with Skeet. He's like a father to us. Yes, a well-loved father, indeed."

"Hmmm . . . and he'll vouch for you, if I decide to give him a call?" asked the police officer.

"But, of course," said Ripp.

"I actually grew up in Atoka," said the officer. "I have very fond memories of Skeet Carney. In fact, one winter our entire family caught the flu. Dad couldn't work because he was so sick. We really needed the medicine, but we had no money, so Skeet opened a line of credit right there on the spot. He's quite a guy."

"Yes," said Ripp while nodding his head, "quite a guy, indeed. I dare say that Sir Carney would hold you in great favor if you could find room in your bosom to release his two most cherished employees."

The police officer gave Ripp a hard stare. "I thought you quit workin' for him so you could go to school?"

"True, true," Ripp said with a smile. "But once you start working for Carney, on the inside . . . you always work for Carney."

Kirk couldn't believe the show Ripp was putting on. He never knew Ripp was such a big ham.

"Hmmm . . ." said the police officer, while thinking. "Well, it is Sunday and I've been workin' all night. I'm awful tired and . . ."

"You do look tired," said Ripp, who closed his eyes for a moment. The cuffs were so tight, they were cutting into his wrists. He gritted his teeth and continued. "Look, why don't you take these cuffs off and we'll be on our way. We'll go get our spare part for the hood and be out of town before you get home to take a nap."

"I thought the spare part was for the grill?" asked the police officer.

"Grill, hood, it's all the same."

The police officer nodded, then turned Ripp's body and unlocked his handcuffs. Ripp smiled.

"The next time you're in Atoka, you can come by the drugstore and I'll personally buy you a soda," said a beaming Ripp.

The police officer said nothing. He just walked to his car and drove away. Kirk looked to Ripp, who was staring out the windshield with wide eyes and a blank face.

"Well, you can't say we didn't have some excitement today," said Kirk.

"My life flashed before my eyes," said Ripp. "Do you realize what my dad would have done to me if I'd been thrown in jail?"

"They would have felt the aftershocks all the way to Stringtown."

Ripp shook his head. "Shit. They would have felt them in Los Angeles."

After several moments of giving thanks to Jesus, Ripp put the car in drive. "So, where do you want to go?" he asked.

"I don't care," replied Kirk. "Comin' to McAlester was your idea, so it's your call."

"How 'bout the movies?"

"Sounds good. What's showin'?"

"They's a movie called 'Double Indemnity'," said Ripp. "It's a thriller 'bout a couple who plot to kill off her husband for the insurance money, then get to suspectin' each other."

"Or we could go throw rocks at cars," said Kirk.

Ripp shook his head. "Naw, you need to go get yo'self some culture."

Kirk looked confused.

"Now, why in the hell would I need to go do something like that?"

"I learned about drama in college. Women love that kinda stuff."

"Trust me, I'd just as soon throw rocks at cars."

"See Kirk, that's what bothers me about you. You're actin' like you're from Atoka. Don't be like that. They's a great big world out there. You got to go get yo'self some of it."

"What good is drama gonna do for me? Do people in big cities pay folks to know about drama?"

Ripp shook his head. "Of course. What if you wanna become a writer or a filmmaker, or even a film critic? You got to verse yo'self in art. And drama is art."

Kirk shook his head. "I'll stick to the math and sciences, thank you very much."

"Ain't nothin' wrong with that, but just keep yo' mind open, Young Henry," Ripp said, while poking Kirk's chest.

"Yes sir, Mr. Carney. I will do that, sir," Kirk said, then laughed.

By the time Kirk and Ripp finally made their way inside the lobby of the theater, the box office was practically uninhabited, which was good because it meant the white folks had already paid and entered. It was an unspoken rule that blacks were to never enter the lobby before the whites. Most of the time, blacks would wait out on the street until the movie started to ensure the white folks had plenty of time to enter.

Same with refreshments. Blacks were only allowed to buy popcorn and sodas after the whites had plenty of time to go first. And just in case things weren't bizarre enough, blacks were allowed to buy ice cream, but were not allowed to eat it in front of whites. Neither Kirk nor Ripp understood the rules, but nonetheless, they abided.

Since Kirk and Ripp were running a little late and the previews had already started, the concession stand was empty, except for the clerk. They were quick to buy two sodas and a big popcorn, then headed on up to the balcony.

After being seated, Kirk laughed as he watched the cartoon that played before the main attraction. Sadly, that was about the only entertaining facet of the experience. After watching the film for thirty minutes, Kirk looked at the bag of popcorn. It was empty. He looked around the old theater, trying to entertain himself. After a few minutes, he could simply take it no more.

"Hey Ripp," Kirk whispered.

"Yeah."

"You know how you brought me over to McAlester to get my mind off all the crap that's been happening in Atoka?" Kirk whispered.

"Yeah," said Ripp.

"This movie is beginning to make me feel worse."

Ripp wore a confused expression. "Why's that?"

"It's just so damned boring," Kirk replied. "I'm thinking it might be more fun to go back to Stringtown and get chased around by thugs."

Ripp smiled. "I was thinkin' the same thing. Lead the way."

By the time Ripp and Kirk made their way back to the Buick, a fairly thick layer of clouds had formed in the sky, covering the afternoon sun. Ripp placed the shifter into drive and the two were soon cruising the streets of McAlester. While driving, Ripp pulled out his billfold, and quickly inspected the amount of folding money inside.

"You know, Kirk, we ain't spent near enough of this money," said Ripp. "Since I left school and became a working man, I'm not used to havin' so much cash. I got to be honest, it's burning a hole in my pocket."

"Well, we've been to the movies. I don't really know what else there is to do on a Sunday afternoon."

"You hungry?" asked Ripp.

"I just ate a fifty pound sack of popcorn, but I am a growin' boy," Kirk said with a smile.

"Let's get something to eat. Do you know of any restaurants in McAlester?"

"I don't," said Kirk. "Let's drive around until we find one."

Ripp drove the car around all the main drags in McAlester in hopes of finding a place to eat. After driving around for an hour and finding nothing but closed restaurants, the two gave up hope.

"I guess nothin's open," said Ripp. "I see a grocery store up ahead. Wanna try it?"

"Sure," Kirk said. He looked at their surroundings and saw he and Ripp had inadvertently driven into a seedy part of town. All of the businesses were run down, the paint faded and chipped. As the old Buick pulled into the parking lot of an old, decrepit grocery store, Kirk noticed a strange sight on the corner of the street. A group of black women stood together, yelling as cars passed by.

Ripp parked and opened the door. Kirk remained seated.

"Aren't you goin' with me?" asked Ripp.

"No, I'm gonna stay here."

"What do you need me to get for you?"

"I trust your judgment," said Kirk, eager for Ripp to leave the car.

"That was your first mistake," Ripp said with a smile. "I'll be right back."

Kirk's reasons for staying in the car were twofold. For starters, he'd been feeling bad all day about Ripp paying for everything. He knew Ripp was happy to spend the money and he would never hold the debt over his head, but Kirk was uneasy about not being able to pay his own way. The other reason for staying in the car was his piqued curiosity about the women on the corner. Kirk had never seen such a colorful spectacle.

While Kirk sat in the Buick and sporadically glanced over at the women, one of them spotted him and began yelling. Unable to make sense of their words, he stepped out of the car and walked toward them.

The woman who was yelling at him was the tallest of the group, and far and away the prettiest. She had a slender build with long braided hair and wore a lime-green tank top and a neon orange short skirt.

"What's a cute young boy like you doing in a place like this?" asked the woman.

Kirk was a little embarrassed and didn't know what to say. "We're just visitin'."

"Are you lookin' for a good time?" asked the tall woman.

Kirk's eyes widened when he realized what the woman was.

"Oh," said Kirk while he walked back to the old Buick. "Uhm, no, we're uh gonna get something to eat over here at the uh, grocery store."

The tall woman inched up her skirt. "You look like a nice young man. Ever been with a woman? I'm running a special for virgins."

Still trying to make his way back to the Buick, Kirk was embarrassed like never before. He prayed Ripp would come out of the grocery store and save him.

"Well, actually I have been with a woman, uh, actually several women, at once. So, thanks for the offer, but I don't think I uh, qualify for your special."

Wearing an evil smile, the woman casually walked straight to him and rubbed her hands over his shoulders.

"Well, if that's the case, then I'm running a special on seasoned young men, men who know what they doing. Young men who can satisfy several women at once."

"What's going on?" said Ripp as he barreled through the grocery store's front doors.

Kirk let out a sigh of relief. He stepped away from the woman and stood by his friend. As soon as Ripp realized who the woman was, he smiled.

"So what's a gorgeous momma like you doin' in a place like this?" asked Ripp.

Fearing Ripp wasn't fully aware of the situation, Kirk intervened. "I think she's a lady of the night. We should probably get on outta here."

Ripp smiled. "I think we'll be alright," he whispered back.

"I'm tryin' to find someone who's lookin' to have a good time," said the woman. "Are you two up for havin' a good time?"

Kirk rolled his eyes.

Feeling brave, Ripp decided to push it a little further. "How much would it cost for the both of us to 'have a good time?'" he asked.

Kirk was boiling with embarrassment. He lightly punched Ripp on the arm.

"What are you doing?" he whispered loudly.

Ripp laughed. "I'm sorry, Kirk. I'm just havin' some fun."

The tall woman inched her skirt up farther. Even though her legs looked enticing, Ripp and Kirk quickly looked away.

"We'd better get," said Ripp. "We're just visiting, but now we need to get back home."

The woman was visibly let down, but remained hospitable.

"Where are you two from?" she asked.

"A little town about an hour away," said Ripp.

"Does this little town have a name?" asked the lady.

"Yeah. Atoka. It's just a bump in the road. You've probably never heard of it."

"Oh, Atoka," said the woman. "Actually, my best customer is from Atoka."

Kirk and Ripp looked at each other. "Really?" said Kirk.

"Yeah," replied the lady. "He won't tell me what he does for a living, but I think he's a banker."

Kirk's stomach dropped. "So, what's his name?" he asked.

The woman looked around and inspected her surroundings.

"I'm not supposed to say," said the woman. "He told me I was never to let anyone know. He said bad things could happen if I did."

"I understand," said Ripp. "It's really none of our business anyway."

"But I'm not afraid of him. He sometimes gets rough with me, but he pays me so well that I don't mind. His name is Jereboam or something like that. It's a name right out of the Bible."

"Jereboam?" said Kirk.

"Yeah. Weird name, huh?"

"Jereboam, Jereboam, where have I heard that?" asked Kirk.

"He's a real tall nester," said the lady. "I'll bet you he's over six foot, five inches."

With their wheels turning, Kirk and Ripp look at each.

"Butch?" said Kirk.

"Are there any other distinctive qualities about him?" asked Ripp.

The lady looked confused by the question.

"Is there anything else about him that's unique?"

"Oh," said the lady. "Well, he has a big scar over his right eye. He told me that he got into a fight with a gang of black men and that while he was killin' them, he got cut on the face," the lady said, then paused. "But I'm pretty sure he got the scar for not paying one of the other girls."

"No kidding?" said Kirk.

The lady opened her purse and pulled out a small dagger. "That's what happens to folks who don't pay."

"He said he was in a fight with a gang of blacks?" asked Kirk.

"Yeah, but I think he's full of shit. Truth of the matter is, I don't think he likes black folk."

Kirk laughed. "But you're black," he said. "That doesn't make any sense."

"Nesters sometimes don't make sense," said the lady.

Everyone laughed.

"Look," said the lady, sincerity showing in her expression. "I probably shouldn't have told you. This is gonna sound crazy, but we do live by a code here and one of the things we try to do is keep everything confidential. It's just that Jereboam is such an asshole, I don't really mind givin' his name out. But please don't tell no one you heard it from me."

"You have our word," said Ripp.

Both Ripp and Kirk entered the old Buick and watched the lady walk back to the group of prostitutes. Ripp wheeled the car back onto the street. In just a matter of moments, they were back on the highway headed to Atoka.

"That was odd," said Kirk. "Never seen anything like that before."

"I should have warned you," said Ripp while he laughed. "I wish I had a picture of your face when I asked her how much for the both of us."

"I was ready to kill you. That wasn't funny."

As the Buick rolled down the open highway, Kirk looked through the back window and saw that McAlester was out of sight. Ahead, he saw nothing but open prairie on both sides of the highway.

"Who do you think that woman was talking about?"

"Well, there's not a lot of tall bankers in Atoka besides Butch."

"Yeah, that's what I was thinking. He's tall, has the scar on his right eye and on top of that, he's a raging asshole. It definitely sounds like Butch."

Ripp laughed. "Yeah, I think he's our man. But why do you think he called himself Jereboam? Is that just a name he picked out the blue?"

"I don't know," replied Kirk.

"It could be his middle name. I've read before that a lot of criminals use names they're familiar with so it's not too hard to remember. That happened a lot with members of the KKK."

Kirk felt like he had been hit by a truck. "Of course!" he shouted.

"What?"

"That's it. The Ku Klux Klan."

"What are you talking about?" asked Ripp.

"The picture. Remember the picture I showed you? The one I found up in the attic of the drugstore?"

"Yeah. So?"

"It was a picture of the Klan. Remember, I was afraid it was Carney."

"And we proved it wasn't," said Ripp. "Judging by the height of the parking meter, the man in picture was pretty tall, probably taller than six-foot-four inches."

"Right. Do you remember what it said at the bottom of the picture?"

"Jereboam," Ripp said.

"That's right."

"Jereboam," said Ripp. "It's Butch."

"That's right. Butch is our man."

"Holy cow," said Ripp. "Butch is our man."

Chapter 20

The church's Sunday-noon bells rang throughout Atoka as Butch and his wife walked down the church's cement steps and onto the sidewalk. A quiet week had passed through the town and brought the only thing worthy of news: A warm front, which raised the overall temperature several degrees. All the people in the surrounding area were out and about on this Sunday morning, hoping that an early spring was in the air.

Butch wrapped his arm around his wife's waist and walked over to Brother Jay, the pastor of the church. Butch shook his hand.

"Mighty fine preaching today, Brother Jay," said Butch.

"Why thank you, Brother Butch," said the old Irish preacher who'd served in Atoka for several years. "Tell me, did you be feeling the warmth of God's hand lay upon your bosom today?"

"Indeed I did," said Butch. "I especially enjoyed the sermon."

"Oh?" said Brother Jay, with raised eyebrows. "And tell me, which part of God's Word spoke dearest to your heart?"

Butch's heart rate instantly spiked. Throughout the sermon, he'd been slipping in and out of sleep and hadn't a clue which part spoke to him, nor even what the sermon was about.

"Well, uh, I uh, especially like the scripture you used when you spoke of uh . . . that thing God said."

"Are you referring to *Galatians 3:28*, which says, 'You are all sons of God through faith in Christ Jesus, for all of you who were baptized into Christ have clothed yourselves with Christ. There is neither Jew nor Greek, slave nor free, male nor female, for you are all one in Christ Jesus?'"

Butch smiled. "Yes," he said with arrogance. "That scripture just grabbed me."

"As well it should, Brother Butch. And what might you be knowin' of said scripture?"

Butch just looked at the preacher, like a deer caught in the headlights.

"What did God's words mean to you, my dear brother?" repeated Brother Jay.

"Oh," said Butch. "Well, it meant that we should all wear clothes. God's clothes." Satisfied with his answer, Butch smiled as he patted Brother Jay on the back and began to walk away.

"The Good Word is telling you not to be so fast to give judgment to your brothers and sisters. It's telling us sinners to love our neighbor, no matter what the color of their skin nor the makeup of their past. That applies to colored folks, Mr. Banker," said Brother Jay, with piercing eyes.

The words cut Butch to the bone. He raised his hand and stuck a finger near the pastor's nose.

"Watch your tongue, preacher," he said, then looked up and noticed that the congregation was gathering behind Pastor Jay. He pulled back his hand.

"The eyes of God are watching you, lad," said Brother Jay with a smile. "There not be a way to evade Him, no matter how cunning one thinks himself to be."

Butch gave the pastor a hard stare, then turned and walked away. As he and his wife reached their car, he looked back and saw Pastor Jay busy shaking hands and conversing with the congregation. Butch gazed through the crowd for a few minutes, then got in his car. Geddy shook his head, then stepped up and shook hands with Pastor Jay.

After dropping off his wife at their house, Butch drove to the bank and parked his car. He grabbed the deposit bag, which contained the church's offerings for the day and entered the bank. After laying the deposit bag on his desk, he unlocked the bottom drawer and took out a bottle of cheap Tennessee whiskey. Throughout the years, he'd found he enjoyed a little nip every now and then. Well actually, more now and less then.

Butch inspected the deposit-slip information. Since he was the town's most prominent banker and an active member of his church, the church elders gave him the responsibility of counting and depositing the money every week. Butch was happy to oblige.

He quickly counted the money from the small individual envelopes, those that contained the congregation members' names, and found the sum totaled $175. He looked at the deposit slip booklet and found that last week's total was $115. Butch quickly pulled $50 from the collection money and placed it in his pocket. He wrote the date in the deposit booklet, then recorded $125 in this week's collection column.

The only remaining task was to record the money given by those members of the congregation who didn't use an envelope. This money came from individuals who didn't want credit for the money they gave the church. This money was Butch's favorite. He opened the ledger book, which revealed the amount of money each member of the church had given. He then counted the money that had been placed openly in the collection plate. Beside his name in the ledger book, he recorded that amount. The feeling of generosity caused Butch to smile and puff out his chest. He folded the money and placed it and the deposit slip into the bottom drawer of his desk. Just as he locked the drawer, he heard someone walk into the bank.

"From afar, it looked like you were about to punch Brother Jay in the face," said Geddy with a smile. "Did the Holy Spirit move you that much today?"

Geddy walked into Butch's office and sat down in a chair in front of his desk.

"No, the damned Mick got to mouthin' about inequality among the minorities," said Butch. "He had no right preachin' to me about such a thing."

Geddy laughed. "Yeah, the nerve of that man. Who does he think he is, a man of God?"

Butch gave Geddy a scornful look. "What did you want to meet about today?"

"Just a friendly meeting among business associates," said Geddy. "We need to discuss a few things about our venture."

"Such as?"

"For starters, a couple of weeks ago, my secretary, Josephine, found a document from your company in the mail. It looked like a listing of expenses, paper and ink costs and such. Care to tell me why you decided to mail that to the prison?"

"Son of a bitch!" shouted Butch. "I was wondering where it went. My secretary must have found that on my desk and saw your name on the small piece of paper attached to the document. That's how I keep things straight, by names of my associates, rather than by the name of the venture. I bet she saw your name and thought it was suppose to be mailed to you. I'm gonna kill that idiot."

"I don't think you should be mad at her. I think I'd be mad at myself. And besides, why are you creating a paper trail, especially with my name attached to it? You're gonna get us caught."

"It's for tax purposes," said Butch. "I'll use the expense of our little printing business as a write-off."

Butch's words incensed Getty. "You have got to be kidding me! You're gonna file our illegal coupon counterfeiting operation on your taxes?"

"No," said Butch. "I'm gonna say the eleven thousand plus dollars was a donation for prison supplies. You know, helpin' with the war effort. I keep all the records so at the end of the year you can give me a receipt showing I have been generous by supplying the prison with paper and ink and such."

"That's just plain stupid," said Geddy. "You're makin' an incredible amount of money on this deal. Why do you want a tax write-off? You're showing a great deal of hubris about this whole venture."

Butch didn't understand the definition of the strange word, so he took it as a compliment. He smiled widely. "Well, thank you, Geddy. I'm glad you appreciate a good businessman when you see one."

"You don't even know what hubris is do you?" fumed Geddy. "It means someone who shows excessive pride before the fall. One who is over confident to the point of taunting his victim. In this case, you are taunting the IRS. You're getting sloppy and it's gonna get us caught."

"I don't know why you're worried," said Butch. "You're not involved in this."

"Bullshit! I'm the dolt who's forcing my prisoner to counterfeit the coupons. How am I not involved?"

"You're not out there selling them on the street. If they're gonna get someone, they'll get the people on the street. The feds won't come after us."

"What twisted reasoning makes you think that?"

Butch smiled. "'Cause I'm using my ties in the Klan to sell the coupons and, trust me, if they get caught they won't tell the feds where they bought them. It's their code. We're safe, I assure you."

Geddy looked distressed. "I'm not so sure the risk is worth the reward."

Butch laughed. "Surely you jest. This thing has gone beyond my wildest dreams. I never imagined it would be so successful. I never envisioned there would be enough affluent people who didn't want their lives interrupted by rationing. Even though the profit is small on each coupon, we've sold such a high volume, the money we've made is staggering. And my connections with the Klan extends our network to almost a national scale. I've even heard of our coupons making their way to the mob in Chicago and New York. We almost have a monopoly on this industry."

"You don't understand," said Geddy. "Since I'm the ration officer of this district, I'm the one who'll take the heat."

Geddy looked down the floor. Butch's arrogance was making him extremely nervous. Geddy was a student of human behavior and, through the years, he observed the one sure-fire way of getting caught was the most basic of human emotions: pride. Throughout the course of mankind, pride has always been man's tragic downfall. Geddy had a very bad feeling he was seeing it now, firsthand.

"You're worried about nothing," said Butch. "Trust me."

"I can't trust you or anyone," said Geddy. "Don't you see I'm in a world of shit here? Since I'm the ration officer and, therefore, the one who has federal authority to distribute and monitor the usage of these ration coupons, it's my head that will roll if we get caught."

"The fact you're the ration office is why this operation is foolproof and why we will never get caught. It's why I chose you. The feds will never find out about this, much less your involvement."

"What if Bartz talks?"

Butch laughed. "No one's gonna listen to a Nazi, trust me."

"I don't know," said Geddy. "He's our weak link. Since he's the one who's designed and printed these coupons, he's the feds' smoking gun."

"Stop worrying. He'll be taken care of soon enough. By the way, how's he doing?"

Geddy shook his head, stood, and began walking around the office.

"The damned kraut is driving me crazy," said Geddy. "He keeps whining about his wife and kids, that he wanted no part of the war, blah blah blah. The Nazis still want him dead, too. I'm tired of keeping them at bay."

"A pain in the ass he might be, but that kraut is our ace. Those coupons he's been printing are damned-near indistinguishable from the real thing."

"They ought to be. He spent years working with the Nazis trying to counterfeit the British pound."

Butch smiled. "We've got ourselves quite a racket going on here," he said. "Just keep 'em coming."

Geddy turned his back to Butch and walked to the bookshelf. He placed his head in his hands.

"About that," said Geddy hesitantly. "I'm afraid this racket has run its course."

"What!" Butch walked over to Geddy. "What are you talking about?"

"Haven't you been reading the newspapers? Our forces are marching through Europe. The war is almost over."

"You let me worry about that," said Butch. "Even if the war is over tomorrow, the country will probably be on rations for months. This war came at one hell of a price."

Growing more distraught, Geddy closed his eyes and bumped his head on the bookshelf.

"I don't think you're hearing me," said Geddy. "We've made our money and we've been damned lucky to not get caught. Let's end this now, before something happens that we regret."

Geddy could see the veins in Butch's head flaring. He knew Butch was getting angry.

"You're acting like a fool!" screamed Butch.

"Maybe you don't know what it's like to be incarcerated, but trust me, I know and I don't want any part of it."

Butch grabbed Geddy around the throat and pressed him against the bookshelf. Geddy struggled to breathe.

"You're in too deep to pull out now, Geddy. We can't afford to make foolish decisions. I'm asking you nicely to think long and hard about this decision."

Butch released his hold. Geddy staggered, then bent over, breathing heavily. After a few moments of gasping for air, Geddy returned to an upright position.

"As long as you're asking nicely," said Geddy, "I guess we'll stay with the plan."

A twinge of remorse crept into Butch's consciousness. He patted Geddy on the back.

"Look," said Butch, calm again. "I've established a vast network with my associates in the Klan. This thing is too big to pull the plug. It will be over soon, but not until I say so. Do you understand?"

Pulling on his collar to get more air, Geddy nodded.

"Good," said Butch, as he returned to his chair. "There's something else I want to talk to you about."

Geddy looked up and frowned. "Great," he muttered.

"There's a nigger boy that's gettin' too close to our operation and I need some help rubbin' him out."

Geddy finally managed to catch his breath. He sat down on the chair.

"What's this boy's name?" asked Geddy.

"Well, Skeet calls him Henry, but I've heard others call him Kirk, so I'm not sure," snapped Butch.

"Skeet? What's his association to Carney?"

"He works for Skeet, down at the drugstore," said Butch.

"Whoa! You're gonna try to kill the boy who works for Carney? Are you out of your mind?"

"I'm not gonna just try, I'm gonna get it done."

"Would you mind explaining why? How is he getting too close to our venture?"

"Well, he actually doesn't know anything about us counterfeiting coupons, but he's been real mouthy. He's tried to humiliate me a couple of times in front of white folk. He even did it in front of Joni Nugent, just when I thought I was gettin' somewhere with her. I'm not gonna stand for it."

"It sounds to me like he's done nothing," said Geddy. "Could it be that you don't like him because of the color of his skin?"

Butch smiled. "Oh, that's definitely a part of it. But it goes much deeper. He's crafty, so I'm gonna need some expert help. I tried to have him taken care of over at Stringtown a week ago, but he was ready. I need some real muscle."

"Being as how I don't do a lot of assassinations, I'm not very well versed in who to call when you want someone killed, so I can't really help you."

"What about the Nazis?"

Geddy almost fell out of his chair. "I think it's time for me to get on back to my wife and kids. If you get a chance to catch a train back to reality, give me a call."

Butch was stunned to see Geddy walk out of the bank. He stared at his desk for a moment, then had an epiphany. His wife would be thrilled if he brought home something to eat. He smiled and reached for the deposit bag, as he took one last nip from the hooch in his bottom drawer.

Chapter 21

Kirk's stomach rumbled as he walked to Mrs. Parker's front door and knocked. He could smell the aroma of her cooking and it made his mouth water in anticipation. Since he hadn't eaten a home-cooked meal in longer than he cared to remember, he'd been looking forward to this visit for quite some time. After waiting several seconds and not hearing any movement inside, he knocked again. Still no response. Kirk walked to the window and looked inside. He saw Mrs. Parker slowly walking toward the door. She was still dressed in her church clothes. Since he missed the service that let out around an hour ago, he knew he was about to be ribbed.

Kirk looked to his watch and saw it was noon. I have plenty of time, he thought.

"Why hello, Henry," said Mrs. Parker. "I was thinking you might be coming by today."

"Yes, ma'am," replied Kirk. "It's the last Sunday of the month. I'm here to collect your newspaper bill."

"That's right." She reached inside her purse and retrieved an envelope. To Kirk's horror, she opened the door, handed him the envelope, then began to close it.

"Is there anything you're needing help with around the house?" asked a desperate Kirk.

Mrs. Parker smiled. "Oh, no. I'm fine. Thanks for comin' by. I'll be seein' you next time," she said and closed the door.

Kirk could feel the drool on his chin growing cold from the light wind. He let out a long deep sigh, then turned and walked away with his head hanging low. Before his foot touched down on the old wooden steps, however, he heard a sound behind him.

"You gonna let all this food go to waste, Henry Kirkland?" said a perturbed Mrs. Parker.

Kirk smiled. Her words were the sweetest he'd heard in a long time.

"Well, I'd hate for that to happen," he said.

Before Mrs. Parker could fully open the door, Kirk stepped inside and walked toward the table. It was perhaps the most beautiful sight he'd ever seen: fried chicken, along with mashed potatoes, gravy, green beans, rolls, and a salad. Kirk's first impulse was to jump on top of the table and eat his way to the bottom.

"Best wash yo' hands," said an authoritative Mrs. Parker.

"Uh, yes, ma'am," Kirk said with hesitancy, still staring at the food. After a few moments, the words finally sank in and he walked to the bathroom.

For over an hour, Kirk sat with Mrs. Parker, eating and listening to her tell stories about the good old days. After three pieces of chicken and equal helpings of all the fixin's, topped off with apricot cobbler for dessert, Kirk sat back in his chair. He struggled to keep his eyes open.

"You sure know how to cook," said Kirk. He looked down and noticed his bulging stomach. "I haven't eaten this well since before our boys took Normandy Beach."

"Glad you liked it," said Mrs. Parker. "And by the way, I didn't see you at church today."

Kirk frowned. "Yes ma'am. Sorry about that. I overslept. I guess I'm pushin' myself too hard with school and all my jobs."

He hated to lie, but he was certain Mrs. Parker wouldn't take it well if he told her the truth. Since the run in with the thugs at Stringtown a week ago, he had hardly slept at all. Most nights, he lay in bed awake, staring at the holes in the roof, jumping out of his skin in fright at each random sound the creaky old house made when the wind blew.

Mrs. Parker placed her hands onto Kirk's. "I know what happened over at Stringtown last week. You did the right thing by shooting at those bastards, Henry Kirkland. Sometimes a man's gotta do what a man's gotta do."

Kirk was in a state of near shock by Mrs. Parker's hawkish stance. He'd never heard such words from her mouth. Throughout the years, she had given him advice on many occasions, from problems he'd encountered at school to social dilemmas at church. The advice was always threaded together with a unifying theme of Christian principles and values. This was a bombshell. He listened with mouth agape.

"Thank you," Kirk finally muttered. "I wish it didn't happen, but I'm afraid they gonna come after me again."

A cold look crept over Mrs. Parker.

"You still got the gun?" she asked.

"I do." He reached into his pocket and felt its presence.

"Good. And do you sleep with it?"

"Yes ma'am."

Kirk looked at Mrs. Parker's face. It was as if she'd mutated into a new person. She arose from her seat, walked to the kitchen, and opened one of the cabinets. She retrieved a bag, which looked to be quite heavy. She carried it to the table and set it down in front of Kirk. She then reached inside and pulled out a .44 Magnum handgun and a handful of bullets.

Kirk figured he must be dreaming. He pinched himself on the arm.

"Do you know how to handle yo' gun?" asked Mrs. Parker with cold eyes.

"I know a little," replied Kirk. "Uncle Willie has shown me a few things."

Mrs. Parker set the ammunition down on the table, then popped open the gun's chamber. She spun it around to make certain it was fully loaded with six bullets. She then closed the chamber and handed the gun to Kirk.

"It's loaded, so be careful," she said.

"Gosh," Kirk said as he grabbed the pistol. "I never dreamed you had a gun."

"I didn't until my husband passed on," said Mrs. Parker with misty eyes. "But I realized soon after that they ain't nobody gonna protect me, 'cept myself."

"I hear that," said Kirk, while he stared at the gun.

"Sometimes I'll drive out past Boggy Bend, to the countryside, and shoot rocks. It helps me keep a feel for the pistol. If you ain't used to shootin', it can be a bit scary."

Kirk smiled. "I can testify to that."

Mrs. Parker grabbed the gun from Kirk's hand and set it on the table. She then sat down beside him.

"I'm worried about you, Henry. So much that I pray for you every day. I don't know who or what is out to get you, but it scares the hell outta me," she said while her eyes watered over. "I don't want what happened to poor Rudy James to happen to you. I just can't bear the thought of losing you."

For the first time in his life, Kirk felt a deep connection to Mrs. Parker. She'd always been a friend of the family, despite her incessant storytelling, but he never thought of their relationship as anything more. She felt much closer now.

"Don't you worry about that," he said. "Ripp and Uncle Willie are usually around to watch my back. I'm in good hands."

Mrs. Parker wiped her eyes on a napkin, then cleared her throat.

Kirk looked at his watch and saw it was already two o'clock. "Wow," he said. "I didn't realize it was so late."

"Oh?"

"It's already two o'clock. I'm meeting some friends in a few minutes. Can I help you with all these dishes?"

"Oh, no," said a proud Mrs. Parker. "You run along and play with your friends. I would like a receipt, however."

"Sure. Sorry I forgot."

Kirk immediately pulled out his receipt booklet and recorded the amount Mrs. Parker paid for her newspapers, along with the date and time. He signed the receipt and gave a copy to Mrs. Parker.

"Thank you, Henry."

"No, thank you for the food. That was the best eatin' I've had in a long, long time."

"Glad you liked it."

Kirk held his stomach as the two walked outside, to the porch.

"Just because we're Christians doesn't mean we can't protect ourselves," she said. "You do know that, don't you?"

"I struggle with the idea of violence," Kirk said somberly.

Mrs. Parker grabbed his hand firmly. "Do you remember a few Sundays back, when the sermon talked about when Jesus went into the temple and found men selling cattle, sheep, and such?"

"Vaguely," Kirk said.

"Well, Jesus saw those men sitting at tables exchanging money in the Temple, of all places. As you can imagine, seein' such a thing in his Father's Temple made him mad, so he made a whip out of cords and drove them out."

"He did?" said Kirk, somewhat surprised.

"He did," affirmed Mrs. Parker. "Now, I know they's a lot of difference between shooting someone and driving them out of the Temple, but the point of the story is that sometimes you've got to do what you've got to do."

Kirk stared at the floor in silence. His mind was racing, trying to understand the full meaning of Mrs. Parker's words. Suddenly and without warning, Mrs. Parker started chuckling.

"What's so funny?" asked Kirk.

With a big smile on her face, Mrs. Parker lifted her head so her eyes met Kirk's. "Henry Kirkland, most folks would never believe that I read much, but I actually read just about anything I can get my hands on. Your teacher, Mrs. McCutcheon, lets me check out books from the Dunbar School library."

"Did you read a funny book?" asked Kirk, a little confused.

"No, but I just finished a book about Scotland. It so happens that in old Scotland, the man who lived near the church and cared for the church was named Kirkland. And even more, to this day, most people in Scotland refer to the church as 'Kirk'. Can you believe it?"

"Ain't that something?" said Kirk.

"You are a special boy, Kirk. Remember, God's not finished with you."

"Thanks, but I'm a little confused. Isn't murder a sin?" Kirk asked. "I thought it was pretty black and white."

"It is," replied Mrs. Parker. "But self-defense isn't murder."

"Are you telling me if I was to kill someone who's trying to kill me, Jesus will understand?"

Mrs. Parker bent over until her head was next to Kirk's.

"I'm telling you that the next time those hooligans jump you, take yo' gun and drive they ass out of the Temple, Kirk!"

# # #

Kirk made his last stop collecting newspaper money, and walked sluggishly toward his house. His stomach still ached from his over indulgence at Mrs. Parker's dinner table, but it was slowly beginning to digest. Besides, it was a small price to pay. Opportunities to eat food like that didn't come around every day, and Kirk knew he'd probably eat even more on his next visit.

Kirk looked at his watch and noticed it was already fifteen minutes after two. He and Ripp had planned an afternoon basketball game at two-thirty at the Dunbar gym. Kirk knew he would probably be a little late meeting Ripp because he still needed to go home, change clothes, and head over to the gym.

The thought of meeting Ripp at the gym gave Kirk a warm feeling. Sunday basketball pickup games were one of his favorite things to do and, due to his current emotional climate, he expected it to provide a much-needed break.

As Kirk picked up his pace, he saw Eric Morman, one of his classmates from Dunbar, running toward him. Eric was a senior and Kirk didn't know him very well. A loner, both of Eric's parents had been in and out of prison several times. The lifestyle of finding trouble was already evident in Eric, as he had scrapped with the Atoka police on several instances. He'd even spent a short sentence at the Atoka County Jail.

"Hello Eric," said Kirk. "Are you going up to the gym today?"

Eric hardly looked at Kirk as he quickly ran on by. Judging by the troubled look on his face, Kirk immediately sensed something was wrong.

Without warning, a gunshot blast roared through the neighborhood. Kirk looked down the hill, toward the source of the sound, but could see nothing out of the ordinary. The one-story houses that sat alongside the street and down the hill appeared quiet and normal. Suddenly, a short woman ran out of Eric's house and headed toward Kirk at full steam, kicking up dust from the dirt road.

Before Kirk could step out of the way, the woman was upon him.

"Paper boy, paper boy, I done killed him!" she screamed. "I shot his ass and I done killed him!"

"Who?" shouted Kirk. "Who did you kill?"

"My husband, Johnny. He's dead I tell you! Dead!"

Kirk recognized the woman as Eric's mom, Marie Morman. She was crying uncontrollably as she stepped closer and closer to Kirk.

"That sum bitch will never beat me again. Never!"

"What do you want me to do?" asked Kirk. He had no idea of the proper protocol in such a situation.

The woman rubbed her face, which was swollen under both eyes. Kirk deduced that she'd been beaten when the shooting occurred.

"He's never gonna hurt you again," said Marie while she rubbed her face. Kirk assumed that she was talking to herself.

"What do you want me to do?" Kirk begged.

"What am I gonna do?" screamed the lady. "What am I gonna do?"

Marie placed her bloody hands on his white shirt. Not knowing what to do, Kirk embraced her while she cried on his shoulder.

"Are you sure he's dead?" asked Kirk.

"I don't know! I don't know!" she screamed. "What am I gonna do?"

"Tell you what. I'll go check and see if I can help," said Kirk. "Why don't you call for an ambulance?"

As Kirk walked toward her house, he saw Marie running as fast as she could in the opposite direction. The sight of her running and screaming with blood all over her body was the most surreal thing he had ever witnessed. As fear shot up his spine, Kirk ran as fast as he could to Eric's house.

Just as he made his way to the front porch, he saw Mr. Morman lying in a pool of blood. Judging by the splattering and origin of the blood on Morman's blue jeans, he appears to have been shot in the groin.

"Mr. Morman? Mr. Morman?" asked Kirk.

Johnny Morman made no sound, other than heavy breaths. His eyes were open, so Kirk decided to approach him. As Kirk neared him, however, he brushed against the rocking chair beside Johnny. A .410 gauge shotgun that had been sitting in the chair fell. Kirk was quick to catch it in midair.

The sudden movement alerted Johnny. He started bellowing something incoherent while flailing his arms wildly. Kirk surmised he was probably in shock and tried to calm him.

"Mr. Morman, it looks like you've been hurt badly. You're gonna have to relax and calm down. You're losing a lot of blood, so you've got to stay calm."

Kirk was amazed by his own ability to stay composed, especially in lieu of all the blood and gore that surrounded him. He'd never seen such horror. The closest he'd ever come to such an atrocity was by reading old novels about World War I from his school. Just as in those dramatic scenes in the novels, he knew Mr. Morman was close to death and that he must do something.

Kirk knelt on one knee to try to calm Mr. Morman. To his surprise, however, Morman reached up and tried to grab the shotgun from his right hand. Kirk instantly turned his body, keeping the shotgun out of Morman's reach. Knowing time was of the essence, he tossed the shotgun into the hedge bushes that stood outside the front porch. He turned around and saw even more blood gushing out of Morman's blue jeans.

Kirk knew from first-aid classes to apply pressure to the wounded area. Morman resisted, but Kirk pressed down on the area below the groin, on Morman's right leg. To Kirk's dismay, the bleeding didn't stop. Kirk knew Morman was doomed.

Kirk looked down and saw his arms, hands, and upper body were covered in blood. Knowing Morman was dying, Kirk's heart began racing furiously. He saw drips of sweat falling onto Morman's legs. Try as he might, the bleeding would not stop.

Kirk heard something behind him, so he turned and saw several neighbors.

"Are any of you a nurse or a doctor?" Kirk asked, knowing the answer.

"What're you doin' boy?" asked someone from the crowd.

"I'm tryin' to stop the bleeding!" Kirk shouted. "This man is gonna die if we don't stop the bleeding!"

Not a single person stepped up to help.

"Would you at least call an ambulance?" pleaded Kirk. "This man is going to die if we don't do something!"

One of the men in the crowd walked over to the hedge bushes and spotted the shotgun.

"Damn, son. What'd you do, get mad and shoot Johnny?"

Kirk ignored the comments and continued to apply pressure. Suddenly, the blood stopped gushing. Fearing the worst, Kirk looked up and saw the wounded man's eyes had glazed over. Johnny Morman was dead.

"Damnit!" shouted Kirk.

Kirk stood to his feet while one of the neighbors walked over to him. The sirens from the ambulance blared in the background.

"Why did you kill poor Johnny?" asked the neighbor.

"I didn't," replied Kirk. "I heard a gunshot and saw his wife, so I came down and tried to help."

"Well, he's dead now," said the neighbor.

"I know," said Kirk somberly. "I know."

The ambulance personnel rushed the porch and frantically tried to aid Morman. After a few minutes, however, they stopped and shook their heads. As they walked back to the ambulance, they passed Sheriff Bill Cain. With a disgruntled look on his face, he walked straight over to Kirk.

"What's your name, boy?" asked the Sheriff Cain.

"Henry Kirkland, sir."

"Get on back to my Sheriff's car. I've got some questions that need answers."

Kirk let out a sigh, then looked at his watch. It was now well past three o'clock. Guess there won't be any basketball today, he thought.

Chapter 22

Kirk let out a great sigh as he waited patiently in the passenger seat of Sheriff Cain's car. He'd been sitting in the same position for over forty-five minutes and had seen neither hide nor hair of the Sheriff. All of the law-enforcement officials, as well as the paramedics, were still inside the house, inspecting the crime scene. Kirk wondered what was taking so long. Johnny was clearly dead. Surely the paramedics could see that.

Due to a warm day as well as his fractured state of mind, Kirk was sweating profusely. His imagination was running wild with thoughts of what the Sheriff was going to ask and do to him. He tried to envision himself sinking the game-winning jump shot for the Sooner basketball team, but each time his imagination would envision himself dribbling the ball up the floor, he'd glance at the cheering fans and see Johnny Morman, pleading for help while bleeding to death. The fans didn't seem to mind, but Kirk couldn't shake the image from his mind.

In order to break up the boredom, he stuck his head out the window of the Sheriff's car to get a better look at the crime scene. The only thing he could clearly make out on the front porch was the paramedics, who had their backs turned to him. They were looking down at Johnny's body. It didn't appear they were working on him any longer. They just stood and gazed down, almost as if they didn't know what to do next.

The Sheriff made his way through the paramedics and walked over to the neighbors. After speaking to them briefly, he walked to the bushes that surrounded the porch. He milled around for a few moments, then retrieved the shotgun. He shook his head, briefly looked at Kirk, then turned and walked back into the house.

Kirk sat back down in his seat. Beads of sweat dripped from his forehead and mixed with the dried blood on his hands. It looked more and more like his day was ruined. Frustrated, he wiped his brow, then placed his hands over his head.

The strong aroma of blood suddenly grabbed him like an iron fist. He could even taste it. It was a sweet metallic taste that reminded Kirk of weekends he'd spent with his grandparents, just outside of Stringtown. They raised cattle and hogs. In the summer, Kirk and his dad would help butcher the hogs. It was always a brutal day that Kirk dreaded. His visits to the farm were peaceful and quiet, except on butchering day.

The event would begin by Kirk's grandpa, Sam Colbert, walking into the hog pen with a hammer. He would find the hog he wanted, then hit the hog right between the eyes. The hog would fall, but would not be dead. Grandpa Sam, usually a gentle kind man, then took the razor-sharp knife and slashed the hog's throat from ear to ear. As the hog's blood gushed everywhere, Kirk's job was to help drag it to the scalding vat. Before the day was over, he would be covered in blood.

As Kirk sat in the Sheriff car, he suddenly realized that swine blood must be similar to human blood because he smelled exactly the same as he did when he butchered hogs with his granddad. The thought sent a chill up his spine.

He wondered why he didn't notice the smell earlier, when he stood over Johnny Morman's body. He surmised his mind was probably in shock while trying to save Johnny's life, and he hadn't smelled much of anything. Kirk winced as the terrible memory flooded his mind again. The whole thing was surreal. Never in his life had he witnessed something so horrific. He actually saw a man die, right before his eyes. Ripp would never believe this. As a matter of fact, Kirk could hardly believe it.

Without warning, Kirk felt a catharsis. Try as he might to stop the flood of emotion, he couldn't help it. He felt his eyes well up, and soon he was crying unabashedly. His life felt in total ruin. A week ago, he'd been jumped by thugs who would have possibly ended his life and now this. What in the hell was going on, he thought.

As Kirk wiped his eyes and shook his head in disbelief, he looked up and saw Sheriff Cain, who was now walking around the car. Kirk sat up in his seat and watched the Sheriff. In what seemed like slow motion, the overweight white Sheriff walked around the front of the car, then opened the door and was seated. With a nasty scowl on his face, he retrieved a notepad from his shirt pocket and began writing.

"You've got some 'splaining to do, boy," said Cain in a very condescending tone. "What was this about? Whiskey? Drugs? Revenge? Or was it just random?"

"I don't rightly know," said Kirk. "I've heard Johnny hadn't been very faithful to his live-in wife, Marie, and that he smacks her around from time to time, but I don't really know what would have prompted her to . . ."

The Sheriff jumped back in his seat.

"Are you tellin' me Marie put you up to this?"

"Put me up to what?" asked Kirk with blank look on his face.

"Killing Johnny Morman."

"What the hell are you talking about?" asked an incensed Kirk. "I didn't kill him. I was trying to save the poor bastard."

"Save him?" said a disbelieving Sheriff Cain.

"Yeah, save him. He was bleeding somethin' terrible when I got here and I was trying to stop the bleeding."

"So, you're telling me you didn't kill him?"

"Hell no, I didn't kill him. I was walkin' home from my newspaper route and heard a blast and then . . ."

"I thought the newspapers were delivered early in the morning?" interrupted the Sheriff.

Kirk grew impatient with the Sheriff's accusations, but a voice inside his head warned he'd better not show it.

"The papers are delivered early in the morning," Kirk said calmly. "I collect money for the papers on the last Sunday of each month. I had just finished collecting all the money and was walking home when this happened."

Kirk looked up and noticed quite a crowd of neighbors gathered in front of Sheriff Cain's car. There must have been fifteen of them, all facing Kirk and the Sheriff. They were pointing directly at Kirk while they talked. Kirk suddenly felt crushed by an enormous burden of guilt, like the kind he felt when he got caught lying to his mom, only a hundred times more pronounced. Even though he was innocent, he presumed they all thought him as the monster who killed their neighbor in cold blood. He would never live this down, he thought. And his poor mom. She'll be devastated when she hears the news.

He looked over and studied the Sheriff's face, and could tell the wheels were turning inside the lawman's mind. As he thumped the pen down harder and harder on the notepad, the Sheriff appeared to be growing angrier with each passing second.

"I know this doesn't look good, but I promise, I didn't kill Mr. Morman, I swear to you, I didn't kill him."

Cain slowly turned his head and locked onto Kirk's eyes.

"Would you like to know what I think?" asked the Sheriff.

"Yes, sir."

"I think you're a gawddamned liar!" screamed Cain. "Everyone knows Marie liked to mess around with everyone in town. Why do you think he beat her all the time?"

Kirk's mind went blank. He could feel his legs moving toward the door. He tried to reach for the latch to make his escape, but extreme fright took away all feeling in his arms.

"I didn't even know Marie, much less mess around with her and I promise, I didn't kill her husband," Kirk said in a weak voice.

"I have witnesses that say they saw you throwing the murder weapon out in the bushes. Care to explain that?" the Sheriff screamed.

"I threw the shotgun out in the bushes because Mr. Morman tried to take it from me when he woke up. I don't think he knew what he was doing. I swear to you, I didn't kill him."

"Then who did?" yelled Sheriff Cain with a condescending inflection.

Kirk paused for a moment. After several moments of feeling mentally numb, his intellect came back. He tried to keep calm and gain perspective. As he sat in silence, breathing slowly, a cold feeling came over him. Maybe the Sheriff was trying to force a confession. Through the years, Kirk had heard of black folks taking the fall for crimes others committed. Maybe that's what the Sheriff was doing.

"I can't say for certain who shot Johnny," said Kirk in a stronger voice. "I wasn't there. However, I did see Marie run out of the house."

"Oh, really?" said the Sheriff. "Did you talk to her?"

Kirk nodded. "She was actin' very irrational."

"What exactly did she say?"

"She said he would never hit her again," replied Kirk. Due to his heightened emotions, his memory was still a little fuzzy. He tried to remember all the details, but his only strong recollection was the dust flying from her feet when she ran toward him. He tried with all his might to remember her telling him that she confessed to the murder, but he just couldn't remember.

"Did she say Johnny would never hit her again?"

"I suppose she was referring to Johnny, but I'm not sure."

"And did you see Marie shoot Johnny?"

"No."

With a smirk, the Sheriff nodded slowly, as if to indicate he knew Kirk was lying. He threw his notepad on the dash of the car.

"I'm getting real tired of playin' games with you, boy."

Kirk grew more suspicious that he was being railroaded.

"I'm getting tired, too."

"I think you need to come down to the station."

"Okay," said Kirk in a shaky voice.

Sheriff Cain opened his door and jumped out of the vehicle. "Get outta the car!"

Kirk stepped out of the vehicle, and the Sheriff strode over to where he stood. Cain spun Kirk's tall thin body around and forced him over the car hood. He then frisked Kirk down from head to toe. When he felt the gun in his pocket, he stopped.

"Gawddamn, boy! What's this? You sit in my car talking about how damned innocent you are. Now I find you're carrying a gun!"

Kirk's mouth was so dry he could hardly talk. "My Uncle Willie gave it to me for protection. My parents just left me all alone," he muttered.

"Who's Uncle Willie?"

"Willie Neal."

"Holy Mother of God!" Sheriff Cain exclaimed. "Willie Neal is your uncle? That doesn't help your case, my friend."

"They's nothing illegal about carrying a gun in this town. And I have never hurt anyone with it," Kirk said in a shaky voice.

"What's your name, boy?" the Sheriff asked as he reached for his handcuffs.

"Henry Kirkland, Jr."

"Boy, I know every family here in nigger town and I know that there ain't no Kirklands over here. Stop lying about your name and tell me who you are. Who are your parents?"

For a moment, Kirk had a hard time remembering the name of his parents. Finally, he forced out the words. "Henry and Laura Colbert."

The Sheriff pulled Kirk up off the car and stared at him. He placed his hands on his hips. "Laura Colbert is your mama?" he asked.

"She is," said Kirk.

"I didn't know that," the Sheriff said calmly. "She worked for me down at the Sheriff's office for years. She's quite a lady."

"Yes, sir."

After several moments of contemplation, Sheriff Cain patted Kirk on the back.

"Tell you what," said the Sheriff. "I know your mamma pretty good and I don't think she raised a murderer. Why don't you get on home and when I have more questions, I'll come by your house."

"Yes, sir," said Kirk in a weak voice.

The world was spinning so fast, the next thing Kirk saw was a trail of dust following the Sheriff's car as it drove away. He looked around and saw the neighbors staring and pointing at him. He quickly turned and began his walk home.

At that moment in time, giant spiders could have began devouring all the houses Kirk passed on the way home, and he wouldn't have been surprised in the least bit. After what he'd just experienced, astonishment would forever be nothing more than an old acquaintance.

Chapter 23

Kirk looked down at the old washtub and noticed the water's reddish tint, from all the dried blood he'd scrubbed off his body. He used an old washcloth to scour himself, scrubbing in places he'd never scrubbed before. Mom would be proud, he thought. After the shock wore off over Johnny's death, the thought of having the dead man's blood on his body gave Kirk the worst case of the willies he'd encountered. He had scrubbed his arms so hard they were raw. He looked at his hands and noticed Johnny's blood still underneath his fingernails. Kirk let out a great sigh and continued to scrub.

He shivered, naked in the cold house. Kirk inspected himself and found all of the blood seemed to be gone. He stepped out of the wash tub, dried off, and got dressed. After he'd placed a log in the woodstove, he walked into the living room. He could never remember a time in his life when his body and his mind were so drained. He sat down on the couch, let out a great sigh, and closed his eyes.

Kirk had only been asleep for a few minutes when he heard a loud knock on his door. He jumped up and ran to the kitchen, where he found his pistol lying beside the washtub. He cracked open the chamber to make sure it was loaded, and proceeded back to the front door. Just as the visitors knocked loudly again, Kirk aimed his gun at the door.

"Who is it?" screamed Kirk.

"It's Ripp. Open the damn door."

Kirk walked to the window and looked outside. He saw Ripp and Battle Axe waiting outside. Kirk unlatched the door and opened it.

"What took you so long?" asked Ripp, as he walked into Kirk's house.

"Sorry," Kirk said. "I was sleeping. Been a rough day."

Battle Axe was quick to walk over and give Kirk a long and firm hug. "We just heard about what happened. Are you alright?"

Kirk nodded. "Yeah," he said. "That's about the only thing I can be."

He shook his head while he walked to the kitchen counter and set down the gun. He then sat on the couch and stared out the window with a blank expression on his face.

Battle Axe looked to Ripp, who shrugged.

"Are you sure you alright?" Battle Axe asked again.

Kirk shook his head, but said nothing.

Ripp and Battle Axe walked to the couch and sat beside Kirk.

"Judging from the gossip that's goin' round town faster than a striped-assed ape, I'd say you've had a pretty bad day," Battle Axe said softly. "Are you sure you're alright?"

Kirk stared at the wall across the room and said nothing. He shook his head slightly.

"You didn't kill Johnny, did you?" asked Ripp.

Battle Axe reached over Kirk's back and popped Ripp on the back of his head.

"Mind yo' manners, boy! Can't you see poor Kirk is ate up on the inside and don't wanna talk? Yo' actin' like a damned fool, askin' such a thing!"

Kirk shot Battle Axe a look of gratitude. "Thanks."

"No problem," replied Battle Axe.

After a few moments of dead silence, Battle Axe could take the suspense no longer.

"So did you kill him?" he blurted.

Kirk placed his head down in the hands. Ripp reached across and popped his dad on the back of the head.

"I'm sorry," said Battle Axe. "I'm just concerned, that's all."

Not knowing what to do or say, Ripp and Battle Axe just stared at Kirk. After a few moments, Kirk removed his hands from his face and leaned back on the couch.

"Thanks for coming," said Kirk in a weak voice. "It means a lot."

"Would you rather be alone?" asked Battle Axe. "'Cause we can leave if you'd rather . . ."

"No, please stay," interrupted Kirk. As he placed his head down in his hands once again, he could hold it no longer. Tears ran down his face. Battle Axe placed his right arm on Kirk's shoulders.

"What's buggin' you? Did things get out of control and you did what you had to do?" asked Battle Axe.

"No," Kirk said as he cleared his throat. "I didn't kill Johnny, if that's what you mean. I just happened to be walking home and heard a gunshot. His wife ran up to me and started screaming that she killed him, then ran off. I figured something bad had happened, so I walked down to they house and saw him on the porch, bleeding to death."

Both Battle Axe and Ripp let out a huge sigh of relief.

"You don't know how happy we are to hear you say that," said Battle Axe. "People is talkin' and they sayin'..."

"I don't care what folks are sayin'! That don't make a damn to me!" Kirk shouted, then paused. "I just saw a man bleed to death and I couldn't help him. I did everything I knew to do and I still couldn't help him." Kirk began crying uncontrollably.

"We know you did," said Ripp. "We know you did everything you could."

"I tried with all my might to stop the bleeding, but I couldn't slow it down," Kirk sobbed. "I tried everything I knew!"

Battle Axe turned and hugged Kirk. For several minutes, the room was silent as Kirk sobbed uncontrollably and Ripp patted him on the back.

Trying to break the moment, Ripp stood up, walked to the kitchen and found a dish towel. He returned to the couch and handed it to Kirk, who released his hold on Battle Axe and wiped the tears from his face.

"Did you know Johnny?" asked Ripp.

"No," said Kirk. "Never met him."

"Then why you takin' this so hard?"

Kirk paused for a moment. He wiped his face again, then stood and walked to the kitchen.

"It's not just Johnny, it's everything," Kirk said. "I've been jumped by some goons, some crazy damned banker is after me, and a man just died, practically in my arms. I have no family here. I'm all alone, and there's a hole in the roof of my house. Ever since my family left, I've had nothing but bad luck."

Ripp scratched his head. "I hate to make you feel worse, but uh, everyone in town thinks you killed Johnny."

"Shit!" yelled Kirk. "You're kiddin' me?"

"No," Battle Axe and Ripp said in unison.

Kirk jumped off the couch, walked to the counter and picked up a fork. As he thumped it against the counter, he contemplated. Ripp and Battle Axe sat and watched, unsure of what to say.

"Sheriff Cain thought that, too," said Kirk. "He interrogated me in his car. I thought he was gonna arrest me, right there on the spot."

"What did you tell him?" asked Battle Axe.

"The truth. As I was walking home to get ready to go to the gym, his wife stopped me and told me Johnny wouldn't beat her no more. I told the Sheriff, but he didn't seem to buy it. He was going to arrest me, until he found out who my momma is."

"Oh, that's right," said Battle Axe. "Your mom used to work for him. Seems like they got along pretty good."

"Well, she saved my butt," said Kirk. "I'd be behind bars right now if it weren't for her."

"This is not good," Battle Axe said with a grim look in his eye. "It ain't nothin' for the man to frame a colored. This has happened before."

"What do you mean?" said Kirk.

"If white folks get theyselves into a jam, they ain't above blamin' an innocent black man."

"I know, I know," said Kirk. It's sad that I have to deal with this."

"One of the worst cases happened up in Tulsa, just a few years ago. A black man by the name of Jess Hollins was sentenced to death for allegedly raping a white girl. The police brought him in and questioned him. He was illiterate, yet he signed a full confession and was given the death penalty."

"Damn," said Ripp, still sitting on the couch.

"The jury at his trial was all white and the judge made sure the trial went very fast 'cause he remembered the Tulsa Race Riot and didn't want no mob violence. The white gal Hollins allegedly raped was a floozy who frequented black bars. She got around, if you know what I mean. They was witnesses who came up on 'em when they was doing they thing and the witnesses said it was consensual. Didn't matter though. He went to trial three times and was found guilty three times."

"Did he die in the electric chair?" asked a terrified Kirk.

"No," replied Battle Axe. "On his third trial, he was sentenced to life in prison. He died a young man in prison of a broken spirit, or so they say."

"Don't that beat all?" said Ripp.

"The point is that black folks don't always get a fair shake. As unfair as it is, sometimes they take the blame fo' things they didn't do. Marie is a white girl, she'll get 'white justice'. You my boy, won't be treated the same. It's a shitty thang, but it be the truth."

Kirk sat down beside Ripp. "You're not makin' me feel any better."

Battle Axe walked to Kirk and Ripp. "Look, I'm not tryin' to scare you. I just want you to know what yo' up against."

"I know," said Kirk. "I appreciate the truth. And I appreciate you both coming over."

Battle Axe looked to the window and saw that it was nearing dusk. He looked at his wristwatch. "Damn," he said. "Ripp, yo' momma's gonna kick our butts if we don't get home and eat. Would you like to come with us, Kirk?"

"Thanks, but I really need to rest," said Kirk. "I'm a little worn out."

"We understand," said Ripp. "Want me to come over after dinner and stay? I don't mind."

Kirk patted Ripp on the knee. "Thanks, but that gun makes me feel pretty safe."

"Alright, but if I hear a shot in the middle of the night, we'll come a runnin'," said Ripp as he and Battle Axe walked to the door.

"Goodbye," replied Kirk.

Battle Axe and Ripp walked through the door at the same time. As their shoulders simultaneously hit the door frame, their bodies were pushed toward each other, forcing their heads to knock together. An ugly grimace formed on Battle Axe's face as he popped Ripp on the head with his hand. The scene made Kirk chuckle as he remembered the cartoon he saw in McAlester at the movie house. Ripp and his dad would be good in the movies, thought Kirk.

He smiled and sat down to gather his thoughts. Once again a slight tap came at the door. Kirk saw Ripp standing on the small porch as he opened the door.

"What did you forget?"

"Well, when we got in the car, Dad had an idea," Ripp said quietly as he cleared his throat several times.

"What sort of idea did your old man come up with? I'll bet it's interesting," said Kirk.

"Well, you know, he thought maybe we should give you something."

"Is it a sack full of money?" Kirk joked, "'Cause a sack full of money sure would make me feel better!"

"No," Ripp muttered, "It's this." Ripp opened his hand, revealing a silver dollar.

"I hate to sound ungrateful, but that doesn't help near as much as a sack full of money," Kirk said jovially.

"It should make you feel better, because this is the dollar Skeet gave me when I left for college," Ripp said with moist eyes.

"Oh, man, I can't take your dollar from Skeet," Kirk said, staring at the iconic coin. "I know how much this means to you because he gave me one when I started at the store."

"Yeah, I know, but we want you to have it. I think you need it more right now. It will give you strength and also be a constant reminder you will make it through all this shit."

Kirk didn't want to take the coin, but knew his best friend was pained by the current predicament. After he thought about it for a few moments, Kirk realized Ripp and Battle Axe probably needed to feel like they contributed something in his time of need. Kirk grabbed the coin and looked into Ripp's eyes.

"This is very thoughtful, Ripp. Thanks. Be sure to tell Battle Axe I appreciate it."

Ripp slipped through the door and headed for Battle Axe's car. Kirk looked down and admired his newest prize possession.

# # #

Kirk shut the door and walked back to the old couch. Just as he closed his eyes, he was awoken with yet another knock. Alert, he ran to the kitchen and picked up the gun.

"Who is it?" he yelled.

"It's me, Young Henry," said the voice.

Kirk scratched his head. That can't be, he thought. He walked to the window and looked outside. Even though it was dark, he easily recognized Mr. Carney.

"What the hell?" said Kirk. He opened the door and in walked Skeet.

"Hello, Young Henry," Carney said while removing his hat.

"Good evening." Kirk hid the gun in his pocket.

"I'm sorry to bother you at this hour on a Sunday night, but I just heard the news."

"Yes, sir," replied Kirk.

"Are you alright?" asked Carney.

Kirk walked to the couch and sat down. Carney followed.

"I guess so," said Kirk. "I don't rightly know how to feel, though. I've never been through such a thing."

"What exactly happened? There's talk around town you had something to do with . . ."

"I didn't kill him," interrupted Kirk. "He was dying when I got there. I did my best to save him, but it was too late."

"I see," said Carney. "I know rumors can sometimes run wild in small towns."

"Please believe me. I had nothing to do with killing Johnny. It was his wife. She told me right after she did it."

"I believe you. Have you talked to the authorities?"

"Yes. Sheriff Cain asked me a lot of questions right afterward."

"And he let you go?"

"Yes, sir."

Carney smiled. "Well, then. I don't think there's much left to worry about. Sounds to me like this will work itself out."

"I sure hope so."

While Carney looked at Kirk, his smile slowly disappeared.

"There's something else," said Carney. "I also heard you recently got cornered over at the Stringtown dance and pulled a gun."

Kirk froze. His right hand made sure his gun was still in his pants' pocket. After feeling it and knowing the gun was safely concealed, he paused. He didn't want Carney to know the truth, but he also knew he was cornered.

"That is true," said Kirk. "Me and Ripp were on a date with some girls and these goons jumped us. I really didn't have much of a choice."

Carney looked down to his hands. Kirk sensed he was uneasy.

"I hope that doesn't disappoint you," said Kirk. "Uncle Willie gave me the gun. He said he'd been hearing some bad people were coming for me."

Again, Carney failed to respond. He just sat on the couch without saying a word. The silence was killing Kirk, who now had a lump in his stomach the size of Atoka.

"You read the Good Book, don't you, Young Henry?"

"Yes, I read the Bible," Kirk replied. "Why?"

"Now, I'm not one to go around spoutin' off verses to impress people, but I read it as much as I can," said Carney. "The Book of Matthew tells us to 'enter through the narrow gate. For wide is the gate and broad is the road that leads to destruction, and many enter through it.' And He says flat out that narrow is the gate and difficult is the way that leads to life.' Do you know what the scripture is telling us?"

"I figure it's saying it's easier for us to choose evil, which is the road most folks take."

"I think you're right," said Carney. "And that's what worries me. I'm not upset you had a gun. As a matter of fact, I'm glad you had a way of defending yourself when those goons jumped you. The thing that worries me is why are goons after you?"

"I don't know," said Kirk. "I've done nothing I know of to make people upset with me."

"Is there anything I need to know? Something you haven't told me?"

Kirk wanted to tell Carney he strongly suspected Butch to be behind the attack, but he wasn't sure how he'd take it.

"No sir," said Kirk.

Carney nodded.

"If that changes and you need to talk to me, please don't hesitate. Henry, you are standing at the gate. The next few months you will decide which one to choose. I can only do so much for you. You have to decide the narrow way to life on your own. There is a gate out of the crime and poverty that surrounds you. I am here if I can help."

"Yes sir," said Kirk.

Carney walked over to Kirk and extended his hand.

"Do you promise?" Carney said with a solemn expression.

Kirk stood and shook Carney's hand. "I promise," he said.

"Good," said Carney. "Now, I'd best get home before Jo calls the Sheriff. And, by the way, if you have any more problems with him, you come to me first."

"Yes, sir," said Kirk.

Carney put his hat back on and walked to the door.

"How did you know where I live?" asked Kirk. "I was kinda surprised to see you in this part of town."

"As were your neighbors," laughed Carney. "I was relying on memory. I came here once to bring your mother some medicine back when you were a baby. On my way here today, I accidentally drove to your neighbor's house. Let's just say they were a little surprised when I knocked on their door and asked for Henry Kirkland."

Kirk laughed. "They probably thought I was in trouble with the law. Especially after what happened today."

"Probably so," said Carney as he walked through the door. "Would you like to come to our house for dinner tonight?"

"No, thanks. I have some homework and other things to do. But thanks."

"No problem," said Carney. "You remember what I said."

"I will," said Kirk. "I promise."

Chapter 24

Weatherford, Oklahoma, 1989

"So what does the coin Ripp gave you represent?" asked Wade with curiosity.

"It stands for hope," said Dr. Kirkland. "I'll be honest with you, Wade, when I sat at my house that evening before Ripp, Battle Axe, and Carney came by, it was one of the lowest points in my life. I felt like I was going to get railed down the line of the justice system. It was terrible."

"What was it like for Sheriff Cain to grill you like he did?"

Dr. Kirkland rolled his eyes. "It was terrible. Have you ever been to jail?"

"No," said Wade.

"It's the most helpless feeling you can encounter," said Dr. Kirkland. "You have absolutely no rights. When they put those cuffs on you, you're at their mercy. They can do whatever they want and your only option is to take it."

"But why did the Sheriff back off so fast?"

"Because he had worked with my momma. She was quite a lady. I promise you, the only thing that kept me out of jail was my mom's good reputation."

"Did you really feel like you were going to take the fall for a crime you didn't commit?"

"I thought there was a chance," said Dr. Kirkland. "Back then, if some powerful white person wanted a black man to take the blame for a crime he didn't commit, it happened. Again, it was a much different world back then."

"Did you want to go to Langston, to be with your parents?"

"I did, until Ripp came by and gave me the coin. I don't really know why, but it really reassured me things would be alright, if I hung in there. I know it sounds silly, but it gave me hope. Another thing that really lifted my spirits was the shoes."

"Did Skeet never mention the shoes again?"

"Nope," replied Dr. Kirkland. "I don't think he ever even looked at them again. I was too shy to say thanks, so I wrote a quick note of thanks and left it on the counter in the pharmacy. He never said another word. I tell you this, I've never met anyone like Skeet Carney. He was the most trusting, generous man I ever met."

Suddenly, Wade was hit with an epiphany. "That's why you carry the toy gun in your briefcase," he said. "It's because you had to carry a gun when you were a kid."

"Ha!" laughed Dr. Kirkland. "I've never thought of it like that. To be honest, I just like watching the reaction from the students."

"Why do you think Butch disliked you so much?" asked Wade.

"He was truly a bigot. Any black man in the room would make him mad. Most folks just viewed blacks as 'invisible', meaning they didn't really mind them as long as they didn't bother anyone. Butch, on the other hand, just hated blacks, period."

"I can't imagine living in such a time and place without my family. It's truly amazing you made it, especially with the random violence and dead bodies."

Dr. Kirkland laughed. "Things had calmed down by the time I was a kid. You should hear some of the stories my dad, Henry Colbert, told us about when he was a kid. It was rough and dangerous."

"Sounds to me like it was pretty tough," said Wade.

"Oh, it gets worse," said Dr. Kirkland, with a stone face. "Much worse . . ."

Chapter 25

Atoka, Oklahoma,

1945

Sheriff Cain looked at his watch in disgust. It was now nine-thirty, which meant that he'd been waiting outside Butch's office for more than an hour. Making customers wait was the standard protocol for Butch, but it always incensed Cain more than he could bear. Butch discovered early in his career that people who came for loans at the bank were so eager to get the money they would put up with just about anything, much like patients waiting for a doctor. And since doctors also came to him for loans, Butch deduced he was simply the most important professional in the community, which entitled him to wealth, power, and privilege. Butch even directed his secretary to double book appointments, just so customers could wait.

As Sheriff Cain simmered, he couldn't help but overhear Butch's conversation with his old friend, Terry Brooks. Terry was a vibrant seventy-three-year-old man who'd been ranching his whole life. Back before Cain was elected Sheriff of Atoka County, he worked for Terry as a hand on his ranch, located north of Atoka. He always stayed in contact with Terry and considered him to be a very good friend.

Sheriff Cain could tell by the conversation Butch was trying to pull a fast one on Terry. The scene brought a smile to Cain's face because Terry was a kind, gentle man who was known for his charity and even temperament, but he had a much meaner side if the right buttons were pushed. While the lackadaisical old man didn't appear threatening and mean, he could be as ferocious as a lion, if cornered.

"I was reviewing your accounts and found the amount of money you owe me, I mean the bank, is greater than the value of your land," Butch said in a sympathetic voice.

"I realize that," said Terry.

"This creates a little problem for us," said Butch. "I just got word from the bank's board of directors they need more collateral."

"More collateral?" asked Terry, stunned. "But why? Collateral has never been a problem before."

Watching through the window of Butch's office, Sheriff Cain saw Terry was growing uneasy.

"Yes, I know, Terry, but the bank has implemented some new changes in our lending procedures and we're tightening down the policies."

"Tightening the policies, huh?" Terry said with disbelief.

"What I'm trying to say," said Butch in a calm voice, "is that we're going to be forced to call the note if we can't get some more collateral."

"But I'm not late on any payments," said Terry. "You can't change the rules right in the middle of the game."

"Oh, no," said a smiling Butch. "We're not changing the rules. In fact, these new policies have been put in place by the bank to protect you, not the bank."

Terry shook his head. "That doesn't even make sense. How could this possibly help me?"

"Because our mission with these precautions is to make sure you don't become late on your payments. Therefore, if you're never late, you won't ever face foreclosure," Butch said with a beaming smile.

"This doesn't make a lick of sense!" shouted Terry.

Sheriff Cain could see Terry's face turn red. Cain smiled. He knew fireworks were on their way.

"Now, now," said Butch condescendingly. "No need in getting upset about this. I just want you to know we're going to have to work something out in order for us to maintain the good standing status for your account."

"If it's not one thing with you leeches, it's another."

Sheriff Cain laughed while he eavesdropped on the conversation. He loved the fact someone was making Butch's life difficult.

"I know we can work this out," said Butch. "There are things we can do to prevent going into foreclosure."

"Such as?" snapped Terry.

"Well," said Butch. "I've noticed you have an enormous amount of oil and gas minerals underneath your property."

"How did you know I own those?" asked Terry. "What did you do, go down to the county courthouse and check?"

"I didn't personally," said Butch, "but it is the policy of the bank to know our customers. Which makes me curious. The money you owe the bank is all operational debt. Why do you keep borrowing money, year after year, when you continue to lose money? Why don't you just quit farming?"

"I've just had some bad luck, that's all," said Terry, who was still in no mood to make small talk. "I figure next year will be better."

Butch laughed. "But you always say that. Why don't you just call it quits and stop using your land as collateral to buy seed and fuel?"

Terry wasn't amused with Butch's commentary. His silence didn't stop the chatter, however.

"I remember old man Peterson telling me about this very thing after he received a huge check from an oil well they hit on his land. He said he would farm until all the oil money was gone. Sure enough, when the oil money ran out, what did he do? He dragged his pitiful ass down here with his tail between his legs and his hand out," Butch laughed boisterously.

Terry failed to see the humor in Butch's belittlement of his occupation.

"You should be grateful for men of the land like Peterson and myself. Without us, leeches like you would be cleaning toilets somewhere," said Terry with a stone face.

Terry's comment wiped the smile from Butch's face.

"I like to think I would be running the financials of a big company if I weren't here," Butch said glumly.

"I'm sure you would like to think so." Terry folded his arms. "Now, why don't you quit dancing around and tell me what it is you want."

For the first time in the conversation, Terry's words rattled Butch. He knew Terry wasn't buying into his con. Growing more and more nervous with each passing second, his appearance was overshadowed by the fear in his eyes. He looked hard at Terry.

"I have a lot of persuasion with the board," said Butch. "If you and I could come up with an agreement, I think I could sway them into forgetting about adding additional collateral to your note."

Terry rolled his eyes in disgust. There was no doubt Butch was about to drop a bomb.

"And what kind of 'agreement' might this be?" Terry asked.

"A very simple one. A very, very simple agreement."

"So simple, I can't refuse, right?"

Butch turned around and retrieved some paperwork from his briefcase. He laid the papers on the desk.

"If I could get some commitment from you that you're serious about paying your note, then I'll make sure the board backs off," Butch said in a shaky voice.

Sheriff Cain was surprised to see the banker so rattled. In all the years he'd known Butch, he'd never known him to act this scared. Maybe it was because he wasn't used to confrontation.

"Again, you're dancing, Butch. Tell me what it is you're asking."

"If you'll sign over your minerals to me, then I'll direct the board to back off. After they agree, I'll sign your minerals right back over to you. See, it's a very simple agreement."

Terry froze. After a few seconds, he looked to the ceiling and shook his head.

"Are you out of your mind?" said Terry in a calm voice. "I owe this bank sixty-five thousand dollars and you're asking me to sign over to you five thousand acres of minerals?"

In too far to back out now, Butch knew he had to at least show strength.

"It's a great deal, isn't it?" said Butch. "Those minerals haven't been leased out to oil companies for a couple of years. They're just sitting there, not making you any money at all. With my proposal, you can make them work for you now. When all this is cleared up and some company wants to lease them to drill a well, I'll sign them back over. See, it's win-win for you."

"I have a brother who is a lawyer in Oklahoma City. He once told me a banker actually did this very thing to a farmer in Oklahoma City. When the old farmer finally figured out that the minerals were actually valued over one hundred times more than the bank paid him, he sued and won the minerals back, plus several hundred thousands dollars in punitive damages."

Butch knew the jig was up, and that he wasn't dealing with an ignorant farmer. It was time to retreat.

"Maybe this deal is not for you," said Butch.

Growing more and more incensed, Terry stood and walked over to Butch's side.

"How many little old ladies have actually fallen for this line of shit?" Terry's voice thundered.

"I don't know what you mean," said Butch, who was now sweating.

"Is this how you've made your fortune? You use fear and intimidation to coax old ignorant farmers into signing everything over to you and then you sell the minerals before they ever know what hit them?"

"I take great offense to what you're implying. This is an honest bank and I am an honest banker."

Terry stepped close to Butch and stuck his finger in his face.

"The only honest thing you've ever done in your life is not serving in the military because you're such a damned coward. I'm an old man, Butch, but if you have hair one between your legs, you'll come outside with me right now."

Cain knew things were about to get out of control, so he entered Butch's office.

"Morning, Sheriff," said Terry. "I guess you overheard what this piece of shit was trying to do to me?"

"Uh, no sir," said Cain. "It's not my nature to eavesdrop on conversations that aren't intended for my ears."

"Well, let me fill you in. In an effort to protect me from the bank's board of directors, sweet ol' Butch was using fear to force me into signing over a million dollars worth of minerals for a sixty-five-thousand dollar debt," Terry said, looking down on the banker. "So tell me, Butch, how many old widows have you tried this on and actually succeeded? How many children are broke and hungry now because you took their rightful inheritance?"

Knowing the Sheriff was there to protect him, Butch's confidence grew. He jumped out of the chair and stood nose-to-nose with Terry.

"I'll not have you diminish my good name," shouted Butch. "This meeting is over. You can either leave of your own free will or I will have you thrown out."

Knowing that he'd done plenty to damage Butch's ego, Terry ended the confrontation.

"I've never in my life met a bigger coward. You're the lowest of the low, Butch. Calling you a criminal would be an insult to criminals everywhere. If you ever decide to grow a pair, you let me know. I'd love to beat some sense into that thick head of yours," said a calm but infuriated Terry.

Before Terry turned to leave the office, he looked down and spit a mouthful of tobacco spit on Butch's fancy dress shoes. He looked Butch in the eye, then turned around and walked out of the room.

"Heathen," said Butch, his face flustered. He grabbed a tissue and wiped his shoes. As he walked to the trashcan, he used the tissue to wipe off sweat from his face, leaving tobacco spit on his cheeks. It took everything in Cain's power to keep from laughing, but he kept a straight face.

Without warning, Butch grabbed a boat-anchor paperweight from his desk and threw it with all his might at the wall. Sheriff Cain's jovial mood instantly turned fearful.

"The nerve of that man!" screamed Butch. "To think he can talk to me like that. Who does he think he is?"

Sheriff Cain noticed a hole in the wall. He sighed, and turned to face Butch.

"You should calm down," said Cain. "I'm sure the other customers in the bank are getting concerned."

"I don't care!" screamed Butch. "This is MY bank and if I want to drive a car through the wall, I damn well will."

"I don't know why you needed to see me this morning, but I'm not going to sit here and watch you throw a fit like a little girl." Cain walked to the door. "Call me after you've grown up."

Sheriff Cain's insubordination riled Butch. His face turned a beet red. "Sit your ass down in that chair! You'll not walk away from me until I tell you to walk away from me."

Butch's threatening demeanor did little to intimidate Sheriff Cain. He continued his walk toward the door.

"Don't you walk away from me!" screamed Butch. "I'll call every note! I'll file the foreclosure paperwork myself!"

Knowing Butch's threats were real, Cain stopped walking. Unlike Terry Brooks, Cain didn't have the capital nor the assets to go about it on his own. He and his farm were saddled in debt, and it grew worse each month. He couldn't survive without the bank and Butch knew it.

When Cain turned around and looked at Butch, the sight made him weak in his knees.

"What do you want from me?" Cain asked

"Sit your ass in that chair," said Butch, still wearing Terry's spit on his cheek. Cain smiled and sat down.

"Why did you want to see me this morning?" asked Cain.

Butch walked over and closed the door. He returned to his desk.

"Where are you in the investigation of Johnny Morman?"

"It's all but finished," said Sheriff Cain. "Why?"

"What have you found out?"

"Well, I shouldn't really be talking about this, but I've interviewed everyone involved over the past three days. It's pretty obvious Johnny had been beating Marie for months. She had enough, so she shot and killed him."

"How do you know someone else didn't kill him? How do you know it was Marie?"

Sheriff Cain was growing impatient with Butch's questions. Nonetheless, he knew the banker held the cards.

"Because she told me. She admitted it when I told her I understood why she would do such a thing. What's more, she'll probably get off without serving time. Juries are pretty sympathetic to abused women."

Butch reached into his desk and removed a flask of whiskey. He took a snort, then slammed it on the desk.

"She's very poor, right?" asked Butch, with sweat running down his face.

"Well, yeah. Why?"

"How much do you think it would take to make her recant her story?"

"Pardon?"

"How much do you think it would take to bribe her into saying she didn't kill Johnny?"

Sheriff Cain looked around the empty room, as if he were checking for invisible people hiding behind the chairs.

"Have you forgotten that I'm the Sheriff?" asked Cain.

"Have you forgotten that you owe me more money than you can pay back in a lifetime? You're not the Sheriff. You're my property, and you'll do as I say."

A sick feeling rumbled around in Cain's guts. Of course, he was extremely aggravated by Butch's words, but unfortunately, Butch was right. Cain let out a long breath. "What are you getting at?"

"Pin it on the nigger boy."

"What?" said a shocked Cain.

"That nigger boy who works for Skeet. Pin it on him."

"What in the hell are you talking about?" asked a disbelieving Cain.

"Are you deaf? I want you to frame that wise ass boy. It's very simple. Pay off Marie so she'll recant her story, then frame the nigger boy."

"Do you know what you're saying?" asked Sheriff Cain. "Do you know the trouble you could get into if you get caught? Come on, Butch. You'll never get away with this."

"No one's gonna give a damn about that boy. There's no way we'll get caught."

"Why are you so hell bent to hurt this kid? If your plan were to work out, he'd go to jail for years, maybe worse."

"He deserves it," said Butch. "He's humiliated me for the last time."

"There's a lot I'll do to keep my farm, but I'm not so sure I can . . ."

"Don't go ridin' the moral high ground on me, Sheriff Cain," Butch interrupted. He reached into his desk and removed a stack of paperwork. "Do you see what I'm holding in my hand?"

The paperwork was blank foreclosure notices.

"I do," said Sheriff Cain.

"And I'm guessing I don't need to connect the dots for you, do I?"

The sick feeling in Cain's gut was more than he could stand. He stood and walked toward the door.

"You're a sick man, Butch. A very sick man."

Butch knew he was losing him. It was time to pull out all the stops.

"I hear your granddad homesteaded your farm. It sure will be a shame to think you're the sorry bastard who lost it to the bank. Your shame will be the talk of the town."

"It'd be an even bigger shame if I sent an innocent boy to the electric chair," Sheriff Cain said.

In a bold and brave move, Cain walked through the door. As he turned to close it again, he found Butch right behind him.

"I know that place means a lot to you, Sheriff. What're you gonna tell your kids?"

Sheriff Cain tried to close the door, but was stopped by Butch's hand. Knowing all attempts had failed, Butch had only one option up his sleeve. It was do or die.

"I'll forgive your debt," said Butch.

Sheriff Cain raised his eyebrows.

"That's right," said Butch. "Every last dime. You do this for me and you'll be a new man, free of debt."

As the notion of financial freedom swirled around in his head, Butch's request suddenly seemed less appalling. After a few moments of weighing the possibilities, Cain made his decision. He turned and walked away from Butch.

"You just think about what I'm proposing," Butch said. "You'll never have an opportunity like this again. Don't let it pass you by."

Sheriff Cain nodded slightly and continued out of the bank. Butch shook his head and he watched him walk away.

Chapter 26

While Josephine poured water onto the ferns that hung beside the huge office windows, movement outside caught her eye. She looked out and noticed a bus of prison transports had driven up to the security gates of the Stringtown Interment Camp. She'd been hearing about the new prisoners' arrival for the past few days. She wasn't sure what was happening, but judging by all the recent havoc created by the hardcore Nazi prisoners, she knew it was big. Not only had they been loud, restless, and disrespectful toward the guards, but they'd been committing random acts of violence toward the non-believer Nazi prisoners. Four prisoners had been admitted into the hospital and several others sported stitches due to cuts from crudely made shivs.

Josephine was confused as to why new prisoners were arriving at the prison. Due to overcrowding at Stringtown over the past few months, some of the prisoners had been shipped to other Oklahoma interment camps. Why would they bring in more? Josephine looked at the ferns and shook her head. She learned long ago most things in the prison camp didn't make sense and it was best to accept it and go on.

After placing the empty pitcher of water in the break room, Josephine walked to her desk and saw an overlooked official Army form, requiring Geddy's signature by one o'clock. She picked up the form and hurried to Geddy's office. As she entered the hallway, she heard a familiar voice.

"Guten Morgen, Yosephine," said the voice.

Josephine knew it was Karl. She turned around and saw him sweeping the outside hallway.

"How are you doing this morning?"

"Maybe not so *gut*," said Karl, while he swept.

"Do I need to contact the Sooner Schooner?"
"Ja, but I'm not so sure . . ."
"What's the matter?" asked Josephine.
"Zee Nazis have become very much restless."
"I've noticed that," said Josephine with great interest. "What's going on?"
"They are awaiting zee Jews."
"The Jews?" asked Josephine. "I don't know of any Jews coming to this prison."
"They are coming here."
Josephine was confused. After trying to wrap her head around the idea for few seconds, she gave up.
"I don't understand. Why would innocent Jews be coming to serve time in our prison?"
"They are not innocent Jews," said Karl. "They are Nazi Jews."
"Yeah, right," laughed Josephine. "And Johnny's is a five-star diner."
Karl tilted his head. "Who is Johnny?"
Josephine knew explaining American sarcasm to Karl would take hours, so she decided to just nip the joke in the bud.
"Forget what I said," Josephine replied. "And please forgive me for laughing. I would never take delight in the plight of the Jews. I just found it absurd that Jews would actually be serving in the Nazi military. So absurd it's actually funny."
"I guess I do not understand this American funny business."
"Not to worry, most of it's not so funny anyway," quipped Josephine.
"Yes. Zee same can be said of the funny business in Deutschland."
"I bet so. What did you really mean by the term, 'Nazi Jews'?"
"Zee Nazi Jews are zee Jews who did not flee Deutschland when zee Nazis came into power. They hid their identities and became Nazis."
"Oh my lord!" exclaimed Josephine. "I had no idea."
"They are here now and will face much violence with zee Nazi prisoners."
"I had no idea. Do the guards know?"
"Ja, but the Nazis' will succeed in their madness, nonetheless."
"Let's hope not," said Josephine.
"Ja, und how."
Josephine looked at the form and remembered needing Geddy's signature.
"I hate to run," she said, "but I really need to get my boss's signature on this form. After that, I'm going to lunch. Maybe you could stop by in the morning when you're picking up the trash."
Josephine noticed Karl's face turn pale. He forced a frightened smile, which made his appearance seem bizarre.

"Is something the matter?" asked Josephine.

"I might not be here tomorrow," said Karl.

Josephine's eyes grew wide and her smile seemed to cover her face.

"Are they releasing you early due to the overcrowding?" she hopefully exclaimed.

"No," Karl said solemnly.

"Are you getting transferred?"

"No," Karl said, still forcing a smile.

"I don't understand."

"Last night, the Nazis had my trial und I was found guilty."

"What? What do you mean? Guilty of what?"

"For talking to zee Americans."

"What?" asked a shocked Josephine.

"They had a trial und I am guilty," Karl said, trying earnestly to control his emotions.

"So what does that mean?"

"I will be . . ." Karl was on the verge of tears.

"You will be what? What's going on?" pleaded Josephine.

With tears streaming down his face, Karl pulled his finger across his throat, the universal sign for death.

"Are you saying they're going to execute you?"

After wiping his nose on his shirt sleeve, Karl nodded.

"That's absurd," Josephine said frantically. "They're prisoners, not the judges. They can't determine the outcome of people's lives."

"That is not all," said Karl, crying. "You must know I have been doing things to make my wife und kids very ashamed."

"Like what?" said Josephine, still trying to understand the bomb he'd just dropped.

"I am a master printer. In the war, one of the things I did for Hitler was to counterfeit the British Pound. I am very good at doing such things."

"Okay," said Josephine. "So what are you saying?"

Geddy's office door burst open. Before she could turn around, Geddy was face-to-face with Josephine.

"I'm off to lunch," said Geddy, holding a stack of papers. "If anyone calls, tell them I'll be back after twelve-thirty."

"Uh, what?" asked Josephine, still trying to grasp Karl's predicament.

"I'm going to lunch," Geddy said slowly. "You know, that thing people do when they are hungry? What's a matter, did you forget to take your medication this morning?"

Josephine was so stunned by Karl's admission, she felt as though she would faint.

"I, uh, I need your signature," Josephine said after a long pause.

"Can't it wait until after lunch?"

"No, it can't," said Josephine. "The commanding officer dropped it off this morning. It's about the new prisoners. He wants it back before one o'clock."

"Fine." Geddy rolled his eyes. "I'll sign it in my office."

Geddy returned to his office. Josephine turned around so she could tell Karl to wait, but the German was nowhere to be found. She called his name and walked down the hall, but to no avail.

"I'm in a hurry, Josephine," Geddy shouted from his office.

Knowing her boss was in no mood to wait, Josephine gave up her search and walked to Geddy's office. As she approached his desk, she looked down to the stack of papers he'd been holding in the hallway. They were receipts for Jereboam Industries, similar to the first one she saw weeks ago. Geddy quickly covered the papers.

Josephine laid the form on the desk. Without saying a word, Geddy signed the form and handed it back.

"Are there any other pressing issues?" asked Geddy.

"Well, actually..." Josephine said, then paused. She knew any pleads for Karl's life would fall on deaf ears.

"Well, what?"

"Nothing."

"Good. I'll be back after twelve-thirty. Matter of fact, make it after one."

"Yes, sir," said a deflated Josephine.

After the two exited the office, Geddy turned and locked the door. He placed his keys in his pocket and proceeded down the hall. He was stopped, however, when Josephine's fear for Karl overcame her common sense.

"Isn't there some way you can protect Karl?" pleaded Josephine. "I just spoke to him and he's very fearful for his life."

"Write you congressman." Geddy walked around Josephine and continued down the hall. "I'm just the auditor."

"But please! He's a human being, same as us. He has a wife and kids. He has a reason to live. Can't you find it in your heart to at least have him put in an isolated cell?"

Geddy stopped and faced Josephine.

"No, I can't. He might be a husband and a father, but more importantly, he's a Nazi."

Wearing a boisterous smile, Geddy turned around and continued down the hall.

"But don't you have a heart? Don't you even care?"

Instead of replying to Josephine's pleas, Geddy whistled as he walked down the hall. Josephine shook her head and sobbed. After wiping her nose with a tissue, she went back to her office and picked up the phone.

"Honey, it's me. Saddle up the ponies. We've got ourselves a Sooner Schooner emergency."

# # #

"I should get an award for dealing with idiots," Geddy said as he joined Butch at a table in the Stringtown Diner. He sat at the booth and laid his paperwork on the table.

"You know I don't like to wait," scoffed Butch as he played with the salt shaker. "I do have an empire to build."

"If you'd play along with my anecdote, I think you'll soon know why I'm late."

"Enlighten me." Butch tossed the shaker on the table. The top came off as soon as it hit, scattering salt all over the table.

"Could you please do something to save Karl? Poor Karl is fearful for his life," Geddy said in a soprano voice, mocking Josephine. "I swear, that secretary of mine is driving me crazy."

"You want me to have her taken care of, too?" Butch said, his eyes cold.

Butch's words incensed Geddy. He looked around the café to see if anyone was listening. "Do watch what you're saying. The last thing I need to have is Skeet Carney up my ass because of his wife."

"Skeet Carney don't scare me one bit," Butch said with a stern voice. "I eat pukes like him every day."

Geddy laughed. "Pissing on Skeet's boots is the last thing you want, trust me. That man has more than power, he has Atoka's hearts and minds, all at his disposal. A wise man knows when to fight and when to run. Never pick a fight with a man like Skeet."

"Skeet doesn't scare me at all," said Butch nonchalantly.

"Touché," said Geddy. "Touché."

"What can I get for you fellas?" asked Rhonda, a pretty young waitress, who seemed to appear out of nowhere. She looked at the spilled salt on the table and frowned. "What happened?"

"Defective salt shaker," said Butch. "It was just sitting there and all the sudden, the damn thing just shattered. It was the damndest thing."

"I'll get it cleaned up," said the waitress.

"Don't worry about it," said Geddy. "We're in a hurry."

"What can I get for you guys?" asked Rhonda.

"I'll have a cheeseburger with fries and a water," said Geddy.

"I'll have what he's having," Butch said, without looking up from the table.

"Sure thing." Rhonda darted off to the kitchen.

Geddy scooted the receipts toward Butch, who grabbed them off the table. "I hope this will suffice for your needs."

"I think it will," said Butch, while looking over the receipts.

"On the receipts, I wrote down that you paid for prison labor."

The waitress set down two glasses of water. Butch gave her butt a hard stare, then winked. He laid the papers on the table and took a drink of water.

"This ought to work."

"It's the dumbest thing we've ever done," said Geddy. "I can't believe you're wanting to actually use a tax write-off and jeopardize this venture. Haven't we made enough money?"

Annoyed, Butch set his glass of water on the table and sat back in his chair.

"Even if I get audited, which I won't, there's no way anyone can put this back on us. My story is I bought some paper, brought it to the prison, and I paid the inmates to print letterhead on the paper. What's so wrong with that? The write-off will cover the cost of the actual paper I had to buy for the coupons. It all works out."

"Let's hope," said Geddy.

"Where are we on the printing?" said Butch.

"It's done," said Geddy. "The kraut finished them last night. You need to come by the prison tonight and pick up the coupons."

"And the kraut?"

"Karl is definitely a liability, due to his mouth. If we continue this venture in the future, we'll have to get a new monkey to do our printing. With this in mind, I told Dietrich to take care of him tonight," said Geddy.

"Who's Dietrich?"

"He's the leader of the crazy Nazi prisoners. He wanted to kill Karl months ago, but I persuaded him to hold off until we had our coupons printed. I gave him the go ahead yesterday."

"So when's it going to happen?"

"Tonight's the night," said Geddy.

Butch smiled. "Good," he said. "I would say things are working themselves out."

"I'd say they are," said Geddy. "The only thing left to do after you pick up the coupons is to deliver them and collect the money. I expect you have those items covered."

"It'll be my pleasure," Butch said.

"I'm sure it will be," said Geddy. "I want those coupons picked up tonight."

"Tonight's not good," said Butch. "I'm picking up some brown sugar in McAlester."

Geddy's mood became less jovial.

"I don't think you understand. I want those coupons out of my prison tonight."

"I understand perfectly, but I'm busy tonight. I'll come by tomorrow," said Butch.

Geddy took a slow drink. As usual, Butch was making the situation difficult.

"Then we do it now," said Geddy, while rising. "The coupons are all inside a supply closet. We can't take any chances. Someone could stumble across them and ..."

"After we eat," said Butch. "I ain't about to have my brown sugar on an empty stomach."

Knowing Butch's thick head and enormous appetite would never relent, Geddy sat back down.

"You never cease to amaze me," said Geddy with a scowl.

"I'll take that as a compliment."

Chapter 27

Terry Brooks had just placed several blocks of alfalfa in the hayrack when he heard the dogs barking, just outside the barn. Barking dogs were a common occurrence on the Brooks ranch, so he didn't pay much attention. Knowing it was time to eat, the horses trotted to the hayrack and immediately began chowing down on the blades of alfalfa hay.

Terry walked to the feed room and measured three gallons of oats in a five-gallon bucket. He stepped out, locked the door, then walked to the feed trough where he dispersed the oats in three separate places, one for each horse. Terry then glanced at his watch and saw it read six-thirty. If he hurried, he and his wife would be able to drive from his ranch in Boggy Bend to Atoka and watch the high school basketball game.

Terry walked around the barn to make certain all the gates were closed. Through the years, he had become obsessive about this practice, as horses are notorious for finding open gates, then eating everything in sight. This could be very dangerous, because if they eat too much, they will founder, which can lead to death. Terry and his family were fortunate this had only occurred twice, but with no serious permanent ailments.

After he triple-checked each gate, he walked toward the exit door. The fact he'd finished all his chores was great because it meant they could make it to the game. Tuesday night basketball games were a huge part of the social scene in Atoka. Anyone who was anyone was always there. It looked like Terry and his wife's streak of not missing a game all year was going to stand.

Just as he reached for the handle, Terry heard the dogs bark again.

"Dally!" Terry screamed. "What's the matter?"

Dally was the old blue heeler dog that was the leader of the other two ranch dogs, Spencer and Flash. Since the dogs were outside the door, Terry couldn't see what they were so upset about, but judging by the tone of Dally's bark, she was distressed.

As Terry turned the doorknob, the barking immediately ceased, followed by a whimper. Terry knew something was very wrong. He turned and quietly ran to the saddle room. He walked to the shelf that contained all the spare horse bits and retrieved a pump-action twelve gauge shotgun used to shoot skunks in the barn. A box of shells sat nearby. He loaded the gun, and walked back to the door.

Terry heard people talking on the other side of the door. Rather than turning off the barn lights and escaping, he decided it best to stand his ground and see if the intruders came through the door. In total silence, he stared at the doorknob. Finally, he saw it turn. Using his forefinger, he found the safety switch on the gun and disengaged the feature. The gun was ready to fire.

After the doorknob turned a full rotation, the world stopped. Terry saw everything pass by in slow motion. Seconds seemed like minutes. The door finally cracked open. In full stealth, Terry stepped back two steps.

"We got somethin' for you, compliments of Butch, you dirty nester!" shouted one of the men.

Terry swallowed hard and braced himself as his felt his heart race in triple time. Suddenly, the door flew open. Three black men rushed through, each brandishing a butcher knife. Terry took aim and shot, pumped the gun, shot, pumped the gun, and shot and pumped the gun. With a horrid look of disbelief, all three men fell to the floor of the barn.

Through the open door, Terry saw a fourth man run away, into the darkness. He hurried through the door and shot, then pumped the gun. Knowing he didn't hit his target, he shot and pumped the gun again. This time, he heard a moan. His bullet made its mark.

Terry came upon the man, bent over, but still on his feet. He didn't recognize the man, due to the darkness, but he knew he was close enough for a final, fatal shot. Terry stepped closer and pulled the trigger. Click. The shotgun was empty. As Terry scrambled to find the box of shells in his coat pocket, the man stepped toward him. He raised his butcher knife, but then stopped.

"I'm real sorry," said the man, "but this ain't my fight. I'm sorry."

Holding his arm, the man turned and limped off into the darkness.

Terry finally located the box of shells in his coat. After reloading the gun, he ran back to the barn. The men were still lying on the ground. Terry was shocked by the amount of blood that covered the barn floor. He'd never in his life seen such a sight.

He cautiously walked to the first man. With is foot, he pushed the man, but immediately found the man was dead. He found the same results with the other men. Relieved, he exited the barn, and walked to his house.

Terry met his wife at the backdoor. Wearing only a bath towel, she was terrified.

"What in the world is going on?" she shouted.

"I got jumped by some thugs in the barn."

"I heard shots as I stepped out of the shower. What happened?"

"I killed three of them. One got away."

In disbelief, Terry's wife covered her mouth with her hands.

"I need to call the sheriff," said Terry.

He walked to the phone, dialed the operator, and asked for the Sheriff's department. After being connected, Terry tried to compose himself.

"I need to report some killings," said Terry.

"Who is calling?" asked the Sheriff's office dispatcher.

"Terry Brooks."

"Hi, Terry. How you doin'?"

"I've been better. You might want to send over the coroner. I've got three dead men here in my barn."

"Are you still at Boggy Bend?" asked the dispatcher.

"Yes," replied Terry.

"I'm sorry, but we don't send out any units to Boggy Bend after dark. You'll have to wait 'till morning."

"What do you mean? You have to send someone now. There're dead men in my barn."

"I'm sorry, but due to the population segment of that particular area, it isn't safe for us to send people during this time of day."

"But one of the assailants wasn't killed. I wounded him and he's out there, somewhere, bleeding to death."

"I'm sorry, Terry, but it's our policy. We don't send any of our personnel to Boggy Bend after dark."

"I see," said Terry. "Please send someone out as soon as you can in the morning."

"Will do, Terry. I'll put out an all-points bulletin to the hospitals for anyone with gunshot wounds."

Terry heard the line go dead. He shook his head and hung up the phone.

# # #

"So what's all this about?" asked Battle Axe.

As the old Chevrolet roared through the night toward Stringtown, he fiddled with the AM radio. "Why we doin' this in the evenin' instead of early in the morning?"

"Don't rightly know," replied Mark. "I received an urgent call from Russo saying that Project Sooner Schooner was needed ASAP. That's when I called you."

"Hmm," said Battle Axe. "I wonder if they's something wrong?"

"I think there is," said Mark. "From what I've been told, our kraut prisoner's health has deteriorated significantly. Plus, he's fearful for his life because of the other Nazi prisoners."

Battle Axe looked deep into Mark's eyes.

"Can I ax you a question?" said Battle Axe.

"Shoot."

"What have we been delivering to the prison these last few months? What exactly is this 'project Sooner Schooner'?"

"You know I'm not supposed to talk about that. The less you know, the better."

"Come on, Mark. We're all adults. The least you can do is tell me what's going on. I feel like I have a right to know."

Mark contemplated Battle Axe's question for several moments.

"I think it's the least you can do," said Battle Axe. "If we get caught, I'm sure I'll be the one to go to Big Mac, since I's the only black man involved in this."

Mark laughed. "Trust me, if we get caught, you won't be doing time at McAlester."

"Then tell me, what's been going on?"

"If I tell you, you have to promise you'll never let Russo or Skeet know I told you," said Mark. "You've got to act dumb. Get it?"

Battle Axe laughed. "Actin' dumb is one of my specialties. That's something I picked up from you nesters."

"Ha, ha," mocked Mark. "Project Sooner Schooner is simply us delivering medical supplies to the German prisoners. They don't receive the medical attention they should, and Josephine's friend, Karl, has diabetes. If it weren't for us delivering his insulin, he would have been dead long ago."

Battle Axe was floored. "You gots to be kiddin'!" he shouted. "All this time, I thought we was deliverin' something illegal, like contraband or something. Is you tellin' me all these boxes are just medical supplies?"

"Sorry to burst your bubble," replied Mark.

"Then why all the secrecy? Why has Russo been so keen to keep it quiet?"

"'Cause we're not sure what the folks in Atoka would think if they found out the town's fathers were delivering medicine to the Nazis. It would only take one or two nuts to get on the anti-Nazi bandwagon and before you know it, we'd get run outta town."

"Shit, there's more than one or two nuts around these parts," said Battle Axe. After a brief pause, he shook his head. "And all this time, I thought we was doin' something illegal."

"Sorry," said Mark.

"You damned nesters is crazier than a shit-house rat," laughed Battle Axe. "All this over a few bottles of medicine."

"Remember to keep your mouth closed."

"I don't know nothin'," Battle Axe said with a smile as he pulled the Chevrolet off the highway and onto a back road that ran alongside the rear yard of the prison. After driving a few feet, Battle Axe pulled the car over and parked near a gate in the chain fence.

"Why are we stopping here?" asked Mark.

"This is the spot where I always drop off the stuff, per Skeet's directions when we first started doing these runs," replied Battle Axe.

Mark looked over to the main prison building and noticed a prisoner exiting through a back door. The prisoner walked toward them. "Who's that?" he asked.

"That's the Kraut," said Battle Axe. "That man has the run of this place. Evidently, he's a model prisoner, 'cause he always picks this stuff up and takes it inside."

Mark looked to the gate. "How's he gonna get through the gate? It's locked up tighter than a drum."

"I have never asked. The less we know, the better."

Karl quickly approached and unlocked the gate. He looked down the dirt road and saw the nearby highway. The thought of making a break for it flashed through his mind, just as it had done a thousand times during his stay at Stringtown. The thought was quickly quashed, however, when Karl realized that he'd never make it very far without food and insulin. And besides that, when word got out that an escaped Nazi was roaming the hills of Atoka County, the crazy rural Americans were sure to use his German ass for target practice.

"*Gutten tag,*" Karl said when he reached Battle Axe and Mark.

"Howdy," said Battle Axe. "We got yo' supplies."

"*Danke shon.*"

"Need any help carrying this stuff in?" asked Mark.

"No," replied Karl. "I think it's okay, maybe."

Battle Axe and Mark helped Karl unload the package from the car. They walked the package through the gate and set it down on the ground.

"You sure you gonna be able to carry this over to the prison? Looks like a big load for one man," asked Battle Axe.

"Before the war in Deutschland, I worked all day delivering ninety-pound blocks of ice to customers. This gave me big muscles. As you Americans say, I am strong like fox," Karl said with a big smile. Both Battle Axe and Mark looked at one another and rolled their eyes.

"I guess that makes us crazier than an ox!" Battle Axe chuckled to Mark.

Why do the Americans think oxen are crazy, thought Karl. He quickly thought he'd just add this to the long list of things he didn't understand about Americans. After a few moments of uncomfortable silence, Karl reached down and tried to drag the package to the prison. Since it was several feet long and heavy, he made little progress, so Battle Axe and Mark grabbed the back end of the package and assisted his efforts.

After several minutes, the men reached the back door of the prison. Walking backward, Karl led the men into the prison. As soon as they were inside, Karl set his side of the package down and walked to the door. He removed a set of keys from inside his coat.

"Whoa there, cowboy! Don't go lockin' us up in this joint!" said Battle Axe.

"But it is protocol," said Karl.

"To hell with yo' protocol," snapped Battle Axe. "They ain't no way I'm gonna allow you to lock that door."

Karl shrugged and walked back to the package. Once again, he picked it up and walked backward down the hall, toward the janitor's closet.

As they walked, Battle Axe looked up and saw that a German prisoner was walking quickly down the hall toward them. Assuming the prisoner was coming to help, Battle Axe failed to say anything to Karl, who had no idea someone was approaching him from behind.

Karl stopped his backward walk when the men reached the janitor's closet. The closet had been the hideout for Karl's insulin and the prison's other medical supplies for several months. Just as Karl sat his end of the package on the floor, the German prisoner pulled out a crude shif from his coat, grabbed Karl's forehead with one hand, and slit his throat with the other. Karl immediately fell to the floor. Without saying a word, the prisoner casually turned around and walked back down the hall.

"Dear God!" screamed Mark.

As Karl's blood flowed down the hallway like water, Battle Axe was quick to remove his coat and wrap it around Karl's neck in an attempt to stop the bleeding. His efforts were futile, however. As his face turned pale, Karl did his best to communicate to Battle Axe.

"Please tell *meiner kinder und meiner vife* that I'm sorry und . . ."

"Hang on," said Battle Axe.

"*Und* give them all *meinen* love," said Karl, as his head fell back. After a few moments, Karl's eyes closed and he stopped breathing. Battle Axe and Mark knew he was dead.

"Let's get the hell outta here," said Battle Axe.

Both men barreled down the hallway and out of the prison. They didn't even lock the gate. Battle Axe started the car, shot a quick U-turn and raced to the highway. Once there, he floored the old Chevrolet. A plume of smoke followed the car as it raced back toward Atoka.

Chapter 28

Vanessa reached for Kirk's hand as the two walked down the hallway of Dunbar High. The eight o'clock bell had just rung, signaling that classes would start in fifteen minutes. As usual, Kirk and Vanessa shared a candy bar and a soda. They were rushed this morning, however, due to a big event that had been scheduled for weeks by Mrs. McCutcheon. The whole school was abuzz with excitement about this morning's program. In order to get good seats, all the students were quietly moving toward the gymnasium.

"Guess who I talked to last night?" asked Vanessa.

"Bob Hope?" replied Kirk sarcastically.

Vanessa laughed. "Yeah, he called and wants me to dance with Patty Thomas on the USO tour."

"I think the troops will get a good laugh out of that," Kirk said with a smile.

"You best watch it," Vanessa said while hitting Kirk on the shoulder. "Seriously, guess who called."

"I really don't know."

"Clarice," said Vanessa.

"Oh. What did she say?"

"She wants the four of us to go on a double date."

"Sounds good to me," said Kirk. "Wanna go back to the creek?"

"I don't see why not. Are you sure Ripp wants to go?"

"I kinda think he will," Kirk said with a smile. "He kinda likes her."

"Good," said Vanessa. "I'll tell Clarice."

As they entered the gym, Kirk was immediately greeted by the familiar smell of the wooden floor, which gave him a warm and contented feeling. Throughout his life, this building had served as a key setting for many happy memories. From basketball games to dances, to plays to award ceremonies, this gym was a staple of his youth. Kirk squeezed Vanessa's hand and smiled as the two made their way to the front.

As the two walked past chairs aligned in neat rows, Kirk looked to the stage and noticed Mrs. McCutcheon talking to a man in uniform. Seated behind the side curtain, they looked like two friends catching up on old times. Mrs. McCutcheon looked up and noticed Kirk. She smiled and waved as he and Vanessa walked down the front row.

Kirk was happy to find so many open seats on the front row. He and Vanessa smiled and talked as the entire gym slowly filled with boisterous students. As usual, the kids acted as though they'd been locked up for several months and were getting their first taste of freedom.

Suddenly, the crowd was hushed. Mrs. McCutcheon walked to the podium at the east end of the stage, very near where Kirk and Vanessa sat.

"Today, I have a special treat for the students of Dunbar," said Mrs. McCutcheon. "As you're all well aware, the United States has been engaged in a world war over the past few years. As civilians, we don't really have a sense of what life is like for the young men who are in Europe and beyond, fighting the war."

A few students were talking loudly, and Mrs. McCutcheon stopped. Like a laser, she peered at the students, who quickly got the message.

"Today, I am thrilled to announce we are welcoming home one of our own and a former student of mine. His name is Leon Nelson, I mean Captain Leon Nelson. Captain Nelson graduated from Dunbar High School in 1938. Some of you may know him and his family. He has graciously agreed to regale us with tales of his experiences overseas. Captain Nelson is a hero who fought valiantly in the war and has made it home with honors. Students, please help me welcome back a former student at Dunbar High, Captain Leon Nelson."

The gymnasium erupted in thunderous applause by the students and teachers. Kirk had never heard anything like it. The noise created from the applause far exceeded anything he'd heard during basketball games.

Due to Kirk's vantage point, he could see Nelson behind the curtain, struggling to get out of his chair. Then Kirk noticed the black man had only one leg. Because Nelson was seated behind the curtain and behind Mrs. McCutcheon, she had no idea he was having problems. Kirk took matters into his own hands. He jumped up on the stage, darted around the curtain, and helped Nelson with his crutches. After a few moments, the army hero limped toward the podium.

An eerie silence blanketed over the audience. Some of the kids pointed to his empty pant leg, which pinned up below his knee. As he struggled to climb the stairs of the stage, Mrs. McCutcheon came to his aid, but his pride wouldn't allow it. He politely refused her help and painstakingly made his way up the stairs. He projected pride and honor with each excruciating step. Finally, he reached the podium. By his side, Mrs. McCutcheon announced:

"Students, please welcome Captain Nelson!"

The gymnasium again filled with applause. Dressed in his officer uniform, Nelson's appearance was sleek and dapper. Just the sight of the soldier made Kirk feel like a better man.

Captain Nelson took a good look at the crowd. Not a single student was talking.

"My, what a serious crowd!" exclaimed Nelson. "Mrs. McCutcheon has a way of getting our attention, doesn't she? Not much has changed since I was here last."

The students laughed nervously. Still at his side, Mrs. McCutcheon smiled.

"Before we start, I'd like to thank Mrs. McCutcheon for having me back. It's been quite a homecoming and I'm eternally grateful for the warm reception you've shown to me."

More applause.

"I'd like to change the format a little," said Mrs. McCutcheon. "If it's alright with all of you, I'd like to ask the captain some questions."

"Sounds great to me," Captain Nelson said.

"For starters," said Mrs. McCutcheon, "Please tell the students about your service in the war and particularly about your involvement in D-day."

Captain Nelson smiled. "Sure. First of all, do you folks know what D-day was?" asked Nelson.

Freddy Pierce sat by Kirk. Not known for his shyness, he blurted out, "That's when we kicked all them krauts' butts in France."

Just as Freddy hoped, his comment created big laughs. Mrs. McCutcheon gave him a look so cold it would scare an Eskimo. Freddy didn't seem to mind, though.

"That's one way of putting it," replied Nelson with a smile, "but I hope you will understand it a lot better when we are done here today."

"Were you involved in D-day?" blurted out a student.

"I was," replied Captain Nelson. "D-day occurred on June the 6, 1944, in Normandy, France. Before the invasion, I was in England in the small town of Dover, which is on the coast by the English Channel. My unit was an all-black group called the 320th Anti-Aircraft Balloon Battalion."

"So you invaded France in a balloon?" asked a freshman girl.

Captain Nelson laughed. "No, but that's a good guess. From Dover, we boarded a small ship very late in the night on June fifth. Our ship traveled across the English Channel, which is the water that separates England and France."

"Can you describe the conditions when you arrived in France?" asked Mrs. McCutcheon.

"Sure. After we arrived in the harbor at Normandy, we sat in the boat and awaited our orders. You simply cannot imagine the number of ships around us. One guy in our group joked that we were going to flood the Germans out with all those ships. The weather conditions were horrible due to the cold and rain. We stood out on the deck without any cover."

"And what was your unit's mission?" asked Mrs. McCutcheon.

"Our unit was responsible for setting up large balloons filled with helium, then placing them on the beach which was going to be invaded by the Allies. There were five areas of the beach given unique code words. Some of our group went to Omaha Beach, but I and others were ordered to go to Utah Beach. Unfortunately, we lost our rudder along the way. We had power but no way to steer the ship."

"Oh, my gosh," said Mrs. McCutcheon. "What did you do?"

Captain Nelson laughed. "We didn't. We floated around in the channel for a couple of hours, until a ship came along and towed us along behind them. This ship was headed to Omaha Beach. By this time, the first of the soldiers had made their way to the beach."

"If I may interrupt," said Mrs. McCutcheon. "This is where the story gets rather unsettling. If you have a weak stomach, you can go back to your classroom."

Captain Nelson and Mrs. McCutcheon looked out into the audience. Not a single student left.

"As Mrs. McCutcheon said, some of you may find this to be upsetting, but it is the truth and you need to know. As we approached the beach, we saw many dead bodies floating in the water. I ordered the guys to pull in as many bodies as they could and remove their dog tags. We had to release the bodies back into the water because we had nowhere to put them. So those brave men were buried at sea. We took their dog tags because it was important to identify as many as possible so they could be listed as killed in action rather than just missing."

Captain Nelson looked out into the crowd and saw the students were completely engaged in the story. No one said a word. Even the class clowns like Freddy Pierce were silently absorbing everything, not just the words said but the way he said them. For the first time in their lives, the students understood the war was real.

Many students, like Jewel Dean Kirk, wiped tears away as the captain told of the details concerning the dead bodies in the English Channel. Kirk was simply overwhelmed as he tried to process all the information. He wondered if the war would be over by the time he would be old enough to go serve. Never in his life had he understood just how horrible war could be. He remembered reading letters from his uncle, Joseph Neal, who joined the army before the war. The letters were a bit unsettling, but nothing like this.

Captain Nelson continued. "So there we were, being towed by a boat into, what we felt, was certain death. We jumped out of the boat and onto the beach around ten o'clock in the morning. At that point, the fighting was still very intense. The Allies hadn't made much headway. Fortunately, the area where we landed was somewhat calmer than other places, but it was still very intense."

"Could you tell the students about the German occupation on the beach?" asked Mrs. McCutcheon.

"Yes. The Germans had four years to get ready for us and they used it wisely. They were positioned in large concrete bunkers containing machine guns and high caliber weapons. Their position was also integrated into the cliffs and hills overlooking the beach. Essentially, they were shooting fish in a barrel. They had the high ground and it was very very difficult for us to take the beach."

Gary Lee Allen, a sophomore, raised his hand. "When you jumped out of the boat, did you think you were going to die?"

Captain Nelson smiled. "The thought did cross my mind," he said, then turned somber. "I remember when we left the boat, we all huddled together and said a prayer. In my mind, I wasn't afraid. I told myself if I died, it would be for the greatest good."

Kirk could see Captain Nelson's eyes shining as he composed himself. In a few moments, Mrs. McCutcheon intervened.

"So now that you're on the beach, what was your mission?"

"Our job was to unload the large balloons and fill them with helium. When they were filled, we floated them over the beach to protect our guys from German planes. We used cables to connect the balloons to each other.

And just to make it more dangerous, these cables had bombs on them. If a German pilot tried to fly between or around the balloons, the plane would hit the cables and make the bombs explode. We actually brought down three planes before it was over."

"Wow," said Mrs. McCutcheon. "That is a fascinating story. So, did you incur your injury there at the beach? If so, how did it happen?"

Captain Nelson smiled. "Well, I'd like to say it was in hand-to-hand combat or some other heroic thing, but the truth is that I stepped on a bomb. The Germans had placed bombs on the beach, in the surf. I was just unlucky enough to step on one when I was on my way to get something out of the ship. Finding these bombs was like finding a needle in a haystack, and man, oh man, did those needles pack a punch."

"Were you hospitalized in France?" asked Mrs. McCutcheon.

"No, I was eventually taken back to England, but they were not able to save my leg. About a week after the injury, I had a below-the-knee amputation."

"Did that end your Army career?" ask Mrs. McCutcheon.

"Actually, it didn't," answered Captain Nelson proudly. "I spent a couple of months in the hospital to recover. During this time, I had to learn how to walk with one leg and use crutches, which I'm still learning. One of the most interesting things that happened then was meeting with some German soldiers who were also injured in the war. As our troops took over France, we captured many prisoners of war."

"What were the Nazi prisoners like? Did they want to kill you because you are black and not part of the 'master race'?" asked Freddy Pierce.

Captain Nelson got a very serious look on his face, "It may sound strange, but I actually did make some friends with those Germans. The odd thing about it was I quickly learned most of them were no different than us. They were caught up in the war and fighting for their cause. Most of the German soldiers were not evil Nazis that wanted to overtake the world. They just wanted the war to end so they could go back home and see their wives and kids."

"What was it like serving in the war as a black man?" asked Mrs. McCutcheon.

"At the beginning, I definitely felt like an outsider. Blacks did not serve with whites in any units. We were not considered able to fight on the front lines even though most of us were bigger and stronger than all those white city boys. We were put together, but after the D-day invasion, a very interesting thing happened. The generals must have decided that despite the difference in our skin color, we all bled red blood. Also, they needed every man still alive to regroup and form units to proceed across France. So all the guys in our group who weren't killed or injured were reassigned to white units. This was probably the first time the idea of 'separate but equal' was removed from social standards. Some of my black friends who went on to serve bragged they didn't have to sit in the back of the tank!"

Kirk looked around and noticed everyone in the crowd laughed. The laughter was hesitant at first, but when the students realized everyone else was having a good time, the laughter became more and more lively.

"How many of you have ridden a bus out of Atoka?" asked Captain Nelson.

Only a few of the students raised their hands. Kirk looked around to see if he knew any of the world travelers.

"So, you know what it means to sit at the back of the bus, right? Up to now, the motto in our country has been 'separate but equal'. Well, how can someone be equal if they have to be separate?" Captain Nelson said, then paused. "Someday, we will truly be equal. It will take some time. And I know you can't imagine it now, but someday, there won't be black schools and white schools. There will be just schools. Someday, you will be able to drink out of any fountain you want. You will be able to go to the movie and sit in any chair you like. You will be able to sit on the front row of the bus if you so desire. Who knows, there might even be black doctors and lawyers, and politicians or even a black president of the United States."

The captain's statement made the crowd laugh. Kirk wondered if Captain Nelson had suffered brain damage along with his other injuries. After the laughter subsided, Kirk's mind reeled. Maybe everyone was laughing because they'd never heard anyone say things like this. They'd never imagined life would ever be any different.

"Do you realize we have been free for less than one hundred years?" asked Captain Nelson. "In 1865, my grandfather walked off the farm where he lived as a slave. He had lived there his whole life, in Russell County Alabama. A man named Nelson owned him. He took his owner's name and headed down the road for a better life. Where do you think our names came from? I promise you there were no Jones, Nelsons, Smiths, or McCutcheons imported from Africa."

After a deliberate pause in the captain's speech, Mrs. McCutcheon took the captain's speech a step further.

"This is all very interesting," said Mrs. McCutcheon, "but what can these young people do right now to survive in a 'separate' world?"

"Hey, I don't have all the answers," replied Captain Nelson, "but you must all make a decision. Just like I had learned Germans were not all monsters, it will take time for whites to understand we are people, too, just like them. The decision you have to make is how you will respond to the injustices of the past. When we become equal, and trust me, we will, being angry and bitter will not help you survive in this world. You will face enough obstacles as it is. Be strong and remember you represent the struggle for all blacks. Keep pressing on for equality, but look forward, not backward. You are fighting the struggle for your kids someday, so study hard, stay out of trouble, and do everything Mrs. McCutcheon tells you to do."

"Captain Nelson, we appreciate your time and your service to our country. I understand you will likely go back overseas in the next month or so?"

"That's right," replied Captain Nelson, "I still have more to give."

"Please join me in showing our appreciation to Captain Nelson for spending time with us today, and also for helping to defend our great country."

The entire student body rose to their feet and clapped. Kirk searched his memory of going to school at Dunbar and couldn't think of a single time anyone received a standing ovation. He was more than impressed. So impressed, in fact that he decided to approach the stage and tell Captain Nelson himself. As the crowd mingled with one another, Kirk looked to the stage and found the captain was making small talk with some of the Dunbar school officials.

"I'm gonna go speak to Captain Nelson," Kirk said to Vanessa, who was chatting with one of her girlfriends. "Then I'll walk you over to the school."

"I'll be right here," replied Vanessa.

Kirk maneuvered himself through a sea of bodies toward the captain. Upon reaching the stairs that led to the side of the stage, he felt a bold grip on his left arm. He looked up and saw that Sheriff Cain was upon him. Startled, he stopped walking.

"Can I help you?" asked Kirk.

"I need you to come to the station. I have some more questions about the Johnny Morman murder."

Kirk was shocked. "What?"

"We can do this the easy way or the hard way," Cain said and pointed at his handcuffs.

"No, no no. I'm not gonna give you any trouble. I'm just confused. I thought this was all taken care of," said Kirk.

"You thought wrong," said Cain. "That's the problem with you criminals, you're always assuming the authorities believe your story."

"Criminal?" said Kirk. "Did you call me a criminal?"

Sheriff Cain rolled his eyes and pulled on Kirk's arm.

"Let's go," he said, and led the way to the gymnasium's exit. While they walked, Kirk searched through the crowd, hoping to spot Vanessa. Since Sheriff Cain was wasting no time escorting him out of the gym, Kirk's efforts failed.

Still standing on the stage, Mrs. McCutcheon saw Kirk and the Sheriff leave the building. She quickly excused herself from her conversation with Captain Nelson and ran to the office of the school, where she found a phone.

# # #

Kirk looked up at the clock on the Atoka County Jail. It read ten-fifteen. He'd been waiting for over twenty minutes. Upon his arrival at the jail, Sheriff Cain placed Kirk in a small room with two chairs and a table. Kirk assumed that Cain's efforts to make him wait were merely tactics to make him nervous, and provoke a full confession. Kirk told himself again that a confession wasn't going to happen, no matter how poorly he was treated.

Without warning, the Sheriff opened the door, slamming it into the wall of the room. The bang startled Kirk, and he jumped in his seat.

"You nervous, boy?" said the Sheriff as he entered the room.

"No, sir," replied Kirk. "You just scared me, that's all."

"That's 'cause you killed a man and your conscience is weighing down on you like a ton of bricks, isn't it? You don't want to talk, but believe me, you're gonna talk today and we're gonna get this case solved."

"I killed no one. And I'm more than happy to answer any questions you might have," Kirk said with a lump in his throat. "What exactly are you needin' to know?"

Sheriff Cain removed his notepad from his front pocket. He quickly flipped through the pages, stopping near the back.

"You claim you were over at Mrs. Parker's house just before the killing. Yet Mrs. Parker says you weren't there at all. She said that she hasn't seen you in weeks."

Kirk's eyes grew as large as potatoes. Maybe they are tryin' to frame me, he thought.

"That's absolutely untrue," said Kirk, "and I can prove it."

"You can?" said a shocked Sheriff Cain.

"Yes," said Kirk. "The reason I was at her house was because I was collecting money for her paper route. I have her signature, which includes the date and time, all which occurred seconds before the murder."

Sheriff Cain was taken aback. His tactics weren't working. He felt his stomach begin to rumble, a sure sign that guilt was on its way.

"Did you go back and write that receipt, right after you murdered Johnny?"

"No, sir," replied a cool Kirk. "Mrs. Parker will testify that I gave her the receipt as I left her house, which was only seconds before the murder."

Suddenly, the cracked door opened. In walked Carney, who appeared to be very perturbed.

"I've seen the receipt myself," said Carney. "I'm here to tell you there's no way Henry could have killed Johnny. He simply didn't have time."

"How long have you been out there listening to our conversation?" asked Sheriff Cain.

"Long enough," said Carney. "Look Sheriff, you know damned good and well Young Henry didn't commit this horrible crime. I thought this was all cleared up. I thought Johnny's wife admitted to killing him."

"She recanted," said Sheriff Cain, who stared at Carney for a few moments. He then wiped his brow. "I need some water."

Carney emitted a look of disbelief, then opened the door and walked into the entrance of the jail. He returned with a cup of water. Cain gulped it down.

"Are you feeling alright?" asked Carney.

"I've had better days," replied the Sheriff.

Carney placed his hand on the Sheriff's back.

"What's this all about?" asked Carney. "You know damn good and well Mrs. Parker can vouch for Henry's whereabouts in the moments prior to the murder. Why are you tryin' to stick Young Henry with this heinous crime?"

Sheriff Cain looked to the floor then placed both hands over his face.

"Is someone pressuring you into framing Young Henry?"

The Sheriff nodded slightly.

"And you know whatever this person has promised you is nothing compared to the guilt you're going to feel when Young Henry gets the electric chair at Big Mac, don't you?"

"I do," said Sheriff Cain, still looking at the floor.

The door to the interrogation room swung open. Deputy Atha entered the room.

"You ready, Sheriff?" asked the deputy.

"Ready for what?" replied Cain.

"To go to the Brooks place."

With a look of confusion, Sheriff Cain scratched his head. "What are you talking about?"

"No one's told you?" said Deputy Atha.

"No. What's going on?"

"Last night, Terry was jumped by some thugs in his barn. He killed three of them, but one got away."

Sheriff Cain remembered Butch's threat to Terry after the incident in the bank. He also remembered warning Butch not to harm Terry or trouble would find him. If Butch disregarded my warnings and broke the law, thought the Sheriff, then I'll be forced to arrest Butch, which meant . . .

"Young Henry," said Sheriff Cain, "you're no longer a suspect in this case. I'm very sorry for the inconvenience this may have caused you."

Kirk and Carney both let out a deep breath.

"Thank you," said Carney.

"Yes, thank you," repeated Kirk.

"Oh, and Sheriff," said Deputy Atha. "One of the suspects got away and is currently at large."

"Any description?" asked Sheriff Cain.

"It was dark and Terry couldn't see well," said Atha. "But he did shoot the suspect in the leg. So far, we haven't found anyone in nearby hospitals with leg injuries."

"So, we have a criminal at large?" asked Carney.

"It appears so," replied Sheriff Cain.

"Kirk, you be on the lookout," said Carney. "Matter of fact, why don't you spend the day with me at the drugstore? It sounds to me like things are about to get very interesting here at Atoka."

Chapter 29

Using an old water-soaked rag, Kirk scrubbed on the counter of the soda fountain so hard, he could practically see his reflection on the surface. Even though he'd been away from the Atoka County Jail for several hours, the experience he'd encountered there earlier stayed with him. So much, in fact, he felt his heart still beating at a quickened pace.

Since it was Friday, the after-school rush was over earlier than usual, which made Kirk happy because he had big plans with Ripp and the girls later that night. Since most of the high-school kids had dates or other activities planned for the first night of the weekend, Friday evenings were generally pretty slow at the drugstore.

"Looking good, Young Henry," said Carney as he walked to the fountain. "Looks like we're gonna get outta here early tonight. It seems as though this day is going to end better than it started, my friend."

"Yes, sir, you can say that again," replied Kirk. "And I am looking forward to some fun."

"Indeed," said Carney. "Is someone going to bring by your homework since you missed most of school today?"

"Yes sir."

The sound of the ringing cowbells alerted both men's attention to the front of the store. They immediately recognized Mrs. McCutcheon.

"Speak of the devil," said Carney.

"Hi, Mrs. McCutcheon," said a surprised Kirk. "What brings you here?"

Mrs. McCutcheon held up a bag of books. "I thought I'd bring by your homework," she said.

"Oh," said Kirk. "I expected one of my classmates to bring it by, but it's always a pleasure to see you."

Mrs. McCutcheon smiled. "Workin' with Skeet has either made you much more polished and well-mannered," she said, "or you've become a really good liar."

All three laughed.

"I can attest Young Henry is not lying," said Carney. "He thinks the world of you, and not just when report cards come out."

"I'll take that compliment. How has everything been around here? Has it been quiet?"

"As usual, Young Henry has worked his tail off," said Carney. "We've been fairly busy, so the day has just flown by."

"We've been sick with worry since the Sheriff took you, Henry. How are you feeling?"

"I'm fine," replied Kirk. "It was a little rocky there at the jail, but things cooled down when Mr. Carney came in. Sheriff Cain suddenly came to his senses."

"Good," Mrs. McCutcheon said with a sigh. "I do appreciate your call letting me know everything was okay, Skeet. And thanks for going down and looking after Henry at the jail."

"It was no problem," said Carney. "I was happy to help."

"Henry's becoming so good at running this place," said Carney with a laugh, "I'm afraid I'll soon not be needed. Before long, he'll be running this place all by himself."

"He has a bright future," said Mrs. McCutcheon. "Speaking of which, could I have a word with you, Skeet?"

"Sure," replied Carney. "I have some things I need to do back in the pharmacy, anyway."

"Is something the matter?" asked Carney, while he closed the door.

"Yes," replied Mrs. McCutcheon. "I don't really know how to say this, so please forgive me if I trip around words."

"Please speak your mind," said Carney with a smile. "I've known you for years and can honestly say you are a woman of impeccable integrity. I can't think of a single thing in the world you could say that would offend me."

"Thanks," said Mrs. McCutcheon. "Let me start by asking this question. What do you know of Henry's recent troubles?"

Carney scratched his head. "Well, obviously, I know of the events this morning. And I know he was jumped by a group of thugs over in Stringtown a few weeks ago. Why?"

"Do you think these events are isolated?"

Carney thought for a moment. "I have no evidence to believe otherwise. Do you?"

Mrs. McCutcheon stared at the floor. "I think you need to sit down," she replied. Carney immediately suspected she was about to drop something big.

After both found seats beside the pharmacy counter, Mrs. McCutcheon reached into her purse and pulled out a cigarette. She put the cigarette to her mouth and lit it.

"I didn't know you smoked," said Carney.

"I don't," said Mrs. McCutcheon. "This is my second cigarette all year. I only do it when I feel the world pressin' down on me."

"Just out of curiosity, what made you smoke the first one?" asked Carney.

"When I found out my husband's brother had been captured in Japan and is routinely tortured at a Japanese prison camp."

"Oh," replied a stunned Carney.

"What I am about to tell you is based on years of observation in Little Dixie," continued Mrs. McCutcheon. "And it's not that I think you and I are any different, but the reality of the matter is that we are and . . ."

Mrs. McCutcheon shook her head, then closed her eyes. Sensing she was troubled, Carney placed his hand on her shoulder.

"Both of us have lived most of our lives right here in Atoka," said Carney. "And I know there are differences, but I can't believe that's why you asked to speak to me."

Mrs. McCutcheon took a deep breath.

"It's all related," said Mrs. McCutcheon. "Skeet, you may not realize this, but most whites in Atoka don't even notice there are blacks in this town. Now, don't get me wrong, most folks are not mean or prejudiced, blacks are just invisible to most white folks. We know our place, be it right or wrong."

Finished with her cigarette, Mrs. McCutcheon rubbed the cherry onto the metal trashcan. She then discarded the butt.

"I must stop you there. There's nothing right about the way things are," said Skeet with sincerity. "Someday, I think things will change."

"I'm sorry, Skeet, but you're missing the point."

"Okay," said Carney. "Tell me, what is the point?"

"Us black folk aren't even here. I hear white folks talking about all sorts of personal things right in front of me, like they don't even see me. Because of that, we know much more about this town than white folks do.

I know things about people in this town that would shock you, because everywhere I go, I'm invisible. Be it on the street corner, in Woods' Brothers store, or anywhere else. And it's all been going on, right under your nose."

Carney shook his head. "So what are you trying to say?"

"That there's a bad secret that involves Henry and it's worse than you can possibly imagine."

Carney scratched his head. "I need to know," he said.

Mrs. McCutcheon reached into her purse and pulled out another cigarette.

# # #

As Kirk was finishing his cleanup chores at the soda fountain, he wondered why Mrs. McCutcheon wanted to see Carney privately. It couldn't be about school, he thought. His grades were just as they'd always been: straight A's. Maybe it was something personal about one of her recent prescriptions.

As the cowbells rang out their dull clanking sound, Kirk looked to the front of the store and saw it was none other than his best friend in the whole world, Ripp. He wore a huge fake grin as he strolled down the aisle toward Kirk.

"That's undoubtedly the biggest shit-eating grin I've ever seen," said a laughing Kirk. "What brings you here?"

"Who, me?" Ripp said while looking around the room. "I just came by to see the jailbird. Think they'll let me visit you tonight while you're in the joint?"

"I don't know, but you'll feel right at home," jabbed Kirk.

"Ouch!" quipped Ripp. "Now that was low."

"Sorry," Kirk said. "I couldn't resist."

"What the hell got into Cain?" Ripp asked sincerely. "He just showed up at school out of nowhere and arrested you?"

"He didn't really arrest me," replied Kirk in a somber tone, "but he might as well have. He took me to the jail. Before I knew it, Skeet showed up and Cain finally calmed down. But it got real weird after that. All of the sudden, a deputy shows up and tells Cain about a shooting out by Boggy Bend at some farmer's place. The news got to Cain. His face turned red, then he just let me go. It was the damndest thing."

"I heard about that. The farmer's name is Brooks. Maybe Cain knew him and was worried about his safety."

"No," Kirk quickly interjected. "It was more than that. He looked real mad, chewing nails mad. I don't know why that would be, but he wasn't concerned. He looked more like he was more ready to kill someone."

"Interesting," said Ripp. "But what's really weird is what happened out there. Those three black men Brooks killed were out-of-towners. They found a butcher knife on one of them. It kinda makes me think they might be the same scum who jumped us over at Stringtown."

"Oh?" replied Kirk.

"Yeah. And get this: The police found an abandoned yellow Highlander nearby.

"You're kiddin' me?" said Kirk with shock.

"No, sir," said Ripp. "Remember what those thugs drove at Stringtown?"

Kirk was visibly shocked. He sat down on one of the soda fountain stools.

"A yellow Highlander."

"That's right," said Ripp. "A yellow Highlander."

"I wonder what they had against Terry Brooks?"

"I don't know, but it sounds to me like those fellows didn't visit him to have tea."

Sitting on the stool, Kirk was lost in thought as he stared at the floor of the soda fountain.

"Forget about it," said a smiling Ripp. "I've got some good news."

Kirk shook his head slowly back and forth. He simply couldn't believe what Ripp had just told him.

"I said, I have some good news," Ripp said in a loud voice.

Still receiving no response, Ripp walked to Kirk and waved his hand in front of his face. "Anyone home?" asked Ripp.

Finally, Kirk looked up. "I can't believe this is actually happening. This is like something out of a movie."

"Are you listening to me? I'm trying to tell you I have some good news."

"Yeah, yeah," Kirk replied as he awoke from his trance. "What is it?"

"I've just been informed we'll be accompanied by a couple of beautiful ladies tonight on a trip to our most favorite place in the entire world, The Bog."

"Oh?" said Kirk.

"It appears you mentioned it to Vanessa today at school and she liked the idea so much she and Clarice went ahead and planned the whole thing," said Ripp. "Things are beginning to look up."

"What time?" asked Kirk.

"I'll pick you up around six-thirty."

Kirk looked to his watch. "I'd better hurry," he said. "That doesn't give me much time to get ready."

"We've got the entire evening, so take your time."

"Sounds great." Kirk gathered up wet towels in the soda fountain. "Do we have a car?"

"I'm sure I can find something at the Chevrolet place. As long as Dad doesn't find out."

"We're just askin' for trouble by doin' that," said Kirk. "If your dad ever finds out we've been taking his customer's cars out on joy rides, there'll be hell to pay."

"That's exactly why he can't find out."

"Indeed. See you at six-thirty."

Ripp turned and walked to the front door of the drugstore. Before he reached the door, the cowbells sounded as Josephine came in the store. She said hi to Ripp as they passed.

"Why, hello, Mrs. Carney," said a smiling Kirk. "It's very nice to see you here."

"Likewise," replied Josephine. "Is Skeet here or is he making a delivery?"

"He's in the back, speaking to Mrs. McCutcheon," replied Kirk.

"Oh," replied Josephine. "Got time to make me a soda?"

"It'd be my pleasure. I don't usually work the fountain, but I think I can draw you up a one."

Kirk had just finished serving the soda to Josephine when Mrs. McCutcheon and Carney came out of the pharmacy. The two were still talking as they walked toward the fountain.

"Why, hello, dear," said Carney, upon seeing his wife. "I wasn't expecting you to come in today. Did you get off work early?"

"The prison is still crawling with investigators trying to figure out who killed Karl," said Josephine. Her eyes misted over while she spoke. "I told Geddy I needed to leave."

"I don't blame you," said Carney.

"Hello, Josephine," said Mrs. McCutcheon. "It's very nice to see you."

"And you as well."

"I hope you haven't been waiting long. I'm sorry to keep you from your husband."

"Think nothing of it," replied Josephine, while composing herself. "I was having a great time talking to Henry."

"He has a way of growing on you, doesn't he?" asked Mrs. McCutcheon.

"That he does," replied Josephine.

"Thank you very much for your time, Skeet," said Mrs. McCutcheon. "And Henry, I expect you to have all that homework done by Monday."

"Yes ma'am," said Kirk.

"I'll see what I can do," said Carney. "Put your mind at ease, though. I'll take care of things."

"Thank you," Mrs. McCutcheon said as she walked to the front door. As soon as she exited the building, Carney locked the front door, and flipped over the closed sign. Kirk wondered what was going on.

"Young Henry, we need to talk," said Carney.

Surprised, Josephine assumed this was a signal for her to leave.

"I'll head on to the house," said Josephine. "Give me a call when you're leaving."

"No, no," said Carney. "You might as well hear this, too. I need all the able minds I can get to figure this out. Both of you, please sit down."

Kirk and Josephine gave each other a confused look as they were seated.

"Now Kirk, you've worked for me for a good while now, and you probably already know I'm a straight shooter."

"Yes, sir," replied Kirk.

"That's why I'm gonna get straight to it. Mrs. McCutcheon tells me Butch is a man who is quite astute at wearing masks. Evidently the real Butch is much different from the Butch I know. She also tells me he's out to get you. Would you care to explain?"

Kirk simultaneously felt happy, embarrassed and ashamed all at the same time. He wasn't sure how much Carney knew, but he was certain the man he was speaking to wasn't in the mood for any bullshit.

"I don't know what I've done to anger Butch, but he definitely doesn't care for me. He's been out to get me ever since I met him."

"What has he done?"

"I can't prove it, but I'm pretty sure he sent those thugs to get me in Stringtown. Uncle Willie heard on the street they were after me. He gave me a gun in case I had trouble. Had I not had it, I'm not so sure I'd be here now."

"Henry, do you remember us talking about the wide path to destruction and the narrow path to life?" asked Carney with intensity.

Kirk quickly replied with confidence, "Sure I remember. I think about that narrow path every day."

"Okay then," responded Carney, "Now, my question to you is this: Have you been doing things you shouldn't have been doing with Butch and his ilk?"

"Look, Skeet, I'm either workin', studying, or playing basketball. I lead a very boring life. If you don't believe me, ask Vanessa."

Carney walked over and placed his hand on Kirk's shoulder.

"I don't need to ask Vanessa," said Carney with conviction. "I know you're a good kid, Henry. I just had to ask."

Kirk could see Carney felt bad for questioning his morals. It was pasted all over his face.

"Understood. What do we do now?"

"I'm not sure," said Carney. "I knew something was amuck when Sheriff Cain re-opened the investigation of the murder. Johnny's wife admitted killing him. Cain was certainly pressured by someone to go after you. Now we know who that someone is."

"There's more," said Kirk.

"Go on," said Carney.

"Around the time I started working here, you sent me upstairs to clean up the Christmas ornaments."

"I remember."

"When I went up there, I came across an old chest. Now I realize I shouldn't have been snooping around, but I opened the chest and saw a picture of a KKK'er right here in downtown Atoka. I didn't know who it was, but it had a name on it. A name I didn't recognize."

"So what does that have to do with Butch?"

"The day after I got jumped in Stringtown, Ripp wanted us to get outta town for a while, so we went to McAlester. We went to the movies, then got bored. As we were about to leave town, we accidentally came across a prostitute."

Carney laughed. "Accidentally, huh?"

"I promise. Anyway, this girl was just talking to us. After we told her we were from Atoka, she told us her best customer is from Atoka. His name is Jereboam."

Josephine's ears perked up when Kirk mentioned the name.

"Jereboam?"

"Yeah," said Kirk. "I didn't realize it at first, but that's the name that's written on the KKK photo, the one I found upstairs in the chest. If you look at it closely, the height of the guy in the picture looks to be the same height as Butch. She also said Jereboam has a scar on his forehead just like Butch."

"Come to think of it, that chest has been in the attic of this drugstore for years. It was here when I opened the store."

"Who owned this building before you opened the drugstore?" asked Kirk.

"The bank," said Carney.

"Now I know!" shouted Josephine. "Jereboam Industries."

"What does that mean, honey?" asked Carney.

"I've come across several receipts at the prison for Jereboam Industries. It's Butch! I asked Geddy who they were for, but he got mad and told me to forget about it."

"What kind of receipts?"

"It doesn't say, but there have been several. Matter of fact, Geddy just had some the other day."

"It sounds to me like Butch is more than a banker who has a seedy past with The Klan," said Carney.

"I'll say," said Josephine. "This guy sounds very dangerous."

"And there's something else. Kirk, do you remember this morning when Cain found out about the murders out at Brooks' ranch? All of the sudden, he said you were no longer a suspect. I'll bet that was the tipping point."

Josephine rose from her chair and walked to the soda fountain.

"I still don't understand," said Josephine. "How would he be involved in that?"

"I don't know either," said Carney, "but we've got to be very very careful. What are you doing tonight, Young Henry?"

"Me and Ripp are going on a date."

"It might not be a bad idea to stay over at Ripp's tonight."

"Will do."

Chapter 30

Ripp turned off the lights to the 1941 Ford Coupe as the car passed under the trees that surrounded North Boggy Creek. He put the transmission in neutral, turned off the engine, and steered the car as it coasted into the woods.

Clarice wore a smirk on her face. "What are you doing? Tryin' to set the mood so you can scare us again?"

"Oh, I'm sorry, ladies," said Ripp with a big smile. "But sometimes my military training automatically takes over my actions. I'm so used to covert missions I sometimes forget I'm among civilians."

Vanessa laughed while Clarice rolled her eyes.

"Ripp Masters, you're more full of it than a Christmas turkey," said Clarice. "You've never been in the military. You outta yo' mind."

Still smiling, Ripp knew he couldn't stop now.

"Yeah, you just keep believing that," said Ripp. "Trust me, I can kill a man just by looking at him."

"Okay," said an animated Clarice. "The government uses you to kill their enemies. Is that what you're saying?"

"That's right," beamed Ripp.

"And where do these secret missions occur? In yo' bedroom in yo' mama's house?"

Everyone in the car, including Ripp, erupted in laughter.

"That was cold," said Kirk. "But damned funny."

"Alright, alright," said Ripp with authority, "let's get this stuff unloaded."

Ripp popped the trunk while the teenagers stepped out and walked to the back of the car. They unloaded two grocery bags of food and supplies for the campfire. Bags in hand, the foursome walked down the trail Kirk and Ripp had worn into the grass. After a few minutes of traveling, they finally came upon their destination.

"There it is, girls," said Ripp with a proud smile. "The Bog."

"Such a mystical place," said Clarice with sarcasm. "I'll be sure to tell my mom I actually visited Xanadu."

"I think you should go easy on making fun of The Bog," whispered Vanessa. "This place means an awful lot to the boys."

"Alright," said Clarice. "I'll play along."

Kirk and Ripp gathered fallen tree branches and other spare wood they found on the ground. After a few minutes, a roaring fire lit the dark wooded area. Using wire hangers, Vanessa speared several hot dogs, then placed them in the fire to roast. By the time the food was fully cooked, Clarice had readied the buns and chips.

Several hotdogs later, Ripp and Kirk were still eating, while the girls sat back down against an old log.

"My gosh," said Clarice. "I think I'm done. I can hardly keep my eyes open."

A wicked grin appeared on Ripp's face. He reached into one of the grocery bags and pulled out a blanket.

"Where did you get that?" asked a suspicious Clarice.

"It was in the trunk of the car," said Ripp. "I found it while we were unloading the groceries. It was covering up a box of stuff."

Clarice was unconvinced. "Are you sure you didn't bring it from home, just in case we wanted to get down on the ground?" she asked.

"Hell, yes, I'm sure," replied Ripp. "I figured you ladies might want to sit a spell after we ate. Ain't no sense in gettin' all dirty."

Clarice nodded, then helped Ripp spread out the blanket. The foursome found comfortable spots.

In a bold move, Ripp lay himself down on the blanket, right beside Clarice, who was still sitting.

"You ladies cold?" asked Ripp.

"I am," said Clarice.

Ripp reach up and grabbed Clarice by the shoulder and gently nudged her down. To Ripp's disbelief, she obliged and lay down next to him, snuggling up to his body for warmth. Ripp couldn't help but smile as he placed his arm around her neck.

Kirk and Vanessa followed their lead and laid down on the blanket. Soon, all four teenagers were staring into the night sky.

"I have an uncle who tells me he once went to New York City," said Ripp. "He said there's so many lights, you can't even see the stars."

"Really?" said Vanessa. "I love the stars. I can't imagine not being able to look up at them."

"I didn't know you were into astronomy," said Kirk.

"Ah, yeah," replied Vanessa. "Just about every night I go out into the backyard and look at the constellations. It helps me escape."

Kirk looked hard into Vanessa's eyes. "Just what are you trying to escape from?"

"I don't know," said Vanessa. "Living in a small town and having no future. I sometimes fear I'll graduate high school, get married, then buy a house in Stringtown and never leave. It really scares me."

"Well, you don't have to stay here," said Kirk. "There are plenty of colleges out there that we can go to and . . ."

"Plenty of colleges?" quipped Clarice. "And what good will that do? You think havin' an education will make any difference? Ain't no whites gonna hire a black, educated or not."

"I don't know," said Kirk. "Mr. Carney says things will change. He's always telling me, someday I'll leave Atoka 'cause they ain't nothin' here for me."

"You're takin' advice from a white man?" asked Clarice.

"He's not just a white man," said Kirk with confidence. "He's a good man who happens to be white."

"How can you put your trust in him, when his grandfather could very well have owned your grandfather? Doesn't our past mean anything to you?"

Kirk sat up and placed his hand on Clarice's shoulder.

"I'll do you one better. Mama has always told me grandpa Kirkland was a slave in Dale County Alabama until he was fourteen. His owner was killed in the Civil War, and grandpa finally got his freedom after the war," said Kirk.

"And had his owner not been killed and the north not won the war, he would have died a slave," flared Clarice.

"But that's the past," Kirk reasoned. "Look at what his grandson is doin' now. I'm sittin' here on this riverbank with a full belly, having a great time with my good friends. I'm a free man and there's a whole big world out there just waiting."

"You looking at the world with rose-colored glasses," said Clarice. "I think whitey done got to you."

"Look Clarice, the past was terrible and it was rotten, but it's gone. If I spend all of my time dwelling on it, I'll always be bound by those chains."

"But I don't see how Carney could be right. I don't see how a day will ever come where we'll be equal," Clarice said, then shook her head.

"I don't know when that day will be," Kirk said, "but I tell you this: I will be ready. I'm going to college and getting my degree. Then I'm going out into the world and I'm going to give it a fair try. If they call me a nigger and tell me to get my black ass back to Atoka, then I'll personally come back here and buy you a Coke at Carney's drugstore."

Ripp was confused. He sat up and looked at Clarice.

"Not long ago, you were nagging on me because I dropped out of school. Now you're telling us it don't make no difference no how?"

Clarice was silent. She sat up and looked at Ripp.

"Sorry," Clarice said. "I guess I was just takin' my frustrations out on y'all."

"I don't understand," said Kirk. "You're beautiful and you make good grades. What do you have to be frustrated about?"

Ashamed, Clarice looked down and held her head with her hands.

"'Cause I'm not smart like you guys," Clarice said. "School don't come easy for me. I have to work real hard."

"That's crazy," said Ripp. "You're much smarter than I am, I know that for a fact."

"But you have a gift," said Clarice. "You got a free scholarship because of your athletics. I'm just a dumb black girl with poor parents. I ain't got no hope."

"You've always got hope," Kirk said. "That's one thing they can never take away."

Kirk felt Vanessa's hand on his leg. He looked over and saw her smile. The sight was intoxicating. He pulled her close with his left arm.

Ripp looked over and noticed Kirk and Vanessa making out, so he sat up and moved his body close to Clarice.

"If it's worth anything, I don't think that you're hopeless," said Ripp. "I think you're the smartest, most beautiful girl in Atoka County."

Clarice smiled. "Thanks."

"I only have one question," said Ripp.

"What's that?"

"Can I come with you when Kirk buys you a Coke at the drugstore?"

Clarice rolled her eyes and snickered.

"I think you'd better shut your mouth and kiss me."

"Yes ma'am," said Ripp.

# # #

As Kirk steered the Ford through the maze of county roads that led to Highway Sixty-Nine, he looked in the rear-view mirror but couldn't find

Ripp. When they packed up their belongings at The Bog, Ripp insisted Kirk drive and he and Clarice use the blanket in the backseat to warm themselves. They'd been in the car now for over ten minutes. The inside was plenty warm, yet Ripp and Clarice were hidden from view, underneath the blanket.

Since the only time Kirk had ever driven was on his Grandpa Colbert's farm in an old pickup, he was takin' it slow. Ever since America entered the war, the speed limit was thirty-five miles per hour, but Kirk was driving the car at an even slower pace. He looked down to his watch and saw that it read ten-thirty p.m. Since the girls needed to be home by eleven, everything was going according to plan, despite the slow travel.

"Are you doing anything tomorrow night?" asked Vanessa.

"No, not really. Why? Do you wanna go out?"

"Sounds good to me," Vanessa said. "Maybe we could go dancing."

"I'd like that," Kirk said as he wheeled the car onto Highway Sixty-Nine. The car picked up speed and cruised down the highway. Kirk found the experience invigorating.

"I sure like the way this car handles," said Kirk. "A man could get used to this. Wonder when Ford will start making new cars again?"

"I didn't know they stopped," said Vanessa.

"They stopped production due to the war," Kirk said.

"I guess you learn something every day."

Kirk smiled, then patted Vanessa on the leg.

Without warning, the steering wheel jumped out of Kirk's hands and the car headed for the ditch. With a full death grip on the wheel, he tried to gain control of the car. Finally he steered the vehicle back onto the highway, but could definitely feel something was wrong. He took his foot off the gas and coasted to the side of the highway.

"Ripp, we have a problem," Kirk said as the car rolled to a stop. "Ripp?"

Kirk turned on the interior light of the car, then turned and looked to the back seat. He reached down and tapped on the blanket. Kirk pretended to hold a police microphone in his hand.

"Ripp Masters, this is Sheriff Cain. Please get your tongue out of the young girl's ear and step out of the car," said Kirk.

Ripp quickly raised the blanket and looked up. He found Kirk and Vanessa staring down on him.

"What's the matter?" Ripp asked.

"They's something wrong with the car. I need some help," said Kirk.

"Okay, okay. Turn the light off and I'll meet you at the front of the car."

After waiting outside for a few minutes, Ripp finally stepped out of the car and joined Kirk. They walked to the front of the car and quickly noticed the problem.

"We've got a flat," said Ripp. "Let's hope they's a spare."

Ripp grabbed the keys and walked to the rear of the car. He popped the trunk.

"Who's car is this?" asked Kirk.

Ripp laughed while he fumbled through the trunk, looking for the spare. "You don't want to know," he said.

"What's so funny? Who's car is it?"

"It's your banker friend's."

Kirk's eyes grew to be as big as his hands. "You've got to be kidding! Why didn't you tell me?"

"It's not that big of a deal," said Ripp. "Besides, what are you going to do?"

Standing beside the trunk, Kirk thought for a moment.

"Well, nothing now, I don't guess. Still, do I need to remind you Butch has it out for me?"

"What's this?" said Ripp while searching through the trunk.

"I don't know. What's it look like?"

"I don't know," said Ripp. "It feels like Butch created some secret compartments here in the trunk. Holding a few pieces of paper in his hand, Ripp held them up in the moonlight.

"It looks like war coupons," said Ripp. He quickly walked to the front of the car and held the paper in front of the headlights. "Sure enough, they're war coupons. Bring that box up here."

Kirk grabbed the huge box and walked to the front of the car.

"Oh my gosh!" said Kirk. "There must be thousands of pages in here," he said.

Ripp flipped through the pages of coupons. He found different types of coupons positioned in the box.

"Dear Lord," said Ripp. "This is unbelievable. What's he doing with all these rationing coupons?"

Kirk scratched his head. "How'd he get so many?" he asked. "I thought the government only gave out a few to each family. Something ain't right about all this."

"I have to agree," said Ripp. He placed several sheets in his pockets.

"When is Butch picking up this car?" asked Kirk.

"In the morning. We serviced it today. He said he was going on some long trip."

Kirk grabbed a few of the coupons and placed them in his pockets. He and Ripp quickly changed the tire and returned the car back to the road. The two were so shocked by what they had seen, they hardly even spoke to the girls on the trip back to town. Ripp drove while Kirk shook his head over and over.

"You know," said Kirk. "You could tell me you're the queen of Egypt and I wouldn't be anymore shocked than I am right now."

"I don't know why," said Ripp. "You know damn well he's not above trying to outsmart the system."

"Yeah, I know," said Kirk. "I know."

"What are you guys talking about?" asked Vanessa.

"Oh, nothing," said Ripp. "Probably better if you didn't know."

# # #

The hour was well after midnight when Butch finally parked his wife's car in front of Johnny's Café. He looked down Court Street and found there were no signs of life. Assured he was alone, Butch stepped out of his vehicle and walked around the building, into the alley. He turned the corner and passed Johnny's back entrance, one of a few well-lighted spots in the dark alley. He looked around, then proceeded down the increasingly dark alley.

"Ollie, Ollie in free," Butch said in the darkness. Upon hearing no reply, Butch reached into his coat and retrieved his .44 Magnum. He pulled the hammer back.

"Anyone here?"

"Just me," whispered a voice in the darkness.

"And who might you be?" asked Butch while he raised his gun.

"I'm yo' cleanup man," said the voice.

The man then stepped into a dimly lit portion of the alley. Butch recognized the man's silhouette and smiled.

"I saw you park on Court Street," said the man as he stepped back into the shadow. "Did you buy a new car?"

"No, that's my wife's car. Mine is getting serviced," said Butch. "I'm taking it to Dallas to make a special delivery on Sunday. I figured I needed to get it serviced before I take it on such a long drive."

"Why'd you call so late and ax me to come here?" said the voice.

"A couple of reasons," said Butch. "One, you botched the Brooks' job and you owe me. That mistake cost me three good men."

"Sometimes things don't work out," said the voice. "I s'pose you could start doin' them yo'self."

"That's the second reason we're meeting," said Butch. "Things are getting rather heated 'round here. There's a boy who's causing me some grief and I need your help."

"What kind of grief?" asked the voice.

"Earlier this evening, I went over to McAlester to get my weekly fix of brown sugar. It seems as though this punk and his punk friend accidentally ran across my girl recently and asked some questions. Well, the stupid bitch told them some things that don't need to be repeated."

"Who might this boy be?"

"A black kid named Henry Kirkland. He lives in nigger town near the nigger school."

The man gave no response. The dead silence concerned Butch. He looked straight ahead, but saw only darkness.

"Are you still there?" said Butch.

"Yeah," replied the man. "Who was with the boy at McAlester?"

"The Masters boy. His first name is Ralph, but they call him Ripp I think."

Again, the man in the shadows didn't respond.

"We'll deal with Mr. Ripp later. I just want to focus on Henry for now."

Butch listened for a response, but heard nothing.

"Are you havin' a problem hearing me?" said Butch.

"Not sure I want to have anything to do with killin' a kid," said the man.

"Kids," said Butch with a smile. "And that's a funny thing to hear from you of all people. Since when did you grow a conscience? Besides, you remember our deal."

"I've done a lot of work for you, but you've never axed me to do such a thang. Not on a kid."

Butch's temper flared. "You'll do as I say or I'll put the bullet in your head myself. Do you understand?"

A few moments of silence eased by.

"I s'pose."

"Good," said Butch. "Now Henry comes down to Johnny's every Saturday night to get his scraps through the back door. He always comes right down this alley. When he comes through here tomorrow night, I want you to hold him up right over by the light at Johnny's backdoor."

"Then what?" asked the man in the shadows.

"Then I'll come up behind him and exterminate the little bastard. I want it to happen near the light, because I want him to know it's me."

"You're quite a man," said the voice after a long pause.

"That's what they tell me." Butch placed the gun in his pocket, then walked back to his car. The man in the shadows walked to the end of the alley and watched as Butch's taillights disappeared into the distance.

Chapter 31

"How's Skeet?" Sharon asked, counting the cash from the weekly deposit.

Kirk laughed. "Oh, he's workin' like they's no tomorrow," replied Kirk. "You know Skeet, if he's not working, he's not happy."

"I hear that," said Sharon. "I've known him since I was a little girl and I can't think of a single time when he was just sitting when he could be working."

"I guess some things never change."

Sharon laughed. "You can say that again. You know I worked for Skeet at the fountain when I was a kid. When I graduated, he called the manager at the telephone office and got me a job there. Most of the girls at the telephone company worked the drugstore fountain when they were young. If you worked hard for him, he would always make the magic call and get you a job. Darlene worked for him, too. The experience at the telephone company landed us both this great job here at the bank."

Kirk smiled. "He's quite a guy."

Since Kirk began making the Saturday deposit weeks ago, he'd formed a kinship with the bank's clerks, Sharon and Darlene. Each week, he would learn a little bit more about their lives. Even though the visits to the bank usually lasted five to ten minutes, he felt as though he knew them fairly well.

"How's you son Brad doing? Is he still ropin' those steers?" asked Kirk.

Sharon rolled her eyes. "That boy eats and sleeps on the back of a horse. I'm starting to get a little worried."

"I would, too," laughed Kirk.

While Sharon continued counting cash, Darlene walked up behind the counter.

"Oh, hi, Henry," said Darlene.

"Hi, Darlene. How are things?"

"It's Saturday, the sun is shining, and today is payday. I'd say it's pretty good," Darlene said with a smile.

"They ain't nothin' wrong with any of that," Kirk said while flashing a big smile.

"Henry, can I ask you a question?" asked Darlene.

"Sure."

"How long have you known Mr. Carney?"

Kirk looked into the air, trying to remember. "I don't know, just a few weeks," Kirk said.

"You didn't know him before you started working at the store?" asked Sharon.

"No ma'am."

"Wow," said Darlene. "He must really trust you."

"Why do you say that?" asked a puzzled Kirk.

"As you know, Skeet is a very organized person," said Sharon. "Many kids have worked for him over the past few years, but he's never allowed any of them to make the weekly deposit. He always brought it down himself."

"We were just wondering why he chose you," said Darlene.

Kirk was dumbstruck. He opened his mouth to answer, but no words came out.

"We don't mean to pry," said Darlene. "We're sorry."

"No need to apologize," said Kirk. "But to be honest, I really don't know."

"We were just curious," said Sharon.

Inside, Kirk was beaming. He couldn't remember a time when he was more proud. An ecstatic smile covered his face ear-to-ear, and a natural high consumed him.

"He's quite a man," said Kirk as he accepted the deposit bag from Sharon.

"He sure is," Sharon said with a smile.

As Kirk turned to face the entrance of the bank, he noticed the closed door to Butch's office. The sight quashed his jovial mood.

"Where's Butch?" Kirk asked, as he looked around. "He's usually here on Saturday afternoons, isn't he?"

"That's a good question," replied Sharon. "He's supposed to be here, but I haven't seen him since yesterday."

"I see," Kirk said. The thought of Butch made his stomach drop, but he quickly shook it off. "Tell Brad to let that poor horse rest."

"Will do," Sharon said with a big laugh.

"See you next week," said Darlene.

"Yes ma'am," Kirk placed the deposit bag in his coat and walked to the door. His heart rate escalated as his fingers touched the wad of coupons taken from the trunk of Butch's car. It was a stark reminder of the talk he was going to have with Carney. He'd tried all morning, but Carney was never alone. Kirk hoped his luck would change when he returned.

Kirk walked through the front doors of the bank, out onto the street. The March sun shown on his face and made him feel warm and safe again. He stopped and looked down Court Street, toward the drugstore. The sight reminded him of the first time he made the Saturday deposit. He let out a deep breath, then began his walk to the drugstore.

So much has changed in the last few weeks, he thought. So much, in fact, that he really couldn't remember how he'd felt when he first began working for Carney. He remembered constantly questioning himself and feeling inferior and unworthy. Over time, those feelings passed. Kirk realized he'd acclimated to his new responsibilities so quickly, this new world was already routine.

Kirk had often yearned to feel needed and to be held responsible for something bigger than just taking out the trash and doing the dishes. Now he had it. He was only fourteen years old, yet he was earning his own keep, making good grades in school, and excelling at his job. He was performing remarkably well in an adult world, yet he was still a kid. For the first time ever, Kirk felt like a success. As he reached to open the front door of the drugstore, he smiled. The last few weeks had been rough at times, he thought, but he'd answered the call. And even more important, he wanted more.

As was the case on most Saturday afternoons, the drugstore was mostly empty. Anxious to speak to Carney, Kirk searched the building to see if his boss was alone. He quickly found he wasn't. Kirk spotted Carney and a couple of ladies at the pharmacy, listening intently to the radio. Since they weren't speaking to one another, Kirk assumed they must be listening to something very important. As Kirk approached the three, he recognized the women to be Joni Nugent and Barbara Ellen. The sight of Joni's beautiful face made Kirk feel warm and tingly inside.

"Hi, Joni," said Kirk. "What's going on?"

Joni smiled, but instead of responding, she placed her finger to her lips, implying she wanted him to be quiet and listen.

Kirk recognized a news show reporting the war. His interest peaked when he heard the sounds of exploding ammunition in the background, indicating the report was actually being broadcasted from the battle zone. Kirk sat in a seat and listened:

"The island of Iwo Jima was declared secure today, March 14, 1945, in a ceremony commenced by the United States Military," said the reporter. "However, there has been no pause in the massive deployment of artillery from both the Allies, nor the Japanese. One Marine was heard to say, 'if this place has been secured, where the hell is all this gunfire coming from?' This reporter concurs," said the voice.

"I don't see how they can say the island has been secured," said Carney. "I can hardly make out what the reporter is saying due to all the gunfire."

Both Joni and Kirk nodded in agreement.

The reporter continued. "The majority of the fighting has been performed by Marine infantry against a desperate Japanese defense. While most of the Navy has already left for Guam, air support was continued by the P-51 Mustangs with their machine guns, bombs and rockets. Spirits were temporarily lifted by a rumor the war in Europe had ended, but morale fell again as this was quickly revealed to be a hoax. I spoke to a Marine who was being shipped off for yet another assignment. He told me quote, 'as we left Iwo, I thought of my friends that had fallen and were buried there. I felt like we were leaving them back there alone, that we were deserting them. We are Marines, fighting men who are supposed to be hard, with no feelings, but we have them. We talk of our fallen buddies as though they were transferred—we sound indifferent, but when we are alone we cry. A buddy is something precious, and to lose that buddy is a hard blow', unquote."

Kirk looked up and noticed everyone wiping their eyes. He too, felt the sadness. He stared at the floor while Carney turned off the radio.

"Thanks, Skeet," said Joni. She grabbed her prescription off the counter and shoved it in her coat pocket.

"If you're still feeling bad in a couple of days, let me know," replied Skeet.

"Will do, that pink pill always does the trick!" said Joni, who then looked at Kirk. "I'm going to be mad if you don't come by and see me at the shop."

"I will," Kirk said. He grabbed a broom and began sweeping up the tile floor. As soon as he heard the cowbells ring, signaling Joni had exited the building, he looked over and saw Carney was alone in the pharmacy. Now's my chance, he thought. He sat the broom down and walked toward Carney.

"Can I speak to you for a moment," said Kirk in a shaky, nervous voice.

Carney looked up, and immediately sensed something was awry.

"What's a matter?" asked Carney with a smile. "Did you get some girl pregnant?"

"Uh, no sir," replied a somber Kirk.

Carney patted Kirk on the back. "I'm just kidding."

"Uh, yes sir," said Kirk.

The two walked to the back room and sat down. Beads of sweat from Kirk's head dropped on the table.

"I have a feeling something is really bothering you," said Carney.

"Yes sir," said Kirk.

"Tell me what's on your mind, Young Henry."

"Something bad has happened and I don't know what to do."

Carney was suddenly horrified because he knew Kirk had bad elements in his life. He'd been doing so well for so long . . . Maybe he'd fallen to temptation.

"It doesn't matter what you've done," said Carney in a fatherly tone. "Just be honest with me and we'll work through it."

"You don't understand," said Kirk. "It's not me."

"Is it Ripp?"

"Yes and no," Kirk said, then paused. "This conversation is going in the wrong direction."

"Take your time."

"Okay. Last night, Ripp and I went on a double date. As usual, we used a car from the Chevrolet shop Ripp and his dad were servicing. It just so happened that last night, we coincidently were driving Butch's car."

Carney rolled his eyes, "Oh, boy. So what happened? Did you wreck his car?"

"No, no," replied Kirk. "Nothing like that. We actually had a flat and then we had to change the tire."

"And you didn't get the lug nuts on tight, so the tire came off when you were driving it on the highway, causing a massive crash?"

"No!" Kirk said firmly, then paused. "I'm sorry. We didn't have an accident."

"I'm sorry," said Carney. "Please finish."

"Thanks," replied Kirk. "While we were changing the flat, we accidentally found a box hidden in a secret compartment in the trunk. We got curious and opened the box."

"And what did you find?"

Kirk reached into his coat and retrieved the coupons. He threw them on the table.

"A whole bunch of these."

Carney picked up and inspected the rationing coupons. "What the hell?"

"That's what I want to know.".

"I'll bet these are counterfeit," said Carney. "Why else would he have them?"

"I don't know."

"How many did you find?"

"Thousands."

"Oh, they're definitely counterfeit. Why else would he have so many?"

"That's what Ripp and me wondered."

Carney held the coupons up to the light.

"I don't really know what to do," said Kirk. "The man hates me enough the way it is. I'd hate to be the reason he goes to jail."

"You did the right thing," said Carney. "I'll get these over to Sheriff Cain. They'll get a search warrant and we'll let them . . ."

"He can't know they came from me," interrupted Kirk. "I don't want anyone knowing that I had anything to do with it."

"Don't worry," said Carney. "I'll tell him it's an anonymous tip."

Kirk let out a deep breath. "You've got to be sure about this, man."

"Don't worry, Young Henry. You have my word."

After thinking about it for a few seconds, Henry nodded. "Okay," he said.

"Good. Is there anything else that's on your mind?"

"Well, actually there is."

"Please tell me."

"It's about Russo."

"Oh?" Carney said with a raised eyebrow.

"I think he's done something bad," said Kirk. "Several weeks ago, I was picking up my newspapers for my route. It was early in the morning and I saw Russo and Mark, my boss, loading up something in their car and I think it was . . ."

The cowbells rang throughout the store. Carney walked to the back room door. He looked into the store and saw a customer entering.

"Looks like we have a customer," said Carney. "Let's take care of them and we'll talk as soon as they leave."

"Okay," Kirk said, disappointed.

He had barely made it to the door when he ran into the customer.

"Why hello, young man. Is Skeet here?"

Kirk recognized the old man. It was Mr. Lucas, probably back for more cough syrup.

"He should be at the pharmacy," said Kirk, pointing.

Lucas poked his head around the corner and spotted Mr. Carney. He walked to the pharmacy counter.

"Evening, Skeet," said Lucas. "Glad I caught you before you closed."

"Hi, Mr. Lucas. What can I do for you today?"

"My damned cough is back," Lucas said. "Could I get a refill?"

"Let me see if I have any made up," said Carney.

"You know," said Lucas, "the last one I got was pretty weak. The one before, now that one hit the spot. I don't know who did the mixin', but let me tell you, the fellow knew what he was doing."

Carney looked over at Kirk and smiled. He then located the cough syrup and refilled the bottle.

"You're gonna have to make this last you for three weeks," said Carney. "I won't fill it until then."

"Yes, sir," said Lucas. "I should have it worked out by then."

Once again, the cowbells rang out, and Kirk noticed several young school kids headed for the soda fountain.

To Kirk's dismay, the next two hours were filled with his normal Saturday afternoon chores. While he washed windows and swept the floor, he looked to Barbara Ellen working the soda fountain and hoped the school kids would leave so he could speak to Skeet. It really didn't matter, though. Skeet worked nonstop in the pharmacy, so he wouldn't have been able to talk anyway. After the kids left the store and the prescriptions were filled, Kirk met Skeet at the soda fountain.

"Whew," said Carney. "That was some kind of rush."

"Indeed it was," said Kirk. "I'm beat."

"Barbara Ellen, would you mind boxing up those empty prescription bottles?"

Happy to get away from the soda fountain, Barbara Ellen nodded as she walked to the pharmacy.

"Boy I am tired," said Carney. "And I almost forgot, it's your payday."

"I guess it is," said Kirk

Carney went to the cash register and retrieved eighteen dollars and fifty cents. He handed it to Kirk.

"Here's your normal pay, plus a three dollar bonus."

Kirk wore a confused look. "What's the extra for?"

"Take Vanessa out and do something fun tonight, on me."

Kirk smiled and took the money. "Thanks."

"You're more than welcome. Now what were you telling me before we were interrupted?"

Kirk looked around the store to make sure it was empty. After several glances, he looked back to Carney.

"It's Russo," Kirk said. "Early one morning, I saw him and Mark loading something into their car. I'm pretty sure it was a . . ."

Once again, the cowbells rang throughout the store. Upset that his story was interrupted once again, Kirk mumbled "damnit" under his breath. His eyes doubled in size and his jaw dropped when he noticed who walked through the front door.

"Why hello, Russo," said Carney.

"Evenin' Skeet."

As Russo walked toward the soda fountain, his eyes never left Kirk. His stare seemed to pierce through Kirk's soul. After gaining control of his senses, Kirk turned and tried to casually drink his soda.

"What brings you in this evenin'?" asked Carney.

"The wife has a cold and asked me to come down and get something for her cough."

"Well I can sure help with that," said Carney. "We'll have her feeling better in no time."

Carney quickly walked to the pharmacy to fix a bottle of cough syrup. Instead of following him to the pharmacy, Russo stood right behind Kirk. Sensing someone was near, Kirk turned around.

"Is there something I can help you with?" asked Kirk.

"Depends on if you have something I want," Russo said in a cold and dry voice.

Kirk could feel his heartbeat jump. "How 'bout a soda?"

"I suppose."

Anxious to get away from Russo, Kirk practically jumped over the bar and began preparing a soda. Working as fast as he could, he looked up periodically to see where Carney was, but never spotted his location in the pharmacy. His nerves shattered, Kirk prayed Carney would hurry.

"So what have you been up to lately, Henry?" asked Russo.

"Uh, just workin' and going to school," Kirk said while pouring the soda.

"You been snoopin' around in places where you got no business?" Russo asked without hesitation.

"Uh, no," said Kirk. He looked down and noticed he was spilling the soda all over the fountain. He tried to stop pouring and clean up the mess, but his hands were shaking too severely to follow commands.

"How's you paper route? You still gettin' an early start every mornin'?"

I'm in some serious shit, thought Kirk. He's telling me he knows what I saw. He knows I know and he's gonna kill me before I can tell anyone else, just like they killed poor Rudy James.

"I try to," said Kirk. "You know what they say, the early bird gets the worm."

Kirk looked up and finally saw Carney walking to the soda fountain with a bottle of cough syrup in his hand.

"Thank God," Kirk said silently.

"Does he get the worm or does he spy in places where he ain't got no business?"

As Carney neared the soda fountain, Kirk knew his only chance for survival was to take action.

"I saw Russo and Mark load a dead body into Russo's car one morning!" screamed Kirk. "I think it was poor Rudy!"

Both Russo and Carney were shocked.

"What?" said Carney.

Kirk walked to Russo and stuck his finger in his face.

"You heard me," said Kirk. "This happened one morning before I did my paper route. I saw Russo and Mark load a dead body into his car, then they dumped the body over in Stringtown, by the prison."

While Carney's mouth dropped to the floor, Russo started laughing.

"What in the world are you talking about?" asked Carney.

"He knows what I'm talking about," said Kirk. "Don't let his laughter cover it up."

Carney walked over to Kirk and Russo. "Could someone please tell me what the hell is gong on?" he asked.

Russo was laughing so hard he could hardly stand up straight. Kirk was so mad, he thought he was going to implode. Carney looked like a confused dog.

"He's talking about Project Sooner Schooner," said Russo.

"What?" asked Carney.

"He was picking up his papers one morning when Mark and I were loading up the medical supplies for the Germans down at the prison. He saw us loading up the bags of medicine and thought it was a body."

"Oh," said Carney.

"What are you talking about?" said Kirk.

"Well," said Carney, "being that Jo works down at the prison, the Germans often complain they aren't getting the proper medical treatment. For the past year or so, me, Russo, and Mark have been dropping off medical supplies to the prisoners. We have to keep it secret because the townspeople might not understand if they knew we were helping the Nazi prisoners. Unfortunately, one of the main prisoners we were helping was killed, so Project Sooner Schooner was sidelined."

"Oh," said Kirk. "But what about the body they found over by the prison?"

"I don't know anything other than what the newspapers have reported," said Russo. "That's just a terrible coincidence."

"We called the project 'Sooner Schooner' so we could talk about it over the phone," said Carney. "It was sort of fun, playing like we were secret agents or something."

"I guess I'm sorry," said Kirk. "I didn't know."

"I knew you saw us that morning," said Russo. "I must admit I've been having a little fun teasing you. I figured you were too freaked out to say anything to anyone."

"I see," said Kirk.

Russo walked over and grabbed the cough syrup from Carney. "I'd stay and reminisce, but the wife really needs this medicine, plus I need to drop by Woods' Brothers before heading home," said Russo.

"Give her my best," said Carney.

"Will do," said Russo.

"Henry, sorry. I probably took it a little too far."

Russo extended his hand. Kirk was slow to shake it.

"Good evening," Russo said, then walked out of the store.

"Does that clear up everything?" asked Carney.

Still dumbfounded, Kirk was trying to figure out what just happened. "I guess it does," he said.

"Good," replied Carney. "It's almost six o'clock. What are you doing after work?"

"Guess I'll head to Johnny's like I always do. Me and Ripp are taking the ladies out afterward."

"Sounds good," said Carney. "Well, you best get on outta here. Barbara Ellen and I need to get ready for the crowd that always comes before the early movie starts."

"Do you need me to stay and help?"

"No," said Carney. "Go out with your friends and have a good time."

"That's a great idea," said Kirk. "A great idea."
With a smile on his face, Kirk walked quickly to the front door.
"Oh, and Young Henry," said Carney.
"Yes?"
"Keep a watch out for you-know-who tonight."
"I will," said Kirk. "I promise."

Chapter 32

Kirk was still shaking his head in disbelief as he walked to Johnny's. Back at the drugstore, Russo did more than just confuse Kirk's young mind, he blew it all to hell. Kirk's memory of the morning when he saw Mark and Russo load the body wasn't fuzzy in the least bit. He knew he saw them load something that strongly resembled a body wrapped in blankets, but he couldn't say with one hundred percent accuracy. And without one hundred percent accuracy, Kirk had nothing. Still, the incident was driving him mad.

What about the Sooner Schooner story? Was there any possible way Russo's explanation could be true? Carney did nod his head in agreement when Russo told the story, so maybe it had validity. And Kirk agreed the townsfolk in Atoka wouldn't take it well if they knew some of the town fathers had been smuggling medical supplies to save the wicked Nazis. The secrecy they were forced to maintain would explain Russo's paranoid suspicions that Kirk had witnessed them loading something at the newspaper shop. As the incident with Russo swirled around in his mind, Kirk began to believe he was wrong. Carney had a lot of respect for Russo, but he would never let him get away with murder. Kirk shook his head. The incident occurred early in the morning. Maybe Kirk's eyes were playing tricks on him. Maybe he'd been wrong all along.

While Kirk continued to mull the story over and over again, the thought of Johnny's chili slowly made its way into his psyche. Throughout the day, the drugstore was so hectic Kirk never even had a chance to eat lunch. He was famished. Even though Johnny's was a good two blocks away, his stomach rumbled with each step. He could even smell the distinct deep-fried-grease smell that could only be Johnny's.

Kirk finally reached the cross street of Ohio Avenue. He walked south until he reached the alley. Aided by only a few street lights and no moon, Kirk's heart rate quickened as he was surrounded by total darkness. He turned east and began his walk through the dark alley that led to Johnny's, a mere two blocks away. Without the aid of a light, Kirk found it difficult to see where he was going. Fortunately, each of the businesses ahead had a nightlight that shone down on their dock. Using these nightlights, Kirk was at least able to navigate his way down the alley. However, the range of the nightlights was limited. Each time he walked past the dock of a business, he found himself walking in total darkness again.

The contrast in light and darkness reminded Kirk of the night in Stringtown, just after the dance when he, Ripp and the girls were jumped by the thugs. His thoughts soon shifted to Butch, which sent shivers down his spine. Suddenly, he felt a lump in his stomach. Suddenly, he wasn't so hungry anymore.

Up ahead, Kirk heard the opening of a door. With a quick glance, he saw a man leaning against the handrails of the dock on Woods' Brothers Store. As soon as the figure saw Kirk, he froze, as did Kirk. While he stood motionless, Kirk had a bad feeling he was being stalked.

"Who's there?" asked the man.

Still frozen in his tracks, Kirk remained silent.

"Henry, is that you?"

Kirk's heart rate jumped off the scale. How did he know it was me, he thought.

"Young Henry, I know it's you. Come on up here in the light, where I can see you."

Kirk's mind raced. Only one man ever referred to him as "Young Henry" and that was Carney. He couldn't make out who the mysterious figure was, but he knew by the man's voice it wasn't Carney.

Kirk thought long and hard. I know the voice, he thought. I've heard it before, not often, but I know the voice.

"Don't be afraid, Young Henry. I'm not going to hurt you. Just come up here by the light, where I can see you."

Even if Kirk wanted to walk toward the figure, he was so scared, he wasn't sure his legs would cooperate. Instinct ruled his mind now. The will to survive told him danger lurked ahead. The only viable option was to run. He turned around and walked quietly toward the street. His only fear was to be spotted by the nightlight that was now directly ahead.

"Don't be afraid. It's me, Duke Russo," said the figure.

Kirk quickly turned around and looked at the figure. Sure enough, it was Russo, but the thought did little to comfort him. He stood and watched as Russo walked down the steps of the dock, onto the alley.

"I didn't mean to scare you," said Russo. "I knew you would be coming through here to go to Johnny's and I wanted to talk."

"How long have you been waiting?" Kirk blurted out.

"Not long, just a few minutes. I was in Woods' Brothers', buying a shovel."

"What you be needin' a shovel for?" Kirk asked with suspicion.

"It's not to bury a body, if that's what you're implying," Russo said with a laugh.

Kirk didn't find his words amusing. In fact, he was becoming very angry.

"What you needin' a shovel for?" Kirk demanded.

Knowing he'd pushed Kirk far enough, Russo quickly decided to stop playing games.

"My wife wants me to plant some trees when it gets a little warmer. I promise."

"You sure 'bout that?"

"Look Henry, I just want to talk. Please?"

"Then talk," Kirk said boldly.

"But I can't see you. Can't you come up here, in the light, where I can see you?"

Kirk's instincts told him once again, to run, but his intellect argued that Russo was, at least in an indirect way, his boss. Besides, Kirk could outrun him with two broken legs. He hesitantly walked toward Russo, but stopped before walking into the light.

In an act peace, Russo extended his hand. Kirk stared at his hand, but did not accept the gesture. Russo took his hand back.

"I'm sorry 'bout the way I've been treating you over the last few weeks," said Russo. "I hope you understand we weren't loading a body that morning. We were loading medical supplies wrapped in a blanket."

Kirk wanted to understand, but at the same time, he was very skeptical of Russo. He still wanted to turn and run, but figured it wouldn't hurt to let the man talk.

"But why would you be so concerned about them damned Nazis, especially when there are just as many people in Atoka who need help?"

"That's a good question and I have a good answer. The truth is, Skeet and I do help folks here in Atoka who need assistance with their medicine, especially folks in your community. People just don't know about it."

"I didn't know," said Kirk. "So how did it happen with the Nazis?"

"Skeet's wife, Jo, works at the prison. Over time, she befriended one of the Nazis. Because of the poor medical conditions at the prison, this fella was essentially dying from his diabetes. That's when me and Skeet, along with Battle Axe and Mark decided to help."

"Battle Axe is in on this?" said Kirk.

"He is," said Russo. "He delivers the medicine and helps with some other things."

Kirk smiled. The thought of Battle Axe being part of something so righteous made him proud.

"I can hardly see you, Kirk. Why don't you step up here in the light? There are a couple of other things I want to talk to you about."

Under normal circumstances, Kirk wouldn't have batted an eye to comply with an adult's wishes, but something still didn't feel right. Although he was warming up to Russo and was beginning to feel comfortable, he was still afraid.

"I'm more comfortable back here," said Kirk.

Russo stepped toward Kirk and reached out with his hand.

"Come on, Young Henry, I'm trying to make amends."

Russo's sudden movement startled Kirk, so he stepped back farther. On his way, he bumped into someone from behind, which sent a blast of adrenaline through his veins. Before he could react, however, the unknown person's dark shadow flashed across the illumination of the nightlight and pinned Russo against the dock's handrails.

"What the hell is going on?" shouted Russo.

Kirk immediately recognized the dark figure, whose hands were around Russo's neck: It was Uncle Willie. Judging from Russo's gasps for air, it looked like Uncle Willie was seeing red again.

"Uncle Willie!" shouted Kirk. "What are you doing?"

Hearing no response, Kirk quickly decided to intervene before Uncle Willie's rage killed another man. He ran to the dock and grabbed his uncle's arms.

"Please, Uncle Willie, stop!" Kirk shouted. "If you kill him, you'll go to Big Mac for the rest of your life!"

Kirk's mentioning of the state prison in McAlester struck a nerve with Uncle Willie. He slowly released his grip on Russo's neck. Although his actions indicated he was regaining control of himself, he quickly made it clear he was still very upset.

"That's my blood, Mr. Man," Uncle Willie screamed while pointing at Kirk. "What was you gonna do to the poor boy?"

Russo struggled, but was finally able to stand.

"Nothin'," said Russo, still breathing heavily. "I just wanted to talk to him, that's all. I promise."

"Why was you walkin' toward him like dat? Looks to me like you was about to do something that would anger Uncle Willie. It ain't good for society when Uncle Willie gets mad."

"I just wanted to talk, I swear," said Russo. "I've been sorta mean to him over the last few weeks. I just wanted to talk."

After hearing Russo's words, Uncle Willie stood in silence for a few moments. Kirk noticed that his hands began to shake, indicating that he was becoming angry again. Suddenly, Uncle Willie walked over to Russo and slapped his face.

"Why you makin' Uncle Willie see red?" he shouted. "Why you makin' Uncle Willie see red?"

Kirk was quick to subdue Uncle Willie. He pulled him away from Russo, into the alley.

"It's okay, Uncle Willie. I'm alright, I promise."

"You alright 'cause of Uncle Willie. I look out for yo' ass, Kirk. I always be lookin' out for yo' ass."

"I know you do," said Kirk. "I know you do and I appreciate it very much."

"Damned right," said Uncle Willie. "I'm always there for you, Kirk. How many times have I saved yo' ass?"

"I don't know," said Kirk. "You seem to always be there when I need you."

"You damned right," said Uncle Willie. "Let's walk on down to Johnny's."

"That sounds great," said a relieved Kirk.

After the two walked down the alley, they passed the last nightlight before Johnny's. In the ample lighting, Kirk looked down and noticed that Uncle Willie's hands began to shake. Upon closer inspection, he also saw beads of sweat streaming down the sides of his face. As they walked past the lit area and into another pocket of darkness, Kirk stopped Uncle Willie.

"Why are your hands shakin'? asked Kirk. "Is something on your mind?"

Uncle Willie never looked at Kirk's face. Instead, his glazed-over eyes looked straight ahead.

"It's time to go on, Kirk," said Uncle Willie.

"Johnny's can wait," said Kirk. "Tell me what's on your mind."

"You wouldn't understand."

Still looking straight ahead, Uncle Willie grabbed Kirk by the arm and led him into the nightlight that shone down onto the dock of Johnny's

Café. Confused, Kirk smiled at first, but when he felt Uncle Willie's grip tighten on his arm, he became concerned.

"Uncle Willie, what's going on?"

"It's yo' time to move on, you get on outta here!"

As the two entered the circle of light, Kirk's instincts signaled again that big trouble loomed. Kirk stopped walking alongside Uncle Willie, but was dragged a few more steps. As Kirk's stomach dropped well below his knees, he knew it was time to act. He grabbed Uncle Willie's arm.

"Uncle Willie, what the hell is going on?" shouted Kirk.

"Your work is done now, Willie," said a voice in the darkness.

Kirk immediately looked in the direction where the voice came from. He knew the voice. Dear God, did he know the voice.

"No, Uncle Willie," said Kirk with tears in his eyes. "Please tell me you didn't."

"Oh, he did," said the voice.

With a few moments, Kirk's worst fears were realized as Butch stepped out of the shadow and into the light.

"I told you to back off, Henry, but you just wouldn't listen. You had to test me and now you're going to experience first hand just how powerful I am.

"Do something, Uncle Willie. Help me, Uncle Willie!"

"Oh, he's not of much use to you, Young Henry," Butch said after a boisterous laugh. "You see, Willie works for me. Matter of fact, he's worked for me for a long time."

"This can't be," Kirk said. "Tell me this can't be."

Uncle Willie remained in his stoic stance, staring into the distance. He acted as if he wasn't even aware of what was going on.

"I grew up with Willie's kind. You see, Henry, I came from scum, poor white trash, but I made somethin' of myself. And I'm not going to have some nigger boy destroy the mighty empire I'm building."

"I don't know what you're talking about," said Kirk. "Me and Uncle Willie just want to get something to eat at Johnny's, that's all."

"You don't know your uncle very well, do you?" asked a smiling Butch. "Do you remember when you got jumped in Stringtown?"

"Yeah," said Kirk. "What about it?"

"Who gave you the gun?"

"Uncle Willie. That's what saved me."

"How do you think he knew you were gonna get jumped that night?" asked Butch.

Kirk looked to Uncle Willie, who was staring at the alley floor. Kirk instantly knew he was guilty.

"You set that up!" exclaimed Kirk. "That's how you always knew."

"Willie, your work is done," said Butch. "Get on outta here!"

Kirk walked over and stood nose-to-nose with Uncle Willie, who failed to acknowledge his presence.

"You promised my momma you would look after me," said Kirk, with tears streaming. "I believed in you, Uncle Willie!"

"Your work is done Willie," said Butch. "Get outta here, now!"

Still acting withdrawn, Uncle Willie turned around and walked away. Kirk watched him walk into the darkness.

Butch pulled his .45 Magnum pistol from his pocket. He pulled the hammer back and stepped toward Kirk.

"On you knees," said Butch.

This is it, thought Kirk. And to be sold out by my own blood. What's my poor mother going to think?

"On your knees, boy!" screamed Butch.

Knowing he had no options, Kirk quickly decided his own demise was unavoidable. The only appealing thought that flashed through his mind was to die with dignity. And it didn't include him dying on his knees. He looked up to Butch and smiled.

"I know there's little soul left in that rancid mind and body of yours," said Kirk, "but you're still gonna have to look me in the eye when you pull the trigger."

Butch's smile suddenly vanished. His inability to fully control the situation shot pangs of anger through his entire being. He gripped the butt of the pistol and aimed for Kirk's head.

"The Lord is my shepherd, I shall not want," said Kirk. "He maketh me to lie down in green pastures, he leadeth me beside the still waters."

Butch was first shocked Kirk was praying, but suddenly gritted his teeth and firmly gripped his pistol.

Kirk heard an unimaginably loud blast echo off the walls of the buildings in the alley. His knees hit the hard ground first, then his arms. Certain he was dead, Kirk closed his eyes as his head lay on the cold ground.

That's funny, thought Kirk. For a man who's just been shot, I don't feel any pain. Maybe I'm in shock. Maybe I'm about to die and my body is covering up the pain.

"Put that gun down, you dirty nester. My work here has just begun. I'll smoke you some mo' and you know it. They be pickin' pieces of yo' ass out of that brick wall for years to come."

Kirk opened his eyes. To his shock, he looked up and saw Butch on his knees in front of him, still holding his pistol.

"Put it down," screamed Uncle Willie.

Kirk looked over his shoulder and saw Uncle Willie holding a pistol. His hand twitching, he took dead aim and fired again.

The shot hit Butch in the right shoulder. He dropped the gun and fell to the ground.

"Now my work here is done, you sorry bastard," said Uncle Willie.

Kirk smiled. That's my Uncle Willie, he thought.

"You alright?" asked Uncle Willie.

"I think so," said Kirk. "How 'bout you?"

"I'm a lot better now," said Uncle Willie. "Much better now."

Chapter 33

Weatherford, Oklahoma

1989

"Oh my God!" exclaimed Wade. "Butch was seriously going to kill you!"

"He was," replied Dr. Kirkland. "That man really had it out for me."

The thought of being stared down with a gun in a dark alley prompted Wade to jump to his feet and pace the office. He was reminded of the lack of space, however, when he bumped into his former teacher, and sat back down and expelled a deep breath.

Still rattled, Wade shook his head. "I'm having a hard time processing all this. There you were, a fourteen year old boy, living alone in a house that had holes in the roof, all the while being stalked by a narcissist banker and his thugs who were trying to kill you. How in the world did you survive?"

Dr. Kirkland laughed. "I didn't have any choice."

"But you could have moved to Langston with your parents," said Wade. "At least you would have been safe there."

"Who's to say there wasn't a crazy banker in Langston?"

Wade laughed. "So you're saying it didn't matter where you lived, trouble was going to find you? That it was your destiny?"

"Oh, I don't know," Dr. Kirkland said softly. "I suppose if your number is called, there's not much you can do."

"But, Butch was such as scumbag. I can't believe he was allowed to harass and kill people and get away with it," said Wade.

"The good news was that Butch's reign of terror ended that night."

"Did he die from Uncle Willie's gunshot wound?" asked Wade.

"No, he didn't die, but he was finally brought to justice. At the time of the shooting, Skeet was at the Sheriff's office, telling Sheriff Cain about the counterfeit rationing coupons, when someone from Johnny's called to report the gunshots."

"Was Cain able to put aside his fears that Butch would foreclose on his place?" asked Wade.

"Oh yeah. As a matter of fact," said Dr. Kirkland, "Sheriff Cain arrested Butch while he was being loaded into the ambulance. Cain let it slip Carney showed him the coupons and Butch started screaming at Skeet something fierce."

"That's true to his narcissistic persona," said Wade. "Rather than being upset with himself for breaking the law, he got mad at Carney for turning him in."

"So right," said Dr. Kirkland. "When he was able to stand trial, he was charged and convicted of attempted murder as well as uttering a forged instrument."

"What is that?" asked a confused Wade.

"The fed's way of saying he counterfeited war coupons," Dr. Kirkland said, then paused for thought. "I believe Butch spent around forty-five years in federal prison for those offenses. He was released in 1980."

"Did he have a job waiting for him at the bank when he got out?" joked Wade.

"It wouldn't surprise me!" laughed Dr. Kirkland.

After both men laughed, Dr. Kirkland's face turned somber.

"Not much is known about him after he got out of prison," said Dr. Kirkland. "I don't know where he moved to, but he was seen in Atoka a couple of times. He was around eighty years old when he got out, so he probably has passed on by now."

"What about Geddy Wainscott?"

Dr. Kirkland smiled. "He was brought to trial about the same time. He received a similar sentence, but his time in prison was 'cut short', so to speak."

"What do you mean?" asked Wade, as he noticed the snow falling outside.

"Geddy wasn't mean like Butch. Geddy was a somewhat normal person who just got caught up with Butch and his greed. When he arrived in federal prison, the other prisoners knew he was weak. He ended up getting killed by another prisoner with a crude shiv."

"Poetic justice," said Wade.

"Oh?"

"Didn't you say Karl Bartz died the same way? And didn't Geddy pay the Nazi prisoners to kill him?"

"You know," said Dr. Kirkland, "I've never put that together, but yeah, you're exactly right."

"Poetic justice," said Wade.

"I'll say," Dr. Kirkland replied.

Wade scratched his forehead several times, then crossed his legs. Dr. Kirkland sensed Wade was looking for words.

"Is there something bothering you?"

"Sorta. I'm struggling to understand Uncle Willie. Growing up, he was essentially one of your best friends, yet he was also in bed with your greatest enemy, which almost caused your demise," Wade said, then paused. "I'm struggling because I know he's family."

"Yes," said a calm Dr. Kirkland. "Uncle Willie was a very conflicted man, but if you understand his circumstances, you'll better understand the man. Always remember, Young Wade, the key to understanding the universe is to understand different perspectives."

"But Butch used him to lure you into a trap. Because of Uncle Willie, you were almost killed."

"Yes," replied Dr. Kirkland, "but Uncle Willie also saved my life. Remember, he could have walked away. He didn't have to come back and save me."

"You're right," said Wade. "My problem is I'm having a hard time understanding how a man could ever be lured into Butch's web."

"You have to remember, Uncle Willie had served time in jail. Since he was a black convict, it was very unlikely anyone in Atoka would give him a good job. And Uncle Willie didn't really have the social skills to move on somewhere else and start over. Then along comes Butch, who offered him something no one else would, some money and some security."

"So he was essentially a social leper? Is that what you're saying?"

"In a figurative way, I suppose you could say that. I'm not excusing him for getting himself into the set of circumstances he brought upon himself, but he truly was a man of limited means."

"I see," said Wade, while nodding his head.

"The most important thing about Uncle Willie is he came through for me when I needed him the most."

"Exactly. Uncle Willie redeemed himself. After doing all those bad things, he finally saw the light and came to your aid."

"He did. He risked everything when he pulled that trigger. It took a great deal of courage and it was certainly unorthodox, but Uncle Willie did find redemption," said Dr. Kirkland, and then paused. "With me, anyway."

# # #

In dire need of something to drink, Wade and Dr. Kirkland trudged through the snow to the Southwestern Student Union for a soda. Eager to get back to Dr. Kirkland's office, they carried the sodas back to the Old Science Building. Upon his entrance, Wade made a special effort to take in the sights of the relic building. Soon, he'd be moving to the University of Oklahoma for medical school. This old place would be nothing more than a memory. The thought made Wade smile as he sat down in Dr. Kirkland's office.

"Tell me about Ripp," said Wade. "What happened to him?"

Dr. Kirkland smiled. "Old Ripp," he said, then paused as if he were lost in thought.

"Everything alright?" asked Wade.

"Huh? Oh, yeah. Everything's fine. After college, Ripp became a teacher. He ended up at Harding High School in Oklahoma City, teaching math."

"What's he doing now?" asked Wade.

"Sadly, he's not in very good health. He is retired and spends a fair amount of time going to doctors and such."

"Are you guys still tight?" asked Wade.

Dr. Kirkland smiled. "Oh yeah. We always will be."

"I guess that only leaves us with Mr. Carney," said Wade. "Is he still alive, by any chance?"

"No," replied Dr. Kirkland. "He and his wife, Jo, died the same day in a house fire."

"That's so sad," said Wade. "I'm really sorry to hear that."

"Actually, it could be viewed as a blessing," said Dr. Kirkland. "By this time, Skeet had retired from the drugstore and was caring for Jo, who was ill. Her health was failing and she needed constant care."

"So they were together until the very end?"

"They were," said Dr. Kirkland. "This happened in May of 1980. There was never any explanation of how the house caught on fire. They died hours apart."

"Wait a minute," said Wade, as bells went off in his head. "Didn't you say Butch was released from prison that year?"

Dr. Kirkland gave Wade a cold, hard look. Wade wasn't sure how to interpret the gaze, but was positive it didn't need to be explored.

"Have you ever come across an older couple who's truly in love?" asked Dr. Kirkland.

Wade smiled. "I think so. Why?"

"It's more and more uncommon these days, but it does still happen. I have an associate who recently lost his wife. They'd been married for over sixty years. Every evening before he goes to bed, he prays for the Lord to take him so he can be with his beloved wife."

"Wow," replied Wade. "I'd say that's real love."

"Exactly," said Dr. Kirkland. "And that's the kind of love Skeet and Jo shared. That's why I said it was a blessing. Had he survived, I think he would have been miserable."

Again, Wade noticed Dr. Kirkland's eyes growing misty. "He really meant a lot to you, didn't he?"

"I owe him everything," said Dr. Kirkland. "He made me accept the notion I could rise above everything and be successful. Not only did Skeet tell me that over and over, but he showed me through his actions. He made me feel like I had a chance and really, that's all you need."

"Showed you?"

"Of course. By unabashedly giving me enormous responsibility, then he stood behind me, regardless of the fallout. For example, it was unheard of for a black kid from the ghetto to take the drugstore's weekly deposits to the bank. That was a lot of money. I could have run off with the money and never looked back, but Skeet had faith that I wouldn't. And I know he was grilled by the folks in town about it, too."

"I'm sure everyone in town thought he was crazy," said Wade.

"Sure they did," replied Dr. Kirkland. "But his faith in me never wavered and, over time, it permeated itself into my consciousness. It took time, but I finally began to feel worthy of such tasks. I began to believe in myself. And that's saying a lot for a poor black kid from the other side of the tracks."

"I think I understand," said Wade, who looked over and watched the heavy snow fall outside the window. "To me, the most compelling part of your story is all the adversity you've faced in your life. The one thing that seems to separate you from others is you didn't seem to dwell on bad things. You held fast to the notion that goodness will overcome evil and not to dwell on the bad, but open your heart to the good."

"It appears Mr. McCoy has been listening to my story," said Dr. Kirkland.

"Thanks. But you haven't told me what happened next."

"After Butch was gone, things really calmed down in Atoka. I still worked at the drugstore for Mr. Carney. My high school years were filled with work, school, and basketball. After I graduated from Atoka, I went to Langston and earned my undergraduate. I got my first job teaching in El Reno and later moved to Southwestern in 1972. I became the first black professor at Southwestern, and maybe the only black professor, come to think of it. Along the way, I earned my graduate degree, then my doctorate."

"A well-accomplished career," said Wade.

"I've been very fortunate," replied Dr. Kirkland.

"So what's the story behind the third coin?" asked Wade.

"Love," said Dr. Kirkland. "And I received it on my last day in Atoka."

"Do tell," replied Wade.

"Alright, but no interruptions," laughed Dr. Kirkland.

Chapter 34

Atoka, Oklahoma, 1949

"Skeet?" Kirk asked while drying the front window. He smiled when he realized this would be the last time he would ever clean these front windows. He wondered how many times he'd done it over the previous four years.

"What do you need, Young Henry?" replied Carney. He arose from behind one of the shelves in the middle of the store.

"Why are you doing this?" asked Kirk. Even though he knew what he was asking was enormous, he delivered the question with the emotion of an ordinary one, just as if he were asking for the soda syrup recipe or the price of paper towels.

"Doing what, Young Henry?" asked Skeet with raised eyebrows. He walked around the corner of the shelf and waited for Kirk to answer.

Throughout the years, Kirk and Carney had talked about life on many occasions. But since Kirk's time with Carney and Atoka was drawing to an end, he felt compelled to ask some more.

Finally, Kirk forced the words out, his voice cracking with emotion. "Why have you helped me all these years? You came to my rescue when almost no one else would. Now you're sending me off to get an education. Why?"

Carney stood frozen at the end of the counter. He held his head down like he was somewhere far away.

"Why have you done it? As soon as I get on the bus for Langston, our time will be up. You've paid me well, been a solid supporter, heck, you even bought me new shoes and my senior class ring."

"Ah, Henry, it's nothin. I just knew you were a good kid and you'd make it out of here someday. You have no future here. It's time to move on."

"But, why me?" Kirk replied.

"It's complicated. It would take a while to even try to explain," said Carney, his voice fading.

Henry looked around the empty store. It was unlikely anyone would come in at this hour, so he pressed on. "I have the time to listen, if you can tell me something about it," he said.

"I don't know if I know why I did it, Young Henry," said Carney. "Why have you run those railroad tracks all these years? I do remember that familiar look on your face the first day you walked in here four years ago. It was a timid look I was familiar with because I used to see it every morning in the mirror when I was a kid."

"Okay, but you still haven't answered why you helped me?"

"I don't like thinking about what brought me to where I am in life. It has been easier to just put it all behind. Dwelling on the past never gets us anywhere, Henry. All it gets us is brand new bad memories which gives them life all over again," Skeet said softly. He looked up at Henry with moist eyes.

"Did something bad happen to you, Skeet?" Kirk asked timidly.

"Something bad has happened to all of us at one time or another. Something good has happened, too," said Carney, with passion. "It's what we decide to focus on that determines what we become."

Kirk had a thousand questions, but he finally had Skeet talking so he kept his mouth shut. "Go on," he said.

"My old man was a real piece of work. He was a preacher here in Atoka when I was born. I was about ten years old in 1905. Things were tough then. No one had money and the last person to get paid at the church was the preacher. He typically brought his frustrations home."

"What was it like to live with such a man?" asked Kirk.

"It was like living in Hell. Our father had many faces and we never knew which one was coming home. He might be happy and praising the Lord or he might come home cussing and throwing things. More than once he took his anger out on my mother. I am ashamed to say I stood in the corner and watched him scream at her, telling her it was her fault there was no food in the house. One day she tried to respond, and he really got out of control. I just stood there, Young Henry. I let him treat Mama like that more than once."

Kirk reckoned a deep scar was opened. Skeet wiped the tears from his face, took a deep breath, and cleared his throat.

"What happened to your old man?" Kirk asked.

Carney shook his head. "The church fired him because of the way he treated Mama. He left town and remarried shortly after that. They had a kid. Strangely, all three of them died on the same day and are buried over east somewhere near Arkansas."

"Ever visited his grave?"

"Never, not even once. Somewhere along the way, I decided I had a choice to make. I could take care of my family or I could spend the rest of my life hating that old man. As I've gotten older, I understand he must have had his own demons, so to speak. I have forgiven him. Dwelling on the negative will only fester into resentment. And no good can come of that."

"I understand."

"Look at my life, Henry. I have this successful business, my family, and young kids like you come in and out of my life. I have tried to take all the negative emotions and turn them into something good, like puttin' you on the bus in a little while."

"I don't think I can ever repay you, Skeet," Kirk said with a broken voice, fighting back the tears.

"You want to repay me?" Carney said with confidence. "Get yourself out of this place and become a success. Someday you'll see that familiar look in a young kid's face. Then it will be your turn to pull him aside and give him a hand up, build his confidence like I did for you. That will be my pay."

"Understood."

Carney looked at his watch. "It's about time to go to the bus station."

"I know," said Kirk. "I brought my suitcase with me, so I'll just walk down there in a bit. Ripp said he would be waiting for me in Langston."

"I'm so glad Ripp decided to go back to school. He's gonna be alright."

"Indeed he will," said Kirk. "We'll look after each other."

"Well, let's go. You didn't think I would let you walk yourself to the bus station did you?" Skeet said as he pointed to his watch.

As Kirk grabbed his suitcase, he noticed Skeet walkin' around the store, putting things in a small sack.

# # #

The silent three-block ride west to the Atoka bus station seemed to take forever in Kirk's mind. Setting on the corner of Court Street and Highway Sixty-Nine, the bus station transported people from all over the country. As they rode along in Skeet's car, Kirk remembered spending time there in the past watching people. He remembered one day a black man in a nice suit came through and asked Ripp's sister, Wanda, a strange question. He asked, "How many people live in this town of Atoka?" When Wanda said she didn't know, he told her she'd better get to exploring. Not just Atoka, but the whole world. Kirk later discovered the man's name was Hall. He was a lawyer who worked with the famous lawyer Thurgood Marshall. They were trying to get the first black woman admitted to the University of Oklahoma law school. After a long fight, the case went all the way to the United States Supreme Court. They ultimately won the case and Ada Fisher was admitted into law school.

Skeet pulled the car into the bus station parking lot. To Kirk's surprise, he found Jo with their two daughters, Joann and Carolyn. Kirk was really surprised to see that they'd planned such a send off. As Kirk got out of the car, he was greeted by the hot July air.

"Morning Henry," Jo said quietly. "The girls wanted to come along and see you off. You know Joann is headed to OU this fall."

"I did not realize that," Kirk replied with a smile, "I wish you the best of luck."

Jo wished Kirk luck, too, and handed him a small bag with cookies and a sandwich inside. She gave him a hug and whispered in his ear, "You make us proud Henry, we're all countin' on you. Don't forget about us when you make it big."

While Kirk blushed, he felt like the temperature was over one-hundred-ten degrees. After the girls said their good-byes and got into their mother's car, the Carney women drove away.

Knowing his bus was loading up, Skeet nervously shifted his feet. As he performed his ritual nervous tic with his elbows and his belt, he reached into his pocket for his coin. Only this time, he didn't twirl it. Instead, he stared at it for a long time, turning it over several times. Kirk noticed all the writing had been worn off the coin.

"Henry," Skeet said while looking up at him, "I've had this coin in my pocket since I was a kid. I got it as pay shortly after I started throwing papers, when I was a kid. I kept it all these years because I knew if I had this I would never be broke."

Kirk smiled. "Well being that the print has worn off, I'm not so sure what it's worth."

"Henry, this coin has served me well for over forty years. I don't need it anymore. I want you to have it if you promise to guard it and never lose it," Skeet said with a stoic face.

"I can't take this, Skeet," Kirk said with a shocked look. "What will you fiddle with when you're nervous?"

"I'm sure Sharon or Darlene can find me a new coin," Skeet laughed.

"This means a lot to me, and I'll always carry it."

Skeet started shifting his feet. "Now you know when you get on that bus, you have to sit in the back. Be polite, and there will be no trouble."

"I may be young and black, but I'm not stupid. I know the rules of 'the man'."

"The bus is loading, Henry," said Carney. "You need to get on and find your seat. First, there are a couple of things I want to give you. Here are two comic books to read on the bus. And of course your favorite, a Baby Ruth candy bar. I do not see how you stayed so skinny eating all those candy bars over these last few years."

"I imagine the four to five miles a day I ran to work and back had something to do with it," Kirk said.

"And there is something else I haven't told you. I know I already paid you for this week, but here is something else I want to do."

"What is that?" Kirk asked, looking down at what appeared to be checks.

"Here are two blank checks," Carney whispered. "One is for books and one is for tuition. When you need money for next semester, you call. If you need the money quickly, you know my bank, and you can write a check on my account. But if you give me some time I can mail you the checks."

A shocked Kirk stood in amazement. "You can't do this, Skeet. I can't let you do this. You have your own family to care for."

"You let me worry about that, Young Henry," Carney said with teary eyes. "I'm investing in you, and I expect a big return through your success."

In all the years Kirk knew Skeet, they rarely shook hands and they had certainly never hugged. As they embraced, Kirk's six-foot-three inch body towered over Skeet's five-feet-four inches. Neither cared how awkward they looked today, though.

"I love you Henry. Now go make me proud," said a teary-eyed Skeet. "Make us all proud. You'll leave this town in the back of the bus, but someday you'll come back on the front row. Or even better, you'll come wheelin' in here in a fancy car. Thank you, Henry. Thank you for being my friend."

Kirk was so choked up he couldn't speak. He patted Skeet on the back and gathered his belongings. He turned to get on the bus, but stopped.

"Skeet, I love you too. And thank you for everything. I'm going to do my best to not let you down. I'll see you next summer maybe."

As Kirk turned and climbed the steps of the bus to make his way to the back, he wiped the tears away. As the bus drove away, Kirk looked out the back window and saw a little man wiping tears. At this moment, however, the little man looked like a giant in Kirk's eyes.

Afterword

Oklahoma City, Oklahoma, 2010

Even though it's been over twenty years since I sat in Dr. Kirkland's office and heard his incredible life story unfold, I'm affected by his words still today. This work must be recognized as a fictionalized version of his life. Nonetheless, the fact remains that Dr. Kirkland had a major impact on my life and the lives of thousands of students through the years.

Many of us owe our success to Kirk. We are grateful he got up every morning and ran those rail tracks in the cold, rain, or the snow. It didn't matter to Kirk; he knew he had to make it to work or starve. When he got on that bus, he was on his way to many more challenges. However, he met them all. He finished his degree at Langston University. He lived for a while in Oklahoma City, where he met his wife, Viola Johnson. He and Viola have been married for fifty years. They have two children and four grandchildren.

Kirk began teaching at the segregated Booker T. Washington school in El Reno, Oklahoma, in 1962. Later, in 1965, he became the first African American teacher at El Reno High School as a biology teacher and coach. With the encouraging words of Skeet Carney in Atoka, Kirk obtained his master's degree in education at SWOSU. In 1972, he became the first African-American professor at SWOSU. While he held his professorship, he obtained his doctorate degree from Oklahoma State University in Stillwater, Oklahoma. Dr. Kirkland retired from SWOSU in 1996. However, at his current age of seventy-six, he continues to teach animal biology at OSU/Oklahoma City Campus.

About thirty years ago, Dr. Kirkland was in his home in Weatherford, Oklahoma when the phone rang. The voice was a familiar one from the past. Skeet Carney was in town and invited his old friend to breakfast. They caught up on old times. Skeet asked him the same three questions he always did: Are you saving money? Do you have insurance? Are you going to church? Dr. Kirkland replied yes to all the questions. Then, Dr. Kirkland told Skeet he was ready to pay him back for all the money he had given him to go to school. Skeet quietly replied that he was owed nothing if Dr. Kirkland could provide him with a copy of his doctorate dissertation.

Early in my collegiate years, he called me into his office and told me I should pursue medicine. Prior to that point in my life, I never imagined I could become a physician. In fact, I put off taking biology because I lacked the confidence to believe I would do well. I still remember sitting in his small office with our knees almost touching while he wore his red OU sweater. I had multiple excuses for him, but he became my gentle mentor that day. His confidence in me that day infected me with the belief that my future was there for the taking. Over the next few years, when I was in need, I went to him. When I was overwhelmed, I went to him. When I needed a friend, I went to him.

I never knew he affected so many people. I have learned many stories of his influence over these last few years. They are the stories behind the names in his little book he still carries today. Some of these stories are included in the following pages. When Dr. Kirkland could have just been a teacher, he became an advisor. When he could have just been an advisor, he became a mentor. When he could have just been a mentor, he became friends with his students.

We recently had an appreciation reception for Dr. Kirkland. A ballroom full of former students and friends filled the room. Anyone who ever met Dr. Kirkland knows he is special. He has always looked out for the timid, uncertain student. He truly searched for that look Skeet told him about.

About four years ago, Dr. Kirkland and I began to do research for this book. While we were in the midst of our research phase, I received a disturbing call one afternoon that Dr. Kirkland was in the emergency room at the Oklahoma Heart Hospital. I rushed to see him. His long legs were hanging off the end of the bed, but he still had a big grin on his face. It was discovered he had five arteries in his heart that required a bypass. We sat there alone and talked again about our friendship. I told him once more how I owe my success to him. I reminded him that without his encouragement, I would not have become a doctor. I wanted him to know I love him. Once again, he humbly told me I was the one who did the work. Though the staff was treating him with perfect respect, I made them aware I was his doctor and friend, and he should be referred to as Dr. Kirkland, not Henry. I wanted everyone else to show him the respect his students feel for him. Before I left his bedside that day, he told me to finish our book despite anything that happened to him.

This story now spans into its third century. I remind myself of the great privilege of carrying this message forward. Part of the way this message will live on will be through this book. It is my hope this book can reach the weak, the timid, and the uncertain and give them the courage to pursue their dreams.

One could say this story really started in about 1851, at the birth of Dr. Kirkland's grandfather. Doing research on his family, I discovered his grandfather, Henry Kirkland, was a slave in Dale County, Alabama. At a young age, his grandfather was separated from his family and was the lone slave of a family in Newton, Alabama. A white Henry A. Kirkland, who died in the Civil War, owned him. Henry Kirkland, Kirk's grandfather, would have been about fourteen when he received his freedom. By 1880, his grandfather had married Isabelle McSwean and lived in Williamston, Barbour County, Alabama. Through further research, I found my great-great-grandmother McCoy was raised in the same little town of Williamston, Alabama, by her uncle who served as postmaster in the 1820s and was one of the largest slave owners in Alabama history.

Dr. Kirkland and I recently traveled to Barbour County, Alabama. We tromped the same roads as our ancestors did years before they found their way westward. We stood beside the trickling water of McSwean Creek. This creek was no doubt named after the slave owners of Dr. Kirkland's grandmother. As we stood together behind the pulpit at Dexter Avenue Baptist Church in Montgomery, Alabama, where Dr. Martin Luther King Jr. preached for six years, I thought of those words that rang out from the steps of the Lincoln Memorial: "I have a dream that one day, the sons of slaves and the sons of former slave owners will be able to sit down together at the table of brotherhood." I realized once again King's dream had come true. I believe destiny brought Dr. Kirkland and me together 130 years later out of the fertile soil of South Alabama.

My wife, Sarah, and I have raised our children with the knowledge we have a great challenge to carry on the legacy. Our children are given opportunities they would not have had if not for the influence of Dr. Kirkland.

Dr. Kirkland's career as an educator is approaching fifty years. Late in his career, he became interested in paleontology. He actually made his greatest discovery in the county where I was born and raised, Roger Mills County, Oklahoma. He received national attention for the discovery of an eleven-million-year-old prehistoric camel in the grasslands a few miles from the land I farmed as a young man.

Dr. Kirkland and his wife, Viola, live within a mile of our house in Oklahoma City. We talk on the phone several times a week. And we see each other often. Though I'll never measure up to the excitement and entertainment that Ripp afforded him, I like to think I'm now Dr. Kirkland's runnin' buddy. And, just like Ripp Masters, I usually do the driving.

Wade McCoy, MD
February 2011

A Few Student Stories

The Horse Surgeon

He was close to dropping out and going home, until . . .

The year was 1994. I was just beginning college at Southwestern Oklahoma State University in Weatherford, Oklahoma with the ambitions of one day realizing my dream of becoming a veterinarian. Dr. Kirkland played an integral role in the introductory coursework of all students taking courses in biological sciences. It was during my sophomore year, when I was enrolled in Dr. Kirkland's vertebrate zoology course, that I began to finally get a "handle" on the rigors of college course work. For the first time, I could see the early "foundation" of my ultimate career start to fall into place.

About this time, I received painful news that my mother, who lived 1000 miles away, was diagnosed and succumbing to late-stage terminal cancer. My perspective on everything changed. My recently-recognized "foundation" that I had been working hard to build was coming apart at the seams. My grades slipped, my focus failed and I began to doubt myself and the tasks I had undertaken. I strongly considered quitting college altogether. I am not sure how or why, but it was during this time that Dr. Kirkland asked me to stay and see him after zoology lab. In our after five-o'clock meeting, he asked me about my coursework, academic intentions, and career plans. I could tell he had a genuine interest in me as a student and a person; in turn, I developed a genuine interest in him. He invited me to participate in some field work which he was conducting involving paleontology.

Our interactions developed from afternoon outings into a field-research program that produced the opportunity for me to present three posters and two podium lectures at scientific meetings as well as one published manuscript. He would do anything within his power to help me realize my goals. I remember one Friday morning after finals that I planned to meet him at the university to travel to prospect a new study site for our work. I hopped in his little blue pick-up and he said, "You know, I have a better idea. It's early and a weekday; let's go to Stillwater." He had arranged a meeting for us with the recruiting and admissions office at the Oklahoma State University College of Veterinary Medicine! I was so keyed up that it wasn't until reflecting on this trip later that I realized how absolutely generous and unselfish of an act this was. Not many people will go out of their way and forgo their personal agenda, vehicle, fuel and time to arrange such a meeting. This was not his job, but he made it his job, he went far above and beyond what was expected of him. He did this because he cared.

This work, and more importantly, working with Dr. Kirkland, turned out to be a saving grace and the mentorship that ultimately saved me from personal failure. It was only recently that I learned that my "Dr. Kirkland story" was not an isolated incident fueled by coincidence and opportunity, but that many others have similar stories of which I am certain are just as or even more compelling than mine. As disillusioned as I was, it was not only *me* that Dr. Kirkland cared for, it was *his students* that he cared for. This is an inspiring quality to anybody, but even more so to me now in my career teaching in the College of Veterinary Medicine. If I can be so fortunate as to give just one student the gift that Dr. Kirkland has given me, I will truly be blessed. He taught me lessons much deeper than vertebrate zoology and pleistocene epoch paleontology... He taught me perseverance, focus, self-confidence, humility, and that dreams can become reality.

Dr. Kirkland epitomizes the true roll of "teacher". He is an educator, mentor, and friend to all who have been privileged with the opportunity to know him. Dr. Kirkland is an authentic hero to me.

Dustin V. Devine, DVM, MS, DACVS
Assistant Professor, Equine Surgery
Oklahoma State University
Stillwater, Oklahoma

The Uncertain Student

He was called to the scolding room to imagine, and ended up in the imaging room . . .

I remember the small room in the back of the Advanced Biology classroom at El Reno (OK) High School. It had shelves and drawers full of specimens and educational material. There was also a movie projector for showing black-and-white films about various aspects of biology. A wooden table and chairs sat in the middle of the room.

The smell of formaldehyde was a frequent visitor there, as were a few reluctant students. This small room was the "office" of Mr. Henry Kirkland, Advanced Biology teacher. When students were asked to enter there, it was almost a foregone conclusion that, despite their best efforts, they had been caught doing something wrong in class. The other likelihood was that word had gotten out about other misdeeds they thought would never come to light.

It was almost forty years ago to the day that I was asked or, was I told, to enter that room. I wasn't sure why, but knew I was guilty of innumerable infractions which I had hoped no one had discovered. The majority of these infractions were minor, but a few didn't seem so minor at the time (or even now, for that matter).

Fortunately, advice rather than a lecture or scolding, was given to me in that small room on that day. As I recall, it was not lengthy but to the point. At the time, I was undecided about my future but was considering studying law or medicine after graduation. This news had apparently filtered its way to Mr. Kirkland. He subtly but in no uncertain terms, suggested that I would be able to help more people by studying medicine than by studying law.

That advice may not have been the turning point in my decision to study medicine. However, there is no question that it did deflect the needle on my compass toward that direction. I went on to college and to medical school and earned my M.D. with a subsequent specialty in diagnostic radiology.

A lot has happened in the intervening years. I believe we both have had an impact on numerous lives in our own ways, through our professions. We are both now called "doctor." When I look back forty years, I don't see Dr. Kirkland. I see a *teacher* who inspired some to question, inquire and gain knowledge. But most of all, I see a caring and compassionate man in a small room, giving truly heartfelt guidance to one in need.

Jim Bullen, MD
Diagnostic Radiologist, Stillwater Medical Center
Stillwater, Oklahoma

A Thankful Student

It is a great honor to acknowledge the contributions that Dr. Henry Kirkland has made to my life. As a young man searching for guidance, Dr. Kirkland filled the gap as a mentor and caring adviser. When individuals ask me why I became an optometrist, I have to give credit to the encouragement and efforts of Dr. Kirkland. He contributed greatly to my studies and guided me forward in my efforts to complete my education at SWOSU and to obtain admission to the optometry program at NSU. Dr. Kirkland encouraged me to investigate optometry as a career. I would regularly go by his office to visit and get direction. At the time, his daughter was pursuing optometry and there were several students he helped lead in this direction. We took several road trips to Tahlequah with a car load of students and Dr. Kirkland often drove us there. I am truly thankful to Dr. Kirkland for the time and efforts he gave me during our time at SWOSU.

Daniel Woods, OD
Ardmore, Oklahoma

A Grateful Student

Dr. Henry Kirkland went far beyond what could be expected to insure my success as a student at Southwestern Oklahoma State University. I remember him passing me in the hall and actually stopping what he was doing to find out how my studies were going and if there was anything he could do to help me out. I remember sitting in his office while he went over all my courses to make sure that I was on the right path and going to be eligible for early admittance into Optometry school (and he was not even my appointed course adviser). He drove a group of students clear across the state, once a year, to visit the Northeastern State University

College of Optometry, and I think I went with him every year that I was a student at Southwestern. Dr. Kirkland's commitment to his students was very obvious due to the time, effort, and the sincerity that he showed while encouraging students to fulfill their dreams. I told him he couldn't retire until I was accepted to optometry school. I was able to proudly announce at a banquet that Dr. Kirkland could now retire, because I had gotten into optometry school. Other than my immediate family members, I have to give Dr. Kirkland the most credit for helping me reach my potential, and becoming the professional that I am today.

Shelly Rice, OD
Wagoner, Oklahoma

Wade McCoy, MD is a family-practice physician at Gilbert Medical Center in Bethany, Oklahoma. He met Dr. Kirkland in 1986 in an Introduction to Biology class at Southwestern Oklahoma State University. Dr. McCoy is from rural Reydon, Oklahoma, a town of less than 200 people. He currently lives in Oklahoma City with his wife, Sarah, and their two daughters. "Rainbow in the Dark" is McCoy's debut novel.

Patrick Chalfant spent his childhood on a large western Oklahoma ranch, which has been owned by his family over 100 years. He was taught and mentored by Dr. Kirkland in 1989 at Southwestern Oklahoma State University. He currently resides in Tulsa, Oklahoma with his wife and two sons. Patrick is the author of "When the Levee Breaks" and "Bury My Heart at Redtree". "Rainbow in the Dark" is his third novel.

Edwards Brothers, Inc.
Thorofare, NJ USA
June 23, 2011